N Y P D

STORIES OF SURVIVAL FROM
THE WORLD'S TOUGHEST BEAT

N Y P D

STORIES OF SURVIVAL FROM
THE WORLD'S TOUGHEST BEAT

EDITED BY CLINT WILLIS

Thunder's Mouth Press
New York

NYPD: Stories of Survival From The World's Toughest Beat

An Adrenaline Book®

Published by
Thunder's Mouth Press
An Imprint of Avalon Publishing Group Incorporated
161 William Street, 16th floor
New York, NY 10038

Book design: Sue Canavan

frontispiece photo: Times Square Police Station,
© Reuters NewMedia Inc./Corbis

Library of Congress Cataloging-in-Publication Data is available.

ISBN: 1-56025-412-2

Printed in Canada
Distributed by Publishers Group West

for Will Balliett
my partner in crime

c o n t e n t s

viii **photographs**

ix **introduction**

1 from *Brooklyn Bounce*
by Joe Poss and Henry R. Schlesinger

29 *Cop Diary*
by Marcus Laffey

53 from *Buddy Boys*
by Mike McAlary

91 *With the Meat in Their Mouth—I*
by Joel Sayre

115 *With the Meat in Their Mouth—II*
by Joel Sayre

137 from *The Gangs of New York*
by Herbert Asbury

157 from *Collura*
by Bill Davidson

187 *The Last Cop Story*
by Mike McAlary

205 from *Rogues' Gallery*
by Thomas Byrnes

249   *One Cop, Eight Square Blocks*
           by Michael Norman

277   from *Brooklyn Bounce*
           by Joe Poss and Henry R. Schlesinger

289   from *Will the Circle Be Unbroken?*
           by Studs Terkel

295   **acknowledgments**

297   **permissions**

299   **bibliography**

photographs

1   NYPD car and prostitute
     © Chauvel Patrick/Corbis Sygma

29   Crime scene
     © Chauvel Patrick/Corbis Sygma

53   New Year's party in Times Square
     © Copes Van Hasselt Johan/Corbis Sygma

91   New York street scene at Fifth Avenue
     © Underwood & Underwood/ Corbis

115 Police & crowd watching men with barrel
     © Bettmann/Corbis

137 Draft riots in New York
     © Bettmann/Corbis

157 Manhattan skyscrapers beyond Brooklyn dock at dusk
     © Kelly-Mooney Photography/Corbis

187 Abner Louima
     © AFP Photo Stan Honda

205 Broadway, New York, late 19th century
     Hulton/Archive

249 Derelict car, nighttime New York
     © Chauvel Patrick/Corbis Sygma

277 Cop with dead body
     © Chauvel Patrick/Corbis Sygma

289 Police officers near ground zero
     © Paul Colangelo/Corbis

introduction

B ack in the early '70s, when I was a teenager, I saw various versions of a bumper sticker that said "If you don't like police, next time you need help call a hippy." The bumper stickers seemed unfair to hippies. Some hippies were helpful—one gave me rides in his hand-painted VW bug and another taught me some guitar licks.

I didn't dislike cops, either. The two patrolmen who picked me up one night in 1974—a young friend and I were drinking beer at an empty construction sight—handled the situation better than my folks did. The cops had seen much worse, and their reasonable tone soothed me even as they escorted me home to face my parents' wrath.

Since then I've met more policemen. A Louisiana state trooper who lived next to my brother in Lafayette used to tell us funny stories about the crazy people he'd arrested or saved—including a guy whose full-grown alligator escaped on the highway one rainy day. A cop who pulled me over on a highway in New York State to tell me that my car was overdue for an inspection was rude. The New Hampshire cop who gave me my only speeding ticket was efficient and professional.

Cops are scary sometimes. I don't like knowing that I have to do what they tell me to do; that they have so much authority and so many opportunities to abuse it. My brother, who lived next door to the funny state trooper, told me that the worst kid in his high school—the dumbest, the meanest—became a policeman so that he could make a living as a bully.

But when I lived in New York City I was glad to see policemen. New York was not an easy place to feel safe, and knowing that cops were around was a comfort. Occasionally, I'd be reading on the subway late at night and miss my stop and look up to find myself in a new neighborhood; I would have been glad to see a hippy or two then, but a uniformed member of the NYPD would have been much better.

Now I live in Maine, where there aren't many cops or criminals. A policeman recently stopped by my house to help me trap a squirrel that had gained entry through the chimney. The policeman seemed tired, in sharp contrast to the tough and energetic and eccentric New York cops I remember. Those New York cops might have been angry at me for wasting their time, or they might have turned the whole thing into a little party with rough jokes and some noise; they might have made fun of me or been in a hurry. This particular Maine cop made a couple of suggestions and went away.

It's hard to feel comfortable judging cops. We give them a dangerous and stressful job; we don't pay them much; we impose high standards on them. And most cops are like the rest of us—they do their best some days; other days they fall short. Still, it's easy to argue that the hardships and risks and temptations of the job set cops apart. We can say that cops live in a higher-stakes world than the rest of us; that they have to pay attention and they have to make the right choices or innocent people get hurt.

In a place like New York City there are more distractions and more choices to make. So the job sometimes gets harder there, and the stories get better. Even so, we also can read these stories as we can read any good stories—with an eye toward finding ourselves inside of them.

Like cops, we all carry responsibilities that require us to be mindful and decisive; if we fail at those tasks, people may suffer. These stories about good cops and bad cops offer versions of life in the New York Police Department over the years. They also remind us that every authentic cop story is different and that cops aren't entirely different from the people they try to protect.

—CLINT WILLIS
SERIES EDITOR, ADRENALINE BOOKS

from Brooklyn Bounce
by Joe Poss and
Henry R. Schlesinger

Joe Poss grew up in an upper-class Ohio suburb. He joined the NYPD on a bet and was assigned to the East New York section of Brooklyn—one of the city's toughest neighborhoods. He wrote his 1994 memoir with writer Henry R. Schlesinger.

I f you're a white person living in the suburbs or Manhattan, or anywhere that isn't a ghetto, then you've probably never seen a ghetto cop—never *experienced* a ghetto cop.

When most people think of the NYPD, they think about Manhattan and midtown cops. Those cops are slick pretty-boys. Their uniforms and manners are as clean and polished as their cars. Their hair is coiffed. They're in the public eye and they know it. And, more importantly, their commanding officers know it. They know that taxpayers, the media, and people of influence live, work, and play in Manhattan. Midtown is about corporate headquarters, high-priced stores, high-rent apartments, and exclusive restaurants.

Manhattan is not only the city's economic, cultural, and power center, it's also ground zero of political influence in the city. Midtown is about networks of people—hundreds of thousands of relationships, huge invisible webs of influence where you never know who knows who, or who is related. Or who can make a telephone call and get you transferred in a heartbeat. The unruly teenager; he may be the son or daughter of a prominent attorney. The victim of a mugging, the wife of a television executive. And the shoplifter, a diplomat. The ass you kiss in Midtown may save your own.

A midtown cop isn't going to get out of his car and toss (search) some guy in a Brooks Brothers suit or his model girlfriend for loitering outside Tiffany's. How would it sound, even politely? "Er, excuse me Chad, Buffy, would you mind terribly putting your hands against the wall?"

In midtown Manhattan, just the hint of rudeness could shit-can a career. A guy could drop a dime (make a civilian complaint) so quick it would make the cop's head spin. And "the job" would, as they say, entertain it. Even odds would have him catching a heavy one (punishment) from the sergeant and a shit fixer (foot) post for the next month.

Midnight cops in Manhattan see people with money barhopping at three in the morning. They're Manhattanites or bridge-and-tunnel nightlife commuters, in from Long Island, Queens, Jersey, and points beyond. They're spending money, helping the city's economy. If you approach them at all, it's for disorderly conduct. And then you either adjust their attitude verbally or ignore them. It's light duty.

If you listen to the Manhattan radio calls, you're likely to hear some cop screaming for help because he's getting yelled at and finger-poked in a street fight. Not only is he calling in a 10-85 (officer needs assistance) for a fucking scuffle, but the whole city hears it. If a cop did that in the ghetto, he would end up getting his locker thrown into the showers, or "covered" (keyed-out) the next time he tried to transmit a radio message.

Now here's the thing that really gets to me. The brass knows this. They know what the job is like in a "light house" or "C" precinct (one without an abundance of criminal activity); and they know the way we do the job in a "heavy house" or "A" precinct such as the 7-5. They not only know it, but they take advantage of the fact. They exploit it. You go to a parade or demonstration in Manhattan and they'll have all the Manhattan cops on the front lines looking sharp. But they'll keep us

Brooklyn badasses sitting in vans around the corner, waiting in the wings just in case things turn ugly.

Cops adapt to their environment. The ghetto transforms them. Nobody can live there without it changing them, and you can't work there without it taking a toll on your thinking. The ghetto, even more than a place on a map, is a state of mind, an experience, an attitude. The poverty, the abandoned buildings, the burned-out cars and dead-end lives imprint themselves on you. It's not a Black thing, Hispanic thing, White thing, or cop thing. It's a human thing.

Ghetto cops wear the rough-edged camouflage of the ghetto. It's slipped into their manner and into their thinking. It's ugly and it's hard, and outside the ghetto it would be seen as a failing. But inside, within the boundaries of poverty and wreckage, it's been turned around, twisted a hundred and eighty degrees, so that all the flaws are virtues. They're a street code that, translated, means the cop is tough enough and smart enough to survive. It means that he possesses the secret street knowledge that there's no hope for this place.

It is, without exaggeration, as much a part of the ghetto cop's uniform as his collar brass, shield, or blue shirt. I learned it slowly, the same way I learned the landscape, streets, buildings, and alleys. The way I learned about the people, the criminals, and the commerce of street corners. Soon it became a familiar and necessary piece of me. The crack houses and drug locations became as familiar to me as the Tudor estates back home.

The point is, you put the Manhattan cop and the Brooklyn ghetto cop side by side and you would see the difference. Look at a Manhattan cop and you'll see that he's got a shiny new Chevy Caprice bubble car with a computer, a neatly pressed shirt and one of those new waist-length jackets, creased pants, shiny boots, and a short-cropped haircut. Your tax dollars at work. Value for the money. That's how you get respect in Manhattan—by looking professional.

In the ghetto, I get out of my boxy, banged-up Chevy in my old nylon duty jacket with the leather patch on the right forearm worn through from rubbing against my gun. The top button of my shirt is undone, with the clip-on tie clipped through the buttonhole of my left lapel. And maybe a small Band-Aid covering my earing. There's a swagger to how I get out of the car. Watch the Manhattan cops get out of their cars. They're stiff, like RoboCop, hat always on and looking just a little uncomfortable.

Now, who gets the respect in the ghetto? I do. My car has battle fatigue. I have battle fatigue. I'm as pissed-off and stressed out as everyone else who has to work or live there. I've heard every stupid lie and know I'm going to hear them again. I'm as much a part of the environment as the bricked-up tenements, the garbage-filled lots, and the corner bodegas. I have made myself belong there. I am part of it.

Put me in Manhattan looking like that and people would say, "My god, what a mess," like I was some homeless misplaced cop.

In the ghetto, this is the way it works. You pull up to a drug location at three in the morning and toss the dealer, steerer, banker, and look-out under the Right of Common Inquiry. Why? Because they've disrespected you by not "stepping off" (walking away) when you drove by. You know they're running a drug operation, and they know you know it. And the respect they should show is to curtail business for forty seconds at the sight of you.

And if they don't, then you stop the car, get out, and toss them. And it's, "Yo! Motherfucker, take your hands out of your fucking pockets and get on the wall. Don't even fucking look at me, look at the fucking wall." If you said that in Manhattan, people wouldn't even comply, they'd just stand there shocked, or say, "Do you have to swear at me, officer?" Then twenty other questions.

With the drug dealers, what you're trying to do is program them into "getting it." *When I pull up to this corner, you walk. You walk when you see me coming. Okay, you're a new guy, these are the rules: This is my fucking precinct, and you better well fucking show me respect. If you don't, then I'm going to toss you. If you still don't, if you make me get out of my nice warm police car, or my nice air-conditioned police car, depending on the season, and make me put you against the wall, then I'm going to tear this fucking corner apart. Get it? You fucking well better.*

And you have to keep coming back, again and again, until they get the message. But if you make the threat, you better follow through; because anyone who doesn't back up their talk doesn't last. They don't get respect, and maybe they don't deserve it. Even if you have to discon the guy—lock him up for three or four hours at the station house, handing him a disorderly conduct "C" summons in lieu of arrest— he still got locked up in front of his friends, who saw you live up to your threat.

This is the respect every cop in the ghetto wants, and it's absolutely the very best you can hope for. You can't fight the whole system. That's the other reality. You take one drug location out, another takes its place. Lock up one dealer, he'll be out in a day or two. And you can't move against the bigger guys, because the bigger agencies: FBI, ATF, DEA have already claimed them. They've planned the press conferences where they put the evidence—piles of bagged cocaine, triple-beam scales, Uzis, and stacks of money—on a table in front of a podium bearing a federal seal. All for the six o'clock news.

The average cop's job at the street level is a repetitive ritual. There's no progress in busting a street-level dealer, it's just filling time. It's putting on a show for the honest public and maybe making a bit of overtime in the process. Street theater and OT.

Now, I'm coming from the perspective of a late-tour cop. The feeling is, there's no public out in the ghetto to see you at three in the morning. The only people who are going to see you are perps, and who gives a fuck if they think you're professional. The only thing they have to know is that you'll kick the shit out of them if they disrespect you, just as surely as they'd whack (shoot) an underling or rival who disrespected them.

The reality is, if you're wandering around at three in the morning in the ghetto, you're probably up to no good. The decent people that live in the ghetto, and many do, are asleep. And if they're up, they're not leaving their houses because they're afraid.

Do you have a right to be walking around at three in the morning without having some cop jump all over you? Fuck yeah! But overriding the rights, even the laws, in every cop's mind is the reality. The reality is in his face every day. He sees it, he lives it. And anything he does, more than likely, isn't personal. He depends on his view of this little piece of the world for his survival. He knows that if he makes a mistake by turning his back on the wrong person, letting his guard down or just showing something that can be mistaken for weakness, he can get hurt or shot dead. And he wouldn't die a hero. Other cops, after hearing the circumstances, would shake their heads and know that he "died stupid."

There's no political spin, social theory, or direct order that can change his mind. He doesn't have to understand it. Maybe he doesn't want to understand it. As a matter of fact, he'd be happy, fucking thrilled, just to survive it.

Once you pull the RMP out on the street, you're on your own. Every decision you make, from which way to turn at the end of the block to whether to pull over a suspicious car, can come back in ways you never imagined.

Part of it is an independence, knowing that the decisions you make are your own. That's one of the reasons I got into police work. The other thing is cops are always looking for "markers." They're the things that tell you what kind of night it's going to be. Is it warm or humid? Then people will be out on the streets, just hanging around and drinking. And drinking means fights. It can mean drunk and disorderly or a dispute ending in gunfire.

Is it the weekend? Do people have money in their pockets from payday? That spells opportunity, a robber's lottery.

Then you look at the people. There are a thousand different ways to tell if a guy's a criminal. The most obvious is when a bunch of guys on a corner spread out as you pull up. Everyone starts to walk. The guy who walks away and keeps looking over his shoulder is "dirty." You watch how he walks. You look at the arms. You can tell. Since holsters are rare on the street, guns are loose, hidden in waistbands and pockets where they can be pulled (drawn) quickly. Guys who are strapped (carrying) or holding a jammy (gun) will walk short, shuffling along so the gun doesn't fall out or down their pants leg. If the gun's at his side, then you watch the arm swing. One arm will swing naturally, while the other stays plastered along his gun side, pressed against it, concealing the bulge.

If you stop to question him and he bolts, both hands on his waistband, he's dirty. Some guys on the street will lift their shirts and turn 360 degrees in a slow pirouette, just to show you they're not packing. They know the routine.

Personally, I love gun runs, calls for an armed person. A gun is loaded. A gun is physical, undeniable, irrefutable evidence. Drugs and money, on the other hand, are a touchy situation. You can run after a person, and they can throw a gun away. But when you catch him, after scooping up the gun, you still have a case. But drug possession can be denied. And more often than not, perps dispose of drugs during a chase. Guns usually aren't disposed of. Drugs are product, but a gun means survival. A couple of vials of crack can be replaced, but a gun is harder and more expensive to acquire.

The drug trade involves money—and that makes cops vulnerable. It's a shakey and sensitive topic with the NYPD. Dealers regularly lie. If a cop recovers a thousand dollars, the dealer will claim it was two thousand, and the department will investigate his claim. He's a fucking criminal, but the department listens to him. And the dealers know they've caused the cop who busted them a hassle.

It's better to just pull up, take the drugs, toss them down the sewer, and cut the guy loose. Safer still, call a sergeant to the scene to verify the count (number of vials recovered), take the drugs back to the precinct to be vouchered, analyzed, and eventually destroyed.

Either way, the street-level dealer you just cut loose still has to pay for the drugs. The supplier gives them to him on consignment, so he's got to go back to his supplier and say the cops took the drugs.

The supplier is going to come down hard on him: "What do you mean the cops took the drugs and didn't bust you? Where's my money? Where's my drugs?" If that's the excuse the dealer has, time after time, he's in deep shit with the supplier. All the supplier cares about is his money, profit, and drugs. All the supplier knows—all he wants to know—is that he gave the street dealer $500 worth of crack and that $500 fucking well better come back in cash.

The supplier's only insurance against corrupt underlings is fear. He guards that fear jealously, maintaining it with any means at his disposal. Just to prevent a rumor that he's been chumped is reason enough to whack a street dealer.

Every supplier has a nine-millimeter Sword of Damocles hanging over his head. Because even a rumor on the street that a dealer can be chumped fosters speculation by competitors and their ambitious underlings that he's weak and soft. Maybe even too weak to hold his network of corners. That can lead to territorial disputes and corner shoot-outs. A good corner franchise is worth a grand a day or more in the supplier's pocket. And the only thing that keeps him there—free from attack and open for business—is fear.

Cops know this. We use it to our advantage. It's an attitude of: hey, if I can't eliminate the problem myself, why not manipulate the situation at least in my favor? Let them kill each other off . . . let them eliminate each other. If, for no other reason, territorial shoot-outs quiet a corner for a few days.

You can't rationalize it. It's a self-perpetuating game of false hope, dubious motives, and the basest form of justice. It's twisted. But true.

Every cop knows where drugs are sold. They know the faces of the dealers, the lookouts, the steerers. But it's tough to bust them. They have a system that keeps the stash and the dealers separate, guaranteeing that if anyone is busted, it's for possession and not distribution. What appears chaotic on the surface is a structured organization run with ruthless efficiency. It's a machine built on teamwork, designed to keep the drugs flowing to the street while minimizing the risk from cops and competitors. Fortune 500 companies should be run so well.

The first guy, the seller, takes the money from the buyer and ducks out of sight into an alley, unlit lobby, or tenement hallway. Once off the street, in a secured area, the seller passes the cash to the holder, who in turn gives the seller the product. The seller then returns to the buyer with the drugs. This division of responsibility insures that at no time is the seller on the street in possession of the drugs and the money simultaneously. From a legal standpoint, it's the difference between "possession with intent" to distribute and simply "possession."

They'll keep a quantity (say, twenty-five vials) out on the street, hiding them under a rock; in the trash in an old potato chip bag; or in a bodega's security gate track. When these are sold, they go back into an apartment building to drop off the money and pick up more crack. They'll do this during a shift change, when there aren't any cops around. But if business is particularly brisk and they have to re-stock, they'll call in a bogus "10-13" (officer needs assistance), giving an address at the other end of the precinct, assuring that every cop in the precinct will fly to that location.

For cops, a dealer's mere presence is an insult. Here are these scumbags doing business out in the open, and they're untouchable. And they know it. What's more, the anonymous, false "13s," they call in create a seriously dangerous condition for cops.

A couple of years ago, a bunch of us decided to do something about one location on Williams and Newport avenues, in an area called "West of Penn," west of Pennsylvania Avenue, the dividing line that runs through sectors Eddie and Frank. Dealers were selling drugs in front of a corner bodega, but the supply was coming out of a six-story tenement next door.

The problem with this building was there were empty lots to the south, the southeast, and the northeast. There just wasn't any way to sneak up on it. As soon as a cop showed his face, one of the lookouts would shout, "bahando," which is Spanish for "look out" or signal that cops are on the block with a two-note, high/low whistle.

The corner bodega was a small store with a large cinder block wall covered by graffitied murals. The detailed murals were testaments to guys who died on that corner. There'd be a painted headstone with the guy's name that said, "In Memory of" and when he was born and when he died. And along with his name would be something that he loved. I call them ghetto prizes. If the guy liked motorcycles, they'd paint a motorcycle alongside his name. If he had a particularly nice gun, there'd be a spraypainted gun. Or if he was a lady's man, there'd be a couple of women in the picture near his name.

The building had a double doorway of black metal, with small plexiglass windows covered by wire mesh. Maybe five or six bullet holes in the door were left over from the last drive-by. The second door inside, leading from the lobby to the hall, was completely off its hinges. The hall was dark, graffiti covering the marble and plaster.

The guy running the operation was known as "Fat Man" or "Fats," something like that, because he was extremely large. He lived in the first apartment on the ground floor.

The place was untouchable. These guys were smart and organized. We stormed that corner half a dozen times and never came up with anything. But every cop in the precinct was sick of that fucking corner, and sick of the scumbags dealing there. Not only were these guys starting to disrespect us, by not walking away when we drove by, they were calling in "13s" left and right, and we all knew it.

When I worked four-to-midnights, a bunch of us got together before a shift and decided what to do about this location. We were determined to turn the tables on these guys. There were a lot of guns there as well as drugs. The idea was to hit them hard and shut them down for a little while. A perp definitely had to go. We were out to take guns and drugs off the street, and to put a body or two into the system.

This particular day we hit the corner three times. Four or five cars, a couple of footmen just being loud and dramatic as hell. We'd come racing up to the building and run into the hall. All these assholes saw were a bunch of cops, they never bothered to count bodies. After the third time, when everyone ran in, we had a few cops stay in the building and hide on the roof. One cop was on our division radio channel, the other was on point-to-point, which central couldn't hear.

A half hour later, we had a car roll by and toss the corner, putting everyone up on the wall to search them and pretend to look for drugs.

Somewhere on the other side of the precinct, a cop phoned in a "13." The whole squad knew about it, and only a couple of cars responded. The main thing was, the dealers heard the call come over the radio. Instantly, the cops tossing the corner stopped, ran back to their cars, and screeched off.

It was maybe twenty seconds before the cops on the roof reported that the guys had recovered their guns and drugs from the trash and were going to re-stock their supply.

The RMP that had driven off to the bogus "13" did a sharp U-turn around the corner, waited thirty seconds for the cops on the roof to get back downstairs, and doubled back along with three other cars.

Everybody scattered as we flew out of the cars. One of the spotters saw the cars coming and went for his waist. But it was too late; four cops jumped him and started beating the living shit out of the guy, recovering from his waistband, a fully loaded automatic.

I was driving one of the cars, and as I came around the corner, I jammed down on the brake, opened the door, and pushed the gear shift into park—all in one motion. I remember having my gun out, drawing it as I brought my hand down from the gearshift and stepped out the door.

As soon as I was clear of the car, I saw this guy run into the lobby. I followed him through the door, gun raised straight up, down the darkened hallway, and toward the back door. He saw me and went for his waistband. Suddenly I'm joined by three other cops and we tackled him. For a split second after we connected, we stayed frozen like that, nobody moving. Then our weight and forward momentum pushed him tumbling back out into the building's walled-in courtyard.

As we hit the ground, four sets of hands kept his hand away from his waistband as he writhed and twisted across the concrete.

Two cops were trying to take the gun away from the guy, while another cop and I tried to cuff him. But he still struggled and wouldn't let go of the gun. This guy was strong. The other cop trying to cuff him finally stepped on his hand and got him to release the gun. It was a .380 automatic with a full clip and one round in the chamber.

By the time we got him to his feet and hauled him outside, I could see other RMPs filled with suspects.

Someone got on the radio and called a sergeant to the scene. We ended up with three arrests, two loaded guns, but no buyers or dealers. For all our trouble, the thing never went to trial. The defendants pleaded out. Fat Man got away.

But we'd done a bust without the brass knowing, so there was some sense of victory in that. If we had involved a sergeant, he would have wanted to plan the whole thing or at least be involved in it. The guy with the gun wouldn't have been jacked (hit) as hard as he was, either. And if the sergeant had heard what we were doing, everyone involved would have caught a foot post for God knows how long.

More than likely, if we had told the sergeant, he would have shot down the idea. Because if there was the smallest chance it could go wrong, cause him headaches, or make more work for him, he would have backed out.

The corner quieted down for a couple of weeks, but then they just started up with the same bullshit. So we decided to hit it again.

Six or eight of us got together before roll call one night and worked out a plan. This time we decided to hit them in the dark. Two of the cars waited around the corner. I got out of the RMP, took my jacket off, and reversed it so they couldn't see my badge or gunbelt. Then I started walking up the street—just another white boy venturing into the ghetto to buy his drugs.

When I got twenty yards away, the spotter made me and went for his waistband. I pulled my gun and yelled, "Police! Don't move motherfucker!"

But the guy bolted into the building. As I ran into the lobby after him, I called it in. I could hear him running down the hallway to the stairs at the back of the first floor, and out into a back alley. I ran after him into the pitch black alley with my gun out as another cop came around the corner.

The guy had his gun out, saw the other cop, and reversed, jumping up and catching hold of a fire escape ladder to the abandoned building next door. Both of us were yelling for him to stop, but he kept climbing the ladder, the gun still in his hand.

I looked up and saw all the windows of the building were cinder blocked over except for a few. The guy then vanished into one of the opened windows.

Without even thinking about it, I started up the ladder. When I got to the open window the perp had climbed through, I peeked around the jagged edge, hoping not to get my head blown off. Inside, I heard him running up the stairs.

The other cop was right behind me by now, so we climbed in through the window. Inside it was dark; the only light seeping in came from the alleyway floodlight. It smelled like piss and decay.

"You got a flashlight?" I asked, because mine was still in the car.

"No," he said. "It's in the car."

I got through the window and ran across the room.

As my partner followed me through the window, I heard a sharp snap of wood, followed by him shouting, "Oh fuck!" The floor had given out under him, and his leg was buried to the knee in a jagged hole.

"What do we do now?" I asked.

The cop pulled his leg out of the floor and said, "Room to room."

"Room to fucking room!" I whispered back. "We don't have a flashlight. That asshole could have a gun on us now and we wouldn't know it. He can probably hear our radios."

I had one of those mini-mag flashlights in my pocket and pulled it out. By now my heart was going a million beats a minute. And I know, this is just fucking insane. But it was great too. It was the risk and adrenalin that kept us going.

So we started a room-to-room search, working our way up floor by floor in the darkness. And when we got to the top floor, we heard him.

I stopped in the doorway and yelled into the room. I couldn't see a fucking thing, but I could hear him rustling around in there.

The other cop, standing on the right side of the door, yelled in as I shined the mini-mag into the room. The beam was just strong enough to light up one corner. There was nothing in the room, just a closet where he must have been hiding.

I walked slowly to the other side of the living room, watching the closet. I and the other cop had our guns out. And were both yelling.

"Let me see your fucking hands!"

"If I see a fucking gun, I'm gonna blow your fucking head off!"

"Show me your fucking hands, motherfucker!"

With each step closer to the closet, I could feel my finger pulling back on the trigger, tensing, palm hard against the backstrap. And I kept hearing this rustling in the closet. What the fuck was he doing in there?

Suddenly, from downstairs, I heard, "Hey, where are you guys?"

"Up here! Top floor!" my partner shouted back, then added, "Bring flashlights!"

Twenty seconds later, we had four more guys in the room, lighting it up with flashlights.

All six of us started moving again on the closet, inching our way closer and closer. One of the guys stood back, off to the side and slowly opened the door, while the rest of us punched our guns and flashlights around the door jam.

From inside the closet, the guy yelled, "Don't shoot! Please, don't shoot!" An instant later, he stuck his hands through the door.

I pulled on one hand, another guy pulled the other, and together we yanked him out of the closet and threw him on the floor.

"Where's the gun? Where's the fucking gun!"

"I don't have no gun," he said.

"Where's the fucking gun, motherfucker!"

Somebody cuffed him and pushed him back down on the floor.

Using one of the other cop's flashlights, I looked in the closet. No gun.

"You find it?" someone asked me.

"No, I can't see it," I shouted back.

"I told you, there ain't no gun," the suspect said, and tried to rise up a little on his chest, turning his head over his shoulder to see the cop.

"Shut the fuck up," a cop said, then wacked the guy back to the ground.

By now, I was on my hands and knees looking in every fucking corner of the closet. No gun.

Then I saw this hole at the far end of the closet, in the back corner. It looked like a rat hole. I broke off a few more chunks of plaster around the edges and shined the light down into it. And there, just out of arm's reach, was the butt of a gun, wedged between floors.

"You got the gun?"

"No, but I can see it." I said.

"What?"

"It's in the wall."

"What the fuck are you talking about?"

Another cop came into the closet, and I showed him. Now we have a gun, but can't recover it.

Suddenly the sergeant got on the radio, "I want you out of that building, now!" There was no way in hell he was coming into the building. The front door was cinder blocked, and the fire escape was the only way in. And he sure wasn't going to climb up that fire escape. Plus, he wanted to know just how we intended to get the perp out, him being handcuffed and all.

I'm only worried about recovering the gun. Finally, somebody showed up with a wire hanger. I untwisted it and worked the hooked end toward the trigger guard. As I pulled the gun out of the hole, I saw it was cocked.

It's another .380. Uncocking the gun and pulling the slide back, I cleared the round in the chamber. The guy could have shot us at any time.

By now, the sergeant was fucking livid, screaming over the radio as we brought the guy down the stairs. When we reached the opened window, we eased him back out onto the fire escape. Me and another cop held him by the collar and began lowering him down the ladder's rungs, one by one, with his hands still cuffed behind his back.

With two steps left, and a six-foot drop to the ground, we couldn't hang on to him—our arms were already extended as far as they'd go.

"Come on, let'em go, we'll catch him," one of the cops below said.

"Let go, we got him! We got him!" another cop on the ground said, actually reaching up.

We let him go, and the cops on the ground immediately stepped away as the guy fell into a pile of trash.

The guy was pissed off, but wasn't hurt. As we hauled him up and brought him out of the alley, I saw the street was filled with department vehicles—ten or fifteen RMPs: NYPD, Transit, Housing, foot cops, ESU (Emergency Services Unit), and EMS buses (ambulances). And they all had their turret lights going. It was as if we were hauling in all ten of America's Most Wanted, not just some gun-toting spotter from a corner drug operation.

My partner sat down on the rear steps of an EMS bus and pulled his pants leg up. It was soaked from the knee down with blood, and there was a huge gash in his leg. And the funny thing was, after all that bullshit, he was afraid he'd have to get a tetanus shot.

In the end, we couldn't tie the perp to the drugs, but we got him on gun possession and he pleaded the case out.

Working steady midnights in the 7-5 is to witness "ghetto Darwinism" up close. It's a lesson in survival in a place where the big, the fast, and the smart eat the small, the slow, and the stupid.

As cliched as it sounds, a good cop knows the streets and the people in them.

You get so that you know which neighborhood bodega will front a crackhead twenty bucks for the family's VCR or pay cash-on-delivery for a "semi-warm" car stereo ripped out of a Saab in Brooklyn Heights or Park Slope.

On the street, you learn how a car is stripped. First the battery, then the tires, then the alternator, then the interior, and finally the engine.

Some of the things I've seen still bewilder me. Like just how strong a crackhead, at a certain point in their addiction, can be. They subsist on candy bars and other junk food, certainly not a well-balanced diet. Food and nearly every other basic necessity has been knocked off their top ten list of priorities, replaced by their habit. Yet these guys have virtually no body fat—they're all muscle—washboard stomachs, and toned arms. Six months later they could be skeletons—what cops call the "Jenny Crack Diet Plan"—but for a few weeks or months, they're dangerous.

Another thing that surprises me is how fast a fucking thief can run. They can go from a dead stop, crouching beside a car trying to break in, to Road Runner "beep-beep speed" in three strides. And they can maintain that speed for two, three, or four blocks, just far enough ahead of a cop to duck into the nearest alley or doorway. Then they just seem to vaporize.

I've learned how guns are best hidden in the bulk of "Triple Fat" goose down jackets . . . or in the air bag compartments, under the fire walls, in hinged door panels, and armrest consoles of cars. I learned how the "Mister Softee" ice cream man, a familiar sight from my own childhood, could be selling drugs from his truck. And the more I learned, the more there was to learn. It seemed endless. The information required, just to survive, could fill an encyclopedia.

After a couple of months, I began to recognize the skells (homeless drifters) who push stolen post office bins and shopping carts through the streets. They look for bottles, cans, pieces of wire or aluminum—anything that can be collected and sold. These guys are out all night, burning tires, stripping the insulation from copper wire, filling their carts with scrap that they redeem for thirty-five cents a pound. Nobody ever pays them any attention, but in their nocturnal scavenging, they see things. They witness crimes. They hear the rumors.

One of the first things I learned when I was just starting out was that hookers, junkies, and skells are good sources of information. They have no loyalty to anyone.

The public is always surprised and gratified whenever a high-profile crime hits the headlines, and two or three days later there's a photo in the paper of detectives hauling the perps in. *Heroes.*

Cops and detectives in the precinct pursuing an ongoing investigation start leaning on people, street people, known dealers, hookers, skells—anyone. Somebody always knows something, or knows someone who knows something.

If it's a slow night, when you need the OT, there's always somebody doing *something* illegal. It's just a matter of ferreting out the information.

My first partner, Eddie, showed me how it worked. There was this one part of the subway-line that ran along Van Sindren Avenue. Before it was barricaded and gated by the city, junkies used to hang out under it and shoot up.

What we would do was wait in the RMP a couple of blocks away, watching in the shadows until they had the dope in the needle, then we'd pull down the narrow alley fast. They'd either panic and run or just rest the needle down and pretend to be taking a piss.

We'd jump out of the car, put them against the wall, and start asking them questions about who's dealing? Who's carrying (packing a gun)? And what, if anything, they've witnessed?

Usually, we got no answers, just a bunch of stuttering and stammering.

"You got a spike (needle)?" Eddie would ask, reaching into the junkie's pockets.

"No, no spike, man," always came the reply.

If we found one, then the lie earned them a crueller (head blow), because if you got pricked by the needle, you're fucked. Then you must take an AIDS test. But usually these guys told the truth, their spikes and works (paraphernalia used to prepare heroin) were set up, ready to be injected or resting nearby.

Any lack of cooperation resulted in our squirting out the hypodermic's contents into the dirt. We'd do it so they could watch. Twenty bucks on the ground. Wasted. His high and stability for the day soaking into the gravel. If we found a crack pipe, we'd smash it.

"Okay, every time we come back here, we're going to harass the shit out of you. Understand? We're not going to lock you up, we're just going to make your life miserable. Unless you give us information. Understand?"

Obviously, we were supposed to be locking these guys up, but if we hauled in one deck of heroin or two vials of crack, we'd be laughed out of the precinct. However, after a few questionings, the junkies would come up with information—legit information.

Drugs are the major industry in the ghetto. The proceeds from street sales pay rents, buy groceries, and keep the lights and telephones from being shut off. What looks random and haphazard to the outsider is a mercilessly efficient business that keeps the supply cheap and available.

Surprisingly, the kids from the suburbs know it. A large vial of crack, called a Jumbo, might cost twenty bucks on Long Island. For a few bucks worth of gas you can buy the same vial for five bucks in East New York. It's the difference between buying two and a half versus five vials for half the price. It's the difference between buying wholesale and retail.

On a slow night, you can find a couple of RMPs parked in the shadows just off Crescent Street and Pitkin avenues, waiting for these kids from the suburbs. It's a well-known drug location, and a favorite with the white kids from Long Island. It's just off the Conduit Boulevard, which is just off the Belt Parkway, which connects with the Southern State to the Long Island Expressway. Express service. Easy in; easy out.

These kids want to spend as little time as possible in the ghetto. And at this particular location, they can do their business and be on their way back to Long Island in ten minutes or less. It's like a drive-up window at McDonald's.

There's a couple of ways to discourage these kids. First, you can pull up on the car and prevent the transaction. Jump on them as soon as they pull up. Go over to the car and start barking questions in their faces: "What the fuck are you doing here?" "Give me your license!" "What the fuck are you bringing your girlfriend here for?" "You're from

Smithtown: Get your white fucking ass back to Smithtown; I don't want to see you here again!"

That's basically a scare tactic. It's good if it's a busy night and you don't have the time to waste on bullshit. The second tactic is to wait until he gets out of the car and walks around the corner to do the deal. Then give the girlfriend a toss—put her against the car and search her.

"Who's the driver?" "Who are you? Where are you from? Why are you here?" You give her the same routine as before, but now her boyfriend's probably done doing his deal and is hanging back in the shadows somewhere. He has no intention of coming near that car, not with the cops there, and especially not with a pocket full of crack or pot.

And you keep on her. Keep asking questions. You know he's getting sweaty, watching from wherever he is, because he's in the fucking ghetto. After a little while, you tell her to take the car and get the fuck out of there.

"If I see this car again, I'm gonna lock you up," we tell her. "We're gonna take the fucking car away and give it to the city as forfeiture, because you're in a known drug location."

She's scared. She's spent her whole life on Long Island and probably doesn't have a clue as to what cops can and can't do in the ghetto.

She might hesitate, but she's scared because you're a ghetto cop. No Long Island cop in Smithtown, Hempstead, or Massapequa has ever talked to her like that before. What's more, there are Black and Hispanic people here. Mercy. So she puts the car in gear and drives off.

And just like clockwork, five minutes later she's back looking for her boyfriend.

Then you pull up on her again. Now the whole situation is turning into a nightmare for her.

"Get out of the fucking car!" you scream at her.

She may or may not be crying or begging just to let her go again.

"I told you not to come back here!" you say. "Now empty your purse, and I swear, if I find a fingernail file, I'm gonna lock you up for a weapons possession!" If you're not familiar with the city and Long

Island, then you should know that the odds of *not* finding a fingernail file, or a can of hairspray for that matter, on a Long Island girl, are roughly the same as winning the lottery. Twice. Nails and hair are both big on Long Island.

You just know what's echoing through her head. She's saying to herself, "Oh fuck, why would my boyfriend bring me here?" Which creates an awkward situation for him later.

Soon you've got the purse contents dumped out on the hood of the car and start going through it. Probably, there's nothing in there. But by now, your partner is in her face yelling, "Slut," "Bitch," "Whore," and patting her down. Now, she's being touched in public, humiliated. Usually, there's a group of five or six dealers, steerers, and lookouts standing on the corner, and they're laughing their asses off. And the boyfriend, he's probably still hanging back, wondering where the nearest subway station might be, and if he'll survive the walk.

Now, you order her to put her shit back in the bag and throw it in the car. Then you tell her to, "Get your tight little Long Island white ass back in the car and get the fuck out of here! Or I swear, I swear to Christ, I'll throw your ass in a cell with one of those mutts and he'll rape your ass all night!"

You watch her drive away and call for another car to follow her out. As for the boyfriend: he's stuck. Fuck his stuck. He came into the ghetto to buy drugs. So fuck him.

One night on a slow tour, my partner and I were sitting in the shadows parked behind a van facing south, just bullshitting, when we saw this white Monte Carlo pull up. The driver pulled onto a one-way road that goes north.

As we watched, a white guy got out of the car to do his deal, car running, leaving the girlfriend behind in the passenger seat.

So we called for backup, and while we're waiting, he resumed, got in his car, and pulled away. Just then, the other RMP pulled up behind him as he came to a stop sign. At this point his full attention was behind him, focused on the cops in his rearview mirror. And suddenly, everything became legal—the full stop at the stop sign, the right turn signal, everything. He probably hadn't followed all the driving laws since he took his road test, but now, in the ghetto, at three in the morning, with the NYPD right behind him, he's driving like everyone's grandmother. It's what my father used to call "instant religion."

Just as he started pulling away, we came out from behind the shadows, hitting the high beams, turret lights, and spot lights. The RMP behind him did the same thing.

Our car doors flew open, and, with our guns drawn, we bum rushed the car. "Don't fucking move! Put the car in park!" Just like on TV.

At this point, you know they're shitting bricks, especially the girl.

He's got cops behind him, cops in front of him, and bright lights in his eyes. He's probably in a total fucking panic. Cops are yelling and pointing guns at him. But for us, it's like role playing; something to do on a slow night.

A couple of cops came up from behind and opened the doors to his car. They pulled the pair out and put them on the hood. I noticed the girl first. She wasn't bad looking, maybe 19 or 20. Dark, shoulder-length hair, tassled boots, and a leather jacket. The guy had dark hair, a mustache, a leather jacket, and he was shaking like a leaf. Basically, he looked like a loser. Just some kid who works in a mall and didn't know what he was going to do with his life. Everything about him said, "All I have is my babe, my crack, and my Monte Carlo—and I can barely afford all three."

We frisked him, "What's this bulge? Is this a gun?"

"No, no man, it's a pack of cigarettes," he answered, nervous and trying to collect himself.

"Don't lie to me! Don't you fucking lie to me! I'll beat the fucking piss out of you!"

"Cigarettes man, really, really, please."

And he was looking at his girlfriend across the car's hood. I saw everything in that look; it said, "Oh man, I'm going to jail. Help!"

I glanced back and saw a couple of the other guys tossing the car. Totally trashing it. And I knew that someone was going to find their way to the fuse box and pull a couple of the fuses, so it would take forever to find out what was wrong with the lights, blinkers, or stereo.

Meanwhile, I'm saying, "Where is it? Where the fuck is it?"

We didn't find any drugs on this particular guy. The dealer's spotter saw us and turned him away.

The drug dealer's crew were grouped in a loose knot on the corner, yucking it up. Dissing the white boy from a safe distance. The message to the white kid is: Now, how do you like dealing with the man like *you* were some ghetto nigger? How do you like being dissed out in the street?

"Don't you know when you pull up here, don't you know that these motherfuckers are going to rob you? Take your car. Butt fuck your girlfriend? Don't you fucking know that?"

By now, the guy's wimpering on the hood while a couple more cops tear his car apart.

"Don't you know they'll turn your girlfriend into a cheap whore? Rip her ass apart?" Then to the girl, "Did you know that? Every one of those mutts'll fuck you till you bleed."

From somewhere she found some courage. Trying to take control of the situation and establish that she's different from whatever other type of person we may be used to dealing with, she said, "You don't have to talk to me like that officer."

"Oh, excuse me, yes I do," I answered. "Because that's exactly what's going to happen." I grabbed her by the forearm and started walking her to the corner. "Yo, money, c'mere man! You want a fresh piece of ass! I got a fresh piece of pussy right here!"

Of course nobody on the corner moved, but by now they're bent over with laughter. This is great street theater for them. A couple of white kids being tossed by the man.

After half a dozen steps, she started to cry.

"Don't cry like a fucking baby," I said. "If you're woman enough to come in here to buy drugs, you're woman enough to deal with the whole thing."

"Officer, I promise, I promise," she cried. "I'll never come back. I promise, please. I'll do anything."

So I walked her back to the car, where the boyfriend was still on the hood. One of the other cops had pulled out a sterile surgeon's glove we use when we search perps. He's rolled up his shirt sleeve and is snapping the glove up his forearm like Ben Casey.

Looking over his shoulder, the kid's eyes grew wider and wider with fear. Nobody's said anything, but it was clear that this cop intended to do a "full cavity" search out on the street.

By now I'm beginning to envy the guys on the corner, because they're able to laugh. Along with the other cops, I'm having a hard time keeping a straight face. The whole scene had digressed into the sick and sadistic. I knew it then, even trying to keep from laughing, and I know it now, when it hardly seems funny. But now I recognize it for what it was—a sick humor in drawing fear from a helpless person.

The whole thing dissolved after that. I brought the kid up off the hood so he was facing me and started talking to both of them. "How would you feel if those five niggers over there fucked your girlfriend and made you watch? Then fucked you in the ass. Then shot and stabbed her. Or shot and stabbed you. All because your cheap little Long Island white ass wants to come into *my precinct* to buy drugs." The message is: I belong here. Those mutts on the corner, they belong here. You, you fucking don't belong here.

Silence from the two.

"You two, you're fucking pathetic. Now get the fuck out of here."

They drove off a short time later. If they'd gotten lippy or insulting, we could have disconned them, wrote them a summons, and held them for four hours. But instead, we had another car follow them out of the area.

We turned off the turret lights and drove around the block to the other side of Crescent and Pine streets. Now we were going to pinch the corner where the dealers were, by bum rushing it in the same way.

Two cars came up from different angles with the lights out. One car came up Pitkin from Pine, and the other came down Crescent, heading down both streets the wrong way.

Both cars moved slowly and quietly to the corner, until finally, at about thirty yards away, one of the lookouts spotted us. And boom, we hit the corner. Lights on, out of the car, guns drawn. A couple of the guys tried to run, but we caught them and herded them back into the group.

"Okay, up on the wall!"

"Take that fucking hat off," someone yelled and threw the guy's hat on the ground.

"Yo man, why you got to do that to my rim?"

"Shut the fuck up," someone said, and smacked him across the back of the head.

This wasn't acting, this was for real.

"Yo, that fucking white boy just gave you up," one of the cops said.

"What the fuck you mean?"

"Fucking white boy, he gave you up. Don't give me 'what the fuck you mean?' You know what you're fucking doing here."

"Yo, officer, we're just hangin' man."

"You had your laugh when we were tossing the white boy. But he gave you up. Now be a fucking man and take it. And we'll be on our way."

There's no fear here from these guys. This is just a fucking inconvenience for them. Every second we're on the corner, they're losing money. And they resent us for it.

I tossed the nearby garbage can looking for their stash. Someone else was searching them. A cop found a stem (glass crack pipe) and crushed it. Another cop kicked their "boom box" off a milk crate, cracking the case.

"Yo man, why you gotta do that?"

" 'Cause you can buy another one. Cause you can afford a hundred of 'em. Now shut the fuck up and stay on the wall."

After a little while, we took everyone's pedigree (name, address, etc.). As they all squared themselves away, we got them in a little group.

"Here's the deal," I said. "I don't want you fucking guys hanging around here anymore. I pull up, you're gone. I shouldn't have to get out of the fucking car. I get out of my car and toss you again, and again, and again. And if I do it enough, if I lose my patience, I'm gonna lock you up. I'll own your ass for four hours. I'll take four hours from your life, cause I got all the time in the world. Eight and a half hours, I can do anything with it. And I still get paid. I'm gonna take you off the street and for four hours you won't get paid."

"Yo man, we got it," one of them said, while another chimed in, "Yo, hear it."

And you know they did. So I eased off into a joke. "Man, what you selling to white people for? You know they give you up?"

A couple of heads nodded in agreement.

"Man, white people, they don't want to go to jail. They'll give you up in a heartbeat.

More nods.

"Now, step off in the direction you live," I said. "Not into the store down the street. Go home."

They walked off, but ten minutes later, after we'd left, they'd be back and open for business.

The point of the whole incident is that you have to establish one fact: that you control everything. You just controlled the white boy from Long Island, which was observed by the street, and you just as equally controlled them.

If they had all stepped off right after we had tossed the kid from Long Island, it would have been, "Sorry you had to miss the show, but you owe me that respect." Everybody's got to make money. Everybody's got to do their job. For those guys on the corner, it's an economic fact that they have to deal drugs. It's a choice between asking, "Will that be a large Coke with that hamburger?" for minimum wage at Burger King or standing on a corner for a couple hundred bucks a night dealing drugs. That isn't even a choice. But when I come around, show some respect. You step off and let me do my job. At least show me that much.

But the thing that really gets me about these kids who come into the ghetto to buy their drugs is how many of them have a father, or cousin, or uncle who's either a cop or a detective. They're holding a PBA (police union) card with a shield number on it and will give up who they know "on the job," in a flash. That's embarrassing. So I tell them,

"How would you feel if I woke them up, right now, and told them I was holding you here? Told them that you admitted you were buying drugs and you gave them right up? Just because you fucking know someone on the job, that doesn't make it okay to come here and buy drugs."

The saddest thing, which I never say, is that even though I don't know who their friend or relative is on the job, I'm embarrassed, deeply and genuinely. But they'll never know it.

The other thing is, the dealers on the corner probably won't rob or kill the kid who comes in from Long Island to buy his drugs. It's bad for business. When word gets out, "Hey you can't go to that location anymore, because they rob white people," that hurts sales. Sometimes they'll rip them off after the fact, by having another guy rob them of the drugs they just bought and whatever money's left in their pockets. But even that's self-defeating. The first principle of good business, even in the ghetto, is that it's safe to buy here. There's still an element of fear; there has to be. It keeps the outsiders in line. Those white kids don't belong there. The dealers don't talk to them nicely. It's: "Yo man, ten bucks, give me the fucking money!" It's a quick hand-to-hand transaction and a done deal. After which, both players go their own way; each thinking the other is pathetic.

What it is, truthfully, is business.

And that's all it is.

Cop Diary

by Marcus Laffey

Marcus Laffey is a pseudonym for New York police officer Edward Conlon, who writes a regular column for the New Yorker. *His accounts about policing the city offer a window on work that is sometimes horrifying, sometimes funny, and sometimes sad.*

Over the past year, more than a hundred people have worn my handcuffs. Not long ago, in a self-defense class, I wore them myself. There was a jolt of dissonance, like the perverse unfamiliarity at hearing your own voice on tape. Is this me? They were cold, and the metal edge pressed keenly against the bone if I moved, even when they were loose. The catch of the steel teeth as the cuffs tighten is austere and final, and never so much so as when it emanates from the small of your back. I thought, Hey, these things work. And then, Good thing. Because their intransigent grip means that, once they're on the correct pair of hands, no one should get hurt. Barring an unexpected kick or a bite, the story's over: no one's going to lose any teeth or blood, we're both going safely to jail, and at least one of us is going home tonight.

The handcuffs are a tool of the trade and an emblem of it, as are the gun and the nightstick. People—especially children whose eye level is at my equipment belt—stare at them, sometimes with a fearful look, but more often with fascination. Since I hold them from the other end, I regard them differently, just as surgeons don't feel uneasy, as I do, at the sight of a scalpel or a syringe. Police work can look ugly, especially when it's done well: you might see a man walking down the street, untroubled, untroubling, when two or ten cops rush up to him, shouting over sirens and screeching tires, with their guns drawn. You haven't seen the old man rocking on a stoop three blocks away with one eye swollen shut. You haven't heard his story, his description of the man being handcuffed: coat, color, height, the tattoo on his wrist.

The transformation from citizen to prisoner is terrible to behold, regardless of its justice. Unlike my sister the teacher or my brother the lawyer, I take prisoners, and to exercise that authority is to invoke a profound social trust. Each time a surgeon undertakes the responsibility of cutting open a human being, it should be awesome and new, no matter how necessary the operation, no matter how routine. A police officer who takes away someone's freedom bears a burden of at least equal gravity Let me tell you, it's a pleasure sometimes.

I walk a beat in a neighborhood of New York City that is a byword for slum. Even if the reality of places like the South Bronx, Brownsville, and Bed-Stuy no longer matches the reputation, and maybe never did, these bad neighborhoods are still bad. Children still walk through three different brands of crack vials in the building lobbies. People still shit in the stairwells. Gunshots in the night may have become less common in my precinct, but many people, young and old, can still distinguish that hard, sharp crack—like a broomstick snapped cleanly in half—from fireworks or a car backfiring.

The genuine surprise is how wholesome and ordinary this neighborhood sometimes seems, with its daily round of parents getting kids ready for school, going to work, wondering if a car or a coat will make it through another winter. Life in the projects and the tenements can be just the way it is in suburbia, except that it takes place on busier streets and in smaller rooms. Sometimes it's better, in the way that city life, when it's good, is better than life anywhere else. In the summer, you can walk through the projects beneath shady aisles of sycamore and maple, past well-tended gardens and playgrounds teeming with children. There will be families having cookouts, old ladies reading Bibles on the benches, pensive pairs of men playing chess. Once, I went to the roof of a project and saw a hawk perched on the rail. Always, you can see Manhattan in the near distance, its towers and spires studded with lights, stately and slapdash, like the crazy geometry of rock crystal. There are many days when I feel sorry for people who work indoors.

The other revelation when I became a cop was how much people *like* cops. In safe neighborhoods, a cop is part of the scenery. I used to notice cops the way I noticed mailboxes, which is to say only when I needed one. But in bad neighborhoods I notice people noticing me, and especially certain classes of people—older people, young kids, single women, people dressed for work or church. They look at me with positive appreciation and relief. I am proof that tonight, on this walk home, no one's going to start with them. Sometimes they express that appreciation. The exceptions are groups of young guys on the street (older, if they're unemployed). Sometimes they're just hanging out, sometimes they're planning something more ambitious, and you're a sign that this wild night's not going to happen—not as they hoped, not here. Sometimes they express themselves, too.

When I'm working, I wear a Kevlar vest, and I carry a nightstick, pepper spray, a radio, a flashlight, two sets of handcuffs, and a gun with two extra fifteen-round magazines. A thick, leather-bound memo book has been squeezed into my back pocket, and leather gloves, rubber gloves, department forms, and binoculars are stuffed in various other pockets. When you chase someone in this outfit, it's like running in a suit of armor while carrying a bag of groceries. But I'm safe, and it's only very rarely that I feel otherwise. All the people I've fought with were trying to get away.

I walk around on patrol, keeping an eye out and talking to people, until a job comes up on the radio. The radio is constant and chaotic, a montage of stray details, awful and comic facts:

"Respond to a woman cornered by a large rodent in her living room."

". . . supposed to be a one-year-old baby with its head split open."

"The perp is a male Hispanic, white T-shirt, blue jeans, possible mustache, repeat, possible mustache."

The appeal of patrol is its spontaneity and variety, its responsiveness to the rhythms of the street: there will be long lulls and then sudden convulsions as pickup jobs and radio runs propel you into a foot pursuit, a dispute, or a birth. When the action's over, the world can seem slow and small, drearily confined. And then you have to do the paperwork.

When you arrest someone, it's like a blind date. You spend a few hours with a stranger, a few feet apart, saying "Tell me about yourself." You ask, "How much do you weigh?" and "Are you a gang member? Really! Which one?" And you hold hands, for a few minutes, as you take prints—each fingertip individually, then four fingers together, flat, and the thumb, flat, at the bottom of the card. A lot of people try to help you by rolling the fingers themselves, which usually smudges the print; sometimes that's their intent. Crack-heads often don't have usable prints: their fingers are burned smooth from the red-hot glass pipe. Junkies, as they're coming down, can go into a whole-body cramp, and have hands as stiff as lobster claws. Perps collared for robbery or assault may have bruised, swollen, or bloody fingers. You try to be gentle, and you wear latex gloves.

When you print a perp, you're close to him, and because you're close you're vulnerable. You take off the cuffs and put your gun in a locker. Once, I was printing a guy as he found out he was not getting a summons but, instead, going through the system. He became enraged at the desk sergeant, screaming curses and threats, and I wondered if he'd make a run at him or, worse, at me. But I was holding his hands and could feel that they were as limp and loose as if he lay in a hot bath—as if his body were indifferent to the hatred in his voice. So I went on printing as he went on shouting, each of us concentrating on the task at hand.

• • •

The paperwork involved in policing is famously wasteful or is a necessary evil, sometimes both. Often, it reaches a nuanced complexity that is itself somehow sublime, like a martial art. If, for example, you arrested a man for hitting his girlfriend with a tire iron and then found a crack vial in his pocket, the paperwork would include a Domestic Incident Report (for follow-up visits by the domestic-violence officer); a 61, or complaint, which describes the offense, the perp, and the victim; and an aided card, which contains information on the victim and what medical attention she received. The 61 and the aided are assigned numbers from the Complaint Index and the Aided and Accident Index. The aided number goes on the 61, and both the complaint and the aided numbers go on the On-Line Booking Sheet. The O.L.B.S. provides more detailed information on the perp; it has to be handwritten, and then entered into the computer, which in turn generates an arrest number.

You would also have to type two vouchers—both of which have serial numbers that must be entered on the 61 and on the O.L.B.S.—for the tire iron and the crack vial; affix a lead seal to the tire iron; and put the crack vial in a narcotics envelope in the presence of the desk officer, writing your name, your shield number, and the date across the seal. You also fill out a Request for Lab Exam (Controlled Substance and Marihuana) and attach it to the envelope. Next, you run a warrant check on the computer, take prints, and bring the perp up to the squad room to be debriefed by detectives, who ask if he knows of and is willing to tell about other crimes.

The prisoner is then searched again and delivered to Central Booking, at Criminal Court. There he waits in a holding cell until he is arraigned before a judge. At C.B., you photograph the prisoner and have him examined by the Emergency Medical Service, interviewed by the Criminal Justice Agency for his bail application, and searched yet again. Only then is he in the system, and out of your hands. Next, you see an assistant district attorney and write up and swear to a document that is also called a complaint. The entire process, from the arrest to the signing of the complaint, usually takes around five hours—if nothing goes wrong.

There are arrests that cops hope and train for like athletes, and in this felony Olympics, collars for homicides, pattern crimes, drugs by the kilo, and automatic weapons are considered gold medals. But the likelihood that things will go wrong with arrests seems to escalate with their importance: a baroque legal system, combined with the vagaries of chance, provides an inexhaustible source of misadventure. You feel like a diver on the platform who has just noticed that all the judges are Russian.

There was my rapist, a match for a pattern of sexual assaults on elderly women. My partner and I responded to a report that a suspicious person was lurking in the stairwell of a project, one floor up from the latest attack. When the man saw us, he ran, shouting, "Help me! Get a video camera!" We wrestled with him for what seemed like ages; he was limber and strong and sweat-soaked, as slippery as a live fish, and was chewing on a rolled-up dollar bill filled with cocaine. He looked just like the police sketch, and also had distinctive green eyes, which victims had described. He had been staying on that floor with his girlfriend until he beat her up and she threw him out, on the same day as the last attack. He was the rapist, beyond a doubt.

At the precinct, he collapsed, and he told the paramedics he'd ingested three grams of cocaine. At the hospital, his heart rate was two hundred and twenty beats per minute, and he was made to drink an electrolyte solution and eat activated charcoal, which caused him to drool black. He was handcuffed to a cot in the E.R. while the midnight pageant of medical catastrophes was brought in. There was an E.D.P. (an emotionally disturbed person) who had bitten clean through his tongue, clipping into it a precise impression of his upper teeth. Another E.D.P., an enormous drunk picked up from the streets, was writhing and thrashing as a diminutive Filipina nurse tried to draw blood: "Now I prick you! Now I just prick you!" An old man threw up, and another prisoner-patient, handcuffed to the cot next to him, kindly handed him the closest receptacle he could find—a plastic pitcher half filled with urine, which splashed back as he vomited, and made him vomit more.

I'd worked almost twenty-four hours by the time we got back to the precinct, when a detective from Special Victims called to say that my perp had already been taken in for a lineup, a few days before, and had not been identified as the rapist. This meant that we had to let him go. I'd felt nothing toward my suspect throughout our ordeal, even when I fought with him, although I believed he had done hideous, brutal things. But now, suddenly, I hated him, because he was no longer a magnificent and malignant catch—he was just some random asshole who had stolen an entire day of my life.

A few days later, I saw him on the street, and he said hello. I didn't. A few days after that, he beat up his girlfriend again, then disappeared. The rapes stopped.

"Whaddaya got?" This is what the boss—usually a sergeant—asks when he arrives at a scene, to make a decision or review one you've made. You tell him, I got a dispute, a matched pair of bloody noses, a shaky I.D. on a chain snatch; I got a lady with a stopped-up toilet who thinks I'm gonna help mop the bathroom; I got an order of protection that says I have to throw the husband out of the house, but he has custody of the three kids because she's a junkie and they have nowhere to go; I got twenty-seven facts in front of me, too many and not enough, in a broken heap like they fell off the back of a truck, which left yesterday.

When you arrive at the scene of an incident, you have a few seconds to take stock—to make a nearly instantaneous appraisal of a jumble of allegations concerning injuries, insults, histories, relationships between neighbors, brothers, lovers, ex-lovers, lovers again—all this with roots of enmity as tangled and deep as those among Balkan tribes. You say, "No, I just need to know what happened *today*." The outpouring of stories can move like a horse race—a hectic and headlong jostling for position, yet with everything moving in the same direction, toward the same end. Or it can turn out to be like a four-car

crash at an intersection, where all the drivers sped up to lay tri-
umphant claim to the right of way. Brawls often conclude with such a
profusion of contradictory stories that you simply take the losers to the
hospital and the winners to jail.

When we answered an emergency call from a woman whom I'll call
Jocelyn (all the names in this piece, including my own, have been
changed), her complaint seemed to be a simple case of assault; her
assailant, George, who was the father of her infant daughter, had already
left the scene. Jocelyn moved stiffly and was covered with scuffs and
scratches, and one earlobe was notched where an earring had been
pulled out. She was surrounded by a phalanx of female relatives who
let out a steady stream of consolations and curses, all attesting to
George's history of violence. I asked her about her earlobe, and she
said, "Oh, that's old," and, looking closer, I saw that it was, and so were
many of the marks on her. But then she lifted up her pant leg and
showed me a fresh red scrape that covered most of the kneecap, and
the course was clear. I asked for a detailed description and got one:
"He's about five-eight and two hundred pounds, a lotta muscles and a
bald head. Gonna take a lotta you cops to lock him up, 'cause he on
parole for armed robbery and he say he ain't goin' back for nothin'!"

"Does he have a weapon now?"

"Wouldn't be surprised."

When my partner spotted him on the street, I called him over to us,
and he came, without delay. "You George?" I asked, and he said that he
was, in a clear, precise diction that was unusual for the street. He'd spent
his time upstate well. I asked if he'd fought with Jocelyn, and he seemed
mildly embarrassed, as if he had found out that they'd awakened the
neighbor's baby. "Yeah, we did argue, over some stupid little thing."

"Tell you what," I said. "Take a walk with us up there. Let's
straighten it out." The only matter to be straightened out was the "con-
firmatory identification," a procedural nicety in which I was glad to
have his innocent cooperation. His lack of concern was disconcerting,
and suggested either that her story was shaky or that his reflexes and
instincts were wildly askew.

Upstairs, Jocelyn made the I.D. I discreetly put my location and condition—"Holding one"—over the air and gently asked George for a lengthy, time-killing version of events. Even when plentiful reinforcements arrived, and his alarm became evident, he didn't give up, but pulled back as someone tried, gently, to take his arm. Given his strength and the dimensions of the cinder-block hallway where we had gathered, no one wanted a brawl. He began to shake, and to bellow "I did not hit her!" and "I am not going back to prison!" We managed to coax him into restraints while he continued to shout, calling for neighbors to tell us what was really going on.

As we took George downstairs, he began to pitch his version of events: Jocelyn was a crackhead; he had custody of their infant daughter; he was angry at Jocelyn because she left the baby alone; her marks were from a fight she had yesterday; lots of people had seen her attack him earlier that day, and would testify that he had never raised a hand against her. On the street outside, one woman—who looked like a crackhead herself—said she had fought Jocelyn last night, and a man said he'd seen George endure Jocelyn's beating him without protest. Toni, whom George referred to as his fiancée, and who also had a child by him, happened by and joined in, shaking her head in disapproval of Jocelyn. But I still had a complainant, an I.D., a fresh injury, and no choice. And when George admitted that he "might have knocked her down" I didn't feel bad about bringing him in.

At the precinct, George alternated between brooding reveries on injustice and civil, reasonable explanations of his predicament. Then he suddenly assumed a soft-voiced and menacing tone, so that I couldn't tell if he was putting on a mask or dropping one. "I did time, man, time," he murmured urgently. "I know people who rob every day. I know people who sell guns, sell machine guns. I know people sell you a grenade man, I could help you out."

Short of gunfire, nothing has as strong an effect on a cop as the word "gun." Guns are unique in their ability to change nobodies and wanna-bes into genuinely bad men in an instant. And while there is nothing more serious than apprehending a dangerous criminal, it also seems like boyhood itself when you can spend your days trying to get the bad guys. That was why, if I almost believed George when he told me about Jocelyn, I almost loved him when he told me about the guns.

I tried not to let it show, though. I didn't want to get greedy—to let the balance tip from buyer to seller. Not long before, a similar story—completely detailed, wholly plausible, legally sworn—had led me, along with thirty other cops, some equipped with full-body armor and shotguns, to raid an apartment where we expected to find a crate of semi-automatics but instead found a dildo and ten thousand roaches. I knew that if George meant it he'd say it more than once, and for his information to be useful he'd have to be willing to keep talking when he wasn't wearing my handcuffs. So I treated him with consideration—"You got change? I'll get you a soda"—and continued to process the arrest.

As it turned out, however, nothing came to pass. Jocelyn dropped the charges, and even came down to Central Booking to take George home. He was elated as he left, telling me, "Watch, I'm gonna get you a gun collar!" Laughing, I called after him, "Give me your number," and waited to see his reaction. He hesitated, then came back and gave me his beeper number. "I'm telling you," he said.

For a while after that, whenever I ran into George on the street, he would talk to me. The information was always good but never quite useful: he confirmed things I knew, and told me about witnesses to assaults and robberies who wouldn't come forward. I called him once or twice, and my call was never returned.

You often start with these cheesy collars: dice, blunts, trespass. It's not what you signed up for, being a glorified hall monitor, if "glorified" is the word. "Public urinator at two o'clock! Let's move in!" But it's part of the job, so you do it—preferably with the discretion you are empowered to exercise. If a group of guys are hanging out smoking marijuana and I'm walking by, one of two things tends to happen. Either I hear a rapid apology, the blunt is tossed—and if it's down a sewer there's no evidence to recover and no basis for a charge, you follow me, guys?—and the group gets a stern word of caution. Or someone decides to lock eyes with me and take a drag, and someone else calls out some cute remark, like "Fuck the police!" and they decline to heed my word to the wise: "Break out, guys. Bounce!" No? And in seconds, or in a minute if I decide I want backup, they're all up against a wall. I start going into their pockets, taking names.

If someone has I.D., I might run a name over the air, and if there's no warrant out for this person's arrest he'll get a summons for Disorderly Conduct at the scene. But most guys like these don't carry I.D., and you take them into the precinct to search them thoroughly, run the checks, and write the summonses. Often, someone will have drugs on him, or a stolen credit card. One in five will have an active warrant, in my experience, and fully half will come up on the computer as "Robbery Recidivist" or as "Target Narcotic Violator," which means that they have a number of convictions for mugging or dealing. Maybe they were just hanging out tonight, but, as far as I'm concerned, tonight they've lost their street-corner privileges. And now and then you find a prize, like a hard-core felon hiding behind a bottle of Bacardi.

For the most part, the time you spend with people you like and respect occurs at a low point in their lives: they've just been robbed, their child is missing, or their husband has collapsed from chest pains. You are less the bearer of bad news than the proof of it. More often, you become bound up in lives that are dismal and grim: parolees and their teen-age girlfriends, thugs, drunks, and junkies, E.D.P.s taking too much or too little for their pain. Other people you never get to know, even after you've spent some time with them.

The old man lived alone and died crumpled on the floor in a little alley between the bed and the wall. He was wearing a dirty shirt and no pants. His apartment was small and cluttered, and all his clothes were in old suitcases, or were stacked beside them, as if he were packing for a long trip. There were two televisions—one old, one brand-new. A manic kitten darted amid the piles of clothes and rubbish around the old man's body. Because he lived alone, we had to search for valuables, in the presence of a sergeant, and voucher them at the precinct. We found his military discharge papers, his false teeth, and stacks of pornography. The other cops left, and I stayed. It was my turn to sit on the D.O.A., waiting for the Medical Examiner to have a look, then for the morgue to take him away.

A man knocked at the door and said, "I took care of him. I'm his stepson. He wanted me to have the TV."

I told him to get some proof, and said that until then he should take the kitten. He left—without the kitten—and I turned on the television.

Less than an hour later, he returned with a lady friend. Both were completely drunk, and demanded in unison, "We loved him! We was his family! Let's have that TV!"

I closed the door on them and sat back down. There was a phone call. I waited, then picked it up, hoping that no one who cared for him would learn of his death by accident, from a stranger.

"Is Mr. Jones at home?"

"No, he isn't."

"Is this . . . Mrs. Jones?"

"No." But thanks for asking.

"When will he be available?"

"No time soon."'

"When should I call back?"

"Can I ask who this is?"

"Mr. Jones had recently expressed an interest in our low-cost insurance policies, and—"

"He's not interested."

"'And who, may I ask, is this?"

"The police. Mr. Jones is dead. That's why I'm here."

"Well, do you think—"

"Dead."

"There may be some—"

"Dead, dead, dead. He's stuck to the floor six feet away from me, guy. No sale."

"Have you considered whether you have all the coverage you need, Officer?"

I hung up and went back to watching television.

Most of the time, the enforcement of the law follows a simple moral algorithm—the sum of what you should do and what you can. If the perp is there, you make an arrest; if he's not, you make a report. If he runs, you chase. If he shoots, you shoot back. The facts, rather than your feelings, dictate the course of action, but the close correspondence of the two is a satisfaction of the job. Sometimes, though, the victims are less sympathetic than the offenders, and an odd bond develops between cop and perp which can emotionally skew the equation.

One woman called to say that her thirteen-year-old son had locked her out of her house; she had obtained a Family Court order that allowed her to call the police whenever she couldn't control him. For over an hour, we knocked, reasoned, and threatened, and fiddled with the locks. We had ample time to find out about the family.

"Is there anyone—someone he isn't mad at—who could talk to him, get him to open the door?" I asked.

"Oh, he's not mad at me," she said. I let it go.

"Maybe a friend from school?"

"I been tellin' him to go to school since last year," she said, adding that he stopped because the other kids beat him up. Asked why, she said that he wore makeup and women's clothes. My partner went to get a coat hanger, to see if he could work the door chain off. The woman went on about how the boy's father left her, how she worked, how the boy stayed out till dawn. She paused a moment, as if she'd just remembered, and said, "I had a three-year-old—she died. She was pretty." She paused again, then said, "I wish that faggot never was born."

My partner got the door open. The thirteen-year-old, a light-skinned black boy with hair dyed a sunny yellow, was dozing. I told him to get some things together, because he was going to a juvenile holding facility now and to court in the morning. By his bedside I saw a list of around twenty names—all men's, and all but a few with beeper rather than phone numbers. His mother picked up a skimpy pair of gold satin shorts, held them up to her substantial waist, and said, "Who wears these? Not me!"

What friendly or fatherly advice was there to offer? "I didn't peddle my ass when I was thirteen, young man, and now I have a cushy civil-service job"? We drove downtown without saying much, and I haven't seen him since.

Another day, on the street, I noticed that a middle-aged woman was staring at me, in the throes of indecision about whether to approach. I went over to her and asked if I could help. "My husband, he beats me, he beats me very bad," she said. I pressed her for details, telling her how, even if I couldn't make an arrest, she could get an order of protection, but she brushed me aside: "No, no, that's all no good. My daughter, she says she's just gonna get somebody to take care of him."

I told her that if he was beaten he'd probably take it out on her anyway, and again she saw I didn't get it. "I don't mean beat him up," she explained. "I mean take care of him. You know!" She raised her eyebrows, like she was letting me in on a sweet deal. "What do you think?"

"Lady, you noticed that I'm wearing a blue hat, badge, the rest? That I'm a cop? And you want to know what I think about having your husband murdered?"

Before she could ask me to quote a price, we parted, each convinced that the other had only a flimsy grasp of reality. A few hours later, another officer and I responded to a call of a "violent domestic dispute." A burly, middle-aged man answered the door and allowed us in. He was in his underwear and seemed at ease, smiling as he showed us around: there was no one else there, and no sign of a struggle of any kind. Even so, I didn't like him, and the female cop with me had the same reaction, but stronger: he had a corrupt and military air, as if he were an aide to some South American President for Life. As we left, I noticed a photograph of the woman I had spoken with earlier hanging on the wall. She was trying to win our argument, it seemed to me, saying, "Look at him. Look. If this one ended up dead, would you really come after me?"

I continued to have hopes for George. I didn't know if he was much more than a corner hoodlum, but the corners he favored were hot ones. And then he came to my attention again, formally, when he beat up his fiancée, Toni. The night before, she told me, George had knocked her down, shoved her against a wall, and confined her in a bedroom when she threatened to call the police. He'd slept at the door of the room, on the floor, to prevent her from escaping. The next morning, he went out and brought her back breakfast, drew her a bath, and then walked her up to her mother's house, where she called the cops.

When I came for George at his job, his rebuttal was as edgily eloquent and semi-plausible as the last time: Yes, they argued, but, no, he didn't hit her ("Did you see a mark, a single mark on her?"), and if he shoved her once it was because she said she'd have him arrested if he ever left her. A cop witnessed that, he added, and we'd have to find him. He had a letter, in which she made that threat: we'd have to find it. I told him that I still had to take him in. He shrugged his acceptance, and we left for the precinct.

For the past year or so, it's been procedure to debrief every prisoner who comes into the precinct. Most perps won't talk, and many are as ignorant of the local underworld as they are of portfolio management. A detective asks, "Do you have information about robberies, homicides, guns, arson, hate crimes, chop shops, terrorism?" I've had people say, "Chop-chop? What chop-chop?" But when George's turn came he said, "Yes," "Yes," "Yes," "Yes," "No," "Yes," and "What was the last one?"

As it turned out, my prisoner was the Rosetta stone to scores of violent felonies, past and planned. George told us that people approached him to do hits and robberies almost every week. The narcotics king of Atlanta wanted to open night clubs in the city, for dancing and dealing, and had been asking George to run them. A robbery at a bodega was supposed to take place a few hours from now, and he knew the two guys who had planned it, what kind of gun they'd carry, how they knew the owner's brother, a pockmarked Dominican who carried a .357, and how he was the one to watch, to take out if he moved. One of the two had robbed a meat market a few months ago of five thousand dollars, with at least a grand in food stamps, which they moved through a Chinese restaurant. Most important, he knew about another planned hit—on a Brazilian man, a witness in a state case. He wouldn't say more.

It was as if George spread the deck and asked the detective to pick a card, any card—but only one. The detective chose the robbery planned for that night. The exchange was remarkably businesslike: if the bodega robbery occurred and arrests were made quickly, that would be good; if it could be prevented, that would be even better; and either result should be enough to secure George freedom. Though it seemed shabby, and even dangerous, to bargain Toni's distress against the safety of a grocery store, it was just that—a bargain. What was left unmentioned was that George would, in all likelihood, be freed by the judge at his arraignment. Toni's case was weak, even terminal, and if history served as a guide the charges might well be dropped. (I had even found the cop who'd witnessed Toni's threats to have George arrested if he left her.) But George was back in the cage now, and he would do what he could to get out of it. It was a line of thought we encouraged.

As calls were made, and the hours passed, George explained that he had no problem giving up people who weren't close friends and who were going to hurt people. He had hurt people himself, and, while it didn't keep him up at night, he thought it a better thing if people didn't get hurt during jobs. George's efforts at moral understanding had a rote, calisthenic quality: "You think, What if it's your brother, your girl who gets shot in a holdup—how would you feel?" What really bothered him was that here he had information of great value, and he'd had to squander it on an domestic-violence charge. "I'm not gonna say all I know," he told me. "What if they grab me with a gun sometime, what am I gonna have left to give?"

It was after dark by now, and the bodega would be open for only a few more hours. There were countless reasons for the robbery not to take place then: a hangover, a date, the flu, an argument, a bad horoscope, or an arrest. The next night was Halloween, when the robbers could even wear masks without attracting notice. The detective passed the information to the borough robbery squad and sent us on our way to Central Booking.

The password had been spoken, but the gates remained shut. I hadn't quite expected that, and neither had George. This meant that he would have to spend the night with the losers, with their foul smells and sad stories, their tough-guy sheers and choked-back sobs. As I put him in the holding cell, George leaned close to me and whispered that he wanted to talk. "About the Brazilian?" I asked. "About the Brazilian," he said. I loved that part; it was just like the movies. As they say, this is no job for a grownup.

There may be no crime more destructive to the criminal-justice system than a hit on a witness: if witnesses won't work, the system doesn't. For several hours, I pursued district attorneys and detectives to peddle my murder conspiracy, but there didn't seem to be a buyer. After midnight, I went home, determined to keep trying in the morning.

Toni arrived at court in the morning looking fresh and rested, and she remained resolute in her desire to press charges. When we were finished, I was taken aback at the vehemence of the assistant D.A.'s reaction. "Did you see that poor woman? I've never seen such fear!" she said. "I really want to put this guy away!" She had tears in her eyes.

Ordinarily, I would have been delighted with the response. Time after time, I've brought in assault cases, from domestic violence more often than not, and seen them dealt down to next to nothing. At last, I'd met a blazing champion of the downtrodden, and it couldn't have happened at a worse time. My peculiar mixture of motives made me uneasy, but I genuinely felt that her reaction was naïve and awry. There are times when my heart breaks for people; this wasn't one of them.

After Toni signed the complaint, I spoke to another supervising D.A., who sent me to another detective. This time, however, the detective reacted as I hoped, saying that we had to move, immediately, and do whatever possible to get to the Brazilian. But when I retrieved George from his holding cell, it looked as if the case had, again, fallen apart. He'd barely slept or eaten, and he was talking in crazy circles, saying that he could go back to jail and wouldn't care, and then that he'd never go back because he hadn't done anything. Once, he broke down—crying, with his face in his hands—and I thought we had lost him. We moved between paying him sympathetic attention and allowing him moments of privacy; we fed him; we let him call his sister to talk. "Think about your children!" I said. Let me tell you, we were ruthless. Finally, he came around and told us what he knew.

George didn't know if the Brazilian had testified or was scheduled to; if he was an informant or was just suspected of thinking about turning. The Brazilian ran narcotics for another dealer, who was in prison; the dealer suspected that his employee had betrayed him, and had ordered the hit. The fee would be six thousand dollars—half on agreement, half on completion. George also knew the name and address of the Brazilian, because he'd seen a video as a kind of prospectus for the hit: footage of the block, the apartment building, the apartment. In the last ten seconds, the Brazilian himself appeared in the video, stumbling unsuspectingly into the frame on his way home. All this George knew because he had been asked to do the hit.

Throughout the afternoon and into the evening, we worked on the deal. The D.A. wanted to know if anyone could I.D. the Brazilian as a witness or an informant; calls went back and forth between cops and prosecutors, word went up the chains of command, across agencies and jurisdictions. We were determined to prevent a murder, but the D.A., in particular, was terrified of another one, whose headline would read, "D.A. FREES PAROLEE, GIRLFRIEND SLAIN." He had Toni brought back in, to see for himself how she felt, how badly she was hurt, and if she was afraid.

George would not give the Brazilian's name without a promise from the D.A. that he himself would be out, today. The D.A. eventually agreed that it would be enough if the name checked out. George gave up the first name, which was all he remembered anyway—Kari. With this shred of evidence, the detectives started calling around and reporting back to us whatever they turned up.

"The D.E.A. has a Bosnian named Kiri, wants to know if it's your guy."

"'F.B.I. has a Corio, from Naples."

"Naples, Florida, or Naples, Italy?" Never mind, forget it, but keep taking anything close—Brazilian Kari might be Jamaican Kelly after how many guys are passing along the name."

By sundown, there had been no confirmation, but the D.A agreed to let George out that night, in exchange for the Brazilian's address, with the stipulation that he accept the terms of the order of protection, enter a batterer's program, and agree to bring them the videotape the next morning. George gave an address in Manhattan, and a half hour later D.E.A. agents were on a cell phone from a car. No one was home, but neighbors confirmed that a Brazilian man lived there, and several said he was a drug dealer. They had a name. The Manhattan D.A. confirmed that he was a defendant in a drug case and a witness for the prosecution in a kidnapping: his own. The hit had been scheduled to take place that very night, it turned out, but the killers were spooked by the police presence.

And so it finally proved to be a good day's work, though not without its questions and compromises. A life was saved, by freeing the man who'd been asked to take it. The intended victim was the kind of person I'd just as soon arrest as rescue. But he was alive—at least for a little while longer—and George was his unlikely and reluctant savior.

George picked up his life more or less where he left off. Toni decided to drop the charges, and Jocelyn became pregnant by him again: "Gotta keep trying till I get a son," he said. Every week or so, I still run into George on the street, and we say hello. I like him, as far as it goes. The feeling is as mutual as it can be, I think, between two people who wouldn't hesitate to shoot each other. As he's a hit man and I'm a cop, the odds of such an occurrence are less remote than they might be otherwise.

It was near the end of my tour of duty, and I was headed back to the precinct when an aided case came over the air. Aideds are among the most frequent jobs, usually entailing an escort of E.M.S. workers to the scene of an illness or injury. When I arrived in the apartment, I could tell from the smell why someone had called. As I walked down the hall, past what seemed to be numerous, spacious rooms, the rank, ripe odor of decomposition grew stronger, and when an expression-less teen-age girl directed me to the last bedroom I was thrown less by the sight of the still, frail old Puerto Rican woman in bed than the four emergency medical technicians working around her. Two were crying.

The old woman was naked, lying face down, stuck to plastic sheets that made a crackling sound as she was unpeeled from them. She had once been a hefty woman but now looked less slimmed down than deflated: her breasts were empty, pressed against her chest, and the bones of her hips and thighs were plainly visible, draped with loose, lifeless skin. Maggots crawled on her, inchworming along, and pop-ping off like broken watch springs. There was rodent excrement in the bed with her, and one E.M.T., examining her legs, said, with a horrified intake of breath, "Those are rat bites! Whoever did this to her should go to jail!"

The old woman let out a breathy moan as she was rolled over, feeling pain wherever her body was alive. This woman was dying; parts of her were already dead. And she didn't live alone. I turned away, and went to talk to the teen-age girl: "Who takes care of this lady?"

"Well," she said, with a pouty, long-suffering tone, "I'm the one who does most of the work."

"Who lives here? How old are they?"

"Me and my sister and my grandmother. My sister's twenty-three, but she's out now."

"Can you tell me why you didn't feed her?"

"She said she wasn't hungry."

"Why didn't you call a doctor?"

"I'm the one that did."

"Before now, why didn't you call?"

"My mom said not to."

She said that her mother lived in another part of the city. I told her to call her and tell her to go to the hospital. I asked what they lived on, and she said her grandmother got checks and her sister cashed them to run the household. Ordinarily, E.M.S. prefers to have a relative ride in the ambulance with the aided, but when the teen-ager approached the door a no-longer-crying E.M.T. told her, curtly, "You want to visit Grandma? Take the bus."

Back at the precinct, it took some time to figure out how to write the complaint—for, while there are many laws regarding the care of children, the elderly are less explicitly protected. I found a misdemeanor in the Penal Law called "Endangering the welfare of an incompetent person," and named the adult sister and the mother as perpetrators. Since there were checks coming in, "Investigate larceny" was added. And that, I realized, without satisfaction, explained the family's nearly homicidal neglect. The old woman was the keystone of a tidy edifice of subsidies: a large apartment, Social Security, welfare for the teen-age girl. If she went to a hospital or a nursing home, all these benefits would vanish from their pockets. People talk about living from paycheck to paycheck; this family almost let a woman die that way.

Every cop has his gripes and jokes, his epics and anecdotes about life on the job. I grew up hearing them. My great-grandfather was a sergeant, in Brooklyn: a dapper, dangerous figure from the Jazz Age who became Mayor Jimmy Walker's driver. My father was a police officer—briefly, before moving on to federal law enforcement, a law degree, and an M.B.A.—and his brother was a police officer for thirty-three years. My father died before I went on the job, but I think that my decision to become a cop would strike him as an affront to how far we've come from the hardscrabble west of Ireland and the docks of

Hell's Kitchen. For the next generation to pound a beat might mean that his grandchildren would not try cases in the Supreme Court but instead make their livelihood digging potatoes with a stick by the crossroads outside Ballinrobe. Ah, acushla machree.

Now, after a few years on the job, I have my own war stories. On weekends, I'll sit back, lift up my feet, and tell my girlfriend, "I took a bullet out of a lady's living room. It must have been shot from Jersey. It went through the glass, and stopped on the sill. It landed there like a sparrow." Or "I talked a runaway into coming home. She was fourteen years old. All I had to do was tell her I'd lock up her boyfriend's whole family if she didn't." At times, the point of the job seems to be to make it home with an intact skin and a good story. The stories are a benefit, like the dental plan.

And you need them, like your handcuffs or your vest, to control events when you have to, and to cover your back. If you're a cop, you need a quick tongue, to tell the victim, the perp, the crowd, the sergeant, the D.A., the judge, and the jury what you're doing, what you did, and why. Are you ready to make a statement? No? Then you just did. You told me you weren't ready. "Police were unprepared to answer," says the lead in the morning paper. Or the gossip in the locker room, or the word on the street.

I also hear more than my share of stories. And so, aside from the odd Christmas party or fund-raiser, I don't hang out with cops from the precinct. My friends who are cops were friends of mine before I went on the job. And most of the people I see regularly have nothing at all to do with police work. The job has enough of me. For five days a week, I stay off the streets unless I'm working them. And when I'm not in uniform I'd just as soon not see blue.

But I also notice that when I'm out on weekends and there's another cop there—at a wedding or a cookout or a club—I'll often spend most of the time talking with him. There are things you've done and places you've been that no one else has had to do or see in quite the same way.

from Buddy Boys
by Mike McAlary

Mike McAlary (1957–1998) for 12 years fol-lowed the police beat for the New York Daily News. *He had a knack for gaining the trust of corrupt cops, including the pair he profiled in his 1988 book about Brooklyn's 77th precinct.*

I wasn't used to certain things about the way those people lived. When you see people living in shit it takes something away from you. It steals something from you. I saw kids in diapers that hadn't been changed for two or three days and it hardened me. I'd walk into apartments with the linoleum half ripped up off the floor, and grease in the kitchen with hundreds of roaches just swarming around. We had to keep moving in those apartments, stamping our feet. We didn't lean on the walls because we didn't want to take the roaches back to the precinct or get them on our uniforms and take them home.

"I remember going on one job where there was a middle-aged woman with rips in her housecoat sitting at a table eating in the middle of this skelly apartment with roaches crawling around on the table. And she was flicking them away from her plate like they were pets, like it was nothing. It makes you cringe. It makes you cry. But what can you do? We had to go into these apartments and breathe in these places.

"One time I went into an apartment and a big woman was lying on the bed, having a baby. She's heavy into labor. She can't wait for the ambulance. The place is disgusting. Her other kids are running around. I wouldn't go into the delivery room if my own wife was having a baby, but I'm here now. And I helped the lady deliver the baby. I wanted to puke but I didn't. I put my hand over my mouth and helped her. There wasn't time for how I was feeling. We just delivered the baby and got the hell out of there. But what did we deliver the baby to? What kind of life is that kid going to have?

"To make matters worse, the people gave us shit. In the old days, when I first got to the precinct, it seemed like more people had respect for you. Even though they looked like shit, if we raised our voices, they knew they couldn't fuck with us. Now, they yell at us as soon as we walk through the door. 'Who the fuck called you? Who needs you?' Eventually you start asking yourself the same questions. I did. It got so I didn't give a shit what was going on in some places. But I wouldn't leave the precinct either. I was married to the job and the guys. Once I got in the precinct and got comfortable, I never wanted to leave. I loved it there. I loved the guys. It was like a second home to me."

If it's true that one day can change your life, Tony Magno's life was forever changed by what he saw and did in the 77th Precinct on one humid summer evening when the whole city went dark, Wednesday, July 13, 1977.

Tony, the cop who rarely left the sanctuary of his home, was sitting on his living-room couch after finishing a day tour and dinner when the lights went out at 9:34 p.m. Like several million other New Yorkers, he figured that he had blown a fuse. But on the way to the basement, he heard people yelling in the streets. No one in Brooklyn had power. The fourth-largest city in the world was plunged into darkness on a humid ninety-five-degree night.

At first, the blackout was just inconvenient. Tony set up his house, lighting candles, loading fresh batteries in radios and flashlights. His neighbors gathered on stoops, quietly swapping ghost stories. The neighborhood kids all agreed that the blackout was a novelty, a reason to stay up late. But as Tony listened to the radio and heard the call for all city police officers to head into their precincts, he became concerned. Thousands of people throughout Black Brooklyn were rioting and looting, gutting shops and burning down building.

He decided that he had to go into work and fight the ghetto looters, leaving his own family unguarded. It seemed to be a clear choice. He was a cop and on this night the city needed cops.

"You are not going in to work," Marianne advised him.

"I have to go in," he explained. "It's my job."

Assuring his family that they'd be all right, Tony called Zeke Zayas, another police officer who lived nearby, and the two agreed to accompany each other into work. Neither Zeke nor Tony was prepared for what they would see that night—a night of madness when it seemed that every Bedford-Stuyvesant resident had taken to the street, looting shops of everything from cars and bikes to aspirin and toilet paper.

In the next twenty-four hours police made 3,300 arrests and heard 45,000 phone complaints throughout the city. The fire department received 23,722 alarms and responded to 900 fires, 55 of them serious. One hundred cops were injured while trying to restore order. A dozen people were shot dead by armed shopkeepers, snipers, and frightened police officers. Looters in the Bronx broke down the metal door to an automobile showroom and drove away fifty cars. Roving bands in Harlem carried off stolen television sets and stereo equipment. In Queens, looters rushed away from broken stores carrying couches and beds. Airline pilots flying over Brooklyn reported that the borough was aglow with fire. Mayor Abe Beame later described the blackout as "a night of terror."

It was an evening perhaps best captured in one headline and one anecdote—both of them from the *Village Voice*, a week after light had been restored. The article, which included a photograph of several looters running down the streets with televisions and furniture on their backs, was entitled, "Here Comes the Neighborhood." Written by Denis Hamill and Michael Daly, it included the story of one young black man who rushed home to his mother in the middle of the blackout with a stolen air conditioner. Using a flashlight, she plugged the air conditioner into an electrical outlet and pressed the "On" switch. When the machine failed to start after several tries, she was furious and threw the air conditioner out the window. "It don't work," she screamed. "Go get another one."

"We got into the precinct without any trouble. As soon as we hit the shitty area—I hate to say it but it was the black area—we saw a lot of people all over the place. The streets were a mess. There was trash and garbage everywhere. The place looked like one big broken window. We got into the station house and went downstairs to get our helmets. I had never worn one before and I felt like an idiot with this stupid pot on my head. I was scared but excited too. I wanted to be out there.

"I remember one of the first calls was a ten-thirteen on Atlantic and Bedford—assist patrolman, shots fired. As soon as we pulled up I heard a shot, then one or two more. I thought, 'Oh, fuck. What did we get ourselves into here?' All the guys were ducking. Some of us had our helmets on backwards. No one knew where the shots were coming from. There must have been twenty cars there, and we all just got back in them and left. There was utter chaos. We didn't know what to do.

"Then we went out on patrol, if you can call it that, in two cars— one unmarked car followed by a patrol car. The unmarked car would pull up to a store and drive up on the sidewalk, pointing the headlights into the store so we could see what we were doing. The place was a shambles, it didn't even look like a store anymore on the inside. One group of guys would run into the store and start slamming the looters with their sticks. I figured, I ain't going in there and get hit by a stick. I stayed outside and put my deviant mind to work. They could only hit one person at a time inside the store, but I could get six people as they ran out of the store. I stood by the door and waited. And I got every one of them as they came out. Whack, whack, whack. I couldn't hit the women in the face. They'd come out and say, 'Officer, please don't hit me.' I had my stick raised but I said, 'All right, I won't hit you.' But as soon as they ran past me, I hit them in the back of the head. I couldn't look them in the face. And it kept going on like that for hours and hours. I was Babe Ruth that night. No one got away from me.

"People fired at us later on that night too. We didn't know where the shots were coming from. It was crazy. The only light on the street was coming from a burning Thom McAn shoe store. People were still inside the burning store stealing shoes. That really got to me. Guys were taking a chance on burning up for a pair of shoes. I really let those looters have it with the stick. I hit this one guy right in the face and he didn't even look like a human anymore.

"One time on Nostrand Avenue we turned around and just starting firing back down the street toward a building. The shooting stopped. They were like rats out there. We'd walk into a store and the place would be crawling with them. They cleaned out the jewelry stores and the grocery stores. I mean everything. And I knew some of the people I was hitting. I was just about to bash this one lady and she yells, 'Tony, it's me.' I looked and it was the school crossing guard. I couldn't believe it. I told her, 'Just drop the shit and get the fuck out of here.' Even the people that I liked, my friends in the neighborhood, were out there looting. I lost all respect for the neighborhood after that night. There were some cops taking things too. Guys were loading up their trunks with stuff. I saw a lot of liquor being passed around the precinct that night."

"I was never so happy to see the sun come up in my life. My arms were falling off. I couldn't swing the nightstick any more. I was exhausted. I couldn't hit another person. But even after daylight people were still out there looting. We got called to a furniture warehouse on Grand Avenue, and people were running down the streets with couches and beds on their backs. They just wouldn't let the stuff go, either. We split their heads with the stick and they'd still hold onto the shit. It was like they already owned it. It scared me to see people like that. It made me think about the neighborhood a lot. Before the blackout, I just figured that we were working with the scum all the time, that there were still good people out there in the community. But after that night, after I saw everybody in the community looting, I just didn't give a shit about what happened on the street any more. I used to just drive through the precinct sometimes and wonder: How far will they go the next time the lights go out?

"It would have made a difference if I could have done something—if I could saved someone's store or something. But when it was all over I felt like a jerk. We went back to the precinct and drank beer. We stayed there and got drunk the whole morning. The cops that came in gave me shit. 'You gotta be some kind of jackass, Magno. You were home with your family and you came into this cesspool in the middle of the blackout?' And they were right. I should have stayed home. All I really did was crack some heads. We didn't arrest anybody. One of the guys told me, "Magno, you batted .900 out there tonight. I only saw you swing and miss once.' Eventually, a day or two later, I got home. But I didn't tell Marianne much about what happened. What was there to say? That I didn't trust people anymore?"

Over the years, Tony rarely took his job home with him. Although he did bring most of his partners home for early morning card games and beer drinking sessions, they rarely talked about work. It was not unusual, Marianne noted, to wake up at 7 a.m. in order to send the kids off to school and discover a half dozen of her husband's friends sitting around her dining room table, drinking beer and arguing. Other cops soon decided that Tony had the perfect wife—she could put up with cops.

Actually, there was only one thing that Marianne hated about being a cop's wife. She could put up with her husband's hours and his drinking buddies. She could put up with his frustration and his brooding silence. But she could not put up with being alone in the house—knowing that her husband was out there working in the city's most dangerous precinct—and seeing a police car stopped on her block.

"If someone ever calls up and says I've been shot, don't believe them," Tony used to tell Marianne. "They don't call you when your husband gets shot. They send a patrol car out to get you. They come to the house."

So whenever Marianne looked out the window and saw a police car stopped on her block, she would freeze, imagining the worst.

"If I saw a car coming down the block slow, I'd get very scared," Marianne said. "I'd think, 'Oh God. Something happened to Anthony.' Thank God they never stopped though. If they had, I wouldn't have been able to make it to the door. It's funny, isn't it? My husband is a cop out working in a car on someone's block and the sight of another cop on my block could send me over the edge."

Tony went through a lot of partners in a lot of cars. He walked into many dangerous situations where bad guys were armed with big guns, but he rarely fired his own and never had to shoot anyone. He got medals too and occasionally made the newspapers, once arresting two men with a loaded gun who had raped and murdered a post office worker on her way home from work. Tony took a gun from one of the men, catching him on a stairwell leading to a tenement roof where the body of the woman was later found.

"I consider this one of the most brutal homicides I have encountered in my police experience," wrote Deputy Inspector William J. O'Sullivan, the commanding officer of the 77th Precinct, in recommending Tony and three other officers for an award of Exceptional Merit on May 9, 1979. "The two perpetrators had taken the victim, whom they did not know, from the lobby of her building by force. During the two hours they held her, she was systematically raped, tortured, and subjected to the vilest abuse until she died. The medical examiner told the officers he had never seen a human body in the condition of the deceased. In this incident, the police officers used initiative and extremely good judgment in their investigation of what might have been passed off as a routine prowler run. They conducted an investigation and arrested two vicious perpetrators, who might have succeeded in escaping less professional officers."

Tony was given a medal and honored by the precinct's community council with a plaque. And for once, he didn't even mind going to court.

Firmly entrenched as a prince of the locker room by 1982, Tony started thinking about semi-retirement—getting off the streets and taking a cushy inside job at the 77th Precinct. Young cops already referred to him as "the next Johnny Massar," and he wasn't insulted by the comparison to the precinct's hard-drinking veteran.

When his partner of six years, Johnny Miller, transferred out of the ghetto to a Staten Island command near his home, Tony took the breakup like a death in the family. On the night they got word of the transfers, Magno and Miller drove through their sector with tears in their eyes, at a loss for words to explain how they felt about each other. At one point during their final tour, the cops were called to a street disturbance. In the heat of their last action, the partners snapped. They struck out at several ill-fated residents who made the mistake of looking at them cross-eyed. Giving someone a beating made both cops feel better.

After Johnny left, Tony started to drop hints around the station house that he'd be willing to work inside all the time, but eventually he got over it and decided to put a few more years in on patrol. As a senior man, Tony was given his choice of new partners. Tony decided that his new partner would have to be an active cop, a veteran who knew the streets and was willing to make arrests and go to court. Tony wanted someone he could trust to back him up in the hairiest of situations and who wouldn't mind him having a beer in their squad car. Finally, he made his choice. He hooked up with a blonde, blue-eyed cop who had a reputation for being a loner and a prankster.

Tony Magno chose Henry Winter.

"First time I saw him he was just like another cop. But I had heard of Henry Winter. The rumor back then, in 1980, was, 'Watch this guy. Did you hear about him? He came over here with a cloud over his head.' I asked the guys, 'What do you mean?' And they said, 'We don't know about this guy. He don't fuck around with the guys. He don't drink. He came over here after his brother-in-law did his thing in the Seven-Five. He's bounced around a few precincts. We're not sure about him. We got a feeling he might have something to do with Internal Affairs.'

"Henry was in another squad then and I didn't work with him. But then stuff started coming back on him. Everybody knew that Henry had a clear head on the streets but was a bit of a flaky-type guy, and he started saying and doing things that were off the wall—jumping on desks with his pants down, burning a drug dealer's money. I don't know how it got around, but everybody knew Henry was doing something weird out there even though he was working with a super-straight guy. He was sneaky about it, doing whatever it was on the side. Eventually he had a falling-out with his partner. The guy just turned around one day and said, 'We ain't partners no more.'

"Then Henry came into my squad and started driving the sergeant, Bill Dougherty, for awhile. They got along good. The sergeant still liked to get involved in making arrests, and Henry liked to make collars, so they gelled. But Sergeant Dougherty was on the lieutenant's list, so of course he made lieutenant and left Henry hanging loose. My partner had left to train rookies. So now I had nobody, Henry had nobody.

"Henry knew I had time on the job and I knew he was all right, real flaky and shit. So I thought, 'What the fuck? Let's hook up.' I asked Henry one day in the latter part of 1983, 'What are you going to do, want to work together or what?' So we did. A couple guys approached me and said, 'Aw, don't hook up with him.' I heard shit like that for no good reason. They just said, 'He's not like you.'

"At this point, I was involved in minor stuff, the type of corruption that was standard operating procedure. No drugs. I'd drink beer in the car. Maybe I'd take some money hanging around in the open at a burglary. I might take a can of tuna fish out of a store along with batteries for my flashlight and cigarettes. But that was it. Everybody was doing that shit. I never came out of an apartment with a million fucking dollars.

"I just had to dance with somebody, and I decided to dance with Henry Winter."

Henry Winter and Tony Magno became partners in crime midway through their first tour together. The cops drove past the corner of Lincoln

Place and Franklin Avenue, an area in the precinct with a reputation for being a drug flea market. Tony spotted a black teenager talking with a group of older men near a stoop. He recognized them as neighborhood cocaine dealers, and saw one of the men slip what looked like a tinfoil package into the teenager's hand.

Smiling, the man turned around to face the street and saw the radio car with the police officers staring at him. The man acted very suspiciously, Henry and Tony later agreed. He ran down the block.

Sitting in the "runner's position"—the front seat on the passenger's side—Henry kicked open his door and bolted after the man. Tony drove ahead of his partner, shutting off the suspect's escape route. As Henry chased him down an alley, the suspect began dropping one-dollar bills. Henry kept chasing the dealer until the money jumped from one-dollar bills to twenty dollar bills. Then he stopped and picked the money up off the sidewalk.

The suspect ran straight into Tony's arms at the end of the alley. Tony threw his prisoner up against the car and frisked him for money and drugs, waiting for his partner to arrive on the scene. A crowd gathered as Tony finished the scavenger hunt, cheering the action.

"Let him go," Henry said, his pockets already stuffed with money. "He's got nothing on him. We can't hold him."

Tony let him go, saying, "We're doing you a favor. We're going to let you go this time."

The caps returned to their car and drove off. They parked a short distance away and Henry pulled out the money—just over four hundred dollars.

"How did you get it?" Tony asked.

"I'm running after the guy," Henry explained with a coy smile, "and he starts dropping it. I backtracked and picked it all up."

Tony made a face and restarted the car. He was afraid the drop was some kind of integrity test. Pondering the situation, he drove around for a few minutes before finally pulling over again.

"Well?" Henry asked. "What do you want to do?"

"Let me count it," said Tony, assuming the role of mathematician.

He counted the cash out into two piles and then looked up.

"Well?" Henry repeated. "What do you want to do?"

Tony held out his hands, weighing both the dollar amount and his decision.

"Ah, fuck it," he said, shoving his cut into his pants with one hand and passing Henry his share of the rip-off with the other. "We're partners, ain't we?"

Most of the cops in the station house believed that the 77th Precinct's newest partners were an ill-fitting couple. In theory, Henry and Tony were in total disagreement on everything from dress and music to politics and sports.

Tony was a dry cleaner's dream. Ever the sharp city dresser, he wore thin black Bally shoes, a sleek black leather coat, finely creased slacks and starched cotton shirts. Henry, the suburban outdoorsman, picked his clothes out of an L. L. Bean catalogue. He wore brightly colored Reebok sneakers, corduroy jackets, dungarees, and flannel shirts.

A check of the AM radio in their squad car confirmed that they were men of different tastes, if not worlds. Tony kept one button preset to an oldies station, while Henry kept another set for a station playing country and western music. On day tours, the partners listened to oldies, with Tony eventually teaching his partner the finer points of doo-wop. On midnight tours they listened to country music, with Henry helping Willie Nelson explain why Tony shouldn't let his babies grow up to be cowboys.

Sporting events presented another problem in Sector Ida-John. Tony lived for the Mets and Giants. Henry died with the Yankees and the Jets. Election nights usually brought more disagreements. Tony would hoist a can of Budweiser to salute victorious Republican candidates, but Henry honked the horn in deference to Democratic winners.

And so it was that Henry Winter and Tony Magno spent much of their time together. They argued, honked horns, sang doo-wops, mimicked Dolly Parton, and laughed. They began to enjoy the time of their police careers. They became the perfect partners. You might even say that they loved each other.

"Tony and I were completely opposite, so whatever he talked about was interesting to me, and whatever I talked about was interesting to him. I could put an experience on Tony, and he could put one on me. It just worked out perfect.

"Tony stayed with the guys after the tour to drink beer and bullshit, but I was on my way home five minutes before our tour ended. Tony didn't make collars, I did. We had nothing in common whatsoever. I talked about hunting and fishing; he talked about other guys on the job and what was happening in the precinct. We always talked.

"It's funny. If you have something in common with someone, you usually become competitive. You can really get on each other's nerves. But we were like magnets. Our differences drew us closer together.

"One thing we agreed on was the car. Tony and I really took pride in it. We started with an old car and then got a new one. We kept it cleaned and waxed. If something went wrong, even if a bulb went out, we'd spend the money ourselves to fix it. Once we were out on a three-day swing and came back to find the car's whole front end demolished. It was destroyed. We didn't get it back for six weeks. Meanwhile we were driving around a shitbox car that was falling apart. Finally we got our car back. We saw them pull it in just as we finished an eight-to-four tour one afternoon. We went over, looked at it and said, 'All right. It's in good shape.' Then we went home. We came in the next day and the car was totaled out again. The guy driving it was some tall Jewish cop—a rookie no less. We called him everything underneath the sun. Tony was really pissed. He screamed at the guy, 'Hey, you can't even drive. You're not a cop, you're a fucking little whore.'

"We were in total agreement on the car. And there was another thing we agreed on too. After a while, neither one of us saw anything wrong with ripping off drug dealers while we were in uniform."

As with most criminals, Henry and Tony started out small. Shortly after they teamed up, they were sitting on a corner in their sector watching a group of suspicious-looking men parade into a smoke shop on Brooklyn Avenue. They decided to get a closer look at what was going on inside. Tony drove to a corner pay phone and Henry dialed 911—the police emergency number. Disguising his voice to sound like a Jamaican black, Henry reported seeing a man with a gun in the smoke shop.

"The mon inside, he have a gun. For sure the mon shoot someone."

He then returned to the car to wait for the call. "Ida-John, Central," Henry said. "We'll handle that job."

With guns drawn, Henry and Tony rushed into the building. Several men fled out through an unguarded rear exit. Inside, Tony found a marijuana-filled cigar box. The cops were disappointed—they wanted money, not drugs. So they led the counter man into the bathroom and forced him to flush the drugs down the toilet.

Within months of that first operation, Henry and Tony were conducting similar raids on numbers parlors in their sector. They would rush into buildings, screaming, their guns drawn, chasing gamblers out into the street through rear exits. Once everyone had left, Henry and Tony would scoop up any money left behind, and leave.

In addition to hitting numbers parlors, they took money whenever they had the opportunity. They once stepped over a dead man's body, discovered in his apartment on the last day of the month, to seek out and steal his rent money.

The cops hit their collective low as thieves on a winter day in 1984. Responding to a radio call of a burglary in progress, they arrived at a Park Place apartment to find a woman standing in the hallway, shaking. She had come home to find her door ajar and jewelry missing from her bedroom bureau.

"I ran out of the apartment," she said. "I was scared the burglar might still be in there. I think he got everything, but I'm not sure."

Henry was interested. "What do you mean you think he got everything?"

"Well I keep a lot of money in the closet, but I didn't dare open it. The money is in a tin box. Could you go in and check to see if it's still there?"

Henry and Tony entered the apartment, leaving the woman in the hallway with a neighbor. Tony guarded the door while Henry removed two hundred dollars from the tin box. Henry stuffed the money into his pocket and the cops returned to the hallway, filling out a burglary complaint report.

"Yep," Henry announced. "They got it all, lady."

Later they split up the cash in the patrol car. Henry felt bad about what he had just done. His conscience bothered him. This wasn't some street dealer or numbers runner they had just ripped off, this was a frightened woman who trusted them. The partners discussed the possibility of returning the money, but Tony didn't want to compound the mistake with a lie.

"Forget it," he decided. "What's done is done. We'll never do it again."

Feeling disgraced, they decided they wouldn't rob anybody but really bad guys. They had to have some code of ethics, they agreed. They were not, Henry and Tony assured each other, complete degenerates. They were businessmen, and even the cruelest businessman had to operate by a set of principles.

But soon they had another problem. They were running out of bad guys. A lot of smoke shops in their sector had closed because the drug merchants had moved to neighborhoods where the cops weren't quite so active and so greedy. Several numbers parlors also shifted their bases of operation, relocating in sectors beyond the reach of Winter and Magno. Apparently shut out, Tony and Henry refocused their attention on the ghetto's burgeoning drug trade.

"We'll become like Robin Hoods," Tony announced one day. "We'll steal from the rich and keep it."

While on patrol one day in late 1984, Henry and Tony rounded a corner on Schenectady Avenue and spotted a man carrying a shoulder bag. He looked at the cops, did a double take, and then sprinted down the street. He entered a storefront that the police listed as "a known drug location" in their intelligence reports.

The cops got out of their car and chased the man into the building. Henry grabbed him in the back of the otherwise empty store and asked, "What are you doing here?"

"Nothing. Just hanging out."

"What are you hanging out here for? There's nobody here."

Then Henry noticed that the man no longer had his shoulder bag and he ordered, "Get out of here. Now."

The man obliged and, once he'd left, Tony found the bag hidden behind a large commercial refrigerator. He opened it and called Henry over.

"What is it?"

"Fucking money. A lot of money."

They returned to their car with the bag. As Henry drove away, Tony counted out more than $5,500. The cops took $2,500 apiece and returned to the station house where they vouchered the bag and remaining $500 as found property. The man they robbed confronted them in the precinct parking lot.

"Please give me the money back. They're gonna kill me when I tell them what happened. They won't believe me."

"We're vouchering the bag and the money," the officers answered. "Tell your boss to come down and prove the money is his. It'll be right here. See the desk officer and tell him where you got the money."

When they turned the bag in, the sergeant discovered an additional $1,500 in a compartment the officers overlooked. Henry and Tony looked at each other and said, "We blew it. How stupid can we be?"

The bag's owner realized he would have to answer some hard questions about the drug trade if he tried to reclaim his cash and he never bothered to set foot in the 77th Precinct.

Henry and Tony were ecstatic. The incident brought a renewed sense of purpose to their work as members of the New York City Police Department. No drug dealer was safe from them. They broke down doors and climbed fire escapes into fortified apartments, getting the drop on surprised dealers.

Within a year after first teaming up, Henry and Tony were hooked on the exitement they felt whenever they harassed drug dealers.

"We always tried to leave the bad guys with a little something. If you go into a place and take everything, they're gonna bitch. They may even come down to the precinct and file a complaint against you. Of course a lot of guys did file complaints against us. They always identified us as 'Blondie and his partner.' Tony used to go crazy when he heard that. He'd scream, 'Keep your hat on when we're out in the streets. Being out here with you is like being with Fay Wray.'

"But if you catch guys and let them go with a little money and drugs they're not going to bitch. They're as happy as a pig in shit. They're thinking, 'I'm not going to jail. So I lost a little money. I'll make it up next week.' Plus they didn't know we were actually keeping the drugs and reselling them. They thought we vouchered the drugs after we let them go. That was easier for them to take than if we walked over to a toilet and flushed one thousand, fifteen hundred, two thousand dollars worth of cocaine away. They got pissed when we did that and said, 'You should have locked me up.'

"Did I feel guilty about what we were doing? Yeah. At that particular minute. When someone handed me money, I felt guilty. I think anybody would feel guilty then. But then all of a sudden we'd get a ten-thirty [shots fired] or something on the radio. And we'd go answer the job and forget about what we'd just done. Once I got through the day, I lived with my guilt. There were times I thought, 'What's going to happen? Holy shit, what am I doing? Taking a lousy couple of dollars. It's not worth it.' But it just seemed like, 'So what?' Who actually is going to come out here and look at us?

"Even though I was a bad guy, I had the feeling, 'Hey I'm bad on one side, but on this side I'm making up for it.' If people really needed us, we were there. We weren't taking anything from honest workers. I know it doesn't matter whether it's an honest worker or a skell, it's still wrong. I know that. But we were taking money that was illegal to begin with. Drug money. It's weird but I never thought I was robbing those people. I was robbing a lowlife. A drug dealer. Someone who shouldn't be there to begin with. The law couldn't touch these guys. If we caught them they just went down and paid the fine. They could afford the fines. Hell, they were making money hand over foot. I know it sounds like a rationalization. But what we did worked. We ripped these guys off and they moved out. They should legalize that. Go in and rip all these guys off and they'll all disappear.

"At first Tony didn't like playing with drugs. He had no problems with money, none whatsoever. He just didn't want to have anything to do with dealing drugs. But after we started selling the drugs back on the street and getting more money, Tony just didn't even think about it anymore. He just did it.

"See, he was set in his ways. He had been on the job for fifteen years by the time I hooked up with him in 1983. He didn't give a shit what the bosses said. If we were going on our meal hour and they wanted to give us a job, we'd try to eat on the job. We'd say, 'Yeah Central, we'll take that job.' But we wouldn't go to it. We'd park somewhere, have our dinner, and after we ate, we'd go to the job.

"If we were goofing off, we'd sit on any job except an emergency call. If the call was a cardiac, we'd go. If we had a young kid suffering an asthma attack, we'd answer it right away. If there was a gun battle in the street, say at Plaza Street: East and Underhill, we'd say, 'Maybe we better take a ride down there because maybe good people are involved.' But if we heard Lincoln and Franklin, a shit area, we'd just sit back and have our dinner. Let them shoot everybody the fuck up. Who the hell cares? We'll just go and pick up the bodies. Everybody else is gone. If two guys are having a gun fight, who do you take? You take the loser. He's sitting there with a bullet in him, so you get to lock him up.

"But really, it all depended on what mood we were in. If we were working a four-to-twelve shift, and Tony came in really early, like maybe around one o'clock in the afternoon, and he partied with the guys downstairs until I came in, then he'd be in a happy mood. He wouldn't care if the precinct turned upside down. We'd handle our jobs. But we wouldn't go crazy to back up another unit or take a job in someone else's sector. We'd do a job and shoot back to Macho's Bodega on Buffalo and St. Johns for a beer.

"We sat in the back on milk boxes, drinking bottles of beer and playing with the roaches, betting on the fastest ones. There were times that we'd have eight or nine cops in the back of the store, hooting and hollering, arguing about who was going to go out to the refrigerator to get the next round of beers. Anthony, a guy who hung out in the store, was an old-type numbers man who wrote everything down on a piece of paper. Everybody played their number with him and so did we. Tony and I hit a lot. He was good. We'd see Anthony on the way into work and he'd wave to us, 'I know, you hit today.' We got everything we ever needed from the bodega—cigarettes, batteries, sandwiches, and beer. All for free. The store owner and Anthony the numbers man both loved us. We were the right type of cops."

In a precinct that seemed to have gone mad, Henry and Tony were regarded as two of the most outrageous characters. Given the right set of circumstances—which was almost any circumstances at all—they could be counted on to commit the most unimaginable offenses. No one in the precinct could match their flair for handling a simple dispute.

One day early in 1984, Tony and Henry responded to a call about a husband-wife dispute in a tiny Park Place apartment. Tony arrived to quell the ruckus wearing shiny new shoes, which he had purchased earlier in the day. The husband, a wife beater, refused to leave the apartment. As Tony shoved the man out of the apartment, he stepped on Tony's new left shoe, landing on it in such a manner that he cut a tiny sliver of leather off the toe. Tony screamed, pointing at his shoe. The dispute stopped.

"I just paid forty fucking dollars for these shoes," Tony yelled, throwing the man around the apartment.

The shaken man pulled out twenty dollars and handed it to the cop. Tony's eyes went wide with a deranged look Henry had never seen before. He pocketed the money and then rifled the man's pockets for more.

"Is this all you got? Twenty dollars? Twenty dollars when I just paid forty dollars for these shoes? You're buying me a new pair of shoes." Tony said.

"Yes sir. But twenty dollars is all I got."

Magno turned on the heel of his good shoe and stormed out of the apartment, rushing back to the patrol car. Winter followed, amazed by his partner's anger. Henry waited until they had driven away from the scene before finally daring to speak.

"You know you just fucking robbed that guy?"

"Fuck him," Tony replied, his face still red with rage. "We're going back next week to get another twenty for the other shoe."

Henry rarely lost his cool. He did, however, once floor a fellow officer who refused to escort a teenaged shooting victim from the site of a gun battle to the hospital. The cop wanted to go visit his girlfriend instead, and Henry sent him off to see his girl with a shiner under his left eye. So on rare occasions Henry, to use a cop expression, "wigged out."

A few months after Tony cut his shoe, Henry entered an apartment to settle a dispute between a Jamaican woman and her landlord. Seeing a uniformed officer at her door, the woman made peace with her landlord, and aimed her sights at Henry, calling him a "blood clot" and suggesting that he engage in a sexual relationship with a goat. Henry took exception to this and raised his flashlight over her head, preparing to strike her. She stepped back into her apartment, grabbed her infant child off the floor, and returned to the fray.

"You blood clot cop. You can't hit me, I'm holding a baby."

Henry stepped forward and whacked the woman on the top of her skull with his flash light, rendering her unconscious immediately. He caught the baby as the woman crumbled, and then placed the child in its crib.

This time it was Tony who looked on mouth agape and stupefied.

"You crazy ass, you've got to be kidding me."

"I couldn't take her no more," Henry explained as they reached the street. "Come on. Let's get out of here."

A week later Tony and Henry returned to the same apartment building to settle another dispute between yet another tenant and the landlord. Henry spotted the Jamaican woman sitting on the stoop holding her baby as they pulled up in their patrol car.

"Hellooo, Officer Winter," she called. "How are you?"

"All right, and yourself? How's the baby?"

"Oh good, good."

Of course, there were members of the community who thrived on testing a police officer's mettle, particularly a cop like Henry Winter who wanted to get along with everyone, cop or thief. On a summer day in 1984, Henry entered an apartment building on Lincoln Place to handle a dispute on the second floor. As he entered the building, Henry met a Jamaican marijuana dealer named Panama Mike, who was selling drugs in the building's vestibule.

"You be gone by the time I come down stairs," Henry said.

He returned a few minutes later only to discover Panama Mike still selling nickel bags of marijuana through a mail slot in the door.

"Have some respect. What did I fucking tell you? I don't care what you do, but when I tell you to be gone, you get the hell out of here."

Panama Mike smiled and said, "Fuck you, Blondie. I'm going to kick your ass the next time you come around here."

"All right, you kick my ass next time I come around here."

Henry continued toward the door, heading for a metal garbage can near the entrance.

"Come on Blondie, me and you, right now."

As they reached the door, Henry grabbed the garbage can and swung it, splitting Panama Mike's nose open. He fell to the floor, and Henry picked him up and put him in the garbage can. Then he left the building.

"How did it go in there?" Tony asked.

"Good. I just left Oscar the Grouch sitting back there in a garbage can."

• • •

"Tony and I got medals for handling one dispute back in the summer of 1984. There was this new kid in the precinct, a guy we called Scoop Mahoney. He was walking a foot post one day and called in a ten-eighty-five—officer needs assistance. Scoop was yelling, 'Man with a knife, man with a machete.' So Tony and I decided to go see what Scoop wanted. There's Scoop on the corner with a guy with a big machete, swinging it like crazy. And every time Mahoney went near him, the guy took a swing at him. The guy was acting really flippy. Other people went after him and he'd swing at them too. Tony and I arrive on the scene and there's all these cops with guns drawn. I said, 'What's he calling in an eighty-five on this for? The guy's got a machete, he's swinging it at you, just drop him. Shoot him.' We're sitting in the car looking and looking, and finally Tony looks at me and I say 'All right.'

"So we get out of the car and now the place is loaded with cops. I don't have a night stick on me. I never liked carrying a stick. I figure if you really have to hit somebody, I mean hit them in the head with all your might, you're gonna kill them anyway, so why not use a gun? Mahoney comes running over to me and says, 'What do I do? I can't get the machete away from him.' I said, 'All right. Give me your stick.' So Tony starts talking to the guy, 'Hey, put down the knife. I'll fucking jack you up.' I tell Mahoney, 'Just get his attention for a second.' Mahoney does it and I walk behind the guy and pow. He goes out cold. I get the machete, I give the machete and the stick to Mahoney, then me and Tony get back in the car and pull away.

"It was Mahoney's collar. We met him back at the station house and he tells us, 'Look, I'm putting in for a medal and I'm putting you guys in for one too.' I says, 'No. No. You handle it.' He says, 'No, I'll put down that I did everything, but you were there, so I'm putting you in too.' And that's the way it went. We got some dipshit medals and Scoop later made detective."

On February 17, 1984, Henry and Tony made the city's daily newspapers for the first time as a team. Henry had narrowly escaped serious injury the night before, when a robbery suspect turned and fired a .357 magnum at him during a chase. The *New York Post* ran an account of the shootout at the top of page four under the headline, " 'I was lucky,' says cop who ducked bullet." The article was illustrated with a large photograph of Henry leading a bloodied suspect away in handcuffs. It was a nice photograph, a graphic picture, the very same photograph that the *Post* later ran on page one to illustrate an even bigger story about Police Officers Henry Winter and Tony Magno.

"It was about one thirty in the morning. Tony and I were out on patrol, driving down Park Place when we reached the corner of Bedford Avenue. Two guys waved us over and said, "We just got robbed," and pointed to five or six guys across the street—like a wolf pack. I said, 'Anybody got guns?' and one kid says, 'Yeah. Two guns.' We drove up to the pack and they took off. I jumped out of the car—I was driving—and took after two guys. This fucked Tony up because now he had to come all the way around the car from the passenger's side to get into the driver's seat. I used to do this to him all the time, it drove him crazy. He used to scream, 'If you're driving, you stay with the car. I run when you drive.' But I always forgot. Sometimes I even forgot to put the car in park. I'd just jump out and start running with the car rolling down the block after me. I'd be chasing the bad guy and Tony would be chasing the car.

"So Tony is running circles around the car and I'm chasing this guy down the block. He got to the corner first and made a right turn down Park Place. I came around the corner and there he is standing in the combat position behind a car pointing the magnum at me. And the fuck fired the gun. The bullet hit the wall behind me and I dove behind it. I stayed there for a minute and then stuck my head out again in time to see the guy rounding the corner with a silver gun in his hand. I ran past the spot he fired at me from and found the magnum. He had two guns. We chased him to a building and then other cops responded to the scene. They found him hiding in the closet of an abandoned building and brought him up to the roof.

"I felt like beating the shit out of him. We tried to take care of him but there were too many people around. I smacked him around a few times but then the guys pulled me off. Everybody was uptight. Some parolee had just shot three cops in the South Bronx the night before, killing one of them. They had to call me off. I was going to kill him. I was going to throw him off the roof. He would have been gone.

"When he heard the shot, Tony broke off his chase and started looking for me. We were both scared. I caught up with him just before they found the guy. He says, 'You okay, shithead?' And then I remembered, we had just ordered chicken wings with hot sauce before all this shit broke, so I said, 'You know we just ordered our food.' So while all this shit's going on, Tony runs down to Nostrand Avenue and picks up our chicken wings with hot sauce. As they're transporting this guy to the station house, we're just sitting there eating our chicken wings and hot sauce in the car, trying to pretend that someone didn't just try and kill me."

In the beginning no one in the 77th Precinct was sure who could be trusted to steal.

Henry and Tony had worked together for six months before they learned that there were other bluefish cops out there, particularly on the midnight tours, running in schools, robbing almost each and every drug dealer they came in contact with.

Throughout most of their careers Tony and Henry worked around the clock. They would work a week on the 8 a.m.-to-4 p.m. tour, then spend another week on the 4 p.m.-to-12 a.m. shift, before finishing out the cycle with a tour on the midnight-to-8 a.m. detail. In the beginning, they stole only when the right moment presented itself, in broad daylight and the dark of night. They used their uniforms for camouflage and their badges as passkeys. Their guns provided security.

But the precinct's most prolific robbers were found on the midnight tour. Police Officers William Gallagher and Brian O'Regan and another half dozen cops lived for the night, when the darkness hid their misdeeds from prying eyes. By late 1984, with their daylight escapades already well known to the men on the midnight tour, Henry and Tony had been welcomed into the After Midnight gang—a group formerly known as Sergeant Stinson's Raiders. They were deemed fit company by Gallagher, a swaggering presence who used his ties to the police union to warn the cops of investigations.

Soon Henry and Gallagher were standing off to the side after roll call, plotting a series of moves that would ultimately land them in reinforced apartments where they were free to terrorize dealers at gunpoint, stealing drugs, money and guns. The cops made up nicknames for each other and talked on the radio in coded messages. Henry became Buddy Boy, Gallagher became Buddy Bee. Brian O'Regan was known as Space Man and the rest of the thieves fell under a single title: The Buddy Boys.

" 'Buddy Boy' was a word that we used among ourselves. 'Buddy Boy' was me. 'Buddy Bee' was Junior Gallagher. 'Buddy Bob' was the code word for what we did. It meant, 'Are we doing anything tonight? You agree to make a little money tonight?' We used the codes over the radio. If Junior was calling our car, he'd say, 'Buddy Boy, Buddy Bob.' That meant, 'Hey Henry, are we doing anything tonight?' If I called Junior it would be, 'Buddy Bee, Buddy Bob.' Pretty simple stuff. But no one listening to the radio could have figured out what the fuck we were talking about.

"Now, if we wanted to hit a place, we'd answer with a 'Hey, two-three-four.' 'Two-three-four' was the code name for a park on Bergen Street between Troy and Schenectady, behind the St. Johns Recreation Center across from a fire house, old Engine Company Two-Three-Four. That's where we got the name. We'd drive into the park and position our cars next to each other between two ball fields and a handball court. If there was anybody hanging out in the park, they'd take off as soon as we drove in. We could see out in all directions, so if the shoofly—some supervisor trying to check up on us—came into the park looking for us, we could see him coming. But nobody ever came. We could talk about whatever we wanted once we got to two-three-four.

"So we'd drive in there and discuss what we wanted to do. I'd say to Junior, 'What place you got in mind?' And he'd answer, 'Two-sixty-one Buffalo. I came in that way before work and scouted it out. I didn't see too many lookouts in front of the place.' And then we'd talk about how we were going to do it. Who's going in the front? Who's going to go in the back? Who went in the back last time? Who got dirty last time? Things like that. Then we'd say, 'All right. Let's do it.'

"We'd drive down the streets with our lights off. We'd give the lead car about a four- or five-second head start to get around the corner first. They'd go in the front or back way and we'd go in the other way. Sometimes we'd even park down the block and walk in, just to get the jump on the lookouts. If it was a heavy drug area, with a lot of lookouts, the scouts would start whistling back and forth as soon as they spotted us, yelling their own code words. We'd sneak up on places through backyards and alleys. It was almost like stalking a deer. Tracking through brush and making sure no one saw you doing anything. It was exciting. We created our own thrills.

"Sometimes it was easy and we didn't even need to show our guns. We'd just knock on the door, they'd open the door up and we'd walk in. They never stuck around to see what we wanted—they just ran, jumping out windows and climbing down fire escapes. We didn't care. We weren't there to arrest anybody. We were there to scoop up their money and drugs and then get the fuck out.

"But we always tried to make them think they were getting away. If a guy stayed and we came up with shit, we'd act all serious. I'd say, 'Whose collar is this?' and Brian would say, 'I got him.' Then someone else would say, 'Take him out in the hallway and put cuffs on him.' But as soon as Brian got the guy into the hallway, we'd call him back on some excuse and Brian would tell the guy, 'Now don't move. You stay right here. You're going to jail as soon as I get back out here.' Then Brian would come back into the room and we'd hear the guy scurrying down the hall, making his getaway. We'd laugh and say, 'Oh, the bad guy just got away.'

"We had this one idiot one time. Gallagher, Brian, me and Tony were on a job. We actually left the guy in the hallway, went back into the apartment, and shut the door. When we came back out five minutes later, the guy was still there. I look at Brian. He looks at me. We can't believe this guy. We go back inside, shut the door, and wait another five minutes. The guy is still standing there. So we closed the door and we ran away. We went out the fire escape because the fucking guy just would not leave. We made some noises in the apartment, and then left one by one, going down the fire escape thinking this was the dumbest fucker we'd ever seen. We had to run away from him! Then we got back in our cars and drove to the park to see who got what and divvy up the drugs and cash."

The Buddy Boys became more brazen with experience. Henry, having nearly broken his foot when he tried to kick down a metal door with sneakers, bought a pair of steel-tipped boots. Gallagher and O'Regan began carrying a sledge hammer, crowbar, and pinch bar in the trunk of their patrol car. They all packed screwdrivers in their attaché cases along with their paperwork.

Some of the cops became experts at kicking down doors and crashing through walls. No door could hold them. They split oak doors with one mighty swing of their hammers and used crowbars to pry metal doors off their hinges. If the cops wanted to get into a third-floor apartment, they would climb to the roof, tie a rope around an elevator housing and then rappel down the side of the building, crashing feet first into the apartment window. Some Buddy Boys also carried ash cans—small but powerful fireworks—which they would light and slip through mail slots, literally bombing people out of their apartments.

If the cops found themselves ill-equipped for a manuever, one of then would rush off to a firehouse to borrow axes and bolt cutters. The firemen, unaware of their role in the burglaries, scratched their heads and asked each other, "What the hell are these guys doing out there?"

One night the Buddy Boys arrived at a building on the corner of Eastern Parkway and Rogers Avenue, only to discover they had no means of getting to an adjoining roof. They had to place a man on the roof to keep the dealer they were after from escaping out his apartment window with his drugs and money.

"We need a ladder for this job," Gallagher decided.

"I saw a ladder at an excavation site on the way in to work today," Henry said.

So Tony and Gallagher sat in the apartment while Brian and Henry tore off in a patrol car, driving to the far end of the precinct where they found a wooden ladder at an excavation site. The cops wedged the ladder between the lights and the roof, ruining the car's paint job in the process, and then sped back to the scene, laughing as they raced through the city streets with an eight-foot ladder hanging off the top of their patrol car. Then they drove the car up on the sidewalk next to the building and put the ladder on top of the car. Henry and Gallagher climbed up the ladder, entering the dealer's apartment. Tony and Brian broke through his front door.

"He was very surprised to see us," Henry later remembered.

"Brian started talking about making his own equipment. He wanted to put together a scaffold that would fit into the back of his car. Then he talked about mailing away for things. He was going to get one of those rope ladders that you throw up, it hooks on, then you pull a string, it comes down, and you climb up. He was actually going to send away for this thing so we could rip places off. I told him, 'Come on. What are we going to do, start a business here? Do you want to get a van, too, and paint "H and B Removal" on the side?' Holy shit. That's what it was like. I mean, I'm not glad this happened to me, but it was getting pretty crazy on the midnight tours. Anything and everything went. You could do whatever you wanted to do and nobody could stop you. Getting a van wasn't out of the question. I think that if this was still going on we'd have a van by now. We would have all chipped in, got a van, and set it up with everything we needed—crowbars, helmets, axes, ropes, ladders, and acetylene torches. We could have parked it somewhere in the precinct before heading into work. Then we could have said on the radio, 'Buddy Bee, Buddy Bob. Get the Buddy-Boymobile.'

"There were a lot of times, hairy times, when we went up against big guns. Sometimes I came through the window, and I said to myself, 'What the fuck am I doing? This is ridiculous.' You're coming in through a window, it's a dark alley, you don't actually know who or what's in there. You just got a tip from one of your squealers, and here you are, four cops, going in with little thirty-eights, surrounding a building, kicking in windows off a fire escape. You don't know what the hell you're getting into. But we did it. There were a lot of times we went in and I could hear my heart coming through my chest. I was so dry I couldn't swallow. I was afraid to go in that window. But when the "Buddy Bob" came over the radio, the foot went in, I dove in that window, wound up on the bed next to a guy with a loaded gun, and came out with forty fucking dollars. I could have been killed. I just took ten years off my life. I got three new gray hairs. And for what? For the excitement of it all, that's what. We were lost in a frenzy.

"It was like we were insane or something. I mean one time we hit this bar on Schenectady Avenue on a late tour. It was Gallagher, O'Regan, Nicky Scaturico, and me. Brian and I jumped over a fence and came in the back way. Gallagher and Nicky came through the front. The idea was to scare them out the back way. Nicky and Junior banged on the front door, trying to sound like Emergency Services cops. So these guys opened the back door and we were right there. Surprise. All in uniform. We tossed everybody. While me and Nicky were in the back searching through things, a line of customers formed. Brian started selling them coke through a slot in the door. And it was a good thing he did, too, because we came up with a small amount of money and a large amount of coke. So O'Regan made more money for us. He did it for about an hour. There was this one guy who came up to the door and wanted to sell his sweater. It was a nice, a brand-new sweater. But there was a long line so we couldn't open the door. That would have been bad for business. Brian tried to get the guy to slip the sweater under the door, but it wouldn't fit. And O'Regan, once he got money, he wouldn't give back change. One guy slipped Brian a fifty and wanted two twenty-dollar tins of coke and ten dollars change. Brian slipped the guy three twenty-dollar tins back. The guy started screaming, 'I don't want this, I want my change.' Brian slipped him another tin. But the guy was insistent, he kept getting louder and louder. And Brian would not give the guy any change. We were screaming now in our best Jamaican dialects, 'Geeve the mon his change.' Brian wouldn't do it. So we had to skate out the back door because the guy was raising too much of a riot."

By mid-1984, the Buddy Boys were in trouble. Not with the cops, but with drugs. They were confiscating hundreds of dollars worth of cocaine and marijuana as well as guns. Originally the cops had been content to flush the drugs down toilets. But being good businessmen, they soon realized that there was a profit to be made in drug dealing. They decided to fence most of their stolen drugs, guns, and electronic equipment through a middle-aged Jamaican drug dealer named Euston Roy Thomas who ran a grocery store and restaurant on Lincoln Place. Nicknamed "Roy," the dealer had ingratiated himself with the cops in the 77th years earlier when he stepped into an argument between a cop and a drug dealer, taking a bullet in the face. Roy still carried the bullet in the back of his head, a tiny mustache covering the entrance wound under his nose.

"Don't worry about me," Roy used to tell the cops. "I got a bullet in the head. If someone comes around here asking about my friends, I don't remember too good. You be amazed at what I remember to forget."

William Gallagher, who had been partners with the cop Roy tried to help out, never forgot the drug dealer. When it came time to fence drugs and guns, Roy was only too happy to accommodate his cop friends. He paid them fifty cents on the dollar for their coke and marijuana and a fair price on their guns, all of which he later resold on the street. No fool, Roy also gave the cops a payoff not to raid his own drug locations, explaining that he did not want to be in the business of buying back his own drugs.

By the winter of 1984, Henry and Roy had developed a certain sympathy. Henry often visited Roy's grocery store on Troy Avenue, asking how his business was going and talking about wives. Roy's Jamaican wife, Grace, was always trying to get her husband to hire her cousins from the islands for his business. Roy preferred kids from the neighborhood. Sometimes the couple's arguments were very loud and violent, and then Henry would arrive at the store and settle the dispute, reminding Grace that it was bad manners to point a loaded gun at one's own husband. Henry would then leave the building with two or three hundred dollars in his pocket and Roy's blessing.

"Buy yourself a cup of coffee," Roy would say.

Roy was well known to the precinct's homicide detectives. A lot of people died on the dealer's block. Although Roy's name figured prominently in discussions of drug-related homicides near the intersection of Troy and Lincoln Place, he was never arrested for murder. Henry knew Roy to be a tough guy but he didn't know him to be a killer. He thought of Roy as a friend, so much of one that when the police officer called his wife to wish her a happy New Year on December 31, 1984, he even put Roy on the phone with Betsy.

"Oh pretty lady," Roy said.

"Goodbye," Betsy said.

When Henry got home the next day, Betsy met him at the door.

"Who was that guy you had on the phone?"

"Oh, that's my friend Roy."

"You got some friends. I don't believe what you do in that precinct!"

Henry could not have known then that some investigators were already thinking the same thing. Homicide investigators assigned to the precinct's detective unit had arrived at Roy's store in January 1985 to inquire about a dead man found on the doorstep. A few days later Tony and Henry came in while detectives were questioning Roy, trying to determine whether he had seen or heard anything relating to the murder. The interrogation proved fruitless. "I got a bullet in my head. Sometimes I forget."

The detectives asked Henry and Tony for help, and Roy was only too happy to talk to them about the case, the detectives noted. One detective working the case, Steve Niglicki, went back to his supervisor, Lieutenant Burns, and reported the questionable relationship between the cops and the drug dealer. Burns filed a report with the Internal Affairs Division.

A set of wheels began to turn at One Police Plaza.

By this time Henry had many street friends in the precinct, and most of them paid through the nose for this relationship. One of them was an elderly black drug dealer named Herbie, who operated a drug business out of an apartment on St. Johns Place. The officers met him while raiding one of his properties, where they found one hundred crack-filled vials in the bottom of a bag in the kitchen. They also found eight hundred dollars on Herbie, which they placed on a counter in the kitchen.

"You're going to jail," Henry announced.

Obviously having dealt with cops from the 77th Precinct before, Herbie seemed unimpressed.

"Look," he said, "We can work out a deal."

The cops walked out of the kitchen, leaving Herbie alone with the crack vials. When they returned, he had stashed the drugs and there was a wad of money lying on the table. As the men continued to talk, Herbie suddenly opened a newspaper and flashed four hundred dollars at the cops. Tony and Henry exchanged glances and then grabbed the newspaper.

"Have a nice day," Herbie said as the cops left his apartment. "Come back real soon."

A few days later, Herbie put out word on the street that he wanted to see the cop called 'Blondie.' Henry drove to the apartment and the two men walked down the street, exchanging pleasantries. Then the cop and the drug dealer got down to business. Herbie explained that he was planning to expand his drug operation and wanted Henry's assurance that certain cops would protect it. He offered Henry two hundred dollars for this assurance, and Henry took the money.

"Be good," Herbie said as the cops drove away.

"We took the money to watch his place but then we got rotated off midnights back to day tours. Herbie got hit three times right after that. Boom. Boom. Boom. And he put out the word that he wanted to see Blondie again. So I went over to see him and he says, 'Look. I'm getting hit on the midnight tours. You're supposed to be watching me and telling me when I'm going to get hit. I need to get somebody on the midnight tours.' So I went back to the station house and told Gallagher about Herbie. I said, 'Billy, you know this guy on St. Johns, he paid us a couple times for watching him, but we can't do it anymore and he wants a friend on the midnight tour. If you want to speak to him, go ahead. Tell him Blondie sent you.' Gallagher went down there and Herbie set him up. At first he got eight hundred a month, but then it went to one thousand and on up to fifteen hundred dollars. Junior and Brian were splitting seventeen hundred a month from Herbie when this whole thing broke."

A third man who bribed Henry and Tony to protect his drug operation was a middle-aged black from Pacific Street named Benny Burwell. Originally Henry and Tony had no idea that Benny was dealing drugs. They believed he paid them fifty dollars a week to keep an eye on his brother's social club. But one day in February 1985, two young cops named Richard Figueroa and Michael Bryan cornered Tony and Henry on the street outside the station house.

"We know what's going on at Pacific and Ralph," Figueroa insisted. "And we want a piece of your pie."

Tony gave the young cops the same look that he gave the guy who stepped on his forty dollar shoes.

"Where the fuck do you guys get off asking for a piece of my pie?" he screamed. "I'm a senior man. I got seventeen years here. You want your action, you go out and get your own piece of pie. Who the hell are you to tell us what you want? This is my contract. You find your own."

But the younger cops were adamant about being cut in on the payoffs.

"Well, we want a piece of your pie," Figueroa insisted. "And if we don't get it, we're going to go harass the guys."

"Do whatever the fuck you want to do," Tony advised them before stalking off.

A few days later Benny called an emergency meeting with Magno and Winter. The shaken dealer explained that two young cops had come into his store and started pushing his customers around, demanding to be paid off. Benny's brother Frankie gave Tony and Henry eight hundred dollars cash, telling them, "Split it with those other two cops. I never want to see them again."

"Hey, we didn't have nothing to do with this," Tony said. "Yeah, okay," said Frankie. "Just take care of those guys and tell them to stay the hell out of here."

Tony went back to the precinct house and split up the money—robbing the cops in the process. He kept six hundred dollars to share with Henry and gave the younger cops two hundred dollars to split. After the initial payoff, Henry returned to Benny's store every other week. He would go in for cigarettes and come out with a brown paper bag filled with money. Tony became a reluctant paymaster, steadily giving the younger cops raises.

Four months later, Figueroa approached Magno in the locker room and told him, "Look, we don't need your Santa Claus no more. We want out. We got enough now." The brash younger cops offered no explanation for their change of heart. Tony was confused. Why would two dirty cops suddenly stop taking free and easy money? They couldn't have developed a conscience all of a sudden. Henry and Tony thought the cops must have heard something that scared them straight.

"Something around here stinks," Tony decided. "I think we just stepped in shit."

"There were investigators tailing us by September 1985. They were easy to lose. We'd spot them and race down one way streets with our lights off. No Manhattan cop could keep up with us when we wanted to lose them. But we knew they were out there. There were too many reports on us by now. They would have been idiots not to be tailing us.

"One day we were going to a job and we saw the shoofly's car behind us. We go to another job, the shoofly follows us. He was constantly following us. So we went on one more job, and came out of the street the wrong way and there's the shoofly, parked on the corner of Park Place and Troy.

"So Tony said, 'Fuck this. Let's call in a man with a gun right on that corner store where he's parked. Let's see what he does. Let's see if he's gonna back us up or take off like a scared rabbit.' We went around the corner, getting in a position where we could still watch him, and called in the gun run from a corner pay phone. And then we watched. We were going to bust his chops, run up on him and say, 'Hey, if you're on the job and a gun run comes over, you back us up, asshole, no matter who you are.' But as soon as the gun run came over the radio, the guy took off like a bat out of hell. He didn't want to get involved in any kind of gun thing. He took off like his pants were on fire. We laughed our asses off over that one."

On a chilly October morning in 1985, William Gallagher called Henry at home. The precinct's union representative had heard some disturbing news from another union official, Ray Lessinger, the Brooklyn North trustee with the Patrolmen's Benevolent Association.

"We got to talk, Buddy Boy. I got some information," Gallagher said.

"All right," Henry replied. "Tell me."

"Not on the ring-a-ding."

"All right, Billy. Where do you want to meet?"

"Meet me at Marine Park tonight. Five o'clock."

The men met outside the park, and then walked. It was a clear evening with a chilly darkness descending as they strolled along, hands behind their backs. For some reason, Henry had hunting on his mind. Deer season would be opening soon. He would pack up his truck and drive north into the Adirondacks to spend two weeks roaming the woods, trying to take home a prize buck or doe.

But William Gallagher didn't have time for small talk.

"Ray says they're running an operation to try and catch you and Tony. One of the guys that was doing undercover work on you got into trouble with drugs. He got bagged himself. But Ray says the thing is still hot. You might not make it to Christmas. Ray says if you make it to Christmas, chances are you'll be okay."

Gallagher went on to explain that the case was being handled by investigators assigned to Internal Affairs and possibly even the Special Prosecutor's Office. Junior also said that as far as he knew only Henry and Tony had been targeted in the probe.

"But look," Gallagher said, putting his hand on Henry's shoulder. "If anything goes wrong, just keep your mouth shut and we'll get you the best lawyer we can. We'll run rackets for you and everything. Money won't be a problem. We'll take care of you."

"Yeah." Henry's body shook with a chill that had nothing to do with the cold. "No problem. You know me, Bill. If they come and ask me any questions, I don't know anything."

The two men shook hands.

"Don't worry about it. Ray says it's not that bad. He just wanted you to be aware of things."

"Tony and I chilled out after that. I went away hunting and told my friend Jimmy the garbage man what had happened. He said, 'Don't worry about it. Even if you do get jammed up, it isn't the end of the world.' But I was scared. I just wanted to make it through Christmas. I didn't want to go to jail at Christmas time. We stopped taking money from Benny. That was over. We weren't doing anything on the streets. I didn't know it, but Crystal Spivey, a black female cop we hung out with, had arrested Benny with major-weight cocaine. And they turned him. Isn't that great? Crystal Spivey busts the guy, they turn Benny to get me, and then they turn me so I can get Crystal. A neat little package.

"So we weren't into anything. Then all of a sudden we got a radio run one day in February to meet a complainant on the corner of Ralph and Pacific. We went looking but couldn't find a complainant. We do see Benny, and he says, 'Hey guys, how you been?' He didn't tell us he'd been collared, and Crystal never told us she arrested the guy. So now Benny is standing there on the corner saying, 'Hey, can I talk to you guys?' We put him in the car and drove away. We had no idea he was wired. We drove away and he told us, 'I'm looking to open a new place. It will be like the old times.' I think I said, 'Yeah. No problem.' This was Benny. We weren't scared of Benny. He handed Tony the money—about two hundred dollars. We dropped him off and drove away. Tony looked at me and said, 'I don't know. Something's not right. Benny was nervous. He was shaking.' We went back and forth for a couple of minutes and I saw a twinkle in Tony's eye and I'm sure he saw a twinkle in mine. I put my hand out and Tony put the money in my hand. I put it in my pocket and forgot about it. That was that.

"They had a truck there. We never saw it. They were running videotape on us. Benny was wired. I think we took money from Benny another four or five times after that. He was always wired. We always took the money. We probably got about fifteen hundred total. It wasn't a lot, but it was enough money to catch us. Enough money to catch us and make us turn in our friends. We did a little better than Judas, I guess. How much is thirty pieces of silver worth anyway?"

With the Meat in Their Mouth—I
by Joel Sayre

Journalist and screenwriter Joel Sayre (1900–1979) in 1953 published a two-part profile of legendary NYPD detective John Cordes in the New Yorker. The first part starts below; the second part begins on page 115.

J ohn Cordes, who retired at the end of 1949 as an acting lieutenant of detectives after thirty-four years' service in the Police Department, is the only man in the New York Department's history ever to win its Medal of Honor twice. No matter what shape the Police Department happens to be in at any given period—corrupt to the core, gleaming with virtue, or somewhere in between—this medal is never lightly bestowed. In the majority of cases it has been awarded posthumously, to men who have been killed while performing valiantly in the line of duty. Every New York cop, however cynical he may be toward all else in life, respects it, as members of the armed forces respect the Congressional Medal of Honor.

Born on Hudson Street in 1890 of an Alsatian father and a North German mother, Cordes (the name is pronounced "Cordeez," with the accent on the first syllable) spent a good part of his childhood in that then squalid neighborhood, which was infested with hoodlums known as the Hudson Dusters, who were one of the toughest gangs in the city and prowled the West Side from Greenwich Village up to Thirty-ninth Street. When Cordes was twelve, his father became ill and could no longer support his wife and five children. Mrs. Cordes, who had once been a practical nurse, moved the family up to Harlem, where she earned the rent by working as the janitress of the tenement they lived in. To help out the family finances, Cordes, who was the second oldest of the children, set up pins in a bowling alley and sold papers; also, for ten cents a head, he used to ride and convoy horses from a brewery at Amsterdam Avenue and 125th Street to a blacksmith shop at Eighth Avenue and 121st Street, and take them back, shod, to the brewery. The blacksmith was James J. Hines, who later became a power in Tammany Hall and was sent to prison in 1940 for owning too large a piece of the numbers racket.

The twelve-year-old Cordes had a racket of his own, which kept him in pocket money. Late at night, he would sneak about the roofs and fire escapes of the tenements near his home, cutting down his neighbors' high-rigged clotheslines and running off with them; next day, he would make a door-to-door tour of the distressed areas, selling new clothesline to the fuming housewives. A number of Cordes' childhood playmates grew up to fall foul of the law; some have died in the electric chair. "The border line between me and them was very thin," he says, in a voice that has been high and crackling all his life. "A little bad luck one way and another, and I might have finished like they did." As a detective, Cordes always maintained a charitable attitude toward the wrongdoers he matched wits and talents with, and beat; it may not have been exactly like shaking hands with a defeated adversary after a fierce battle, but it was akin to it. In his heyday, during the nineteen-twenties, Cordes used to make between two hundred and fifty and three hundred arrests a year. "Most of them thought I was the greatest son of a bitch ever born," he says in referring to the wrongdoers he sent to prison. A stranger, unversed in the Cordes idiom, might not realize that by this statement Cordes means that few of those men harbored lasting grudges against him. In a detached, nostalgic way, Cordes admires the technical skills of many of those he locked up. "He was a good kidnapper out of Cleveland," he will say, or "They were the best fur thieves in town at the time."

At the age of thirteen, Cordes left P.S. 43, where he was in grade 8-B, and got a job as a runner for a brokerage house that traded on the Curb Exchange, which at that time was still operating literally on the curbs of Broad Street. Runners stationed in the street communicated with order clerks up in the windows of nearby brokerage offices by signalling rapidly with their hands. A young Broadway smart named Arnold Rothstein, who was also getting his start in the financial world, used to take a pair of educated dice down to the Curb on paydays and clean the runners out.

Cordes spent the rest of his teens with the Curb Exchange. A bright youngster, brisk and conscientious, he was an excellent runner and order clerk, and at the peak of his career there he was providing the signals for five brokerage offices simultaneously. His employers liked him and used to give him tips on stocks. He played the market successfully; by the time he came of age, he had accumulated a bank roll of twenty-five thousand dollars. For a while, he considered buying a seat on the Curb—one could be purchased for as little as twenty-five hundred dollars at the time—and going into business for himself. Instead, one day when he was barely twenty-one, he impulsively quit his job and left the market. He had always kept in top physical shape, and had enjoyed participating in as many sports as he could find time for—baseball, boxing, handball, wrestling, distance running, and swimming. He had been good at them, too. Now, jaded by frenzied finance, he decided to have fun for a while, so he went over to Newark and became a bicycle racer, competing regularly twice a week at the Velodrome there. The Velodrome bike racers were supposed to be amateurs, but in most cases the designation was laughable. One of them, a pedaller from Utah, was managed by Robert Arthur Tourbillon (known in the underworld, because of his initials, as Rats or Ratsie), who later became internationally famous as a confidence man, blackmailer, badger-game worker, and gilt-edged thief under the name of Dapper Don Collins.

To occupy himself between grinds, Cordes used to return to New York and labor as missionary for the O'Brien Civil Service Institute, a cramming school for citizens ambitious to attain permanent tenure on the public payrolls. His mission was to proselytize on the Institute's behalf, and for this he received a retainer of twenty-five dollars a week, plus five dollars for each proselyte. Cordes specialized in persuading gigantic men engaged in backbreaking labor that they were leading fruitless, futureless lives. Why not, he would urge them, try the Police Department, with its easier work, better pay, and pension on retirement? After all, passing the Department's physical and mental examinations was merely a matter of taking a few months of night courses at the Institute. He hung around docks, car-barns, packing houses, and stables frequented by draymen, preaching the O'Brien gospel; an able evangelist, he sent converts to the Institute in droves.

Cordes was not sold by his own sales talk; in the end, he gambled himself into the Police Department. One evening while he was looking things over in the O'Brien gymnasium, he noticed an enormous fellow, who worked days as a beef lugger in a packing plant, lying on his back on a mat and unsuccessfully trying to lift a thirty-five-pound bar bell that was planted under his neck. Lifting the bar bell from this position was an obligatory requirement for the police physical tests. "Look, friend, it's just a trick," Cordes said to the giant. "Here, let me show you." Cordes slipped off his coat, got down on the mat, and demonstrated the feat with ease. He weighed only a hundred and forty-five, stripped, at that time, and the beef lugger was nettled. "I suppose you think you could get on the cops," he sneered. "Certainly I could," replied Cordes, who had never before given the matter a thought. After some argument, he bet three hundred dollars that he could get on the cops and another two hundred that the beef lugger couldnt't.

Between bike races, Cordes trained in the gym for the next few weeks and boned up on paperwork. (Up to this time, he had believed that his first name was Harry, but upon digging up the birth certificate that had to accompany his application papers, he discovered that his given name was John Henry Frederick. His mother had started calling him Harry in his infancy; at the age of ninety-five, she still does.) Cordes passed the physical and written exams with a rating of 90.91, which put him at the top of the list, and was admitted to the Department in August, 1915, shortly after his twenty-fifth birthday. The beef lugger flunked.

Cordes' police career got off to an unusual start. After graduating from the Police Academy, rookie cops ordinarily pound heats in uniform—first in the company of an older cop, then on their own. The very first day Cordes reported for duty, he was picked out of the ranks at Police Headquarters by Lieutenant of Detectives Daniel E. Costigan, whom the newspapers invariably referred to as Honest Dan, and detailed to plainclothes work. This was during the reform administration of Republican Mayor John Purroy Mitchel, and Police Commissioner Arthur Woods, a former master at Groton, had ordered Costigan to make war on the city's gambling—a burning issue in those days also. Costigan wanted some unknown faces on the special fifty-man squad he was organizing. Cordes didn't look the way a cop in plainclothes is popularly supposed to look. His brow was not low, his head stuck out in back, and his feet weren't noticeably big; his expression was cheerful, and his manner was friendly; he had straw-colored hair that was somewhat curly, thick eyebrows, large, staring blue eyes, a fresh complexion, and not much meat on his bones for his five feet ten. Gambling-house steerers were taken in by his guileless air and had no way of knowing that his forty-three-inch chest was backed by rippling muscles. "There's nobody so gullible as a guy who wants your dough," Cordes says in recalling those days. "They chased me like they was dogs and I was a rabbit." Posing as the ne'er-do-well son of a Canadian millionaire, he occupied a parlor suite at Mrs. Grunnhut's celebrated boarding house on West Forty-fifth Street, where he was constantly receiving telegrams, purportedly from Montreal and signed "Dad," that announced the imminent arrival of large consignments of cash, and in five weeks of sleuthing had no trouble getting into thirty-three gambling joints and obtaining evidence for a big raid that closed them all up. The detectives who raided the joints arrested Cordes along with the rest and put him in jail, so that he could listen to the talk of the gamblers in their cells and strengthen the case against them. "My God!" a dice hustler on his cell tier yelled. "They've even locked up that poor sucker from Canada!" The other gamblers laughed, but they did not the next morning in court when Lieutenant Costigan stepped forward and pinned a police shield on the poor sucker's lapel. Cordes has staggering powers of recall, which enable him still, thirty-seven years later, to reel off the names and addresses of all thirty-three joints: Stony Melville's wheelhouse (Stony was a former Wall Street broker) at 123 West Seventy-second Street; Al Levy's horse room (better known as the Rock of Gibraltar), at 267 Grand Street; Baldy and Warren's crap game (the biggest in New York), on three floors at 203 East Fifteenth Street; and so on.

Costigan, who was made an inspector soon after Cordes joined the force, saw that the young man was a born detective and kept him happily busy on the special squad. Hardly a day passed that Cordes did not remind himself how lucky he had been to escape pounding a beat in uniform. To an up-and-coming young detective, a uniformed cop seemed a sort of watchman—necessary, no doubt, but unglamorous. Cordes' attitude toward detective work was that of a perfervid Boy Scout toward woodcraft, and he brought to it a Teutonic thoroughness and zeal inherited from his mother, and an appetite for competition acquired in sports and in the financial district. Many of his older colleagues, observing him sourly and listening to him pop off (for he was the voluble type), thought he was at least partly insane, and, looking back on his younger self, Cordes is often inclined to agree with them. "Jeezes, what chances I took!" he says. "I couldn't have had good sense."

Cordes loved to masquerade. While still hardly more than an apprentice, he successfully portrayed—in addition to the ne'er-do-well Canadian scion—a ragged hunchback, a soldier, a sailor, a streetcar conductor, a meter reader, a longshoreman, a contractor, and a whole stock company of bums. He also effectively played the role of a chopped-liver-and-Greek-salad glutton in the course of a crusade to wipe out a pre-prohibition institution known as the wine rink, a fore-runner of the speakeasy. Ostensibly restaurants and mostly under Greek management, wine rinks were small, flyblown establishments that violated the excise laws by selling high-voltage wines without a license. Standard equipment in every wine rink was a large sign announcing that "free grape juice" would be served with every table-d'hôte meal ordered. No wine-rink menu ever listed more than two dishes—chopped liver and Greek salad. Chopped liver is self-explanatory; Greek salad is a medley of vegetables, with onions and olives predominating, that is pleasant enough but liable to become monotonous if over indulged in. While obtaining samples of illicit wine sold as grape juice in twenty-nine rinks, Cordes and two other detectives, posing as gourmands, choked down a total of seventy-five portions of chopped liver and Greek salad in three days. (In the light of what prohibition was soon to bring, such sacrifices to such an end seem trifling indeed. Less than a decade later, in broad daylight, Cordes engaged in a fight for his life with two thugs who had kid-napped a pair of bootleggers. It was for thwarting the kidnappers that he was awarded one of his two Medals of Honor.)

Had it not been for a man named Stephen Vassilopoulos, Cordes might easily have ended his police career after six years by quitting in disgust, or, the disgust muffled, he might have gone on and on, to retire finally not as a famous detective but as an obscure desk sergeant in some out-lying precinct. For in 1921, he became a victim of politics. By that time, Tammany had returned to power by electing John F. Hylan as Mayor. Hylan appointed a new police commissioner—Richard Enright, a strange, large man from Steuben County. Enright had come to New York as a country boy, joined the police force, and worked his way up from the ranks. Inspector Costigan was senior to Enright in service, and Enright hated him, claiming that Costigan had once prevented him from being made a captain. One of Enright's first official acts was to

remove Costigan from command of the special squad. Enright continued the squad under another inspector, but the fifty men Costigan
had picked for it were all marked for the guillotine. Early in 1921, "for
the good of the service," Cordes was ordered to buy himself a uniform
and go pound a beat in Harlem. Actually, it was not even a beat; he drew
a fixed post at the corner of 135th Street and Lenox Avenue. Patrolling a
beat, a uniformed cop has at least several square blocks to do his stuff
in; Cordes' demesne was little more than an intersection. He loathed
working in uniform; besides, he had recently got married—to Vera Fay
McCall, a girl from Marion, Indiana, whom he met in Newark during
his bike-racing days—and he felt he owed it to his wife to get back into
the Detective Bureau, where he thought his prospects looked better. At
the end of about six months of helping old ladies across the street, he
saw an opportunity and seized it.

Late one Sunday night in August, three masked hoodlums entered
the bedroom of the man named Stephen Vassilopoulos, who had a
candy-and-soda concession at Brighton Beach, where he also lived.
The intruders bound Vassilopoulos to his bed with ripped-up sheets,
strapped adhesive tape over his eyes and mouth, and set to work jim-
mying a safe he kept in his bedroom. The jimmy broke before the robbers could get the safe open, so they unstrapped Vassilopoulos' mouth
and demanded that he tell them the safe's combination. When he
refused, they began pulling out the hairs of his elegant thick mustache, one by one. Vassilopoulos opened the safe for them. The robbers left with twenty-one hundred dollars in cash and Liberty Bonds.

While this was going on, Cordes was sulking on his fixed post,
working the midnight-to-8-a.m. trick. Shortly after he got home that
Monday morning, a stool pigeon phoned him and said that a young
waiter named Joe Paulse, who lived in a boarding house on West Forty-
ninth Street, was one of the men who had plucked the Vassilopoulos
mustache. Cordes at once changed into plainclothes and started shadowing Paulse; he also persuaded one of the boarding-house tenants to
eavesdrop on the suspect's conversations on the hall telephone. Except
when he was working his eight hours in uniform, Cordes kept after

Paulse unrelentingly until Thursday midnight, saying nothing about the case to anybody. ("Those four days I never took off a shoe," he says.) On Friday morning, he went down to Headquarters, where he called on Assistant Chief Inspector John Coughlin, the head of the Detective Bureau, and told him he could break the Brighton Beach job. Coughlin promised Cordes that if he did, he would he taken back into the Bureau. Cordes said that at eight-thirty that evening Paulse was going to meet another of the robbers, Marino by name, in front of the Strand Theatre, at Forty-seventh Street and Broadway. Marino, he continued, had held out on the booty, and Paulse intended to kill him. Coughlin ordered Cordes to carry on, and promised to send him some help at once, just in case the murder might be attempted ahead of schedule. Cordes went straight to the theatre and took up a cautious watch outside it; in police argot, he took a plant. Soon he was joined by four detectives from the Coney Island station, in whose jurisdiction the Brighton Beach robbery lay. Cordes explained to them enthusiastically that here was a sure opportunity to break the case; evidently, his enthusiasm was not contagious; for after waiting around until four, they knocked off for the day, leaving Cordes alone. On the dot of eight-thirty, a Packard containing five men stopped in front of the Strand, and Marino stepped out of it. From the crowd in front of the theatre, Paulse rushed at him with a drawn revolver, but before he could pull the trigger, Cordes snatched the revolver away from him, knocked him to the sidewalk, and covered Marino and the four other men. He then took all six to the West Forty-seventh Street station house in the Packard. Snatching guns from would-be killers was a specialty Cordes later became celebrated for. According to regulations, cops must carry revolvers at all times; off duty they may carry revolvers of smaller calibre than the one the regulations prescribe, but armed they must be. Cordes, for some reason he cannot precisely define, always hated to carry a gun, and he frequently didn't; because detectives are not inspected as carefully before going on duty as are uniformed members of the force, and because of the fact that, armed or unarmed, he produced results, he usually got away with it.

Police went to Marino's rooms and found a missing piece of the broken jimmy, three masks, assorted weapons and ammunition, Vassilopoulos' Liberty Bonds and quite a lot of his cash, and some keys to the interior drawers of his safe. Within a few days, the third robber, one Mancuso, was captured, and all three were sent to prison for long terms. It was what the cops call a good pinch, and Cordes never worked in uniform again.

Three months later Cordes made another good pinch. During the summer and fall of 1921, there were more than three hundred burglaries in houses and apartments of well-to-do residents of the upper West Side; in one, Eva Tanguay, the actress, lost ten thousand dollars' worth of jewelry and clothes from her apartment at 319 West Eighty-sixth Street. The common denominator of most of the burglaries was that they occurred during the afternoon, when their victims were away from home. After Cordes' return to the Detective Bureau, he was assigned to the West Forty-seventh Street station and teamed with a veteran detective named Patrick Manney, who was short, slight, and the father of fifteen children. For several weeks, the pair worked on the so-called "matinée burglaries." From apartment-house doormen and elevator operators they pieced together descriptions of two of the burglars. Early one afternoon in late November, Cordes and Manney spotted two men who fitted the descriptions standing at the corner of Forty-eighth Street and Broadway. One of the men was dark, the other fair; both were hefty and well dressed. When an uptown streetcar came along, they boarded it and rode to Seventy-second Street; the detectives got on and off with them. All the afternoon, the detectives tailed the two men. They watched outside as the pair entered half a dozen apartment houses, stayed a short while in each, and then came out empty-handed. Finally, the detectives' patience was rewarded when the two men went into an apartment house on the south side of Eighty-second Street between West End Avenue and Riverside Drive, stayed about three-quarters of an hour, then came out loaded. The dark man was carrying a large suitcase; the fair man had what appeared to be a big bundle of clothing over one arm. "We caught them with the meat in their mouth," says Cordes. The pair started toward Riverside Drive with the detectives tailing them.

About halfway down the block, Suitcase crossed to the north side of the street and continued walking toward the Drive; on the south side, Bundle kept right on going. Five or ten yards from the Drive, the two men realized they were being followed, and started to run. On this occasion, both detectives were unarmed. Manney took off after Suitcase and Cordes took off after Bundle. Manney caught Suitcase, who towered above him, on the west side of the Drive, and when he closed in to seize him, Suitcase pulled a two-pound jimmy from his pocket, hit Manney on the side of the head with it, and started to run again. Manney staggered, recovered, caught up with Suitcase, and jumped on his back. Suitcase shook him off and hit him on the head again with the jimmy, but then the father of fifteen whipped his blackjack out of his hip pocket, slammed it along Suitcase's jaw, and stiffened him. Meanwhile, Cordes had chased Bundle down the east side of the Drive, overhauled him, and sent him crashing into a fence by using the chaser's trip; that is, he had flung out the toe of his right shoe and caught Bundle under the right heel. Bundle lay face down on the sidewalk, as though stunned, but when Cordes bent over him, he whirled around onto his back with a .45 automatic in his right hand. Cordes seized him by the wrist with his left hand and turned the gun aside. The two rolled back and forth on the sidewalk as they battled for the gun, flailing at each other with their free fists; Bundle not only hit and kicked Cordes repeatedly but bit him several times. At last, Cordes got possession of the gun and brought its butt down on Bundle's head. Crowds of people had gathered around both fights, and many others were watching from apartment windows and bus tops; it cost money to see this sort of thing in the movies. After Cordes and Manney had subdued their prisoners, they had to convince their public that they represented the law, and not the underworld.

Bundle turned out to be William Neeley, twenty-nine years old, who had served a term in Sing Sing for burglary, was wanted in Atlantic

City for a ten-thousand-dollar jewel robbery in the Traymore Hotel there, and was free on bail on a counterfeiting charge in Asbury Park. Suitcase was Eugene Metuli, twenty-seven years old, who, in Cordes' words, "was wanted by everybody but the Church." More than a hundred keys were found on Metuli; Neeley had about fifty. The loot, which amounted to three thousand dollars' worth of jewelry and clothing, had been stolen from the apartment of Justice Henry W. Herbert, of the Court of Special Sessions. The final sentence from the *Herald's* story reporting the capture of the matinée burglars read, "They [Neeley and Metuli] said they were friends of Waxey Gordon, an old-time gangster, who was once one of the leaders of the Dopey Benny Fein gang, and has served time in prison." Gordon became New York's Public Enemy No. 1 during prohibition and died last year in Alcatraz, where he was serving a twenty-five-year sentence.

The next summer, Cordes was transferred to the East 104th Street station, where he worked for Captain of Detectives John Lyons, who soon came to admire his work as a skillful and dogged shadower of criminals and suspects. Lyons could see that Cordes combined all the attributes of a successful tailer—iron legs and arches, the considerable acting ability a man must have to make himself unnoteworthy, and a sixth sense of anticipation—and he thought highly of Cordes' often repeated dictum: "Be easy and natural, never let the other guy make your eyes, and keep trying to figure out what he'll do next." When Captain Lyons was presently transferred to the Thirty-first Detective Precinct, with headquarters in the East Sixty-seventh Street station, he took Cordes along.

On Thursday evening, March 29, 1923, at ten minutes to eight, Cordes, wearing a green cap and a new camel's-hair overcoat with red and brown checks, was on his way to report for work. He was riding down there from his home in Harlem in a black five-passenger Studebaker driven by his brother Freddie, who owned the car and was a clerk at Lewis & Conger's. On the way downtown, Freddie stopped in front of a United Cigar store at 954 Lexington Avenue, just south of Sixty-ninth

Street and not far from the station house. Freddie had run out of cigars—Optimo Blunts were what he smoked—and his brother had offered to get out and get him some.

By rights, it was Cordes' day off, but during the afternoon a fellow-detective who was getting married that evening had called up to say that the man who had volunteered to take his trick for him had let him down, and Cordes had agreed to take the trick instead. Something had happened that morning that Cordes remembered later. A cross-eyed eight-year-old boy named Tommy Radlup, whose father ran a fruit stand near where Cordes lived, was in the habit of panhandling the detective whenever they met on the street. Cordes usually gave him a nickel or a dime, but that morning he had had no change and had passed the boy up. "Awright for you," Tommy had said. "You're gonna have bad luck."

About five minutes before Freddie stopped the Studebaker for his brother to get out and get him the cigars, two robbers had entered the cigar store and pulled revolvers on William Einhorn, the salesman. They were Patrick Ahearn, twenty-three years old, and John Whitton, eighteen; both were narcotic addicts and both belonged to what was left of the Hudson Dusters. Ahearn towered over Whitton, who was four feet ten inches tall and weighed a hundred and eighteen pounds, but Whitton, known on the West Side as the Mutt, dominated him. The previous Saturday, Whitton had escaped from the East View Penitentiary, in Westchester. He was looking for a stake.

The cigar store was small and had only two showcases, which were placed at right angles, forming an L. The longer showcase, which faced Lexington Avenue, contained mostly pipes and supported the cash register; the other was on the south side of the store, and its shelves were filled with boxes of cigars. In the wall behind the cigar showcase was a small safe, close to the floor. At the north end of the pipe showcase, opposite the door opening on Lexington Avenue, was a waist-high, swinging wooden gate, the only entrance to the rear of the showcases. In the northwest corner of the room was a door that led to a stockroom, from which there was no other exit. Keeping their guns on Einhorn,

Whitton and Ahearn went behind the counter. Ahearn cleaned out the cash register, in which there was $16.98, and then took a stand behind the gate to act as lookout. Whitton gave Einhorn a push. "Get down to the safe and give me the money," he said. The safe contained eighty dollars in bills and coins; the coins were done up in paper-covered rolls. After Einhorn turned the money over, Whitton ordered him to stay crouched on the floor.

Cordes, due at the station house in ten minutes, hurried into the store and was almost at the cigar showcase, which was only a few strides from the street door, when he noticed that the sales personnel were wearing caps and blue work shirts. Something bad was happening, he realized instantly, or had happened already; if it was what he thought it was, to turn on his heel and head for the door without a word might well be the last walking he ever did. The taller man, standing behind the gate, had his right hand in his coat pocket in a way that Cordes did not like at all. Cordes leaned over the cigar case and pretended to study the brands. Behind the cigar counter, and just a bit to his right, stood the runt. When the runt moved slightly, Cordes saw a .38 in his hand, with the muzzle pointing toward the floor. Cordes, as usual, had no corresponding weapon with him.

"I don't see the particular type of cigar I smoke," Cordes said in his high voice, staring at a full box of Optimo Blunts on the top shelf in the case. "Guess you're out of them. Well, I'll be in again." He started to back toward the door.

"Just a minute, Mister," the tall man behind the gate said. "You'll get your smokes." He stared at the runt behind the cigar counter, presumably expecting him to act like a salesman, but the runt interpreted the stare as a signal to produce Einhorn and, looking down at the floor, made a beckoning gesture with his left hand. The top half of a very frightened man, who was more appropriately wearing a mohair jacket, rose up beside him and appealed to Cordes with his eyes. Cordes was almost to the door. "Be in again," he repeated, as though he had not noticed the frightened man at all.

Whitton fired at Cordes' heart, just as Cordes instinctively covered it with his right hand. The bullet was slowed down by the hand, which it pierced through the palm, and by the camel's-hair coat and the clothing underneath, and wound up by merely cutting the flesh on the left side of his chest. Cordes fell to the floor. "Give it to the son of a bitch!" Whitton yelled. Ahearn came running from behind the gate and bent over Cordes to finish him off with his gun. Cordes snatched the gun from him and, firing with his left hand, shot him in the stomach. Ahearn went down. From the floor, Cordes opened fire on Whitton, who had taken shelter behind the cash register. They exchanged several shots. Cordes was still shooting left-handed and his bullets went wild. Whitton hit Cordes in the right shoulder and on the inside of the left thigh near the knee. Then, like Ahearn, he ran out from behind the gate to finish Cordes off. Cordes snatched his gun, too—Ahearn's was by this time out of ammunition—but Whitton got back through the gate before Cordes could fire. Although Cordes' shots kept going wild, they drove Whitton through the door into the stockroom. Cordes dragged himself to his feet, staggered to the cigar counter, found Einhorn lying face down but unhurt behind it, and learned from him that Whitton was trapped in the stockroom, as there was no exit from it. Cordes then lurched out into Lexington Avenue and almost collided with his brother, who, when he realized where all the noise was coming from, had jumped from the Studebaker and dashed toward the store. "For God's sake," Cordes told Freddie, "beat it over to the station house and get my partner! Tell him I got a good pinch here."

Freddie started for the car, but just then there was a shot from the east side of Lexington Avenue that hit John in the back of his right shoulder. It had been fired by a sergeant from the uniformed force in Brooklyn, who was spending his day off with a maid who worked in the Lexington Avenue neighborhood. The sergeant was almost fallingdown drunk. He had, however, obeyed the regulation about being armed while off duty; hearing the shooting and seeing Cordes with a gun in his hand, he had mistaken him for a robber. Stumbling across the street, he fired two more shots before he reached the Cordes brothers. One shot went through the glass of the cigar-store door and broke a mirror that backed the pipe showcase; the other went through a window of a store next door.

Cordes had been knocked down by the shot that struck him in the shoulder, and Whitton's gun had fallen from his hand and skidded down the street. He got to his feet and took his detective's shield, in its leather case, out of his pocket and showed it to the sergeant as the latter came lumbering up. "Please don't kill me, Mister," Cordes said. "I'm a policeman." The sergeant put the muzzle of his gun against Cordes' right cheek and pulled the trigger. The bullet just missed Cordes' jugular vein and lodged in the spongy part of his right mastoid; amazingly, it did not knock him down. He spun around several times, stopped, got his bearings, and kicked the sergeant in the groin. The sergeant fell, his gun went off, and the bullet from it hit Freddie in the left elbow.

Cordes' right jawbone was fractured in three places, and there were two wounds in his shoulder, one in his leg and another in his chest, and a hole through his right hand, but rage overcame the terrible pain he was suffering. He picked up the gun he had dropped, shoved his right forefinger into the hole in his cheek, went back into the store, and, stepping over Ahearn, who was lying unconscious on the floor, entered the stockroom, where he arrested Whitton.

When Cordes got Whitton to the street, help had not arrived from the station house, because nobody had called for it. Freddie, surrounded by a small crowd, was lying on the sidewalk while an amateur surgeon applied a handkerchief tourniquet above his elbow. No uniformed cop was in sight; the drunken sergeant had disappeared. Now pain began to creep up on Cordes, and he was afraid he might collapse and his unhurt prisoner escape before he could deliver him into safekeeping. The East Sixty-seventh Street station was two and a half blocks away; Presbyterian Hospital was nearer—at Seventieth and Park. Cordes, accompanied by Freddie, marched Whitton to the hospital. On the way, Whitton said to his captor, "You're gonna die, Mister. Lemme go and I'll say a prayer for you." Cordes told him to save his prayers. "Anyway," he added, "if I thought I was gonna die, I'd kill you first." The reception clerk at Presbyterian's Park Avenue entrance refused to admit them, insisting that they go to the accident-ward entrance, on the Seventy-first Street side of the building. "So I followed directions and walked around there," Cordes says. From the accident ward, he phoned his partner, Emil Mack, at the station house, and soon Mack and other detectives came to pick up Whitton. Whitton tried to ditch the eighty dollars from the cigar-store safe, but he had dropped only three dollars in rolled-up coins under a cot when a detective caught him at it. Meanwhile, Ahearn had been sent in an ambulance to Bellevue for repairs. Surgeons worked all night over Cordes at Presbyterian, and the next morning, in front-page stories of the shooting, several newspapers said that he would probably die.

Instead of dying, Cordes went home six days later, although not with the approval of his doctor. He would have been home a day earlier if it had not taken him twenty-four hours to persuade his wife to smuggle him in some clothes in which to sneak down the hospital's back stairs and escape.

The Sunday after Cordes had returned home, he was taking a walk in Mount Morris Park when a smiling, ruddy man of middle age, who weighed more than two hundred pounds and was solidly built, called at the Cordes apartment, which was on the ground floor of a building on Mount Morris Park West, near 124th Street. The caller told Mrs. Cordes that he was a detective and an old friend of her husband's, and would like to see him. She said that Cordes would be back any minute, and invited him in to wait. He sat down in an armchair in the living room; Mrs. Cordes excused herself to finish some work she was doing in another part of the apartment. She noticed that the visitor had a rosary in one hand. He kept smiling to himself and fingering the beads.

This man, whose name was Peter James McKenna, was not a detective but an ex-convict who had just been released after serving a year in prison, during which he had become a religious maniac. In 1922, Cordes and his partner at the time, Detective James Sheehan, had arrested McKenna in Harlem, along with a young Canadian named Hector Harold Garmant, for forging certified checks and being in illegal possession of a number of revolvers and blackjacks. Back in 1912, when McKenna owned a liquor store at Second Avenue and 124th Street, he was an important prosecution witness in the trial of Police Lieutenant Charles Becker for the murder of the gambler Herman Rosenthal. Becker was sent to the electric chair. In 1914, McKenna was sentenced to ten years in Sing Sing for grand larceny; two years later, Governor Charles S. Whitman, who had been District Attorney at the time of the Becker case, pardoned him. After arresting McKenna and Garmant in Harlem, Cordes and Sheehan started to take them downtown in a Model T Ford. Sheehan was driving. McKenna, riding in the back seat with Cordes, kept boasting about his friendship with Whitman. "I sent one cop to the electric chair and I'll send you, too," he said, and punched Cordes in the jaw. Cordes picked up a tire pump that happened to be lying on the floor of the car and hit McKenna over the head with it. Whitman, who after leaving Albany had gone into private practice, took McKenna's case and succeeded in getting the forgery charge against him quashed, but McKenna had to serve a year for the Sullivan Law violations.

When Cordes—his right hand and shoulder were still in bandages and his jaw was wired—returned to his apartment from his walk, McKenna rose and pocketed his rosary. "God didn't take you, so I've come to finish the job," he said in a thundering voice, and tried to seize Cordes by the throat. Cordes ducked and dodged. The living-room furniture was too heavy to wield with his one free hand, so he ran into the dining room, where the chairs were lighter, grabbed one, and stiffened McKenna with it first crack. He then dragged him out of the apartment, down the hall to the building entrance, and threw him into the street. McKenna never came back. He eventually died in an insane asylum.

The McKenna imbroglio exhausted Mrs. Cordes' patience and she appealed to Cordes' doctor, who ordered him back to the hospital. Cordes just laughed. The doctor appealed to the Police Department. Cordes was commanded to go to the police convalescent and vacation camp at Tannersville, in the Catskills, and finish his recuperation with no more monkey business. He managed to stick it out there that spring and summer (his wounds healed nicely, although the bull's-eye the sergeant scored on his cheekbone gave him splitting headaches for twenty-five years), but as fall approached he began to get restless. On Labor Day, Commissioner Enright, whose nephew, Syd Enright, was superintendent of the camp, paid a visit of inspection to the place and asked Cordes how he was getting along. "Fine," Cordes said. "And you're gonna make me a first-grade detective." Enright made a harrumphing noise and passed on down the line. He still thought of Cordes as a protégé of his old enemy Costigan.

In early October, the cops at the camp read in their newspapers about a fourteen-thousand-dollar payroll robbery at the International Motor Truck Company, in Long Island City; one of three robbers had critically wounded the cashier, a sixty-year-old man named John Fetzer. That evening, Cordes was playing cards when a stool pigeon phoned him from New York and asked if he had seen the news from Long Island City. Cordes said he had. "Well," said the stool, "I think we can do it all right on the guy who got the cashier." He went on to give Cordes some details, and Cordes told him to call the camp the next night and leave word that Mrs. Cordes' mother was dangerously ill in New York, and probably going to die. Cordes' wife has been an orphan since childhood. There was a freezing hailstorm the next night when the message came, but Cordes, after putting on such a convincing show of being an anxious son-in-law that Syd Enright lent him twenty-five dollars for expenses, hired a taxi to take him to Rhinecliff, where he caught a 3:25 a.m. train to New York.

The man Cordes was after was a man he knew well—Eddie Purtell, a thirty-two-year-old member of a West Side mob that was headed by James Cunniffe and was the hottest stickup outfit in New York. Despite the continuing bitter-cold weather, Cordes took a plant outside the tenement house Purtell's mother lived in on Ninth Avenue, at Twenty-eighth Street, grabbing a little sleep only when he couldn't go on without it. At about four in the morning of the ninth day, he climbed the steps of the Ninth Avenue "L" station at Thirtieth Street to go to the men's room. He went through the turnstile and out on to the platform, and, glancing down at the icy street below, saw that a horse hitched to a Borden Milk Company wagon had fallen. On the edge of a small group of men that had swiftly gathered to look on was Purtell. Cordes hurried back through the turnstile and down the stairs, and went up to Purtell. "Why, hello, Johnny," Purtell said. "I thought you was hurt real bad."

"Superficial flesh wound," said Cordes.

"What brings you out this early?" Purtell asked.

"You," Cordes said, and then improvised, "Coughlin told me to bring you in."

Coughlin, the head of the Detective Bureau, was a magnificently built man, well over six feet tall, who wore a pince-nez and dressed like a banker. Since it was unlikely that he would be at his desk for several hours, Cordes, to kill time, walked Purtell down to the Battery, then back uptown to the neighborhood of Police Headquarters, on Centre Street, where they had breakfast in an all-night restaurant and sat around until Cordes figured Coughlin would be at work. "What's he want me for?" Purtell kept asking. Cordes would shrug, and say, "Search me. All I know is he told me to bring you in."

"What are you doing here?" Coughlin demanded when Cordes appeared before him with Purtell. "You're supposed to be in Tannersville."

"Sure," Cordes said. "But don't you remember you phoned me there last night and told me to bring Purtell in? Well, here he is."

There was a pause before Coughlin spoke. "I did no such goddam thing," he said, but there was a faint note of doubt in his voice.

"I guess you must of been drunk when you called me," Cordes said casually. "Well, anyway, now we got Purtell here, it's a shame to waste him. Let's take him over to Long Island City and have a guy there in the hospital look at him."

At St. John's Hospital, in Long Island City, Fetzer, the cashier, positively identified Purtell as the man who had shot him during the payroll robbery. Later that day, three more witnesses identified him as one of the robbers. Purtell was locked up. "Now are you satisfied that you told me to come down and collar that guy?" Cordes asked Coughlin.

"Yes, I am, you fresh little bastard," said Coughlin.

The following spring, Purtell was given a thirty-year sentence in Sing Sing.

A couple of weeks later, Cordes was not only made a first-grade detective but awarded the Medal of Honor for his gallantry in the cigar-store stickup. Ahearn, whom Cordes shot in the stomach in that fracas, drew an indeterminate sentence, was sent to the Elmira Reformatory, and was paroled after serving eighteen months. Cordes lost track of him for about four years. Then, one day, he received the following letter:

> Pat'k. Ahearn,
> 307 W. 13th St.
> City

> Mr. Cordez
>
> I am taking the liberty, By asking you if you could get me a job. I have been working on the docks but things are slow so I dont get mutch work now.
>
> I seen your name in the paper this morning stating you wer one of the best men in the department, That was What made me think of you. I guss you know who I am. I am the fellow that was playing tag with you that night in the cigar store when you taged me out. Well John how do you feel. I feel pritty good only when I sneeze I get cramped up.
>
> Wishing you luck and hoping to hear from you.
>
> Paddy.

Cordes got Ahearn a longshoreman's job, and kept an eye on him. Ahearn became a respectable citizen and still is.

Whitton, who shot Cordes in the hand, chest, shoulder, and leg, was sentenced to fifteen years and served them. Cordes did not see him again until one day in the spring of 1940, when he ran into him on

Pier 45, on the North River. Cordes had by then become an acting lieu-tenant and was in command of the Manhattan waterfront. "Well, well, if it isn't the Mutt!" Cordes said. "What are you doing here?" Whitton told him he was working on the pier as a longshoreman. "O.K., and good luck," Cordes said, "but if you're gonna steal, I'll throw you back in jail." Cordes got weekly reports on Whitton for several months; the man's conduct was good and he was a first-rate longshoreman.

One Sunday morning in December, the Anchor Line's *Cameronia* docked at Pier 45, and Cordes, who was in the vicinity at the time, was buttonholed by a vice-president of the line. "That fellow Whitton," the vice-president said. "I want him out of here. He's a murderer."

"Give him a break," said Cordes. "He's trying to turn square and he's doing a good job at it. If you kick him out, he'll get bitter and go bad again. He's one of my boys and I'll answer for him. Just leave him to me."

"He's a murderer," the vice-president repeated. "I don't want him around, I tell you."

"It wasn't you he tried to murder," Cordes said. "It was me. And if I don't hold it against him, why should you? I tell you what we'll do. We'll go aboard the ship and leave it up to the skipper." The vice-president agreed.

The captain of the *Cameronia* ordered breakfast in his cabin for his guests. Cordes didn't wait until it arrived. "Suppose there's a kid eigh-teen years old," he said to the captain. "His mother and father are drunken bums who've kicked him around practically since the day he's born. He's got three strikes on him before he can even get up to the plate, and he's already in trouble with the law when he's only fifteen, sixteen years old. All right, one night he runs into me during a stickup. Put yourself in my place, Captain—you're the cop, I'm the stickup kid. It'd be self-preservation, wouldn't it? We're both out to get each other, but I happen to get you first. But I don't kill you, and you get over your wounds pretty fast. O.K., they give me fifteen years, and I pay my debt. Then we run into each other—seventeen, pretty near eighteen years later. You'd forgive me, wouldn't you, Captain?"

"No," the captain said. "I wouldn't. If you shot me, I'd get back at you, if I had to wait till I was a hundred to do it. Now sit down and have some breakfast."

"I don't want no breakfast," Cordes said, "You're worse than this other son of a bitch here. A poor guy's trying to straighten up and do right, and you're insisting that he stays wrong all the rest of his life. And it's bastards like you that are always hollering for more police protection." Cordes slammed the door of the cabin, went down to the dock, and picked up Whitton. Fifteen minutes later, he had Whitton working on another pier.

Within a few weeks, a case of ten disassembled Thompson submachine guns, valued at two hundred dollars apiece, which had been made by the Auto-Ordnance Company, of Utica, and were on their way to the British Army, were missing from a consignment on Pier 54. The police dropped grappling hooks in the North River near the end of the pier and hauled up the case the guns had been packed in but not the guns. On the afternoon of Washington's Birthday, the phone in Cordes' office rang, and a man's voice asked for him. "The lieutenant's not here right now," said the detective on duty. "Can I take a message?" "Tell Johnny," the voice said, "that if he'll go back of the haberdash store on Fifteenth between Eleventh and Twelfth Avenues, he'll find something he's been looking for." Cordes and a detail of cops went to the back yard of the haberdashery and found the ten Thompson submachine guns, all assembled and wrapped in burlap bags.

The following May, Whitton's body was fished out of the North River with three bullet holes in it. Word went around the waterfront that he had got it for stooling on the machine-gun job. Cordes, however, is convinced that this was an unjust accusation. "The Mutt didn't stool and he wouldn't stool," he says. "What happened was he had some of the union leaders, the low brass, scared to death and they decided to get rid of him."

Tommy Radlup, the cross-eyed boy who predicted that Cordes would have bad luck, became a stickup man in later life.

With the Meat in Their Mouth—II

by Joel Sayre

The conclusion of Joel Sayre's (1900–1979) profile of detective John Cordes appeared in the New Yorker on September 12, 1953. (The first installment of his two-part story begins on page 91.)

Back in the twenties, when John Cordes used to be interviewed by newspaper feature writers as the New York Police Department's paragon of detectives, he was always careful to credit luck with an assist. "Crooks are smart," he told a reporter in 1928. "You got to outsmart them. And you got to be lucky." At the time he said this, he had been a cop for thirteen years, had attained the rank of detective sergeant, and was the only member of the Department ever to win its highest award, the Medal of Honor, twice—a distinction he still holds.

Although he is by nature hardly unassuming, Cordes, who is now sixty-three, really meant it when he said he believed he owed a good deal to luck. On duty, he generally wore a green cap that he considered lucky; he has always found dates with the numbers 13, 8, and 5 in them propitious; and he considers Friday his best day of the week. He does not let superstition get the better of him, however. Since the end of 1949, when he retired from the Detective Bureau, as an acting lieutenant, after thirty-four years' service, he has had a job during the winter months with an agency that polices three Florida race tracks. Now and then, when somebody whose judgment he respects gives him a positively sure thing in a race, he will bet a small sum on the horse, but it is his belief that at least ninety per cent of the positively sure things fail to finish in the money, and if he dies broke, it will never be as a horse-player. Cordes, who used to charge, and capture, armed killers with his bare hands, regards horseplaying as foolhardy.

The Cordes concept of luck is broad, flexible, and seemingly illogical. Branch Rickey has defined luck in professional baseball as "the residue of design"—meaning that so-called lucky ballplayers bring about by intelligence and skill most of the "breaks" that occur in a game and know how to take advantage of them. The act of gallantry for which Cordes won his first Medal of Honor, in 1923, illustrates a comparable sort of luck. Cordes, who doesn't smoke, just happened to wander into a cigar store to buy some cigars for his brother one evening on his way to work, found two men holding up the clerk there, and wound up with five bullet wounds in his body and the two thugs under arrest. (In this fracas, as in most of the ones he has been involved in, he was unarmed, for he always had an aversion to carrying weapons and, despite departmental regulations to the contrary, rarely did so.) Another time, out for an off-duty stroll, Cordes recognized a small-time stickup man as he was going into a bank, and followed him inside. Instead of sticking the bank up, the man opened an account in it and deposited nineteen hundred dollars. Cordes tailed him to a Yorkville tenement, where the stickup man joined six other hoodlums in an all-night party. The uproar they created began to draw protests from some of the nearby tenement dwellers, and Cordes, still brooding about the nineteen-hundred-dollar deposit, arrested the whole gang for disturbing the peace. ("Sure, I know you ain't doing any harm, but we got complaints," he told the revellers. "My hands are tied, boys.") It turned out that the gang was wanted for stealing thirty-five thousand dollars' worth of diamonds from a New Rochelle jewelry store. A layman might regard such alertness and astute hunch-playing as a smart, if unspectacular, piece of detective work, but Cordes looks on it as sheer luck.

As an example of such luck, Cordes (pronounced "*Cor*-deez") puts his roundup of the Yorkville hoodlums in almost the same class with the way he once recovered a piece of missing evidence during a grand-larceny trial in a magistrate's court downtown. The linchpin in the prosecution's case was a subpoenaed cancelled check for twenty-five thousand dollars, which had been dispatched to the court from an uptown office by messenger boy. When the boy arrived at the court, he went through his pockets, could not find the check, and swore he must have lost it. Everybody suspected the worst, because the defendant was a lawyer with strong Tammany connections. Losing the check was like having a star witness bumped off, for in those days banks did not pho-tostat the checks they handled. The dismayed prosecution asked for an adjournment until after lunch. It was winter, and the streets were cov-ered with snow and slush. Cordes drove his car several blocks to a restaurant where he had a lunch date with the prosecuting attorney. When he got out of the car, he noticed an envelope sticking to the treads of his left front tire. He idly peeled the envelope off the tire, glanced at the blurred name on it, and saw that it was his own. Inside the envelope was the missing check. The boy actually had lost it, and somewhere between the courthouse and the restaurant Cordes' tire had picked the envelope up and held on to it, God alone knows how. At lunch, Cordes waited until the prosecuting attorney went to telephone and then slipped the check under his plate. When, upon returning, the attorney found it there, he stared at Cordes and said, "You bastard, you picked that kid's pocket."

Over the years, Cordes was usually luckier in breaking cases than in collecting his share of the rewards that were, in some instances, offered for doing so. In February, 1926, representatives of a furriers' organiza-tion complained to Police Commissioner George V. McLaughlin that loft thieves were robbing the fur industry blind. The organization's spokesmen implied that there might be collusion between the loft thieves and certain detectives, and offered a reward of twenty-five thousand dollars for the arrest and conviction of the persons responsible, whoever they were. McLaughlin gave Cordes the assignment, told him to pick any men he wanted to help him, and ordered him to bear down on whatever members of the Bureau might prove to be involved in the robberies. Cordes chose three detectives to assist him— John Morrissey, Lewis Barrett, and Frank Walsh, all old-timers. Then, after studying the techniques employed in the robberies, comparing them with information on fur thieves in the *modus-operandi* files at Police Headquarters, and consulting with Inspector Joseph Donovan, head of the Bureau of Criminal Identification, Cordes decided that the men he was after were Abraham Baum, alias Abe Polub, alias Abie the Waiter, and his partner, Charles (Kiddie) Goldberg. Kiddie was dark, short, slight, and wiry. Abie the Waiter bore a remarkable resemblance to Cordes; he was about five feet ten, husky in the shoulders and chest, and blue-eyed, with light skin and hair. "All you got to do is go out and find yourself," Donovan told Cordes.

Cordes and his three assistants beat around the city for a couple of weeks and alerted all their stool pigeons, but they could discover no trace of Abie and Kiddie. Finally, Cordes, wearied by the fruitless pursuit, went to the Pennsylvania Hotel one afternoon to take a Turkish bath. Walking down a corridor toward the baths, he thought for a moment that he was facing a wall mirror; then he realized that it wasn't his reflection he was approaching but a man who looked like him and who was advancing in his direction. Cordes swiftly averted his gaze, since one of his prime rules for successful shadowing has always been "Never let them make your eyes." With Cordes right behind him, the man left the hotel, took an I.R.T. train up Broadway to 110th Street, and walked to an apartment house on 108th Street near Amsterdam Avenue. It was Abie all right, and Kiddie was living there with him. At the apartment house, Abie went under the delightful alias of Mr. Pelt.

The detectives' aim was to seize Abie and Kiddie in the commission of a theft—"to catch them with the meat in their mouth," as Cordes phrases it. He took an apartment in a building across the street from the one Abie and Kiddie lived in, installed some rented furniture, and put a tap on the suspects' telephone. But Abie and Kiddie had depressingly few phone conversations, and what little they said in the course of them was terse and guarded; it was clear to Cordes that they were afraid their wire was tapped. In March, however, Cordes and his squad became greatly encouraged, for Abie and Kiddie began touring the city almost every day, studying fur lofts; the detectives, of course, were simultaneously studying Abie and Kiddie. "We had to be very careful," Cordes says. "It would sperl it if they seen somebody was sitting on them." (Though Cordes was born on Hudson Street and has lived most of his life in Harlem and the Bronx, several of his diphthongs have a touch of Brooklynese.) In April, the detectives felt sure they were about to strike pay dirt when Abie and Kiddie, without relinquishing their uptown apartment, took another, in a tenement on Twenty-eighth Street, between Sixth and Seventh Avenues, on the edge of the fur district. The two men had a telephone installed there. Cordes rented and furnished an apartment in the tenement, put a sweet-faced elderly Italian woman he knew in charge of it, and ordered the new telephone's wire tapped. With two ménages and the daily comings and goings of Abie and Kiddie to watch over, Cordes needed more help, and he was given a young detective who will here be known simply as George. Cordes planted George at the Twenty-eighth Street post.

Then, for the next five months, nothing happened, as far as Cordes could learn, except that Abie and Kiddie dined in good restaurants and went to the theatre or the movies almost every night. They would sleep at 108th Street and loaf around the Twenty-eighth Street tenement in the afternoons. They discouraged their watchers by ceasing their study of fur lofts and making what phone calls they made from pay stations. Cordes' men grew bored and disgruntled. He tried to whip up their enthusiasm by reminding them of the twenty-five-thousand-dollar reward. (Cordes was a first-grade detective at this time, and made $4,000 a year; the others were second-grade, and made $3,500.) One day during the doldrums, an associate approached Cordes at Headquarters and said, "Say, Johnny, about that kid you got working on Twenty-eighth Street—that George. He's no good, and it's my hunch he's giving you the foot." He meant that George had tipped Abie and Kiddie off to the fact that they were being tailed, but Cordes refused to believe it. Then, in September, Abie and Kiddie suddenly disappeared. The detectives had lost them completely, and Cordes began to think that perhaps George had given him the foot after all. He replaced George at the Twenty-eighth Street tenement, telling him, "You better come and work with me for a while. Maybe it'll change our luck." Thenceforth, Cordes kept an eye on George during working hours, and when George went off duty he was tailed by a member of the Headquarters undercover squad.

Presently, Cordes discovered that Abie and Kiddie had been living at the Second Avenue Baths. In late September, they started using their two apartments again. "Then, in October, they got real busy looking over lofts in the mornings," says Cordes, who has a memory that is more detailed than many another man's diary. "They got particular interested in a five-story loft building at 53 East Broadway. We covered the roofs around it fifteen days and nights straight. We put in dogs' hours—eighteen, twenty a stretch. It was cold that October; the cold bothers you when you have nothing to do. Then, one Friday afternoon about four, we seen the two of them go into the building with a large package, and pretty soon they come out without it. It was burglars' tools that they'd stashed somewhere in the building, we felt sure. Abie went to a Hundred and Eighth Street and Kiddie to Twenty-eighth and spent the rest of Friday. Next morning about eleven, the two of them went into the East Broadway building and didn't come out. We found out later they hid in one of the terlets till the building closed for Saturday afternoon. I sent Morrissey, the best man I had, and Barrett to cover the downstairs front. There was a fur firm on every floor, and they was all protected by heavy locked doors. Walsh and young George and I went up to the roof of an open building next door and crossed over to the roof of the building Abie and Kiddie was in. From up there, we could cover both the roof and the back of the building. About two, three o'clock in the afternoon, we heard prying and ripping and tearing at a door on the third floor, so we figured it must be Abie and Kiddie. We wanted them to get the meat in their mouth good, but I went down and told Morrissey if we hadn't made a score by four o'clock, why, to go to the firehouse next door and borrow an axe and we'd chop the door down. Then I went back up to the roof to wait.

"The trapdoor that opened onto the roof was about in the middle of it. We were standing at the edge of the roof looking down at the back of the building when along towards four we heard a crash and a shot. Then up through the trapdoor comes Abie, with a big sack over his shoulder and a gun in his hand. He drew a bead on me, and I yelled to Walsh, 'Shoot the son of a bitch! Whataya waitin' for?' Walsh fired and hit Abie in the right shoulder. Just then there was another shot, and Kiddie comes flying through the trap with *two* sacks on his shoulder. Morrissey had broke in and gone upstairs just as Abie and Kiddie were getting ready to leave. He'd shot at Abie from the stairway and missed, but he fired at Kiddie from the bottom of the ladder and hit him in the right heel, blowing the heel clear off his shoe. The three sacks had sixty thousand dollars' worth of minks, sables, and ermines in them. Pretty soon, the Police Commissioner showed up, and Inspector Carey of Homicide, because he'd heard there'd been a killing, only there hadn't, and a whole lot of other people, including Murray Dobson that later got to be Governor Lehman's bodyguard. McLaughlin was so pleased about the collar that he made all my boys first-grade detectives then and there on the roof, and even made a first-grader out of Dobson, he felt so good. Abie and Kiddie both got long terms. They were in those fur jobs all alone, and it was the bunk about any detectives being involved. That about young George giving us the foot was also strictly a bum steer. The man that give it to me turned out to be an enemy of his."

An acquaintance to whom Cordes described this case not long ago asked how he and the four other detectives had split up the twenty-five-thousand-dollar reward. Cordes gave the hollowest laugh in the annals of humor and said, "They finally compromised and paid us three thousand dollars, but by that time twelve or thirteen other guys had put themselves in on the pinch, so the five of us ended up with hash-brown potatoes. And every night for about nine months there, we was buying houses!"

Six months after breaking the fur case, Cordes became embroiled in a case of more far-reaching implications. On Sunday, May 1, 1927, around four o'clock in the afternoon, he entered a phone booth in a United Cigar store on the northeast corner of Eighth Avenue and Forty-second Street to call Inspector John Coughlin, head of the Detective Bureau, and ask him if there were any urgent police problems that required his attention. At the time, Cordes was working out of Head-quarters with Detectives Morrissey, Walsh, and Barrett. The Cordes unit had their pick of assignments, and cruised widely about the five boroughs in search of evildoers. It had been a dull day. While his three colleagues waited outside on the pavement, Cordes took the receiver off the hook and dropped a nickel in the slot. But he didn't call Spring 3100, because just as he was about to do so he heard a man's rough voice in an adjoining booth say, "We got your brother and we got the other guy. To prove we got your brother, I'm gonna tear his Elks card in half and mail a half of it to you right away. If you want your brother back alive, give four hundred and seventy thousand bucks to whoever turns up with the other half of the Elks card. Otherwise, we'll give you his head."

Cordes gently put the receiver back on the hook, collected his nickel, left the booth, snatched a stogie out of a can on the cigar counter, and, choking slightly, since he is a nonsmoker, proceeded to light it while he moseyed into position to sneak a look at the owner of the rough voice. The man was large and swarthy, wore glasses, and had a thick, brushy black mustache. Cordes recognized him as Joe Marcus, alias Little Joe, alias Mike White, alias Jack Thompson, who had once been a member of the local Kid Dropper mob but had not been seen around New York for four or five years. He was wanted for the murder of a police constable in Montreal, and a ten-thousand-dollar reward had been offered for his arrest and conviction for robbing a Superior,

Wisconsin, post office of seventy-one thousand dollars' worth of cash and stamps.

Cordes threw the stogie away and hurried out of the store to rejoin the three other detectives. He swiftly described Marcus to them, told them of the telephone call, and ordered Walsh and Barrett to shadow the man until he posted a letter in a mailbox. "Soon as he does that, forget about him, but drop a piece of newspaper in the box right after he drops in the letter," Cordes told them. "Then we'll get the Post Office to open the box and let us take a look at the name and address on the envelope with the Elks card in it." In a few minutes, Marcus came out of the store and obligingly dropped a letter in a mailbox across the street. With Cordes and Morrissey tailing him, he strolled eastward on Forty-second Street until he reached a penny arcade near Seventh Avenue. He entered it, and Cordes and Morrissey followed him in and took up positions at penny-in-the-slot peepshow machines. The spectacle Cordes selected to peep at was "A Night in a Moorish Harem," but he saw little of it, because Marcus was breaking forty-nine clay pipes in succession at the arcade's shooting gallery. "Don't he never miss?" Morrissey muttered with noticeable gloom.

"I can see we're gonna have fun with this guy," Cordes replied thoughtfully.

Marcus paid for his shooting and then, with the two detectives still behind him, took the B.-M.T. at Times Square to the Church Avenue station in Brooklyn, from which he walked to a large apartment house at 30 Westminster Road. Before he entered the building, Cordes and Morrissey saw him stop and talk with a man who had just come out. By means of the colossal catalogue of man-wanted circulars that Cordes has always kept in his brain, he identified the newcomer as Bill Morton—"a good stickup and kidnapper outa Cleveland," says Cordes. Marcus and Morton went into the building together. "I doubt if they got any kidnapped Elks in that house," Cordes said to Morrissey. "We better take a plant." He and Morrissey went down the block and began watching the apartment house from the doorway of a stationery store that had a phone booth.

Cordes left Morrissey in charge of the plant while he telephoned the main desk at Headquarters, from which he learned that the envelope Marcus had posted was addressed to Nate Scharlin; Headquarters had got in touch with Scharlin and found that the Elks card belonged to his forty-year-old brother, Abe, who had been missing for three days. Abe Scharlin, who owned a distillery in Greendale, Kentucky, lived, with his wife and Nate, on West Seventy-second Street, and was regarded by the police as a quiet and peaceful, but big, bootlegger. A few years previously, he had been in trouble in California for narcotics peddling, and he had once owned a chain of stores there that dealt exclusively with Chinese customers. Also missing, Headquarters had learned from Nate Scharlin, was the secretary of the distillery, James (Jeff) Taylor, who was "the other guy" Marcus had referred to in the phone booth. It came to light later that the Marcus mob had snatched Taylor on the evening of April 28th as he was leaving his home in the Buckingham Court Apartments, on Bergen Street, Brooklyn, and had forced him at gun point to call Abe Scharlin and arrange to meet him in front of the Charles M. Schwab mansion, at Riverside Drive and Seventy-fourth Street; obeying instructions, Taylor told Scharlin it was a matter of urgent importance that he couldn't go into over the phone. Scharlin turned up outside Schwab's and was forthwith snatched. Neither man's family had reported his disappearance to the police. Although the kidnapping of bootleggers had been fairly common in the Chicago area, this one was the first the New York cops had ever had to deal with.

Around seven-thirty that evening, Walsh and Barrett went over to Brooklyn and joined Cordes and Morrissey on the plant. Walsh said his wife was sick, so Cordes excused him; Barrett and Morrissey stayed on. At about eight o'clock, somebody came out of the apartment building who instantly aroused the detectives' interest. The *Times* subsequently described him as "a huge man of very rough appearance." He was. His name was Dave Berman, and he was a Chicago thug who, at the age of twenty-four, was wanted for bank and post-office robberies involving a total of almost a million dollars. One robbery, of the Northwestern National Bank in Milwaukee, had yielded $296,000;

another, at La Porte, Indiana, $180,000. Cordes had never seen Berman before, and his mental man-wanted catalogue contained nothing on him, but he instantly got the feeling that the man was no good and figured that he was involved in the kidnapping.

"O.K., Barrett," Cordes said, nodding toward Berman. "There's your man. Give him a walk and see where he goes." Barrett took off after Berman; Cordes and Morrissey stayed on the plant.

At about ten o'clock, Barrett returned. "What became of your man?" Cordes asked him.

"Oh, I tailed him to three stores, and he's only buying shirts and stuff ike that," Barrett said. "Ought to be back any minute now."

All but speechless with anger at this display of negligence, Cordes told Barrett to go home, and settled down with Morrissey to shadow the apartment house all night. Barrett was wrong; Berman did not return. Had Barrett stuck with Berman, the case could probably have been broken that evening, for it later developed that after leaving the third haberdashery shop Berman went to the hideout where Scharlin and Taylor were being held.

At about nine o'clock the next morning, Marcus came out of the apartment house. "You stay here. I'll take him," Cordes told Morrissey, and he tailed Marcus to the Church Avenue station of the B.-M.T. and followed him onto a train. Marcus got off at Canal Street. He made four brief phone calls, and then a longer one, from different cigar stores in that part of town. Cordes, fearful of alarming his quarry, didn't dare stand close enough to any of the booths to hear what Marcus said, but he thought he had a pretty good idea of what was going on. He figured that Marcus's first four calls were to the relatives of one or the other of the kidnapped men—probably Scharlin's relatives, since they were wealthier than Taylor's—giving instructions about the payment of the ransom, and that Marcus had kept them brief because he didn't want to allow the police, who might be assumed to be tapping the Scharlin wire, time to trace the calls. Cordes thought that the longer call was probably a progress report to confederates who were holding the kidnapped men. After making his phone calls, Marcus went over to Broadway, and spent the rest of the morning and most of the afternoon standing in front of Lindy's restaurant, chatting and laughing with various acquaintances who stopped to talk to him. At about five-thirty, he took the B.-M.T. back to Brooklyn and returned to the Westminster Road apartment house. Cordes and Morrissey watched it all night—their second night without sleep.

Shortly after nine o'clock the next morning, a Tuesday, Marcus came out of the apartment building and, as if in the grip of a compulsion neurosis, precisely repeated his routine of the day before. He took the same subway, made the same number of hit-and-run telephone calls from the same booths, garnished Lindy's sidewalk again until five-thirty, and returned to Westminster Road again for the night. On Wednesday it was the same thing all over again. Morton, the good stickup and kidnapper out of Cleveland, had not emerged from the building since entering it with Marcus on Sunday.

There had been only two new developments of any consequence in the case, and both of them were financial. Mrs. Abe Scharlin, whom the police had instructed to answer all phone calls to her house, had proved herself a wizard at renegotiating, for during her three days of spasmodic chats with Marcus she had prevailed upon him to reduce the amount of the ransom from four hundred and seventy thousand dollars to twenty thousand dollars for the two men. The other development was that Nate Scharlin had looked up Cordes while he was on the plant in Brooklyn, and had offered him and his detail twenty-five thousand dollars for Abe's safe return. Cordes had had enough experience in such matters to realize that the donkey never catches the carrot. There were so many others—superiors holding down desk jobs at Headquarters, and last-minute coattail catchers—who were sure to put themselves in on a pinch that the fellows who had actually done the work always ended up, as they had in the fur-robbery case, with hash-brown potatoes. Besides, he needed no monetary inspiration to keep him interested in this assignment. The kidnapping case was a big one, and he loved to work on the big ones. Nowadays, veteran members of the Detective Bureau, who were starting at their jobs when

Cordes was at the height of his powers, still shake their heads at the tenacity and endurance he displayed on this occasion. "There was never anybody like that guy for going without sleep," a captain of detectives said not long ago. "Three, four, five days I've seen him work non-stop without hardly shutting an eye. And all the time he'd be hopped up like a kid playing cops-and-robbers."

After four straight around-the-clock days of tailing and planting Marcus, Cordes was beginning to feel a homicidal impulse every time he looked at the fellow, with his big black mustache and his spectacles. Toward noon on Thursday, the fifth day, he saw a large, dark, clean-shaven man, who was not wearing glasses, come out of the building on Westminster Road. Cordes studied him intently, and then said to Morrissey, "There's our man. That's Marcus for sure. That shave job he's done on his upper lip and ditching the glasses don't fool me. But him taking off that muff looks like things are warming up. I'll give him a walk. See you later."

It was indeed Marcus, and, as usual, he took the B.-M.T. to Canal Street and went into a cigar store to phone. This time, Cordes risked arousing Marcus's suspicions by strolling in and leaning against the booth. "This is the last day," he heard Marcus say. "If you don't have the money up by six o'clock, they won't get another chance." There were, as usual, more calls from other booths, but Cordes did not need to eavesdrop. He had heard enough: Scharlin and Taylor were to be murdered if the ransom wasn't paid by six o'clock. Now, of all times, he must not lose Marcus or make him suspicious. Marcus did not go near Lindy's that afternoon; instead, he took the "L" to Sixty-sixth Street and Columbus Avenue. From there, after doubling back on his tracks several times and glancing cautiously about, obviously to assure himself that he was not being followed, he went over to Central Park West and stood in the Sixty-second Street entrance to the Park. It was two o'clock when he arrived there. At two-twenty, Cordes, watching from across the street, heard what he describes as a "shriek whistle"—the kind boys make by putting two fingers in the mouth and blowing vigorously. Marcus peered in the direction it came from, and down Central Park West ambled Berman, last seen on his Sunday-evening shopping spree.

Marcus and Berman exchanged a few words and then went into the Park, sat down on the grass, and proceeded to converse earnestly in low tones. Cordes crouched behind a nearby bush. He had not shaved or changed his clothes for five days, and he looked like a mission stiff who had wandered uptown from the Bowery. He could see from the way Marcus and Berman handled themselves that they had guns stuffed in their belts. They talked for about forty minutes, after which they got up and started walking south. As Cordes was rounding his bush to follow them, he tripped on a root and fell; getting up, he was assailed by a great ache of weariness. He looked at his watch; it was three o'clock. "This is the last day," Marcus had said. "If you don't have the money up by six o'clock, they won't get another chance." It looked to Cordes as if Marcus and Berman were about to separate. If they did separate, which one of them should he stick with? The one who would lead him to where the kidnapped men were. Sure, but which one was that? Cordes fought his weariness and tried to figure the percentages.

Instead of separating, however, Marcus and Berman stopped and stood looking off to their left, apparently attracted by the music from the carrousel. Indeed, they started walking in its direction, and Cordes, as he stumbled wearily after them, thought, Oh, for God's sake, are these two big lugs going for a ride on the merry-go-round? But it turned out to be a ball game on a diamond near the carrousel that had caught their interest, and they sat down on the grass behind first base and began to watch it. Cordes took a seat on a bench on the side of a hillock to the north of the diamond, picked up a newspaper at his feet, and pretended to read it. The type smeared before his bleary eyes, but he did make out that the paper was the Bronx *Home News*.

After watching the game for nearly an hour, Marcus and Berman got up from the grass and started walking east. Cordes was about to rise and follow when suddenly they turned, skirted the diamond's outfield, and came up the hillock. He lost no time in raising the Bronx *Home News* in front of his face. When they reached the path his bench was on, they turned in his direction and began walking toward him. Out of the corner of his eye, Cordes could see them fifty or sixty yards to his left. They walked slowly, not talking. They've spotted me for a cop, he thought. When they were about a dozen yards away, Cordes saw Marcus, who was walking on the inside, take a gun out of his belt and put it in his right coat pocket, as casually as a man would shift a handkerchief. Under the bottom edge of the Bronx *Home News*, Cordes could see the four big feet coming nearer and nearer. His body grew taut and his fingers dug into the margins of the newspaper. The feet were right in front of him now.

"Think I'll make another phone call," Marcus said.

"O.K.," Berman replied.

The feet kept on moving, and Cordes watched them beneath the Bronx *Home News* until they had travelled far enough for him to lower it.

Marcus and Berman left the Park and went to the Mayflower Pharmacy, at Central Park West and Sixty-second Street, where Marcus made his phone call while Berman waited outside. Then the two walked slowly up Central Park West. Cordes again had the feeling that they were about to separate. Time was running out on him, and he determined to try and seize Marcus and Berman at once. He did not know whether or not the ransom had been paid, but it was now almost four o'clock, and he felt certain that Marcus had just phoned instructions to his henchmen about what to do with Scharlin and Taylor. Nearby, Cordes saw a motorcycle cop stop his machine and dismount. Cordes hurried to him, identified himself, and asked for help. The cop was a youngster named Richard O'Connor. Marcus and Berman had now reached Sixty-sixth Street, and were standing on the southwest corner talking. "Those two guys over there are wanted for murder and robbery," Cordes told O'Connor. "Don't be afraid to shoot, because they're both heeled."

Cordes then sauntered west on the north side of Sixty-sixth Street, sneaking backward glances over his shoulder at Marcus and Berman, who were still talking on the corner. O'Connor remained with his machine on Central Park West, pretending to be absorbed in its engine. When Cordes had gone about a third of the way up the block, he crossed to the south side of the street and walked slowly eastward until he came to 10 West Sixty-sixth, where the high stoop of an apartment house projected several feet beyond a railing protecting the entrance to the building's basement. Cordes took his stand behind the west side of the stoop. Peering around it, he saw Marcus and Berman coming toward him; Marcus was on the inside, and both were still talking. Well behind them came O'Connor.

Just before Marcus and Berman reached the east side of the stoop, Cordes sprang out at them, drove them against the railing, and shouted, "Get 'em up, you bastards!" Marcus and Berman drew instantly, but Cordes was too quick for them. With his left hand he seized Berman's right wrist; with his right hand he grabbed Marcus's gun by the cylinder. "Hurry up and shoot!" he bawled at O'Connor, who was by then about five yards behind. At that moment, Marcus jerked his gun up and fired, but the bullet flew over Cordes' right shoulder. Marcus twisted to his left to fire again. O'Connor fired first, hitting him in the chest. Cordes wrested Berman's gun away and, with its butt, struck him over the left eye, knocking him down; as Berman fell, his eyeball was hanging out of its socket by the optic nerve. Then Cordes sent for an ambulance, but before it arrived O'Connor rushed Marcus to Roosevelt Hospital in a cab; Marcus died shortly after he was admitted. After Berman's eye had been dressed, Cordes took him to the West Sixty-eighth Street station house. Berman insisted that he was Charles Gordon, of Philadelphia, but on the bulletin board of the station house was a man-wanted flier bearing his photograph, his fingerprint whorls, his criminal record, the offer of an eight-thousand-dollar reward for his arrest, and the name David Berman. "Davey, what was you doing here in town?" Cordes asked him. "I was buying merchandise," Berman said.

The killing of Marcus and the capture of Berman made the late editions of the afternoon papers. Because neither Scharlin's family nor Taylor's had reported the kidnapping to the Missing Persons Bureau, this was the first the press had heard of it. In Marcus's wallet was found the other half of Scharlin's Elks card and five checks for three thousand dollars each, made out by Taylor to a man named Charles Kraemer, who was a well-known figure in the New York underworld. Kraemer was picked up that night as he was standing in front of Lindy's; he had recently come to town from Illinois, where he had been released after serving seven years for burglary. Although he vehemently denied knowing Marcus or Berman, the police were satisfied that his role in the kidnapping had been that of front man during negotiations.

Shortly after Cordes delivered Berman to the station house, Inspector Coughlin arrived there, accompanied by a detective who had once been a partner of Cordes'. In deference to the feelings of this detective's descendants, he will be given a name that was not his real one—Joseph Dorley. Dorley was ten years older than Cordes— tall, bony, leathery-faced, and turkey-necked, with a head like an upended cobblestone collared by a fringe of gray hair. He and Cordes had worked together when Cordes was a young detective. They had cruised around nights, and almost every night Dorley would park in front of the Fairfield Hotel, on the upper West Side, and leave Cordes waiting while he went inside; he told Cordes that he was vis- iting a sick old aunt of whom he was very fond. The visits often lasted so long that on winter nights Cordes had started to turn blue by the time Dorley came out. "Very sick tonight," Dorley would murmur, shaking his head. "Poor old soul." It wasn't until some years later, when the two were no longer partners, that Cordes learned that the name of Dorley's sick old aunt was Arnold Rothstein.

Inspector Coughlin questioned Berman and Kraemer but could get no information from them about where Scharlin and Taylor were. After Cordes had washed and shaved, he and Dorley and Walsh went over to Brooklyn to the Buckingham Court Apartments and talked with Taylor's wife until shortly after midnight. Cordes told her he was sure they would get her husband back for her. "It's Friday now," he said. "Friday's always my lucky day." The detectives left the Taylor apartment and rang for the elevator, which was of the self-operated type. When the door opened, out stepped Scharlin and Taylor.

Back in the Taylor apartment, the kidnapped men told the detectives that a short while before, with pillowcases over their heads, they had been driven in a closed car to Greenwood Cemetery and released. After reading in the papers about what had happened to Marcus and Berman, the remaining kidnappers had evidently decided that Scharlin and Taylor were too hot to hold any longer. When Scharlin and Taylor were kidnapped, on the night of April 28th, the kidnappers, who showed up in a car, had not immediately blindfolded them but had made them sit on the floor in back during a long ride to the hideout. Once they got there, pillowcases had been put over their heads and they had been forced to wear them during the eight days of their captivity. They had been cuffed a couple of times by one of the kidnappers, probably Berman, but on the whole had not been badly treated. The kidnappers had provided Scharlin, who was a diabetic, with the special foods his diet required. At one point, a loaded pistol had been shown to Taylor under his pillowcase; with its muzzle nudging his right kidney, he had complied with an order to make out five checks to Kraemer. Before the two men were hooded, they had seen that the hideout was a dingy two-story frame house and that a large window on one side had red and blue diamond-shaped panes. Every day, they had heard chickens clucking and crowing outside. Taylor, a native of Brooklyn, said he was pretty sure the house was somewhere in south Brooklyn. Cordes took Scharlin and Taylor to Headquarters, where, after examining many rogues'-gallery portraits, they identified Marcus, Berman, and Morton as their kidnappers, along with three other men, whom the police hadn't suspected—the Dougherty brothers, Charles and Sam, from Philadelphia, and a St. Louis hoodlum named Chickie Clark.

Taylor's hunch that the hideout was in south Brooklyn proved correct; about five o'clock that Friday morning, he cruised around the Hamilton Park region with Cordes, Dorley, and Walsh, and finally picked out a house at 1146 Fifty-seventh Street. Nobody answered when the detectives knocked, so Cordes entered by a cellar window, went up to the first floor, and let the others in. It was the house, all right. The kidnappers had been in such a hurry to leave that they hadn't taken the time to pack their belongings, which consisted of four hand grenades, four tear-gas bombs, a Thompson sub-machine gun, and a large assortment of sawed-off shotguns and automatics. They also left behind an interesting list of prospective victims. Presumably, if the Scharlin-Taylor job had been a success, the mob would have expanded its New York activities in a big way, for on the list were the names of Arnold Rothstein, the actors Al Jolson and Harry Richman, Big Frenchy De Mange, who was the bootlegging colleague of Owney Madden and Bill Duffy, and Maxie Greenberg, who was a partner of Waxey Gordon's. (Greenberg was later murdered in Elizabeth; Gordon died recently in Alcatraz, where he was serving a twenty-five-year sentence under the Baumes Law.)

All the evils that accompanied prohibition flourished in New York during the fourteen years it was in effect—all, that is, except kidnapping. There was a snatch here from time to time (Big Frenchy was kidnapped by the Vincent Coll mob in 1931, and in the Madden-Duffy saloons the cash-register tills were scraped to get up the ransom money), but the art and science of kidnapping never became a vogue here, as it did in the Chicago area. It seems likely that by breaking up the Scharlin-Taylor snatch Cordes squelched in its earliest stages a concerted drive by kidnappers from all over the country to move in on New York. Arnold Rothstein indicated that he thought so, anyhow. Cordes ran into him in the Great Drug Store, on Seventh Avenue between Forty-eighth and Forty-ninth, one night not long after the case was cleaned up, and Rothstein wrung his hand and poured forth his gratitude. "You rendered a great public service, Johnny, and I want to show you how much I appreciate it," Rothstein said. "I want to take over the mortgage you got on your little house uptown." Cordes grinned at him and said, "And let you have a rope around my neck the rest of my life? No, thanks, A.R., I'll take care of the mortgage myself."

Cordes received another offer, too. Scharlin and Taylor had a sudden change of mind, or change of something, and decided that they couldn't identify any of their kidnappers, but Berman still faced trial for felonious assault on Cordes. One evening shortly before the case was brought to court, Cordes' home telephone—its number was unlisted—rang, and a harsh voice offered him "a hundred Gs if you forget all about any assault." "Look, friend," Cordes said. "Anybody tries to kill me, they got to go and pay for it." And he hung up. Berman was tried, found guilty, and sentenced to fourteen years. Aged twenty-four at the time of his conviction, he was, in police parlance, "a full-grown man when he came out."

As for the rewards, word arrived from the Middle West that all the witnesses against Berman for his bank robberies had disappeared or been bumped off, so there went the eight thousand dollars on that score. The ten-thousand-dollar reward for Marcus had a string attached to it; he would have had to be convicted in order for his captors to collect it, and since he was dead, so was the ten thousand dollars. There was still, however, the reward of twenty-five thousand dollars that Nate Scharlin had promised for his brother's safe return. When, one day a week or so after the return had been accomplished, Cordes was summoned to the office of the Police Commissioner—a new man, Joseph A. Warren—he did not go there with dragging feet. Warren was a shy, gentle, pious Irishman, the type that turns up in Tammany Hall now and again, though not so frequently as to become monotonous. "Johnny," Warren said, "a nice present for you came in here this morning."

"Yes, Mr. Commissioner?" Cordes said, barely able to refrain from rubbing his palms together.

"But it would have besmirched your good character, Johnny, so I sent it back."

"But, Mr. Commissioner!" Cordes said. "I give my blood!"

"I know you did, Johnny," Warren replied. "But bootlegger money's not for a man of your character to be besmirched with."

That August, Cordes and Dorley were sent to Saratoga to keep an eye on the race track there. Stationing a couple of detectives in Saratoga during racing season was an old procedure of the New York Police Department. One evening, Cordes ran into Taylor in the Grand Union

Hotel. They exchanged a few amenities, and then Taylor said, "You got that money, didn't you?"

"No, I didn't," Cordes said. "The Commissioner sent it back. Thought it would besmirch my good character."

"Sure, I know that," said Taylor, "but later on your partner picked it up."

"My partner!" Cordes shouted. "Listen, just don't move from right here for a minute till I get back."

At the United States Hotel, Cordes found Dorley eating dinner, with his napkin tucked in his collar. "Guy at the Grand Union's gotta see you right away," Cordes said.

Dorley wanted to know who the guy was.

"Never mind, he's gotta see you right away," Cordes told him, and almost dragged him to the Grand Union and into Taylor's presence.

"Joe, you know Mr. Taylor, don't you?" Cordes said to Dorley.

Dorley put his right forefinger to his lip and studied Taylor carefully. "No," he said. "I don't believe I do."

"No?" said Cordes. "You don't remember him coming to his apartment from the kidnap last May, or driving around south Brooklyn that morning when he found the hideout for us?"

"Oh, yes," Dorley said. "I remember Mr. Taylor now."

"Well, do you remember collecting some money from him to give to me and then not giving it to me?"

"Why, Johnny, I wouldn't do a thing like that to you," Dorley said. Taylor laughed.

"You wouldn't, but you did, you dirty, despicable son of a bitch," Cordes said, and belted Dorley in the jaw. That was the closest Cordes ever came to collecting his share of Nate Scharlin's reward.

A year later, Cordes was awarded the Department's Medal of Honor, his second, for his work on the kidnapping. On a photograph of Cordes being decorated by Mayor James J. Walker, Commissioner Warren wrote, "Your record to date is the best ever known in the Police Department. Keep up the good work. Congratulations and appreciation."

PROVOST GUARD ATTACKING THE RIOTERS

from The Gangs of New York
by Herbert Asbury

Criminals took over large sections of New York City for several days during the draft riots of July 1863. Protests against a new conscription law quickly led to mayhem, with a mob of 50,000 to 70,000 people looting and burning buildings. Thousands of people were killed. A police force of some 2,300 men opposed the mob. Herbert Asbury (1891–1963) described the riots in his classic book about the city's gang culture.

The second day of rioting, Tuesday, July 14, 1863, began with two murders. After a night of drinking and carousing in the dives and dance halls of the Bowery and Five Points, more than a thousand frenzied men and women surged into Clarkson street before dawn and hanged William Jones, a Negro, to a tree when he attempted to defend his wife and children and prevent the burning of his home. A fire was lighted beneath him, and the mob danced madly about, shrieking and throwing stones and bricks at his body while it dangled above the flames. Another Negro, named Williams, was attacked at Washington and LeRoy streets. While half a score of rioters held him down, their leader smashed his skull with a huge stone weighing more than twenty pounds, which he dropped time after time on the Negro's head. Women who accompanied the rioters slashed his body with knives and poured oil into the wounds, but before they could ignite it were dispersed by a detachment of police under Drill

Officer Copeland and Captain John F. Dickson. This force also defeated the mob in Clarkson street and cut down Jones's body.

It was soon apparent that New York faced a day of even fiercer fighting than on Monday, and that all of the resources of the police and military would be required to save the metropolis from fire and pillage. By six o'clock mobs had begun to assemble throughout the city, sweeping tumultuously through the streets, pursuing and beating Negroes, and looting and setting fire to houses. One of the first crowds to gather appeared suddenly in East Eighty-sixth street and attacked the Twenty-third precinct police station, which was garrisoned only by Doorman Ebling, the patrolmen having been marched downtown to Headquarters soon after midnight. The station house was burned. Another mob made a demonstration before Mayor Opdyke's home, smashing windows and doors with bricks and paving stones before it was driven away by the police and soldiers. A second great mass of shouting men and women surged across Printing House Square to attack the *Times* and *Tribune* buildings, but fled in disorder northward through Park Row and Center street when they saw the Gatling guns and the howitzer which had been moved into position during the night. A third gang burned the home of Colonel Robert Nugent, Assistant Provost Marshal General, in West Eighty-sixth street.

Great throngs of men gathered before daybreak in Ninth and First avenues, and worked furiously, erecting barricades which were to give the police and troops much trouble later in the day. Telegraph poles and lamp-posts were hacked down and laid across the street, and between them the rioters piled carts, barrels, boxes and heavy pieces of furniture stolen from residences and stores in the vicinity. In First avenue the fortifications extended from Eleventh to Fourteenth streets, and in Ninth avenue from Thirty-second to Forty-third streets, with smaller barricades across the intersecting thoroughfares. Throughout the day, when hard pressed by the policemen and soldiers, the rioters sought refuge in these districts, and they were not dispersed and the barricades destroyed until the troops had driven the mob back with heavy volleys of musketry fire.

Inspector Daniel Carpenter mustered a force of two hundred policemen at Headquarters at six o'clock Tuesday morning, and marched them uptown to suppress rioters who had appeared in Second avenue and threatened the plant of the Union Steam Works at Twenty-second street, from which the police had been unable to remove the stores of munitions. The detachment marched into Second avenue a block below the Works, and found a mob which packed the thoroughfare north to Thirty-third street. Hundreds of the rioters possessed muskets, swords and pistols, and boldly confronted the police, while others had invaded the houses on either side of Second avenue between Thirty-second and Thirty-third streets, and lay in wait on the roofs with piles of bricks and stones beside them. As he had done in the Broadway and Amity street battle on Monday, Inspector Carpenter deployed his men as skirmishers, and two lines of policemen marched slowly northward, meeting with little resistance except for a few scattering volleys which passed harmlessly over their heads, or clipped the pavement before them. But at Thirty-second street the rioters on the house-tops suddenly hurled a shower of bricks and stones into the ranks of the police, and many of the patrolmen went down under the shock of the heavy missiles. At the same instant the mob, which had slowly closed in behind the advancing force, attacked front and rear, but Carpenter and his men fought with such fury and discipline that within fifteen minutes they had cleared the street, and the rioters huddled in small and sullen groups a hundred feet from the menacing clubs. With the mob thus frightened, fifty patrolmen dashed into the houses and up the stairs to the roofs, where they fell upon the gangsters. The rioters would not stand up before the slashing nightsticks, and many leaped into the street and were killed. Others were clubbed down, and those who escaped into the street were felled by Carpenter and his men. About fifty rioters had taken possession of a saloon at Second avenue and Thirty-first street, and were firing muskets and pistols through the windows, but were driven out without loss to the police, although many patrolmen had narrow escapes. One of the gangsters fired a bullet through a policeman's cap, but the latter seized him about the middle and flung him through a window, dashing out his brains against the pavement.

Word of the fierce battle reached the Seventh avenue Arsenal, and Major-General Sandford dispatched Colonel H. J. O'Brien, of the Eleventh New York Volunteers, with one hundred and fifty infantrymen of various units, to the aid of the police. The troops were accompanied by two six-pound cannon and twenty-five artillerymen, under command of Lieutenant Eagleson. When he saw the troops marching up Second avenue Inspector Carpenter immediately launched another assault against the mob, but the rage of the rioters had increased and they stood their ground, pelting the soldiers and the police with bricks and stones and keeping up a steady fire from their muskets and pistols. Colonel O'Brien wheeled the troops into company front and the infantrymen fired several volleys, but still the rioters pressed forward with great fury. Lieutenant Eagleson was then ordered to fire his guns, and the six-pounders belched a hail of grape and canister into the close packed ranks of the mob, causing frightful havoc. Six rounds were discharged before the rioters fall back, and then they broke and fled in all directions, leaving the sidewalks and pavement strewn with dead and wounded. One of the killed was a woman who carried a baby in her arms. She fell at the first volley, but the baby was underneath and was not injured, although the mother was fearfully trampled as the mob surged back and forth over her body.

With comparative quiet restored in Second avenue, Inspector Carpenter started on a tour of the eastern part of the city, and engaged several mobs which were surging through the streets. Colonel O'Brien marched his soldiers back to the Arsenal, but three hours later returned alone to the scene of the battle, for his home was in the vicinity and he was concerned for the safety of his family, as well as of his property. He reached his house without incident and finding that Mrs. O'Brien and her children had fled to Brooklyn before the fighting began and were with relatives, started to return to his command. But when he rode into Second avenue he was recognized, and several men attempted to pull him from his horse, while others threw bricks at him. He dismounted and entered a saloon at Nineteenth street and Second avenue. When he came out a great crowd of men and women had assembled, and were urging each other to kill him. With his sword in one hand and his revolver in the other, Colonel O'Brien walked deliberately across the street toward his horse. But he had not gone ten feet before the mob surged forward, and he was knocked down with a club. Before he could scramble to his feet the rioters were upon him. He was kicked and beaten, and then a rope was twisted about his ankles and he was dragged back and forth over the cobblestones. A Catholic priest interfered long enough to administer the last rites of the church, and then departed, leaving Colonel O'Brien to the tender mercies of the infuriated rioters. For more than three hours they tortured him, slashing his flesh with knives and daggers, dropping stones upon his head and body, and hauling him up and down the street with fierce howls of victory. He was then abandoned, and throughout the long, hot July afternoon lay unconscious on the pavement, none of his friends daring to rescue him or take him water. About sundown a great mob of men and women appeared and proceeded to inflict fresh torments upon his torn and battered body, finally dragging him into his own back yard. There a gang of Five Points harpies squatted about him, and after mutilating him with knives, flung stones at his head until he was dead.

The attention of the rioters had been distracted from the Union Steam Works by the ferocity of the attacks led by Inspector Carpenter and Colonel O'Brien, but when the police and soldiers had marched away the mob reappeared and captured the factory after a brief fight with the small guard of patrolmen. But instead of removing the carbines and distributing them, the rioters did not even break out the cases. They garrisoned the plant with some five hundred thugs, evidently with the intention of using it as a headquarters and a rallying point for the rioters operating along the East Side. Two hundred policemen under command of Inspector George W. Dilks marched into Second avenue when news of the capture of the Steam Works reached Headquarters, and the building was retaken foot by foot after terrific fighting. Many of the rioters were pursued to the roofs and killed, and the dead and dying littered the halls and rooms and the sidewalk in front of the structure. A physician of the neighborhood said afterward that within an hour he dressed twenty-one wounds in the head, all of which were fatal.

During the heavy fighting which preceded the invasion of the Union Steam Works by the police the mob was led by a one-armed giant who wielded a huge bludgeon, employing it as a flail with great effect, and by a young man in dirty overalls who fought valiantly with knife and club. The giant was shot and killed, and the young man was dealt such a terrific blow on the head that he fell heavily against an iron railing, and one of the pickets penetrated his throat beneath the chin. A policeman lifted the body from the paling, and the young man was found to possess aristocratic features, well-cared-for hands, and a fair, white skin. Obviously he was a man unused to physical labor. "Although dressed as a laborer, in dirty overalls and filthy shirt," wrote a chronicler of the riots, "underneath these were fine cassemere pants, a handsome, rich vest, and a fine linen shirt." His identity was never learned, for when the police had gone his body, together with the other dead, was carried away by the rioters. It is believed to have been taken to the Five Points in a cart, and buried beneath one of the tenements at Paradise Square.

All of the carbines and ammunition which remained in the Union Steam Works were loaded into wagons and taken to Police Headquarters under heavy guard. Soon after the recapture of the factory a detachment of soldiers joined the policemen, and the combined forces made a tour of the district, dispersing several large mobs. In Twenty-first street the expedition was met by a galling fire from the windows and roofs, and the policemen fell back, while the troops advanced and silenced the sharpshooters with several well-aimed volleys. One rioter who was shooting from behind a corner of a house was killed when a soldier fired through the building. The Police under Inspector Dilks included, among other units, all of the reserves of the Eighteenth precinct, and while these men were fighting the mobs in First and

Second avenues another gang of rioters attacked the station house in East Twenty-second street. Sergeant Burden and three men comprised the garrison, and although they made a determined resistance and kept the mob at bay for half an hour, they were finally driven out and the building burned.

Meanwhile Captain George W. Walling, already noted as one of the fiercest fighters of the Police Department because of his forays against the Honeymoon gang and the thugs of the water front, was having a busy time with a detachment of patrolmen from the Twentieth precinct. Early in the morning they marched into Pitt street, where a mob had surrounded a small body of soldiers, but before they could arrive the troops had fired into the rioters and dispersed them. Captain Walling then marched his men through the Bowery and broke up several large mobs, and an hour later was ordered to the rescue of a company of soldiers who had been attacked in front of Allerton's Hotel, in Eleventh avenue between Fortieth and Forty-first streets, by a gang of rioters who had taken their guns away from them. After defeating this mob and recapturing many of the stolen muskets, Captain Walling marched across town to Fifth avenue and Forty-seventh street, where rioters had broken into and were looting the homes of Dr. Ward and other residents of the vicinity. The detachment finally arrived at the police station in West Thirty-fifth street after several hours of hard fighting, and joined a force which was being organized to attack the barricades in Ninth avenue.

So far as the police units were concerned, the formation of this body had been completed by three o'clock in the afternoon, but it was almost two hours later before regular army troops under command of Captain Wesson arrived to support them. Meanwhile the rioters had strengthened their defenses, and had burned the Weehawken Ferry house at West Forty-second street because a saloon keeper refused to surrender his stock of liquors. At six o'clock the combined military and police forces moved out of the station house and marched into Ninth avenue, where thousands of rioters, armed with muskets, pistols, bricks and paving stones, crouched behind the barricades. Captains

Slott and Walling led a large detachment of police as an advance guard, but met with such a heavy fire from the entrenched mob that they were compelled to retreat. The soldiers then advanced in line of skirmishers and routed the mob with several volleys of musketry, killing between twenty and thirty. The police rushed forward, and with their clubs and axes demolished the first line of barricades, while the troops massed in the rear and kept up a steady fire to prevent a counter attack. Similar methods were employed to capture the remaining fortifications, and within two hours the mob had fled, the defenses had been cleared away and the police were in control of Ninth avenue.

While this battle was in progress another great crowd had attacked the home of J. S. Gibbons, a cousin of Horace Greeley, at No. 19 Lamartine Place, near Eighth avenue and Twenty-ninth street. The rioters swarmed into the house, and were looting it when they were attacked from the rear by a police force drawn from the Broadway Squad and the reserves of the Thirty-first precinct, under command of Captain James Z. Bogart. There was fierce fighting for half an hour, and in the midst of the uproar a detachment of soldiers appeared and fired a wild volley which struck policeman and rioter alike. Patrolman Dipple was shot in the thigh, the bullet entering the bone and ranging upward through the marrow. He died soon afterward. Patrolmen Robinson and Hodgson were also seriously wounded. During the pillaging of the Gibbons residence the women caused the police more trouble than the men. Not only did they fight with greater ferocity, but they clung tenaciously to whatever bit of spoil they had been able to lay their hands upon. They were not driven from the house until the police took to spanking them with their clubs.

Throughout the whole of Tuesday the police experienced great difficulty in keeping their lines of communication open, for the leaders of the mob sent out patrols which cut every telegraph wire they could find; and repair crews, escorted by soldiers, were constantly being dispatched from Headquarters to mend breaks. The rioters also tore down the railroad telegraph lines along Eleventh avenue, and ripped up great sections of the Harlem and New Haven railroad tracks, evidently with the intention of hampering the movement of troop trains. The lines of the Police Telegraph system which remained in operation were congested with important messages, but nevertheless Commissioner Acton suspended all official business for a moment early Tuesday afternoon, and at 1:12 o'clock this telegram was sent to the police of the Fifth Precinct:

> SEND TO DR. PURPLE AT 183
> HUDSON STREET TO GO AS SOON AS
> POSSIBLE TO INSPECTOR LEONARD'S HOUSE. BABY VERY SICK.

A military escort was provided for the physician, and it is of record that the sick baby recovered.

By noon Tuesday the danger to the armories, arsenals, Navy Yard and other government and state property had been materially lessened. The Seventh Regiment Armory was garrisoned by four hundred men and two howitzers, and detachments almost as large were in the Central Park, Seventh avenue and Worth street arsenals. The sub-treasury in Wall street was guarded by a troop of regular infantry and a battery of field guns, under command of Colonel Bliss of the Volunteers. Rumors of an intended raid upon the Navy Yard in the East River were received at Headquarters, and the war vessels in the harbor and in the Hudson immediately steamed up the East River; and soon all the approaches to the Yard were under the guns of the receiving ship North Carolina, the corvette Savannah, and the gunboats Granite City, Gertrude, Unadilla and Tulip. The ironclad Passaic and the steam gunboat Fuchsia had taken up positions off the Battery to prevent an attempt by the rioters to gain a footing on Governor's Island. Warships also lay at the foot of Wall and other important streets, with their guns trained to sweep the thoroughfares with grape and canister at the first sight of rioting mobs.

About two o'clock in the afternoon the bridge over the Harlem River at Macomb's Dam was destroyed, together with the Washington Hotel and a large planing mill at Third avenue and 129th street. There was now fierce rioting throughout Manhattan, and from the Battery to the Harlem River detachments of soldiers and policemen were constantly in contact with the mobs, emerging victorious from a great majority of the clashes. By late Tuesday afternoon Special Volunteer Policemen, to the number of almost a thousand, had been equipped with badges, uniforms and clubs, and were doing garrison and guard duty, releasing policemen and soldiers for active work in the field. Little fighting against the mobs was done by the Specials because of their lack of discipline and experience, although good work was done by a few companies composed of men who had seen battle service against the Confederates. They were led against the rioters by the officers who had commanded them in the South.

A large body of rioters attempted to form a troop of cavalry with horses stolen from the stables of the Red Bird Line, but the horsemen could not manage their steeds and accomplished nothing. Another mob launched an attack against a Negro church in Thirtieth street between Seventh and Eighth avenues, and Captain Walling marched to the scene with a large force of patrolmen. The church was already in flames when the police arrived, and the rioters were fighting back the firemen who were endeavoring to put out the blaze. Walling and his men dispersed the mob, killing one man who sat astride the roof hacking at the timbers with an axe. Meanwhile other crowds were looting gun stores in Third avenue near Thirty-seventh street, and had set fire to the buildings after carrying out the arms and ammunition. Later the occupants of the block on Second avenue between Thirty-fourth and Thirty-fifth streets were notified that their homes would be burned that night, but within ten minutes the mob had applied the torch and hanged a Negro who fled from one of the tenements. Ten houses were burned.

There was practically no halt in the fighting on Tuesday night, bloody battles raging at various points throughout the city. For the fourth time a mob made an unsuccessful attack upon *The Tribune* building in Printing House Square; and between eight and nine o'clock Patrolman Bryan of the Fourth Precinct telegraphed to Headquarters that a huge crowd was threatening to burn Brooks Brothers clothing store in

Catherine street.* Fifty men were rushed to the building under command of Sergeants Finney and Matthews and Roundsman Farrell, but before they could arrive the attack had begun. Patrolmen Kennedy, Platt and Davis, who had been mingling with the rioters in disguise, checked the mob for a few moments, but they were soon overwhelmed and beaten, and the rioters then smashed the doors and streamed into the store. There they lighted the gas and broke out the windows, and when the police arrived the thugs were hurriedly attiring themselves in new suits and stuffing their pockets with neckties, shirts and other articles of apparel. Great bundles of clothing were also thrown from the windows.

The police quickly dispersed the mob in the street, and then charged inside, clubbing the rioters with their nightsticks and chasing them from floor to floor. Many tried to escape down a rope which led through a trapdoor into the basement, but the police waited for them at the bottom and knocked them senseless as fast as they appeared. During the struggle several policemen were shot and seriously wounded, and it was not until Inspector Carpenter appeared with his roving command that the store was cleared. Throughout the night a heavy guard was maintained, and the next day fifty patrolmen, with a military escort, searched the low rookeries of the vicinity and recovered about $10,000 worth of clothing and other property. In one shanty they found fifty new suits, and in another a huge gunnysack filled with neckties and socks.

Governor Seymour issued a proclamation late Tuesday afternoon declaring the city to be in a state of insurrection, and at midnight Mayor Opdyke received a telegram from Edwin M. Stanton, Secretary of War, that five regiments had been detached from the victorious Union Armies, and were being rushed to the metropolis. The message was not made public, but encouraged by the prospect of aid and by the success of the previous day's operations, Commissioner Acton

* Now at Madison avenue and Forty-fourth street

announced in Wednesday morning's newspapers that the backbone of the riot had been broken, and that the police were in control of the city. Nevertheless, there was heavy fighting during the next three days, and especially on Wednesday, when five Negroes were hanged and the soldiers again loosed their howitzers and field guns against the raging gangs of rioters. The five thousand liquor stores within the mob-infested areas remained open, but otherwise business had been almost entirely suspended, and the stores and factories sheltered their stocks of goods behind barred doors and shuttered windows. Except for occasional service on Sixth avenue, all of the street cars and omnibuses had ceased to operate, and the drays and carts which ordinarily rumbled through the city bearing loads of merchandise had been hidden to prevent the rioters using them to erect barricades. The roads of Westchester county and northward were crowded with men, women and children fleeing from a city that seemed doomed to destruction; and from Tuesday noon until the end of the rioting the railroad stations and the piers were crowded with great throngs that fought for places on trains and boats.

Wednesday, the 15th of July, was the hottest day of the year, and the stifling heat was made more intolerable by the columns of black smoke which curled upward from the ruins of more than three score houses which had been fired by the rioters. The fighting began before dawn, but the first conflict of importance occurred about nine o'clock, when a detachment of infantrymen of the Eighth Regiment of Volunteers, under command of General Dodge, supported by a troop of cavalry and a battery of howitzers under Colonel Mott of the Regular Army, marched out of Headquarters to disperse a mob which was reported to be hanging Negroes at Thirty-second street and Eighth avenue, within a block of the present Pennsylvania Hotel, and on the site of the Pennsylvania Railroad Station. When the column marched into Eighth avenue the soldiers found three Negroes hanging to lamp-posts, while a gang of ferocious women crowded about the dangling bodies, slashing them with knives as a mob of men estimated at more than five thousand yelled and cheered. The rioters fell back as the troops advanced, and Colonel Mott spurred his horse into their midst and cut down one of the Negroes with his sword, afterward running the weapon through a rioter who tried to drag him from his mount.

Colonel Mott had scarcely returned to his command when the mob surged forward and began the attack with a hail of bricks and stones and a brisk fire from muskets and pistols. Colonel Mott ordered Captain Howell to bring two howitzers into position in Seventh avenue to sweep Thirty-second street, and the guns were loaded with grape and canister. The infantry and cavalry then charged with bayonet and saber, driving the mob back to Eighth avenue. But the rioters came on again when the troops returned to protect the artillery, and Captain Howell shouted that he would fire the guns unless they dispersed. He was answered by jeers and shouts, and the mob rushed forward, the solid mass of humanity packing the street from curb to curb. Captain Howell ordered his gunners to fire, and scores of rioters fell dead or wounded as the shot ripped and tore through their close-packed ranks. But it was not until six rounds had been fired that they scattered and fled into Eighth avenue, and thence northward. The soldiers broke up into small detachments and cleared the side streets, and then cut down the bodies of the Negroes, after which they marched back to Headquarters in Mulberry street. Half an hour later the rioters returned, carried away their dead and wounded, and again strung up the Negroes. They dangled from the lamp-posts until late afternoon, when they were removed by a detachment of police under Captain Brower.

Artillery was again brought into action about an hour after the fighting in Eighth avenue, when the rioters attacked Jackson's Foundry in Twenty-eighth street between First and Second avenues. Driven away in disorder by half a dozen rounds of grape and canister, elements of the mob poured across the city and set fire to several houses at Twenty-seventh street and Seventh avenue, and when the troops had departed mobs again assembled on the East Side and burned half a dozen dwellings in Second avenue near Twenty-eighth street, although no further move was made against the foundry. During the early afternoon Colonel Nevers led a company of regular infantrymen who frustrated an attempt to destroy the iron clad Dunderberg, which was under construction in Webb's Shipyard. Another military detachment, comprising thirty-three men of Hawkins' Zouaves and a company of regular infantry, captured a house at Broadway and Thirty-third street in which the rioters had secreted several thousand muskets. This expedition was supported by a battery of rifled cannon which had arrived in the city about noon.

Several times on Wednesday afternoon large bodies of troops were routed by the mobs, and two howitzers were captured by the rioters after the artillerymen had been clubbed down. However, the guns were of no value to the mobs, for they had no ammunition. The most serious of the day's defeats occurred about six o'clock, when Colonel Cleveland Winslow marched against a great mob in First avenue between Eighteenth and Nineteenth streets, with a force of two hundred volunteers commanded by Major Robinson, about fifty soldiers of the Duryea Zouaves, and two howitzers commanded by Colonel E. E. Jardine of Hawkins' Zouaves. While the infantrymen were engaging the rioters, Colonel Jardine unlimbered his guns and trained them to sweep the avenue, but before he could fire the mob had scattered into the houses on either side of the street. Within a few minutes a heavy fire was being directed upon the troops from the roofs and windows. More than a score of soldiers were killed and wounded. The howitzers poured a rain of shot through the street with little effect, and the soldiers attempted unsuccessfully to pick off the sharpshooters, but the latter fired with such deadly accuracy that within half an hour half of the military force was dead or wounded. Among the latter was Colonel Jardine, who was shot in the thigh by a rioter who stepped into the middle of the street while the howitzers were being loaded, rested his musket on the shoulder of a comrade, and took deliberate aim. Realizing that his command would be overwhelmed if the rioters made an attack in force, Colonel Winslow ordered the troops to fall back until the police could arrive with clubs and clear the houses, and drive the thugs into the street where the artillery would be effective. But at the first sign of a retreat the mob swarmed from the buildings and launched such a savage attack that the soldiers abandoned their dead and wounded, and their artillery, and fled in disorder, only a few escaping. Colonel Jardine, with two officers of the Duryea Zouaves who had also been hurt, crawled into the basement of a dwelling in Second avenue near Nineteenth street. There two women hid them beneath a great pile of kindling wood, but they were soon found by rioters who broke into the house. Colonel Jardine's companions were immediately clubbed to death, and he would have suffered a similar fate had not one of the leaders of the mob recognized him as an old acquaintance, and prevailed upon the rioters to spare his life. Several hours later, when the district had become quiet, the women carried Colonel Jardine to the home of a surgeon. Eventually he recovered from his wounds.

The victory in First avenue was the last important success won by the mob. The regiments which had been ordered into New York began to arrive early Wednesday evening, and on Thursday morning Commissioner Acton and General Brown were able to supplement their tired forces with several thousand fresh troops who had been hardened by the campaign against the Confederates. The Seventy-Fourth Regiment of the National Guard reached the city about ten o'clock Wednesday night, and was immediately marched through the riot areas, as was the Sixty-Fifth, a Buffalo regiment, which had arrived half an hour later. At four o'clock Thursday morning the Seventh Regiment of the National Guard landed at Canal street, and soon after daybreak marched through the streets of the East Side, to the dismay of its old enemies among the gang leaders. The Sixty-Ninth Regiment detrained Thursday morning, and a few hours later the streets also resounded to the tramp of the Twenty-Sixth Michigan and the Fifty-Second and 152nd New York Volunteers. From then until Friday night troops arrived in the city in ever increasing numbers, and with the additional forces at their command General Brown and Commissioner Acton were able to effect an organization which had hitherto been impossible. Manhattan Island was divided into four districts, and headquarters were established in

Harlem, in West Twenty-second and East Twenty-ninth streets, and at City Hall. In each area large bodies of soldiers and policemen were kept on reserve, while smaller detachments kept up a continuous patrol of the streets, preventing the formation of mobs. Much of this work was performed by the troops, for the police had engaged in such hard fighting since Monday that scarcely a man was unwounded, and the remainder were so weary from constant marching and battling that they could no longer cope effectively with the rioters.

Mayor Opdyke published an encouraging proclamation in the Thursday morning newspapers, urging the citizens to return to their usual occupations, and some of the street car and omnibus lines resumed operations. An official announcement, later discovered to be erroneous, was issued that the draft had been suspended in New York, and would not thereafter be enforced, and the Board of Aldermen held a special meeting and appropriated $2,500,000 with which to pay the exemption fees of all poor men who were chosen but did not want to go to war. But despite these measures fighting continued throughout the day. The most serious encounter was in Second avenue between Twenty-ninth and Thirty-first streets, where a mob defeated several small detachments of policemen and soldiers, and pursued about twenty-five of the latter into Jackson's Foundry, which was besieged. General Brown dispatched Captain Putnam to the rescue with a battery of field guns, fifty policemen and a full company of regular infantry. When the mob attacked, Captain Putnam swept the street with his artillery, killing eleven men and wounding many more. The rioters then scattered into the buildings on either side of Second avenue, but both policemen and soldiers pursued them, and with clubbed muskets and nightsticks drove them into the street, where they were again raked by the guns. They soon fled, and the troops marched to the rescue of their beleaguered comrades in the foundry.

This was the last fight of any consequence, although there were frequent minor clashes throughout Thursday night, and a few on Friday. Another proclamation by the Mayor on Friday declared that the riotous assemblages had been dispersed, and that a sufficient military force was now on hand to suppress any illegal movement, however formidable. At eleven o'clock Friday morning a crowd of some three thousand men and women assembled before the residence of Archbishop Hughes, at Madison avenue and Thirty-sixth street, and the prelate addressed them from a chair on his balcony, as he was so afflicted with rheumatism that he could not stand. He appealed to their religious pride and urged them to cease rioting:

"Every man has a right to defend his home or his shanty at the risk of life. The cause, however, must be just. It must not be aggressive or offensive. Do you want my advice? Well, I have been hurt by the report that you were rioters. You cannot imagine that I could hear these things without being grievously pained. Is there not some way by which you can stop these proceedings and support the laws, none of which have been enacted against you as Irishmen and Catholics? You have suffered already. No government can save itself unless it protects its citizens. Military force will be let loose on you. The innocent will be shot down, and the guilty will be likely to escape. Would it not be better to retire quietly?"

A strong force of soldiers and policemen attended the meeting, but did not molest the Archbishop's audience, which dispersed quietly as soon as the prelate had finished speaking. "They were on the whole a peaceable crowd," wrote Headley in *Sketches of the Great Riots of New York*, "and it was evidently composed chiefly if not wholly of those who had taken no part in the riot. None of the bloody heads and gashed faces, of which there were so many at that moment in the city, appeared. The address was well enough, but it came too late to be of any service. It might have saved lives and much destruction had it been delivered two days before, but now it was like the bombardment of a fortress after it had surrendered—a mere waste of ammunition. The fight was over, and to use his own not very refined illustration, he 'spak' too late.' "

General Brown was relieved by General E. R. S. Canby on the morning of Friday, and on Saturday General John A. Dix took over the command of the Department of the East from General Wool. On orders from General Dix the troops assumed the duty of guarding the city, while the police devoted several days to the recovery of stolen property. Large detachments, some with military escorts, visited the rookeries and dives of the Five Points, the Bowery and the slum districts along the Hudson and East Rivers, and in cellars and garrets found loot of every description, from barrels of sugar and luxurious rugs to tobacco and bird-seed. "Mahogany and rosewood chairs with brocade upholstering, marble top tables and stands, costly paintings and hundreds of delicate and valuable mantel ornaments are daily found in low hovels," said a newspaper. "Every person in whose possession these articles are found disclaims all knowledge of the same, except that they found them in the street, and took them in to prevent them being burned. The entire city will be searched, and it is expected that the greatest portion of the property taken from the buildings sacked by the mob will be recovered."

The casualties of the four days' fighting were never exactly computed, but were as high as those of some of the important battles of the Revolution and the Civil War, including such famous engagements as Shiloh and Bull Run. Conservative estimates placed the total at two thousand killed and about eight thousand wounded, a vast majority of whom were rioters. Practically every man on the police force was injured, although only three died. The losses of the various military units were not disclosed by the War Department, but were at least fifty men killed and some three hundred wounded. Eighteen Negroes were hanged by the rioters, and about seventy others were reported missing. Five were known to have been drowned when mobs pursued them into the East and Hudson Rivers. The police and troops captured eleven thousand stand of arms, including muskets and pistols, together with several thousand bludgeons and other weapons. The property loss was estimated at about $5,000,000, and the loss to business was incalculable, due to the stoppage of trade and the exodus of thousands of citizens, many of whom did not return to the city for several months. More than a hundred buildings were burned, including a Protestant Mission, the Colored Orphan Asylum, three police stations, an Armory, three Provost Marshals' offices, and a great number of dwellings, factories and stores. About two hundred other structures were looted and damaged.

Throughout the rioting the police and military authorities were hampered, and their plans often frustrated, by the politicians, especially the Democratic members of the Board of Aldermen and the State Legislature, who seized the opportunity to embarrass the administrations of the Republican President and the Republican Mayor. These worthy statesmen frequently appeared at Police Headquarters, and at a time when houses were being looted and burned and Negroes tortured and hanged, when business was at a standstill and the streets were filled with surging mobs, demanded that the police and soldiers be withdrawn from their districts, complaining that they were murdering the people. A Democratic Police Magistrate held a special session of his court, brought forward a test case, and solemnly pronounced the draft law to be unconstitutional, and urged the people to resist its enforcement. Most of the prisoners taken by the police during the last two days of the rioting, and during the search for stolen goods, were immediately freed through political influence, and were never brought to trial. Many of the gang leaders of the Five Points, the water front and other criminal infested areas were caught leading their thugs on looting expeditions, but politicians rushed to their aid and saved them from punishment. When the rioting had ceased only twenty men, out of the thousands who had formed the mobs, were in jail. Of these nineteen were tried and convicted, and were sentenced to an average of five years each in prison.

from Collura

by Bill Davidson

Bill Davidson's (born 1918) 1977 book profiles actor Steven Collura, who in 1967 was recruited to work undercover for the NYPD. Collura became one of the city's best agents. But the murder of an informant named Frenchy haunted him—as did his failure to bust the men responsible for a massive heroin shipment to Brooklyn's Pier Eight.

The message came through Joe White on the switchboard, and it was the usual request for Collura to work undercover with a registered informant. Ordinarily he would have turned down the assignment on the ground that he was already busy on similar operations, but one factor piqued his interest. *This* request for his services came from the elite Special Investigating Unit, and to his knowledge, the SIU rarely if ever used undercover detectives. Even in the French Connection case, they had provided the shock troops after Egan and Grosso, who were a field team and *not* undercover, had picked up the first clue at the Copacabana nightclub.

Offsetting Collura's curiosity over why the SIU wanted him was his concern over the fact that the unit just had come under heavy fire from the Internal Affairs Division—the highest the IAD had ever reached into the narcotics-enforcement hierarchy.

Weighing one thing against the other, Collura decided to have one meeting with 2nd Grade Detectives Vinnie Gallardo and Luis

Benitez of the SIU. If it *was* just another marginal street operation, he'd reject it.

So on a rainy night in November, 1972, he rendezvoused with the squat Italian Gallardo and the balding Puerto Rican Benitez in their deceptively beat-up blue Buick, parked opposite the entrance to the Brooklyn-Battery Tunnel at the deserted Manhattan riverfront on West Street. The meeting did not start auspiciously. Gallardo and Benitez had a crack new informant fresh out of Rikers Island, etc. Collura had heard all that before. He only half-listened.

Suddenly he heard Gallardo say, "This dude knows about a big shipment from Marseilles coming into the Brooklyn docks."

Collura lit up like a computer panel. "*Where* on the Brooklyn docks?"

"He mentioned Columbia Street, Pier Eight."

Collura could feel his pulse pounding violently in his temples. His mouth became dry, his underarms wet. He leaned forward in the front passenger seat of Gallardo's car and feigned making an adjustment to his boot while he told himself to play it cool. If this *was* The Big Score, he'd have to be as cautious and methodical as he'd ever been in his life. He straightened up and asked, "What made you guys request me for this?"

Benitez said, in his Spanish-accented English, "We need a guy who is very good in narcotics on the street. We also need a guy who knows a lot about organized crime. So you are two in one."

Collura nodded. "And I'm in charge of the operation?"

"Complete charge. We do it by the book. The undercover calls the shots, like always."

Collura nodded again. "Okay," he said. "Now tell me about your informant. I don't even want to meet him until I'm sure everything smells fuckin' right."

"I don't blame you," said the phlegmatic Gallardo. He then launched into a summary of the events that had led up to this meeting.

Gallardo's SIU team had, for some time, been using a very effective black informant in Harlem, whose code name was, simply, John. Unlike the street-junkie-type informants regularly assigned to Collura, John was a high-class wheeler-dealer in heroin whose knowledge went far beyond the nickel-and-dime-bag arena. He operated on the "heavy" level of wholesaling operations. John was invaluable to the SIU also for pure intelligence. If they wanted to know what was "going down" in a certain case in which they were interested, they'd send John up to Harlem, and in a few days he'd come back and tell them. Instead of using undercover detectives like Collura, the SIU relied entirely on trusted and experienced informants like John. When one of their top-grade informants told them a big narcotics deal was about to take place in such-and-such a building, the SIU would go through a complicated procedure of stakeouts and wiretaps. Then they'd go to court for a warrant to raid the premises—more often than not coming in with a big haul of heroin and important arrests.

John's only weakness was that like most "turned around" dealers, he occasionally could not resist the temptation of doing a little independent heroin business on the side. The last time this had happened was in June, 1972, and he had been arrested by a detective team from Manhattan North Narcotics. With John's long "yellow sheet" of previous arrests and convictions, the best Gallardo's team could do for him was a reduced sentence of six months in Rikers Island Penitentiary.

It turned out to be fortuitous. John was put into a cell with another black dealer he had known quite well in Harlem. John's cellmate was distraught. He told John he had been on the verge of making enough money to last him for years, but had been busted at just the wrong time. He was acting as the go-between on the biggest heroin shipment about to come into New York in a decade, and now he had blown it. John had then cleverly dropped the hint that he was getting out of Rikers soon on appeal, and his cellmate had eagerly suggested that John could probably take over the operation for him—provided John paid him a percentage of the earnings. John then contacted Gallardo with the story, and he *did* get out. The SIU was fascinated and wanted to know more.

Gallardo and relays of other detectives tested John a hundred ways to make sure the cellmate's representations were valid. Everything checked out. Independent groups of heroin entrepreneurs were making deals in Marseille, in the same way that independent groups of refugee Cubans had become multimillionaires by making cocaine deals in South America. A Harlem group could put up $250,000 for a shipment of nearly pure heroin from Marseilles, which would produce a profit of 3,000 percent when "banged out" and distributed in diluted amounts on the street. The only problem at that time was that the Harlem streets were "hot," with the Internal Affairs investigation and the new infusion of black undercover detectives. According to John's cellmate, his people's street-distributor network had been all but wiped out. Therefore, they simply wanted to recoup their $250,000 investment, plus a $500,000 profit, by selling the entire shipment for $750,000 to a big-time buyer elsewhere who did *not* have similar street-distributor problems.

Gallardo had sent John to Harlem to contact his cellmate's "people." John came back to report that the deal was everything the cellmate had said it was. He had also been able to report that his own credentials were good enough for the "people," so that they had accepted him as a substitute for the cellmate as their representative in selling the huge yet-to-arrive heroin shipment. His job was to seek out and find an equivalent representative of a worthwhile potential buyer of the shipment. That was when Gallardo had requested the assignment of Collura to the case. He needed the best cop he could find to pose as the go-between for the "buyer."

When Gallardo had finished outlining all this, Collura asked, "Why don't you use a black undercover? Wouldn't that make more sense in Harlem?"

"It wouldn't work. The black guys in the Department are too new on this gig. Besides, a black go-between would probably be representing a black buyer, which wouldn't look kosher. A nigger buyer would be having the same trouble with 'hot streets' in his area that the seller would."

This made sense to Collura. "Besides," he speculated, "we're talking three quarters of a million here. Who would they expect to be the first to come up with that kind of bread?"

"I think you're getting the point," said Gallardo.

Both being Italian, they disliked using the word "Mafia."

"An interesting idea," said Collura, "but I want to give it some thought. I'll contact you in a couple of days."

Collura met again with Gallardo and Benitez on Wednesday night, November 29. Again the session took place in Gallardo's Buick in the darkness of West Street, opposite the tunnel entrance. Every field detective has his favorite spot for clandestine conferences, and this was Gallardo's. Collura felt vaguely thankful, since the smelly Fulton Fish Market area was known to be a then-popular SIU rendezvous point.

Collura still wasn't sure he was going to accept the assignment, but in his excitement during his two days of considering it, he had developed an entire scenario for a cover story he could use, developing the Mafia theory interposed by Gallardo at the end of the previous meeting.

"Let me try this out on you," Collura said to Gallardo and Benitez. "In the families, especially in Brooklyn, the older guys in the organization still won't touch dope. They think it's a dirty way of making money. So they leave that to the younger guys who're trying to make their bones. I once worked on a case of a prick like that, name of Mike, down on Columbia Street."

Collura paused unconsciously at that point, and Gallardo had to tell him to go on.

"Yeah," said Collura. "Anyway, it would be pretty realistic for me to be representing a family in a three-quarters-of-a-million-dollar junk deal up in Harlem. They'd *expect* a kid my age to be the contact. First, I'm Italian. Second, I can do a bit about my connections with 'good' people. Third, I can make them believe I have the bread and they need me more than I need them."

"Not bad," said Gallardo. "But how do you account for your connection with John?"

"Easy. It's a bit I've used before. I met John in Rikers when I was
busted on a dope charge that my people got dismissed for me. After
John and I both got out of the joint, we bounced around together and
I hooked him up with some good money people on big junk deals."

"Do you know enough about Rikers to get away with that shit?"
asked Benitez.

"Try me. I've been inside."

They then played Twenty Questions, and Gallardo and Benitez were
surprised at Collura's knowledge of the cellblocks, the reception
center, the mess halls, the smells and patois of the penitentiary.

"Okay," said Collura, "now try to pick holes in the *rest* of the cover
story." Gallardo and Benitez did so, carrying on a conversation as if
they were three dope dealers rapping on the street. It was almost like
an actors' improvisational class, and the two older detectives took to it
with unexpected skill, using all the experience of their combined forty-
two years in the Police Department. When Collura faltered on a particular point, they discussed it until he had smoothed out his answers.
It was an hour before they all were satisfied with Collura's mastery of
the role of the young Mafioso negotiating an enormous narcotics deal
in Harlem.

Stimulated by the improvisation session, they sat in silence for a
while, cooling down from it. Finally Gallardo said, "Okay, *we* think it'll
work. How about you?"

Collura said, "I don't know yet. It all depends on the vibes I get
from John. It's *my* ass, and I gotta make sure I trust him. Set up a
meet for him and me in about a week. In the meantime, tell him to
scout the area in Harlem and report to me everything he finds out."

Gallardo shrugged. "Like I said, you run the operation."

At 1 a.m. on Monday, December 4, 1972, Collura sat waiting for
John in the Horn & Hardart cafeteria at 34th Street and Lexington
Avenue in midtown Manhattan. He had deliberately chosen the place
because in the early-morning hours it was frequented by derelicts and

tired whores, whose minds would be on other things. It was not an environment that was attractive to narcotics dealers who might recognize him.

A small, very dark black man walked in, and Collura immediately knew it was John. He wore beautifully cut tan slacks, brown shoes, a white turtleneck sweater and a $200 brown leather jacket. Collura waved him over and he sat down at the table, which was at the rear of the cafeteria and remote from any of the other patrons. John was about 40, but looked older. He turned out to be a slow and deliberate talker, different from the junkies Collura had previously worked with who tended to just ramble on.

Collura said, "Okay, what do you have to tell me?"

John said, "About what?"

"What do you mean? You were supposed to be getting me information. What have you been doing all week?"

"Oh," said John, "I told Vinnie and Luis."

Collura reached across the table and clamped an iron grip on John's left biceps. "Listen, you mothafucka," he said, "when you get information for *me*, you tell it to *me*—not Vinnie, not Luis, not anyone fuckin' else. D'you understand?" He relaxed his grip and John, muffled fear in his eyes, fell back in his chair. "I dig," he said. Collura had crossed the all-important barrier of establishing control. "Now let's start all over again," he said. "What do you have to tell me?"

John said, "I met with the two dudes who are runnin' the deal. Charles and Hank. The big shipment comes into Brooklyn in two weeks."

"Pier Eight?"

"They didn't say this time, but I think so."

"What else?"

"They definitely want to unload the whole bundle in one bulk to one buyer. Most of their dealers are busted, and it's like almost impossible for them to distribute on the street. So they desperate. The people they gettin' the shit from, they have to be paid, so they's no way they can just sit and wait till the streets cool off."

"Where do this Hank and Charles hang out?"

"Two places. The Cecil Hotel at 210 West 118th between Saint Nicholas and Adam Clayton Powell. They live there, and they work outta the Playhouse Lounge in the lobby. Then they's a social club at 122 West 116th between Saint Nicholas and Lenox. They do they business in there, too."

"Any white dudes in this thing with Hank and Charles?"

"Might be. Definitely might be. But I ain't never seen none. Hank and Charles, they my only contac'."

Collura didn't like John. "Okay," he said, "split."

John looked at him blankly. "Split," Collura repeated. "Walk east on Thirty-fourth Street for a couple of blocks and Vinnie and Luis will pick you up in their car at Second Avenue."

John left, and Collura sat at the table for a while, thinking about the conversation. Then he got into his VW and drove up to Harlem. It was now nearly 3 a.m., but he saw expensive Cadillacs and Continentals outside the drab and run-down Cecil Hotel and also at the social club on 116th Street. A couple of the license plates looked familiar, and their numbers matched up with two he had written in his notebook while he was staking out Mike on Columbia Street two years before. The Department of Motor Vehicles had told him the registration numbers were fictitious.

Well, well, well, Collura said to himself.

"What did you think of John?" asked Vinnie Gallardo when Collura met him and Benitez the next night on West Street.

"I'm not sure," he said. "What did he tell *you* about the setup?"

Gallardo repeated the same information about Hank, Charles, the Cecil Hotel and the social club on 116th Street.

"At least he's telling us the same story," said Collura. "He also checks out on the Cecil and the social club." He mentioned the Cadillacs and the Continentals.

"Then you're telling us we got a go on this operation?"

All of Collura's instincts were to say no, that he didn't quite trust John not to try to pull off a piece of the action for himself.

Instead, he said, "Tell John to set up a meet with Hank and Charles in the Playhouse Lounge up there in the Cecil Hotel. After that, we'll see."

Collura slept only fitfully. He knew it was the beginning of one of his periods of chronic insomnia, and he tried to take advantage of every minute of slumber. But a recurring dream kept waking him up. He was in an airline terminal rushing to catch a plane. He'd get on an escalator ascending to the boarding gate, but the escalator would keep going and going and never reach the top. In the meantime, he'd see the boarding gate close, and he'd yell at the agent to hold the plane for him, and his own shout would wake him up.

It was Thursday, December 7—three days after he had first met John in the cafeteria.

Collura was now on an accelerated schedule of phoning the Undercover switchboard every half-hour. At 11:30 a.m., there was a message to call John at a pay-booth number. Collura phoned the number. John said, "We meet the two dudes at eleven tonight. The Playhouse Lounge in the lobby of the Cecil. Do I go in with you?"

"No," said Collura. "You be sitting there with the mothafuckas. I come in alone."

He met with Gallardo and Benitez at 4 p.m. "You're fuckin' crazy," said Gallardo, "walkin' into a roomful of niggers all by yourself. John should be with you."

"No," replied Collura, "a white kid from the mob walks in alone. He shows disdain for having to make a deal on this level. With an entrance like that, he demands and *gets* respect—not only for himself but for all the power behind him, which still scares them shitless up in Harlem."

From the way Gallardo looked at him, Collura realized that for the first time he had *his* respect. "You're fuckin' well right," Gallardo said. "What do you need for backup?"

"Add two more guys from the SIU. Make them both black so they can blend into the crowd outside on the street. If I don't come out in twenty minutes, send 'em in to get me."

"Okay," said Gallardo. "I got two good men in mind. Both gold shields. I'll designate them Team B. Luis and I will be Team A."

"Good. Because when I come out after rappin' with Hank and Charles, I want a loose tail put on them. I want to know where they go."

"You got it," said Gallardo. "Anything else?"

"Yeah. You better rig up a Rikers Island prison record for me and put it in the files. If these guys can fuck around with auto licenses, they can probably check out anything they want in the fuckin' files in this fuckin' city."

But after he left Vinnie and Luis, Collura took one further vital pre-cautionary step on his own. He knew that the Harlem people had connections not only in the state and city bureaucracy, but probably also within the Mafia structure. That was a possibly fatal risk he *had* to try to short-circuit in advance.

He'd been told that the Intelligence Bureau had developed a turned-around contact inside the organization of Carlo Gambino, then Boss of Bosses of the city's five Mafia families. So Collura phoned the Undercover switchboard and left the following message: "If the Gambino contact learns that anyone is asking questions about an Italian kid making a big buy of shit in Harlem, he should vouch for the kid as being connected with the Gallos."

On his next check-in with the switchboard, Collura got a cryptic but satisfying answer. "It'll be taken care of," said Joe White.

At 11:05 p.m., Collura parked his borrowed white Cadillac Eldorado among the others at the curb in front of the Cecil Hotel in Harlem. Black faces stared at him in astonishment as he strode into the lobby of the hotel wearing his gray sports jacket and matching slacks and his Mafia-style pinkie ring and diamond watch, both flashing blue and red in the reflected light of the overhead neon. He was the epitome of bravado, and only his concentration on his performance kept him from being overwhelmed by the terror inside him.

Once in the lobby, he turned into the entrance of the Playhouse

Lounge. The place was jammed with people, all black, swaying to the earsplitting shriek of a Stevie Wonder record at top volume. Heads swiveled around, and he could almost see the words forming on a hundred lips: "What the fuck *he* doin' here?" Collura stared back as brazenly as he could, and gradually the heads began to turn away.

And then John was there in the semidarkness, leading him to a table in the back of the room. "Don't forget to introduce me as Allie-boy," Collura whispered. There was method to this reversion to his childhood nickname. Allie-boy also was the nickname of Alphonso Persico, one of the most feared Mafiosi now running the old Joe Colombo family, and though Persico was in his mid-forties, Collura could well be taken for his nephew.

The introduction must have had some effect, because Charles and Hank *did* rise slightly to shake hands. Charles was very dark, with a bushy moustache, an Afro hairdo and the bulky, broad-shouldered build of a retired heavyweight prizefighter. Hank was more slender, clean-shaven, quite good-looking, with slicked-back "processed" (straightened) hair and the demeanor of a successful black businessman. Both men wore expensive custom-made suits and were laden down with neck chains, bracelets, rings and other jewelry.

A waitress came by to take their order for drinks, and then John said to Collura, "These are the friends I told you about that maybe you could do some business with them."

Collura, moving quickly to take control, said to Hank, "Yeah, bro, what's the story?"

The enormous Charles leaned forward angrily and said, "Now, wait just one fuckin' minute, man. All we know is what John told us about you."

Collura responded with equal heat. "Bullshit. By now you've checked me out from here to Rikers Island. John don't know any more about me than I told him."

Hank jumped in as a peacemaker. "Relax," he said; "we just wanna know who you're repping."

"It's none of your fuckin' business. Just like it's none of my fuckin' business who *you're* frontin' for."

Collura allowed the stalemate to exist for about five seconds, then said, "Let's cut the shit. If you got merchandise to sell, I'm lookin' to buy. I got connections with people who might be able to handle a good deal of junk."

The key words were "connections" and "people." Hank suddenly relaxed. He said guardedly, "We got connections with a big load of junk comin' in. How much can you handle?"

In reply, Collura deliberately used the pronoun "we" instead of "I." He said, "Whatever you got, *we* can handle."

He caught Charles and Hank exchanging a quick glance, and he pressed his advantage: "Have you got figures to throw at me? Otherwise, I'm gettin' the fuck outta here."

Hank looked at Charles again, received a quick nod and said, "We're talkin' about possibly a hundred keys."

Collura had to fight an overwhelming impulse to explode with combined shock and exultation. A hundred "keys" was a hundred kilos—220 pounds—of pure heroin, $75,000,000 on the street: almost double the biggest shipment ever intercepted in the United States—the 51.1 kilos of the French Connection case.

"I know about the hundred keys," Collura said offhandedly. "Do you have it?"

"No, it's comin'."

"Then what the fuck am I doin' here?"

Hank moved in to calm Collura down, and the multi-million-dollar poker game was just about over. "Hey, man," Hank said, "we know what you want."

Collura said, "Yeah, but you're gonna have to lay a taste on me."

Charles said, "Okay, man, we'll let you know when you can pick up your taste."

Collura retorted sharply, "When? Next year?"

Hank said, "No. In a couple of days."

That was all Collura wanted to hear, and he got up to go. So far, he had miraculously pulled off the act without error, and his theory was that the less his exposure to Hank and Charles, the less chance they would have to detect flaws in his cover story. Hank said, "Why don't you stay for drinks and broads, man?"

Collura said, "No, man, I got business." He haughtily dropped a $50 bill on the table "for the drinks," and he walked out with John.

He was totally limp when he got to his car. He told John, "Keep in touch with those dudes and let me know how *they* feel about this meeting. If it looks like trouble, we're not going back."

"Jesus Christ," said Vinnie Gallardo, "a *hundred* fuckin' keys? That would supply every fuckin' junkie in the United States for a fuckin' year."

He and Collura were in his car in the parking lot of the Port Authority Bus Terminal at Eighth Avenue and 41st Street.

"If it isn't bullshit," said Collura. "How about Team B? Did they pick up on Hank and Charles after I walked out last night?"

"The mothafuckas never left the Cecil Hotel. I even added another team, and they watched the place front and back."

Collura said, "Keep a loose tail on them. They may go down to Pier Eight when the ship comes in."

There no longer was any doubt in his mind that the ship *would* come in. Despite his surface expressions of skepticism, he had closeted his trepidations in the back of his mind. His course now was inexorable.

On Monday, December 11, there was a message from John at the switchboard, and he and Collura met at 63rd Street and Central Park West. John said, "They keep tryin' to check you out. They find a record on you somewhere and they seem to think it's pretty good. All they keep askin' me is who is your people and I keep sayin' you come from the very *best* people."

"What about the taste?"

"They keep sayin' they very anxious to give you the taste and start talkin' money."

• • •

It was December 26, 1972—fifteen agonizing days later for Collura. He had spent the entire Christmas holiday in his apartment, waiting for messages from the switchboard. Then there was the call from John. This time they met under the West Side Highway at 56th Street.

John said, "The ship musta come in. They got an oh-zee for you to taste." (An "oh-zee" is an ounce.)

"When?"

"Tomorrow night at eleven."

"Where?"

"I dunno yet. You'll have to pick me up at 116th and Lenox at ten-thirty an' I'll take you there."

Collura dropped John off and rushed to meet Gallardo's expanded task force, now known as Team 16, at the usual West Street meeting place. He caught a glimpse of the two new black team members, but spoke only to Gallardo in his car. He told Gallardo about the arrangements for picking up the taste and said, "Since I don't know where I'm going, put a loose tail on me when I meet John at 116th and Lenox. When I get to the location, I'll circle the block once, before I park. Then the usual procedures go into effect. If I'm not out in twenty minutes, you guys come in."

At 10:30 on Wednesday, John was waiting patiently at 116th Street and Lenox Avenue. He slipped out of the shadows of a deserted store-front and got into Collura's white Cadillac. "Where are we going?" Collura asked.

"305 West 113th."

Collura nodded and headed west and south. He was reassured to catch a glimpse of Gallardo's old blue Buick in his rearview mirror.

Collura went west on 113th and then circled back around 114th, parking in front of the once-ornate deserted apartment building at 305 West 113th. Surprisingly, there were a lot of people in the blitzed-looking street of vacant lots and boarded-up tenements.

The windows of 305 were boarded up too, but the front door gaped open. They went inside and up a flight of rubble-strewn stairs. It was totally dark, but Collura could feel the crunch of broken glass and plaster beneath his feet. Directly at the top of the stairs, John knocked on a closed door. Collura could hear bolts being shot back, and the door opened slightly to reveal the unmistakable large silhouette of Charles, outlined against a dim light emanating from somewhere in the apartment.

"Okay," Collura said to John, "wait for me downstairs."

John looked surprised and reluctant to go, but he obeyed Collura's sharp order.

Fear nearly paralyzed Collura as he stepped inside, but he controlled it. He could see a foyer, beyond which were a small room that had probably been a dinette and, at the front of the apartment, a living room. He was aware that all the walls were brightly painted but that huge chunks of plaster had fallen from them. The only furniture was a battered couch in the living room and, facing it, a cheap plastic coffee table and a nondescript brown upholstered chair. The light came from a single bulb hanging from a wire in the ceiling of the living room. Collura wondered where the electricity came from, since the apartment obviously had not been inhabited for some time.

Charles joined Hank, who was sitting on the couch, and Collura crunched his way across the debris on the floor and settled into the chair. It was bitter cold, and there was no heat in the apartment. They all kept their coats on. They exhaled clouds of frosty vapor.

After a minute of silence, Charles abruptly got up and went into another room. He came back with a glassine envelope, which he flung nonchalantly on the table.

"This is it?" said Collura. "Now what are we talkin' about?"

Collura made no move to pick up the glassine envelope.

"The whole hundred keys," said Hank. "That's what we got on ice."

"What are you lookin' for?" asked Collura.

"Seven hundred fifty thousand for the whole load."

"In installments or all at once?"

"All at once."

The glassine envelope remained ignored in the midst of the conversation.

"That may be too high," said Collura. "I'm authorized to go to five hundred thousand."

Hank said, "No way, man. Do you know what that load of shit is worth to us on the street?"

"Yeah, maybe seventy, eighty million. But what the fuck good is it doin' you? My people know you got no dealers on the street."

Collura noted a tight look cross Hank's face. He waited a brief second, then added, "I dunno. If this oh-zee tests out as high as you guys seem to think, maybe my people *will* go to seven fifty."

There was the slightest hint of relaxation in Hank and Charles.

Collura looked around the wrecked hovel of an apartment. "You're tellin' me you're going to have a hundred fuckin' keys up *here*?" he said.

"You crazy, man?" Charles said. "We do the deal the regular way. If you like the taste, we get ten thousand front money. Then we take your people to the stash and the rest of the bundle gets turned over COD. Seven hundred and fifty thousand."

Collura nodded. "*If* the taste comes back from my lab as good as you say it is. If it don't test out good, you'll never see me again."

For the first time in the conversation, he acknowledged the existence of the glassine envelope lying on the table. He picked it up, stuffed it into his pocket and walked out. He paused only to get a telephone number at which to contact them and for Charles to unbolt the apartment door.

He met John downstairs and roared off with him in the Cadillac. He left John at Manhattan Avenue and, spotting Gallardo's Buick in his rearview mirror, continued downtown to the Port Authority Bus Terminal parking lot. There was no time to go all the way to West Street near the tip of Manhattan.

Gallardo got into the parked Cadillac and they went through the routine of initialing and sealing the glassine bag as evidence. Then Collura drove to the Police Lab on East 20th Street and Gallardo and

Luis rushed back up to Harlem to continue the stakeout of Hank and Charles.

Of all the times Collura had been in the Police Lab, this was the one visit that engraved itself on his memory. Get off the elevator on the eighth floor. Turn right to the little waiting room with its table and six chairs. Go to the little window with the ledge for spreading out your papers. Give the evidence to the clerk, with the detectives working at desks behind him. Watch him take the evidence to the right, where the chemists work. Watch him take evidence from other cases out of the huge bank-type vault to the left. Tell the clerk this is a super-rush job. Tell him it's a special SIU authorization. Watch him check by phone. Sit in the waiting room and try to read the *American Legion Magazine* and *SPRING 3100*. Watch for the white-coated chemist to come out of the back room with the analysis. Guess whether it will be an old guy or a young guy.

It was an old guy, with curly gray hair and wearing a doctor's white smock. He came out at 2:30 a.m. and walked directly over to Collura. There was a gleam in his eyes as if he had just passed a personal scientific milestone. "This heroin is incredible," he said. "It's nearly 88 percent pure. I've never seen anything like it."

"Thank you, Doc," said Collura. He snatched the analysis sheet out of the old man's hands and headed for the elevator.

From a phone booth in the lobby, Collura called the Undercover switchboard and requisitioned a miniradio specifically tuned to the SIU frequency. He had to get in touch with Gallardo at once. He sped downtown to the 1st Precinct Building and picked up the radio. He then headed for the East River Drive, made a left turn and parked at the Downtown Heliport, totally deserted at 3 o'clock in the morning. It was Collura's equivalent of Gallardo's favorite rendezvous spot on West Street.

He extended the radio's antenna and spoke into the built-in microphone: "Vinnie, it's Allie-boy. Allie-boy calling Vinnie. Anybody from Team Sixteen please respond." There was a moment of silence. Then the radio crackled and Gallardo's voice said, "Allie, we've got you. We're on the East River Drive goin' south."

Collura started to tell him about the chemist's analysis, but Gallardo broke in with "Hold it, Allie. Something's goin' down."

"What's up?"

"We're followin' the two black guys you met tonight—*and* John."

Collura was stunned. He said, "Repeat, Vinnie, repeat."

Gallardo said, "Puttin' the tail on the two guys, we picked up John visually. He was gettin' into a black Mustang. Now *he's* followin' the two guys and we're followin' both of their cars."

"What the fuck is John up to?"

"Beats the shit outta me."

Collura then quickly gave Gallardo a summary of the lab results and asked, "Where's Team B?"

"Still uptown and unable to reach."

"If you need me for a tail, my location is the Heliport off the Drive—"

"Not right now. We're on the Brooklyn Bridge."

"Okay, Vinnie," said Collura. "Continue to inform me about the pursuit."

Collura crossed the Brooklyn Bridge, parked near one of the exits on the Brooklyn side and continued to listen to Vinnie's reports on the radio: "The two black guys just pulled up on Columbia Street near Pier Eight."

Collura felt as if his blood pressure were going through the roof of his mouth.

Gallardo said, "One guy's gettin' outta the car. It's the big dude, Charles. I'm goin' to try to follow him on foot."

Next came Luis' voice: "The big dude went into a building on the pier. Looks like a warehouse."

While he waited for the next report, Collura asked, "Where's John?"

"We lost him."

A few minutes later, Luis said, "Here comes the big dude again, outta the pier. He's carryin' a black case."

There was another period of silence, and then Collura heard Vinnie again: "I lost the mothafucka on the pier and he took off in the car with the other dude. We're now tailin' 'em back over the Brooklyn Bridge."

Voice contact faded, probably because of the steel struts of the bridge, so Collura drove to the 61st Street exit of the East River Drive in Manhattan. He shut off the car lights and tried to reach Gallardo again by radio. The voice came back very weakly: "We're sittin' on 'em at the Cecil Hotel location. They both went inside with the case."

"How big is the case?"

"Oh, y'know, one of them overnight jobs that fit under the seat of an airplane."

"How'd you lose John?"

"He cut out near the pier. We figured the other two guys were more important, so we stayed with them."

"Any word from John down at the switchboard?"

"None."

Suddenly delayed realization seemed to hit Gallardo. Even the weak radio signal could not dilute the wonder in his voice as he asked, "Did you say that taste is eighty-eight percent pure?"

And without waiting for an answer: "Christ, that really *is* just off the fuckin' boat."

It was December 28, 1972. New York City was in its snow-frosted festive period between Christmas and New Year's, when the streets were thronged with people rushing from department store to department store exchanging gifts. It was not a festive time for Collura. Once again, he sat in his apartment waiting for a message from John. For the first time in his life, he had forgotten to buy a present for his mother, and in a fit of remorse he phoned Bloomingdale's and ordered her a totally inappropriate red velvet hostess gown for $159.95. There were no girls in Collura's apartment during this waiting period. In his all-consuming concentration on The Big Score, his normal craving for female company had all but disappeared. He didn't realize this at the time because he didn't even think about it.

All he wanted was that one fucking, motherfucking, mother-motherfucking message from the Undercover switchboard that John had called.

John did not call.

On Friday, December 29, he met with Vinnie and Luis at West Street. Gallardo's Team 16 had added two more detectives, and they were out on the streets of Harlem, Bedford-Stuyvesant and even the South Bronx, looking for John.

Collura said, "What got *into* the son-of-a-bitch to take off after Hank and Charles like that?"

"I hate to say it, because we brought him into this," Gallardo replied, "but the only explanation is that he wanted to find out where the stash is, so he could rip off a piece of it for himself and retire for life. He musta got scared off when he realized we were followin' him."

Collura did not mention his own earlier misgivings about John. He said, "So you think he's holing up somewhere because he knows *we* know he fucked up with us?"

"Yeah. But we'll find him and get him back in line again."

"But how can we trust him now?"

"You can generate a lot of trust when you hold a twenty-year rap over a guy."

"I can't stall too long on getting back to Hank and Charles on the taste. What if we don't find John?"

"Then I say we close down the operation and just make a house bust at the Cecil Hotel."

Collura flared at that. "Bullshit!" he said. "We've come this far, and with or without John, we go all the way."

Gallardo said, "Listen, kid, you been bendin' the rules quite a bit already. Twice you went into interior locations alone, and you *know* that's against the regulations for undercovers."

"*Fuck* the regulations," yelled Collura. "If Egan and Grosso didn't bend the rules, there wouldn't have been any French Connection case, and you fuckin' well know it."

"It's your operation," said Gallardo. "But in the meantime we're goin' to keep tryin' to find John."

Eight more detectives were called in to join the search, and they scoured the city through December 30 and 31. In the meantime, Gallardo's Team 16 had been mounting a round-the-clock stakeout on the Cecil Hotel. Hank and Charles were observed leaving the hotel only once. They went to the 116th Street social club, not carrying the black suitcase or anything else, and then they returned to the Playhouse Lounge equally empty-handed.

By New Year's Eve, Collura's insomnia had taken full hold of him. He put on his street clothes instead of his Mafia finery and switched from the Cadillac to the Volkswagen to roam the avenues and byways of Harlem, pushing through the throngs of black celebrants, looking for John personally. On New Year's Day and January 2, he prowled Bedford-Stuyvesant and Brownsville in Brooklyn.

By Wednesday, January 3, everyone had given up the search for John. If Operation Big Score was to continue, it would have to be without him. Collura, as the detective in charge, made the final decision to do so.

He phoned the number Hank and Charles had given him. He said he was "ready for another meet." That meant he had had the taste analyzed chemically, that he was satisfied with the quality of the heroin and that he was prepared to show up with the $10,000 in "front money." The meeting was set for 10 o'clock the next night.

"Where?" asked Collura.

"The same place as last time," said Hank.

That meant the abandoned apartment at 305 West 113th Street.

Then came Collura's hyped-up sleepless night of January 3–4, 1973.

From 11 p.m. until 1 a.m., he toured Harlem and learned from the gleeful junkies on the street that the heroin shortage was nearly over—that a big new shipment from Marseille was about to be purchased and distributed by the Mafia.

From 2 a.m. to 5 a.m., beset by insomnia and anticipation, he paced nervously, back and forth, back and forth, in his East 73rd Street apartment.

At 5:10 a.m., unable to bear the tension, he phoned the Undercover switchboard and requested a meeting with Vinnie Gallardo.

At 5:19, he had his chance encounter with his neighbor, Mrs. Mintz, and her dyspeptic dog, James.

At 6:06, Collura rendezvoused with Gallardo at the Downtown Heliport, and Vinnie tried unsuccessfully to get Collura to abort the showdown with Charles and Hank, substituting a routine SIU "house bust" instead.

From 7:30 a.m. to 7:15 p.m., Collura nervously paced his apartment again and prepared his wardrobe, armament and act for the evening's crucial encounter with Charles and Hank.

At 7:57, he met with Vinnie and Luis at the Downtown Heliport and was fitted with the tiny radio-transmitter "wire."

At 10 p.m., shadowed by his team in their own cars, Collura's borrowed white Cadillac pulled up in front of 305 West 113th Street in Harlem.

At 10:02, Collura muttered into his neck-chain microphone, "I'm going in"—and he headed toward the gaping front door of the abandoned building.

The downstairs hallway was totally dark, except for a fragment of pale reflected light from a street lamp outside. The first thing Collura saw in that patch of light was the huge bulk of Charles, looming up from a hiding place alongside the stairs. Collura had already felt his way up two of the steps, but now Charles was behind him, and so was Hank. They nudged and shouldered Collura up to the first landing, effectively blocking the entire width of the stairs and cutting off any possible retreat. Under the circumstances, Collura found himself abnormally calm. In an unruffled tone of voice, he said to Charles, "Hey, man, be cool. I got the bread. What're you pushin' for?"

Except for jostling him, Hank and Charles hadn't laid a hand on Collura. In fact, once they got Collura inside the apartment at the top of the stairs and had bolted the door, Charles asked in perfectly friendly fashion, "Hey, man, you wanna blow some coke while we doin' business?"

Before Collura could answer, however, Charles had pushed him forward toward what had been the living room. Hank circled in front of him, but in the light of the overhead bulb Collura could see two men sitting on the couch Charles and Hank had occupied on his last visit to the apartment. One of the newcomers was white, the other black.

The white man scrutinized Collura for a brief instant and then shook his head slightly. Almost simultaneously, Charles grabbed Collura from behind, by the collar. From the corner of his eye, he could see Hank holding a gun by the barrel, and the butt came crashing down on his head. Collura sagged and then was deliberately forced to his knees by Charles.

"Beg for your life, you mothafucka," said Charles.

"Beg, beg, beg," said Hank.

"That's where you belong, on your fuckin' knees, you white mothafucka."

"Beg, beg, beg," said Hank.

Collura begged. He said, "Don't kill me. I don't want to die. Take what you want." While crouched over on his knees and pleading, however, he managed to unbutton the blue cashmere car coat that obstructed his access to the crotch holster.

He suddenly rolled sideways toward a corner of the archway that framed the living room. In the same split second, he heard a tremendous roaring ringing sound and his head snapped forward from the force of a bullet clawing at the back of his skull. By the time he fell, face upward, into the corner, his own .38 was out of the crotch holster, and he fired all five rounds in the direction of what was now just dimly perceived motion. It was the first time in five years that he had fired his weapon in action.

He felt warm blood gushing down his neck and cheek. With out-of-focus vision, he saw two men rushing past him toward a window at the back of the apartment. He thought of Frenchy and how he had been OD'd. He heard an incessant earsplitting pounding from somewhere to his left.

He saw nothing for a while.

He saw a lot of flashing lights on police cars.

He saw nothing.

He saw the huge eye of a brilliant single light beaming down on him.

He saw nothing.

Using a baluster from the stairs as a battering ram, Vinnie Gallardo and his men had burst through the bolted door of the apartment not three minutes after Gallardo had heard the sentence of doom on his radio. Collura's "wire" had even picked up the footsteps of the fleeing men as they jumped through a window onto a neighboring roof and escaped.

Inside the apartment, Gallardo saw Collura, huddled in his corner, blood completely masking his left ear. By that time he was unconscious, but breathing noisily through the blood that trickled across his nostrils. Lying on the rubble-strewn floor directly in front of Collura were the bodies of Charles and Hank. Charles had taken just one of Collura's .38-caliber slugs in the chest, but to judge by the amount of blood, the bullet must have severed the aorta. Hank had been hit in the neck, and a shot at such close range had broken it. There was a second gaping wound in Hank's stomach.

One of the Team 16 men had already radioed for an ambulance, and it was there, along with a dozen police patrol cars, before the dust of Gallardo's forced entry had settled. Collura was taken to the street on a stretcher and rushed to nearby Harlem Hospital. There, it was determined that Hank's bullet had sliced across the base of his skull from his left ear to the nape of his neck (probably while he was falling) but had not penetrated the bone to the brain. Also, there was a bad wound of undetermined cause on his forehead. After emergency surgery to close up both wounds, Collura was transferred by ambulance to Roosevelt Hospital in midtown Manhattan.

Collura's records at Roosevelt Hospital identify him laconically as a member of "New York City Police Dept., Narcotics Dept., 1st Pct., Old Slip Station, NYC." The records make note of his wounds, and the diagnosis is listed as "concussion by HX" (high explosive). The principal concern for him now was possible brain damage from the close-range gunshot, and he was kept under rigorous observation for a week. He suffered recurring dizziness and lack of motor control.

On his fifth day in the hospital, Gallardo and Benitez were permitted to see him. They told Collura that John's body had been found. It was in a cargo container about to be loaded aboard a ship at Pier 8 and was discovered only because a longshoreman happened to notice the smell. John's throat had been cut from ear to ear. The medical examiner estimated John had been dead since the night of December 27, when he had pursued Charles and Hank to Brooklyn in his black Mustang. Gallardo guessed that Charles and Hank had had henchmen who had intercepted John—after Vinnie and Luis had lost him in the chase—and had murdered him. Gallardo now was sure that John had been executed for his greed in trying to find the cache in order to rip off part of the heroin for himself.

Collura asked if the big heroin shipment had gotten out on the street. Gallardo said, "Yes, it has. They must've found another buyer. The town's loaded with shit."

Collura said, "And what about the ten thousand dollars I was carrying in the attaché case?"

Gallardo said, "We recovered it. You dropped it in the hallway in the apartment, and that's where we found it."

He and Benitez left shortly after his brief conversation, and Collura had plenty of time to think about what had gone wrong.

From what he now knew, there were three definite possibilities that he had been set up. First of all, there was John. When John had been caught after that insane foray into Brooklyn in pursuit of Hank and Charles, it was entirely likely that he had given Collura away in a vain attempt to have his own life spared. But if he had done so, why hadn't Hank and Charles called him "pig" or "fuzz" when they had him helpless on his knees on the floor of the 113th Street apartment? If they had known he was a cop, certainly they would have taunted him about it before trying to kill him. Instead, they had simply called him a "white mothafucka."

Then there was the unknown white man who seemed to be the signal caller at his near-execution. He could have been an underworld Mafia expert, specifically brought in to ascertain whether or not Collura was a genuine contact of the organization. By that almost imperceptible shake of his head, he might have been sentencing Collura to death as an impostor.

The most painful possibility of all for Collura was that he had been set up by his fellow policemen. The $10,000 he was carrying was typical of the sort of missing-evidence corruption Internal Affairs had been finding in the SIU. If he *had* been set up and killed, how easy it would have been for Gallardo to pocket the money and say, "The ten thousand dollars disappeared with the two perpetrators who escaped the premises." But the money had not disappeared—a fact which Collura confirmed by calling Joe White at the Undercover switchboard. Gallardo had turned it back to the SIU's operating fund.

So all Collura was left with was his own thoughts about his own culpability and what he had come to be after five years. How could I get caught up in such a trip, he asked himself, that I ended up in a Harlem tenement and nearly died? Was I so addicted to the buzz of this thing that I was actually out of my head and trying to commit suicide? Vinnie had warned me. Why did I do it? Why didn't I let them just go in and blow the fuckin' doors down in that apartment? Five years ago, when Mike Asti first recruited me, I told him, "I'm not a cop," and yet how could I get on a trip like this, and why couldn't I back off and let the real career cops do what they do best in a crisis situation? If I continue on the trip, what's going to prevent me from *successfully* getting myself killed the next time? Have I become so close to being a junkie that I'm following their philosophy: "The best high in the world is when you OD, man"?

The painful self-analysis continued after Collura was allowed to go home but still required to report to Roosevelt Hospital twice a week as an outpatient for the next month. The dizziness and fainting spells persisted, and most of his time in his apartment had to be devoted to self-enforced bed rest. He saw no one. He still hadn't told his family anything about his police work, let alone his injury; and he had no desire for the presence of any of his women friends. After a while, he asked his neighbor, Mrs. Mintz, if she could send in her non-English-speaking Korean maid to clean up the apartment a couple of times a week.

On February 15, exactly six weeks after he was shot, Collura felt well enough to check in with the Undercover switchboard. The detective on duty at the phones was not Joe White, and Collura didn't recognize the voice. Collura asked what had happened to the Pier 8–Harlem operation. The detective told him the SIU had closed it down and had moved on to other things. He then said, "By the way, there's a new lieutenant here, and he left word that he wants to talk to you whenever you check in. He ain't here now."

"All right," said Collura, "have him call me when he comes in." He gave the detective his home number. It was the first time he had broken phone security.

While he waited for the lieutenant to call, Collura reviewed all the thoughts that had run through his mind since he had been in the hospital. His addiction was pulling him back to the Department, but he recognized the addiction now. He also realized that he and the Department had grown apart as quickly as they had grown together, and that he didn't relate to it anymore. He quickly replayed all the cases he had worked on and rated them mentally for positive and negative effect. Christ, he said to himself, the most positive thing I did in the whole five years was the Young Lords operation—and that wasn't even police work.

The phone rang at 5 o'clock that afternoon. It was the lieutenant.

The lieutenant said, "Collura, you've made your bones. No more undercover for you. There's a good spot open in Third District Homicide, east-midtown Manhattan, nice and easy. You'll be starting at a sergeant's pay."

Collura said, "No thanks, Lieutenant. I'm resigning from the Department as soon as I can get downtown to fill out the papers on Friday."

Collura's resignation took effect on February 19, 1973, though he was still on sick leave until the end of March. It wasn't until April 5 that he got around to turning in Gold Shield No. 3013. Once again, there was no ceremony. He simply gave the shield to the civilian Chief Clerk, who nodded brusquely and slipped it into a desk drawer.

By the end of 1974, the elite SIU—the Special Investigating Unit of the New York City Police Department—was in a shambles. Of the unit's one hundred or so gold-shield detectives, more than sixty had been charged with official acts of corruption and were being indicted on criminal charges or being dismissed from the Department. Among them were Vinnie Gallardo, Luis Benitez and the other four men in Team 16 of Operation Big Score. Eventually, the SIU was totally disbanded as unreconstructable, and its few surviving members were reassigned elsewhere. All Narcotics Division activities were moved out of the 1st Precinct Building at Old Slip.

Before the move, Collura paid a belated visit to the old Headquarters Building to collect his records. With but a couple of exceptions, the detectives he had known treated him with undisguised hostility. The atmosphere reeked of suspicion. No one knew who was—or had been—an agent of the Internal Affairs Division.

When Collura looked into the files, all the records of his cases had been removed. By the IAD, checking into cops with whom he had worked? By cops protecting other cops? In any event, the records were gone.

It was as if he had never existed.

The Last Cop Story
by Mike McAlary

Journalist Mike McAlary (1957–1998) won the Pulitzer Prize for his August 1997 exposé about the police torture of Haitian immigrant Abner Louima in Brooklyn. Officer Justin Volpe was convicted of participating in the crime and sentenced to 30 years in prison.

I was hoping to be done with cops. On the morning I heard the phone call, I was getting ready to do some publicity for a book I'd written, based on the screenplay for the film *Cop Land*, about some make-believe New York City police officers who are chased down in New Jersey by Sly Stallone and Robert De Niro. Fiction is kinder than reality.

I was even hoping to be done with newspaper columns. I'd planned to leave my job last winter after eleven years, three newspapers, and thousands of columns, but Pete Hamill became editor of the *New York Daily News* and talked me into staying to write once a week. Keeping a hand in day-to-day journalism, he argued, keeps your voice fresh and true. We agreed that the fewer columns about cops, the better.

And then I heard the phone message from a cop pretending to be a hospital worker. He called on August 11, at 7:55 p.m., after I'd left the office to discuss corrupt cops, real and imagined, with readers at a

Barnes & Noble bookstore on Manhattan's Upper West Side. I had hit the delete button on plenty of messages in the last year, on complaints petty and grand. Events in my life had caused a shift in my interest and attention. But as I listened to the thirty-second call the next morning, and listened to it again, I realized that I had one last cop story to investigate.

"McAlary. Mike McAlary," the voice began. "You don't know me, but I am calling you because in the Seven-O Precinct in Brooklyn, on August the ninth at 0400 hours, they, the cops there, sodomized a prisoner. They took a nightstick and shoved it up his behind and up into his bladder. The patient is currently at Coney Island Hospital. His name, his last name, is L-O-U-I-M-A. Now they are trying to cover this up, because it was two white officers. And they did this to a black guy who they locked up for disorderly conduct. And now they are charging him with assault in the second. All this information can be verified if you call Coney Island Hospital or the Seven-O Precinct. I will not call you again."

When you do a city-side column in New York, I have learned, someone is always angrily accusing you of writing fiction. But I hadn't tried much of it until the last couple of years. I'd done three nonfiction books but hadn't tried a novel until I woke up one day last year and realized I might die without ever having written one.

Anyway, too many good newspaper columnists stay too long. Footprints fade from their work and they become cynical bores. I always thought you should pack away the stories, characters, comedies, and assorted miseries in the great trunk of experience until you were ready to draw on the pathos to create fiction. If you never move on from the newspaper to write stories longer than your forearm, you've failed.

As I got dressed that morning, I played the message for my wife, who listened, measured the narrative, and looked at me, horrified. "You have to do it," she said.

"But I am done with the cop stuff. I thought we decided to move on."

She gave me a look that said, "Bullshit," and then added, "If this happened and you ignore the tip, you will never be able to look at yourself again. And nobody will be in such a hurry to read you."

I unclenched my hands and realized they had been rolled into fists since I first heard the recording. Six months pregnant with our fourth child, Alice Argento McAlary walked me to the door. Over the last year, as I had built an exit ramp from the newspaper business, she had been my partner and editor, working on two novels and a major magazine piece that has since been sold as a book and a movie. But she had lived with cop stories as long as I had. She had lived with the death threats and slashed tires, heard cops cry on the phone and heard them confess the lowest crimes. She had held me after I interviewed them and they committed suicide. "This is what you do," she said.

"I'll check it out."

A driver from the film company was waiting outside in a black Lincoln. We had spent the last three or four days together as he ferried me around the city for promotional appearances. The driver, a ponytailed man named Bill Munter had a passion for rock music—that was about it. He wanted to talk about a beach concert being performed that night. I don't know if you've tried it, but having an intelligent conversation at six in the morning about Genesis—either the book of the Bible or the band—is nearly impossible. I had to ask him to turn down his passion while I made some phone calls.

Too many tales that begin with a recorded message shrivel and die when you shine a light on them. I decided to pursue this story until I hit a lie. I ran the name in the message through the Department of Motor Vehicles computer and came up with several Louimas who had driver's licenses with addresses in Brooklyn or Queens. Then, with that list, I called Coney Island Hospital and started with the A's. This is Journalism 101.

"Can I speak to a patient named Abner Louima?"

"He is in our intensive care," the operator replied. "Critical condition but stable. You cannot talk to prisoners."

Bingo. There was a guy there. So what?

Three of the Louimas listed in the computer lived at the same residence in East Flatbush. One number was for Fanie Louima, which seemed an unfortunate name in the middle of this story. When I got her on the phone, I could tell she had been crying. I told her I'd heard a story about Abner Louima and knew he was in the hospital. She said Abner was her son. She had just left a lawyer's office, she said, and gave me his name.

By the time my car reached the Midtown Tunnel on the way into Manhattan from my house on Long Island, I realized that if the Louima story was true, it was so horrible that it would affect every cop in every precinct in America. It would be worse than the videotaped beating of Rodney King. Of course, with King we could see the sticks.

As I rode through Manhattan that morning, I felt something in my stomach that made me afraid. I had gotten sick at the end of last year and had had a cancerous tumor removed from my colon. Thinking about Louima and the prospect of his crude, wanton colostomy, I shuddered again.

By 10:00 a.m., while I was sitting in my doctor's waiting room, I'd used my cell phone to make an appointment to meet Louima's lawyer at Coney Island Hospital. I had already blown off the *Cop Land* interviews, the fictional-cop circuit, to chase down what could be a story about the dirtiest cop of my career.

As the car waited, I was shot up with 5-FU and leucovorin, two anti-cancer drugs that have kept me stable. My heart was ripping through my chest. Some reporters, I know, prepare notes for cancer memoirs in their treatment rooms. They dribble ink on paper as the fluid drips from the IV bag into their arm. I have done that, too.

The Cancer Life, I have discovered, is not unlike waking up one day on death row. Ordinarily, I'm not bitter or even panicked. I'm fine, so long as I don't obsess too much on the possibility of never being a grandfather to my twelve-year-old son's kid or missing my ten-year-old daughter's wedding or being unable to teach my five-year-old boy how to throw a curveball. Or of never being able to walk along a Mediterranean beach, crooked, wrinkled, and gray, with my wife.

I had been able to control the fears and even try to take charge of my future. That helped me decide to try to change the life I had to the one I wanted: less journalism, more fiction; fewer bars, more doctors. But on this morning, I felt I needed to see someone else's doctor. I wanted to find out what happened to Louima before I refocused on what was happening to me. There is plenty of time for cancer-endurance stories, I figured, but an account of the torture of a prisoner surviving a police dungeon isn't just a compelling newspaper story, it is urban catastrophic. Some crimes do more than just stop us—they change us. I put a bandage on my arm and got back in the car.

The film-company driver was no longer interested in book tours or music. As he eavesdropped on my cell-phone conversations, he became enraged. "The cops did what?"

He sped me from the oncologist's office on the Upper East Side to the Brooklyn hospital and waited. I met Brian Figeroux, Louima's lawyer, at the curb, along with Abner's wife and his severely gray father. Micheline Louima, twenty-four, was wearing a little white sailor hat and an orange dress. She was quite attractive, despite a frozen, almost jagged look that I recognized from police funerals. Cop widows at hospitals, wakes, and funerals wear the same look. It is the calm, calculating face that comes over someone when forgiveness becomes impossible. Micheline offered her hand but it felt as cold and sharp as broken glass.

"How could this have happened?" she said.

The father, Jean Louima—who survived another version of police terror at the hands of Haiti's former paramilitary thugs, the Ton Ton Macoutes, to bring his family to America—looked stunned. "My sweet America," he said before a moan overtook his voice.

Figeroux took me aside and explained that a hospital administrator had agreed to let me in the room with a *Daily News* photographer, Tom Monaster. This was a huge mistake by the hospital, and I knew we had only a tiny window of opportunity before another administrator realized the folly of letting a columnist and a photographer into a prisoner's room.

We were Louima's first visitors. I still believed that this story was probably a lie. It has happened before. Three years ago, some conspiring African livery-cab drivers in Rockaway, Queens, claimed they'd been sodomized by a traffic cop. I spent months proving their story a fabrication. I hoped that this one was equally untrue.

Six of us gathered in the lobby. The clock was running, I knew, and I was afraid of being discovered. As we waited for an elevator, a crowd grew, and I tried to act invisible.

"Hey, McAlary!" a voice shouted from across the lobby. "What are you doing here?"

I turned, expecting to see the hospital administrator from hell. Instead, I faced a group of white construction workers, including one guy with shoulder-length gray hair, tattoos, and a worn face who looked a lot like Steve Dunleavy, the rough tabloid-TV star.

"What's the scoop?" he asked.

"Maybe police brutality," I whispered. "I'll tell you more on the way down."

"Well," the guy replied, "if you wait by these elevators, you'll never even get upstairs. They're broken. Grab your people and follow me."

He led us around the corner to a freight elevator and rode with us to the seventh-floor trauma unit. He never asked another question, and the Louimas seemed startled by the man's kindness. As we stepped off the elevator, I heard the familiar beeping of heart monitors. The polished hallways smelled of disinfectant, and I saw a forest of IV bags on metal poles, some swollen and red like fruit hanging on trees.

There was a cop sitting at the door, and I figured we were dead. I took a deep breath and nodded to him. He stood up, nodded back and stepped aside to let us pass. We pulled the curtains behind us, and I managed to mask my surprise. In the months since, I have thought a lot about that police officer. Why did he let me in? He was either the dumbest cop in the city or one of the shrewdest. I prefer to believe he wanted me in the room. I like to think of him as a hero, sort of like the cop who left the message on my voice mail.

Abner Louima trembled in the bed. He wore a white hospital smock that looked particularly silly in contrast to his grotesque wound. It is difficult to judge a man's size when he's in a hospital bed, but Louima seemed scrawny, even delicate. He had a coarse goatee and a flinty mustache. He attempted a smile as we met and offered a bruised, raw hand. His wife touched his cheek and wept.

"Thank you for coming, Mac-Cleary," Louima whispered through his broken, swollen mouth. He did a better job with my name than I did with his.

A plastic tube was running from his torn bladder into a plastic bag. He had an IV running into one arm and a plastic tube sticking out of his abdomen, about four inches below his navel, just above the line of pubic hair. He nervously pulled the smock tighter. He pointed his left hand absently, almost absurdly, at his legs. His urine, now muddy and red, ran down a plastic tube and puddled in a bag hanging from the foot of the bed. The prisoner's right wrist was handcuffed to the side of the bed, and he had to speak over the clanging of the metal.

"I like cops," he said. "Until now, I wanted to be one."

He would tell me as jarring a tale as I'd ever heard, worse than a story Officer Brian O'Regan told me about the night uniformed cops broke into a crack house, scared off the dealers, and sold the vials through a mail slot to unsuspecting customers. Worse than the story Peter Heron once told me about shooting his heroin dealer on the Lower East Side and then framing him for an unprovoked attack on an off-duty police officer. Worse than Henry Winter's account of stealing money from an old lady's closet.

I don't know how police corruption became my life. I'd never even met a cop until 1986, after I moved out of the toy department, which is what the city-side guys call the sports section, and into news. I covered the Yankees and the Mets but believed most athletes unworthy of the attention. By the end of that year, I knew Brian O'Regan and Henry Winter, two corrupt cops from Brooklyn's infamous Seventy-seventh Precinct. Ultimately, they both committed suicide, a decade apart. O'Regan, a former marine, killed himself the night after telling me how he became a corrupt cop. I realize now that he hired me out to write his obituary, which is a tough assignment, but I still carry his mass card and the memory.

I wrote a book about this crew, named Buddy Boys, and became the father confessor to bad cops. They called their precinct the Alamo. It was a fortress in the heart of New York's largest ghetto. The corruption started with bribes and payoffs. Then the Buddy Boys began to enforce their own brand of street justice. Soon they were robbing drug dealers, flying across the precinct with fire-department ladders strapped to the roofs of their cars, breaking into small businesses, burglarizing apartments, and stealing money from the infirm, the wounded, and the dead. I have met too many corrupt cops, listened to their harrowing tales, reported the searing crimes and shaken their hands. But they are not friends. And no matter how much they say they need you or how ingratiating they seem, if you flinch after hearing their stories, you are ruined, too.

Henry Winter killed himself in September 1995, nine years after his buddy and neighbor Brian O'Regan ate his gun. Winter could not live with the rat he had become. Few of them can. He hung himself in his mother's closet, one flight up from the Formica kitchen table where he'd told me his story. I was in Los Angeles, preparing for the O. J. Simpson verdict, when a detective called to break the news of Winter's death. That next day, I watched the verdict come in at a gas station in South-Central L. A. The black mechanics cheered O. J.'s not-guilty verdict, but not because they knew Simpson, who never came to South-Central. They cheered because they knew Mark Fuhrman, who represented every racist cop who patrolled their neighborhood. Today, all cops must live with the infamy of Fuhrman, who gives credibility to every charge of police brutality in every courtroom.

Now Abner Louima was lying in the hospital with a torn colon, a lacerated bladder, and a ruptured intestine. If his story was true, he was about to become a national figure, the victim of a night of torture that would turn law enforcement on its nightstick.

I recognized a dreadful smell in the hospital room. Human feces. Louima, I noticed then, was wearing a crude diaper. I had to steel my hand to write notes in a small black memo book. He had plastic splint bags on his shins. An old woman who had suffered a heart attack was sharing the room with Louima. She struggled to hear from behind the curtain.

"What? What did he say?"

In time, all the town would struggle to hear. The facts of the case haven't changed since Louima whispered the account to me.

Early Saturday morning, August 9, a party was ending at Louima's favorite club in East Flatbush. As the club emptied, there was a fight between two women. Abner, who had just gotten off work as a security guard, didn't know either woman but got caught up in it. The cops showed up to scatter the crowd, and someone slugged Officer Justin Volpe in the face. The punch enraged him. The black civilian who slugged the white cop, witnesses claim, escaped, and the cops grabbed Louima, a slow-moving black face.

"The white cops started with some racial stuff," Abner whispered. "They said, 'Why do you niggers come to this country if you can't speak English?'"

Louima said one cop told him to shut up, pushed him to the ground, and handcuffed him. He claimed he was put in a patrol car and driven away and that the cops stopped to beat him twice before he got to the precinct. He recalled: "One cop was yelling, 'You scum, I am going to teach you to respect a cop!'"

Louima claimed that at the precinct he was taken in front of the desk sergeant and strip-searched.

"My pants were down at my ankles, in front of the other cops," he said. "They took my identification and money. They walked me over to the bathroom and closed the door. There were two cops. One said, 'If you yell or make any noise, I will kill you.' One cop held me and the other one stuck the stick up my behind. He said, 'Take this, nigger.' I was screaming. Then the cop pulled it out. There was blood and shit on it. He shoved it in my mouth, broke my teeth, and said, 'That's your shit, nigger.'"

"What kind of nightstick are we talking about?" I asked. I leaned over so I could show him two nightsticks I had drawn in my notebook one handled and the other straight.

"Not a nightstick," Louima said. "It was the plunger from the policemen's bathroom."

No one in the room had heard this detail before. Until this moment, we all thought he was talking about a nightstick.

"How do you know?"

"I seen the rubber thing on the bottom."

The cops had their name tags covered, he said, with black mourning bands—ordinarily worn to honor a dead cop—but Louima knew a name from his arrest report: Justin Volpe.

"How big was the cop who did this to you?"

Louima measured me from his bed. "Smaller than you," he said. That made him under six feet. "He has black hair, shaved on the side and spiked on top. No mustache."

After an hour, I put my notebook in my pocket and leaned close to him again. The shame of suffering this injury and having to relay his story to a stranger in front of his wife and father must have been overwhelming.

"You will be okay now," I said.

"I know," he said, checking his wife at his left shoulder. He said this for her. This was the only lie he told that I recognized. I walked to the foot of the bed and stood with his lawyers, who I noticed had their hands balled into fists.

I couldn't remember an afternoon like this in the newspaper business. The curtains were drawn, and Louima's family gathered around him to pray, and I stepped back shaking. Before this, I'd always been content just to wade through injustice, write the column, and move on to the next misery. But as I stood there, I wanted to avenge Abner Louima.

"This is not a corruption case," Figeroux said quietly. "This is a torture case. Cops are going to jail."

The victim's information was pretty specific. This was an easy case, I realized, but you had to work it. Identification was not going to be a problem.

"You have to get investigators in here with photographs of cops on the midnight tour."

"We know," Figeroux said. "But the nurses say Internal Affairs just came and left yesterday. They did nothing."

"Where is the Brooklyn DA?" I asked.

"I can't get him on the phone."

That was about right. Charles J. Hynes, the Brooklyn district attorney, is a good lawyer, but ordinarily you have to shine a television light on an injustice to get his attention.

"You call him right now and tell him a reporter was here and I'm going to put this on tomorrow's front page."

They called just as I left and a hospital administrator was padding down the hallway to throw me out. I thanked the cop at the door. Within five hours, investigators from the DA's squad and the NYPD's Internal Affairs Bureau were at the hospital, and two cops were suspended.

The city was reeling by noon the following day. The mayor and the police commissioner were having back-to-back press conferences, and every TV crew in the city was rushing to Coney Island Hospital. As it happened, I had to see a doctor for a consultation at Memorial Sloan-Kettering Cancer Center. The waiting room here is always hopelessly crowded with hopelessly ill people. It seems impossible that there can be this many tragedies gathered quietly in a single room. But, I have noticed, even in a room with sixty patients, I never see anyone reading a newspaper. Even on a day like today, when the entire city was consumed by a story, news of the world does not intrude, or even matter, in the cancer ward.

A half hour later, I was in the examining room, waiting to see a doctor regarded as the world's leading authority on colorectal cancer, when my beeper began to vibrate. Louima's lawyer wanted to speak to me. I'm not sure I would die for a story, but this choice was fairly easy. My CAT scans seemed less important than Abner Louima's X rays. I left an afternoon of further dread to write a second page-one story.

That night, my friend Marvyn Kornberg called to say he had a new client, Justin Volpe. In the background, I could hear his wife protesting. Marvyn is an incredibly capable lawyer. We have worked together on many stories over the years, put cops in jail and gotten them out. He has a sign in his office above Queens Boulevard that reads, KORNBERG'S RULE OF LAW: PRESUMPTION OF INNO-CENCE COMMENCES WITH PAYMENT OF RETAINER. I don't like all of his clients any more than he likes all of my columns, but I'll listen. I did the first interview with Joey Buttafuoco, whom he represented, and was so repulsed by the man and his story that I told Marvyn, "I never want to see that guy again."

It seems odd when I look back at the turns our lives have taken. Marvyn and I were sick at about the same time and helped each other recover. Marvyn had his prostate removed last year but is completely healthy now, a ferocious warrior.

"My bank just presumed Volpe innocent," Marvyn reported. I laughed. Kornberg rose to prominence in 1985, representing a black kid who had been tortured by cops with an electric stun gun. It was the sickest case of police brutality in New York before Louima. Now he was on the other side.

His wife was mad at him for taking the case. Kornberg, I knew, was just happy to be back in the middle of things. "This is what I do," he explained.

"Marvyn," I said, "it's great to be alive."

Within a week of the crime, I met Justin Volpe at an office in Queens. He offered his hand, and I studied it. It was small but powerful looking. I remembered what Louima had said about a cop in gloves in the bathroom. The brutal cop, he remembered, didn't want shit on his white hands.

"It is good to meet you," the suspect said. "I always wanted to talk to you."

He was shorter than me, shorter than I had imagined. His hair was black, as Louima described, long on top and shaved on the sides. He was obviously a weight lifter and was built like a fire hydrant. He was dressed in a white linen shirt and jeans. There was an orange stain on his left shoulder, and he looked as if he'd been sleeping on a bag of Chee-Tos.

I'd known that Volpe had a black girlfriend, Susan, and now they were meeting for the first time since he'd been arrested. They kissed and hugged. It was confusing, and even disconcerting, to see them together. We moved into a room that was terrifyingly small, about the size of the Seventieth Precinct bathroom.

"I am perfectly willing to believe this is a lie," I told Volpe.

"It didn't happen the way they are saying," he said. "Now I know what it is like to be falsely accused."

"Then what happened?"

"It wasn't me," Volpe replied.

"Then who was it?"

"If it happened, it wasn't me."

That is as far as we could go on that subject. Volpe wanted to talk only if I agreed not to press him on the facts. The interview was like walking on ice the morning after the first deep freeze. He was remarkably controlled.

"That picture on the front page makes me look like a gangster," he complained.

But when I looked at Volpe, I saw the reflection of a lot of rogue cops I'd met over the last ten years. As with so many of them, there was a false graciousness to him. They offer their hand, as if to be rescued. They want you to save them. I looked at him and I felt tired.

The entire scene was preposterous. Volpe was holding his girl-friend's hand, their black and white fingers, and lives, intertwined.

"I will do anything to protect her," he said. "I don't care about me."

In the corner, Volpe's father, Robert, wearing a black silk shirt, looked pained. He had been a detective, even a hero cop. His son isn't just accused of doing this to his family. He did this to the old man's department. Robert Volpe has seen convictions in his own cases with less evidence.

"You spend your whole life on one side of the law, and you wake up with a son who is Public Enemy Number One," Robert said. "You always expect a knock at the door and for someone to say one of your sons was shot, but not this."

I wasn't buying. Kornberg wasn't going to like the story I'd write, but he would get over it. I mentioned to Volpe the name of his lawyer's last infamous client, Joey Buttafuoco. Volpe turned his face into a pitted prune.

"Oh, that fellow," Volpe said, sneering. Bad guy.

I laughed at the absurdity. The most hated cop in America looks down on Joey Buttafuoco.

Two days after the attack, Susan had reported for work in the Seventieth Precinct, walked past the front desk and up the stairs to the clerical office. She'd felt the eyes of the precinct on her again as she climbed the stairs.

She'd thought she was past that kind of gossip. She is a black woman in love, she told me, with a white cop. The black cops, she said, see her as a fool; the white cops see her as a whore.

And then someone told her that one of the Seven-O's cops had shoved a bathroom plunger up a prisoner's rectum. "They say Justin did it," the coworker said.

Their life together started to unravel there, but it took a while for her to recognize it. As we talked now in that Queens office, she was struggling. She hoped, almost painfully, that the story was a lie. "If it happened, he didn't do it," Susan said. "Justin wouldn't do this to our life."

It isn't often as a reporter that you take your knowledge directly to the subject of a story. But as Justin moved to the other side of the room that day, I tried it. I was trying to tell her with my questions and demeanor that she should get out of the relationship now. I wanted to warn her out of the house.

"We want to be married, still," she said. The girl grew up in a Coney Island housing project, and Justin Volpe had been her heroic prince.

She didn't realize yet that her world had already changed forever. I felt an odd connection with her. Not so long ago, I'd felt the same vertigo she was feeling when my own future had been suddenly turned upside down.

She folded her hands on her lap and moaned. On this Sunday morning, after church, she was wearing a short black skirt and a white blouse. She had a simple diamond-stud earring in each of her lobes. "If he did this, he did it to our children," she said. "Impossible."

Her bravery in defending an accused lover was humbling, but I wanted her to see what I saw.

"Can you imagine him doing this?"

"I can't imagine being married to this story," she replied.

I caught a whiff of flowers, maybe lilacs, as she flattened her hands on the table and sighed.

I said, "Susan, people are going to say this sounds like the cliche: 'I can't be a racist. Some of my best friends are black.'"

"I know," she said. "But [Justin] is not an evil person."

"Maybe he snapped," I said.

"You can't lead one life and then do that in the precinct bathroom," she replied. "Racism isn't some switch you can turn on and off."

"Maybe Justin did," I suggested.

"We talked about racism many times," she said. "Cried about it at night. Where would we live? How would we raise our kids? We both know what the score is."

She started to cry. And I was uncomfortable. I didn't know how far to take this. I didn't like this role, and I didn't like how her own failing sense of denial made me feel.

I tried to be a reporter again. Although Louima hadn't said it to me, he'd been quoted as saying that the cop who attacked him said, "Dinkins time is over. It's Giuliani time." I asked Susan if she'd ever heard Volpe compare the current and former mayors.

"No," she said, laughing. "Never. [Justin] is not a political person. The thing about its being Giuliani time is silly."

And then she brought a hand to her face. "We thought it was our time," she said.

Once the first round of arrests were made and federal investigators began to take over the case, the story moved on, but without me. The case of Abner Louima went national and then international. Police brutality became a major political issue again. Louima himself remained in the hospital for two months, making a painful and slow recovery, while the talk-show hosts made the most of his ghastly abuse.

One afternoon, in the middle of all this, after hundreds of readers, reporters, and cops called to thank me for getting the story started, I was driving home alone, and I started to cry. I'm embarrassed to admit this even now. I don't think I've cried on a story since Brian O'Regan committed suicide.

My reaction that time was pretty straightforward. But I'm not sure why I got so emotional, so suddenly, this time. In part, it was relief after all the tension and anger and anxiety. This story was a life-changing crisis for so many of the people involved in it, especially for Abner Louima and Susan. The crisis would continue for them but not for me.

I also cried because my self proclaimed last cop story was over, and I didn't want to move on just yet. I would miss the adrenaline rush of winning a news story and the righteous indignation you allow yourself when you write something that actually repairs an injustice.

In some ways, this had been my biggest cop story. Almost like homering in my last at bat. It had changed the case, and it had changed the city somewhat. It had changed me a little, too. Yes, I'd miss the rush. But I also had a better sense of completion than I'd had before I got that phone message. And more confidence to move on.

I could return to my doctors' offices now, and to my familiar dread. That was certainly another factor behind my tears. This story had been a small crisis for me, too, pulling me out of my own life for a time. But that time was over.

When I got home the other day, I had another message on my voice mail. This time, it was from my editor. He'd read the first draft of my novel, and he says we are on our way to another life.

from Rogues' Gallery
by Thomas Byrnes

Thomas Byrnes (1842–1910) as chief of New York's Detective Bureau between 1880 and 1895 terrorized the city's underworld. His Rogues' Gallery, published in 1886, profiled many of America's top criminals. This selection describes intriguing unsolved murders of late-nineteenth-century New York.

The Murder of Doras Doyen, alias Helen Jewett

Although fifty years have passed since the notorious and beautiful young woman, Doras Doyen, otherwise known as Helen Jewett, was mysteriously butchered in her bed at No. 41 Thomas Street in this city, the brutal and unavenged crime has not been forgotten. Many old residents still recall with horror the cruel murder of the fair cyprian, which was committed early on the morning of April 12, 1836. Doras Doyen was born in Augusta, Maine, and at the time of her tragic death was but twenty-three years of age. Her many charms were thus described by an able writer, at the time of the murder:

"She was a shade below the middle height, but of a form of exquisite symmetry, which, though voluptuously turned in every perceptible point, was sufficiently dainty in its outline to give her the full advantage of a medium stature to the eye. Her complexion was that of a clear brown, bearing in it all the voluptuous ardor of that shade.

"Her features were not what might be termed regular, but there was a harmony in their expression which was inexpressibly charming; the nose was rather small, which was a fault; the mouth was rather large, but the full richness of its satin lips and the deep files of ivory infantry which crescented within their rosy lines redeemed all its latitudinal excess; while her large, black, steady eyes, streaming now with glances of precocious knowledge, and anon languishing with meditation or snapping with mischievousness, gave the whole picture a peculiar charm which entitled it to the renown of one of the most fascinating faces that ever imperiled a susceptible observer.

"In disposition this lovely creature was equal to her form. She was frank and amiable. Her heart was kind to excess to all who required her assistance, though the ardor of her temperament rendered her amenable to fiercest sentiments of passion."

A young clerk in a Maiden Lane store, named Richard P. Robinson, was among the many admirers of the comely Helen Jewett. He was strikingly handsome, having a frank, boyish face that was well set off by curling hair of golden brown. Robinson, though but eighteen years of age, was an *habitue* of the fast resorts in the city, where he was commonly known as "Frank Rivers." The long Spanish cloak which he wore jauntily about his shapely person became, after the murder of his mistress, the rage among the young men about town, and was known as the "Robinson Cloak."

It was at a theatre that Helen Jewett and Richard P. Robinson met one night by chance. The clerk defended her against the advances of a drunken ruffian and was rewarded with an invitation to call on her at the house of a Mrs. Berry in Duane Street, known to the wild young men of the day as the "Palais de la Duchesse Berri." There Helen received him in an apartment that would have done credit to the palace of Cleopatra. Other visits soon followed, and within a few weeks her passing fancy for the handsome youth ripened into the maddest infatuation.

For a time all went well, but at last rumors began to reach Helen's ears that she was but a sharer in her admirer's affections. Determined to discover the truth she disguised herself as a young man, and posting herself in front of the Maiden Lane store in which Robinson was employed waited till evening, and followed him first to his boarding-house in Dey Street and from there to a house in Broome Street, where she found him in the company of a rival siren.

Mad with jealousy Helen threw herself on the woman and struck her repeatedly in the face, her diamond rings drawing blood at every blow. She repented her violence and wrote to her lover a few days afterwards imploring him to forgive and return to her. A reconciliation followed, but within a few months, Helen, furious at the discovery of some fresh perfidy on the part of Robinson, taunted him with having caused the death of a young girl whom he had wronged and then deserted. Terrified at the consequences of exposure he professed to be ready to do anything that Helen wished, and finally purchased her silence by promising to marry her. Once more all went well until Helen learned that Robinson not only did not intend to keep his promise but was on the eve of being married to a young lady of wealth and position. In a fury she wrote him a letter threatening the most dire consequences if he failed to keep faith with her.

There is little doubt now that that letter sealed the fate of Helen Jewett. Her life only stood between Robinson and fortune. On April 10, 1836, the day preceding the murder, Robinson received a note from Helen begging him to call on her that night and containing a hint of the terrible penalty in case of a refusal to do so. He replied, promising to call the next night.

The house of Mrs. Townsend, No. 41 Thomas Street, an establishment famous for the magnificence of its appointments from one end of the country to the other, was the place where Helen was then living. Robinson, enveloped in his long Spanish cloak, rang the bell of this house between nine and ten o'clock on the night of Saturday, April 11, 1836. At the door the clerk was met by his young mistress, who was heard to exclaim joyously: "Oh, my dear Frank, how glad I am that you have come!"

Helen an hour afterwards from the head of the stairs called for a bottle of champagne. When Mrs. Townsend brought the bottle of wine up-stairs the young woman received it from her at the room door. That was the last time the poor girl was seen alive.

The inmates of the house one by one retired, and at one o'clock on that Sunday morning all was still. Marie Stevens, who occupied a room directly opposite that of Helen's, was aroused an hour later by a noise that sounded like that of a blow or a heavy fall. It was followed by a long and heavy moan. Getting up she listened at the door. All was then as silent as the grave. Presently she heard the door of Helen's apartment open gently and the sound of feet passing along the hall. Cautiously opening her door she saw a tall figure, wrapped in a long cloak and holding a small lamp, glide down the staircase. Then she returned to her room.

Mrs. Townsend at three o'clock had occasion to go down stairs, and found a glass lamp belonging to Helen still burning on a table in the parlor. Looking around she discovered that the back door was open, and after calling out twice "Who's there?" fastened it and went up-stairs to Helen's room. The door was ajar, and as she opened it a dense volume of reeking black smoke drove her back and almost overpowered her. Her screams of terror roused the house in an instant, and several of the inmates rushed to the spot and attempted to force their way through the smoke. The draught from the open door at that moment caused the smoldering fire to burst into flames, whose flickering light revealed to the horror-stricken women the form of the ill-fated Helen lying bathed in blood in the centre of the room. Her fair forehead was almost divided by a ghastly axe-stroke. The bed linen in which her form was half enveloped was burning brightly. A sickening odor of scorched flesh pervaded the apartment. The awful discovery redoubled the excitement in the house. The women screamed with terror, and in a few minutes three policemen rushed in. With their assistance the fire was soon extinguished.

Helen Jewett's body, clad in a dainty night-dress, lay with the face towards the bed; one arm lay across the breast and the other was raised over the head. The left side from the waist up was burned to a crisp. The examination of the remains showed that death had been caused instantly by the stroke of the hatchet on the right temple, and that the burning had taken place after death.

The room in which the tragedy was enacted was a marvel of luxury. It was filled with magnificent furniture, mirrors, splendid paintings and objects of art, and contained many rare and beautiful volumes.

The trail of the assassin was plainly marked. In the yard was picked up a blood-stained hatchet, and close by the rear fence lay the long Spanish cloak which Robinson invariably wore. The murderer after scaling the fence had found himself in the rear of a small frame house inhabited by negroes. He had forced his way into the cellar and from there had made his exit into the street, down which he was seen to run at full speed by a negro woman, who had been awakened by the noise made in forcing open the door.

Robinson was found apparently fast asleep with his room-mate, James Tow. He showed no emotion when told of the murder, and merely remarked, "This is bad business," as he quietly rose and dressed himself. While he was doing so the policeman noticed on the knees and seat of his trousers were marks of whitewash such as might have been received while scaling the fence in Mrs. Townsend's yard. When confronted with the body he retained the most perfect self-possession and turned away repeating, "This is a bad business."

Robinson's trial began on June 2, 1836, and lasted five days. The court room was packed to suffocation every day of the trial. So strongly did sympathy set for the prisoner in some quarters, that the fast young men of the day flocked to the trial in crowds, wearing in his honor glazed caps such as he habitually wore, which were long afterwards known as "Frank Rivers" caps.

District-Attorney Phoenix conducted the prosecution, assisted by Mr. Robert Morris. The prisoner was defended by Mr. Ogden Hoffman, Mr. William M. Price and Mr. Maxwell.

The weight of testimony was overwhelmingly against the accused. Fortunately for him, Marie Stevenson, the woman who saw him leaving Helen Jewett's room, was found dead in her bed before the trial began.

The cloak was proved to be Robinson's, and the hatchet was identified as having been taken from the store where he was employed. The string which was tied round its handle was shown to have formed a part of the cord belonging to his cloak. His trousers, marked with whitewash, were also put in evidence. A drug clerk swore that the prisoner, under the name of Douglas, had attempted to purchase arsenic from him ten days previous to the murder.

Mr. Hoffman made a sentimental but powerful appeal in the prisoner's behalf and undertook to prove by the testimony of Robert Furlong, a grocer at the corner of Cedar and Nassau streets, that the accused had been in his store until a quarter past ten on the night of the murder and therefore could not have entered the Thomas Street house between nine and ten, as was sworn to by Mrs. Townsend.

Furlong committed suicide two weeks after the murder by leaping from the deck of a vessel into the North River.

The rest of the defense consisted of attempts to impeach the veracity of the inmates of the Thomas Street house. The colored woman who saw the prisoner escape from the cellar door was spirited away before the trial began.

On the evening of the fifth day the case was given to the jury, who, in spite of the tremendous array of testimony brought forward by the prosecution and the feeble character of the defense, brought in a verdict of "not guilty" after a very short deliberation.

It was generally believed that some of the jurymen had been corrupted. The verdict was received with a tremendous outbreak of enthusiasm among the glazed-cap sympathizers of the prisoner, and the court adjourned amid a scene of the wildest confusion.

Robinson immediately left for Texas, where he died a few years afterwards.

The Murder of Mary Cecilia Rogers

"The Mystery of Marie Roget," Edgar Allen Poe's famous story, founded on the mysterious murder of Mary Rogers, "the pretty cigar girl," has made that tragedy known wherever the English language is spoken. Mary Cecilia Rogers was the only daughter of a respectable widow who kept a boarding-house for clerks in Nassau Street. She lived under her mother's roof until she was twenty years of age, when John Anderson, the famous tobacco merchant, heard of her marvelous beauty and conceived the idea of making her serve as an attraction in his store on Broadway, near Thomas Street. This was in 1840.

As "the pretty cigar girl," Mary became famous. Custom flocked to the store. The young swells of the time made the shop a lounging-place, and vied with each other in attempts to win the favor of the divinity of the counter. Her conduct, however, appears to have been a model of modest decorum. She was lavish in her smiles, but repelled all undue advances with a decision that checked the boldest of *roués*.

Once only did the breath of suspicion attach to her good name. She disappeared one day from the store, and was absent for a week, when she returned and answered all inquiries with the statement that she had been visiting friends in the country. A widely circulated rumor, however, had it that Mary had been seen several times during her absence with a tall, well-dressed man of dark complexion. Who this man was has never been ascertained, but it was afterwards rumored that on the day on which she was supposed to have been murdered a man answering to that description was seen in company with her.

A week after her return to the store she suddenly resigned her position and went home to assist her mother in household duties. It was soon afterwards announced that she was engaged to be married to Daniel Payne, a young clerk who boarded in her mother's house.

On the beautiful morning of Sunday, July 25, 1841, Mary Rogers was last seen alive. At ten o'clock she knocked at Payne's door, and told him that she was going to spend the day with a Mrs. Downing, in Bleecker Street. Payne replied that he would call for her and bring her home in the evening. A furious thunder-storm, however, broke out in the afternoon, and during the evening the rain fell in torrents. Payne, who was evidently a rather careless lover, failed to keep his engagement, supposing that his betrothed could just as well spend the night at her friend's house. Next morning he went to his work as usual. When afternoon came and Mary did not return, her mother, who took it for granted that the girl had been storm-bound for the night at Mrs.

Downing's, became seriously alarmed. When Payne came home to dinner, and learned that Mary was still absent, he started at once for Mrs. Downing's house. To his amazement, he was told that she had not been there on Sunday. The police were notified, and a general search was made. So well known was the girl that the news of her disappearance created a great sensation. No trace was found of her until the following Wednesday, when some fishermen, setting their nets off Castle Point, Hoboken, found the body floating near the shore, not far from a refreshment saloon known as "Sybil's Cave."

The corpse was frightfully disfigured, the face having been entirely destroyed, evidently with repeated blows of some blunt instrument. Round the waist was fastened a stout cord, to the other end of which a heavy stone was attached. Encircling her neck was a piece of lace torn from her dress, tied tightly enough to produce strangulation. Sunk deeply into the flesh of both wrists were the marks of cords. The hands were covered with light kid gloves, and a light bonnet hung by its ribbons around the neck. The clothing was horribly disordered and torn. A further examination disclosed the awful fact that a more fearful crime than murder had been committed.

It was established beyond all doubt that Mary had not gone to the house in Bleecker Street on the Sunday on which she disappeared. No one could be found who had seen her after she had left her home. At the end of a week not the faintest clew to the mystery had been found. The authorities then issued a proclamation calling on any persons who might be possessed of any knowledge of the girl's history or habits that might furnish a possible clew to a motive for her murder to come forward. The next day the Coroner received an anonymous letter from a young man in Hoboken who declared that he had seen Mary in Hoboken on Sunday, but had not come forward before owing to what he termed "motives of perhaps criminal prudence."

The writer stated that while walking in the Elysian Fields, then a famous summer resort on Sunday afternoons, he had seen a boat pull out from the New York side containing six rough-looking men and a well-dressed girl, whom he recognized as Mary Rogers. She and her companions left the boat on the beach and went into the woods. The writer was surprised to see her in the company of such rough-looking characters, and noticed that she evidently went with them willingly, laughing merrily as she walked away from the shore. They had scarcely disappeared in the woods when a second boat put out from New York and was pulled rapidly across the river by three handsomely-dressed gentlemen. One of them leaped ashore, and meeting two other gentlemen who were waiting on the beach, excitedly asked them if they had seen a young woman and six men land from a boat a few minutes before. On being told that they had, and on the direction they had taken being pointed out to him, he asked whether the men had used any violence towards the girl. He was told that she had apparently gone with them willingly, and he then, without making any further remark, returned to his boat, which was at once headed for New York.

The author of this letter was never discovered, but the letter was printed in the newspapers, and the next day the two gentlemen who had been walking on the beach came forward and corroborated the story. They both knew Mary Rogers by sight, and said that the girl who entered the woods with the six roughs resembled her closely, but they were not sufficiently near to be able to positively affirm that it was she. The next important piece of evidence came from a stage-driver named Adams, who, after allowing several weeks to elapse, testified that on the fatal Sunday he had seen Mary arrive in Hoboken, at the Bull's Ferry, accompanied by a tall, well-dressed man of dark complexion, and go with him to a road-house near the Elysian Fields known as "Nick Mullen's." Mrs. Loss, the keeper of the house, remembered that such a man had come to her place with a young woman on the day in question, and had gone into the adjoining woods after partaking of refreshments. Soon after their departure she heard a woman's scream coming from the woods, but as the place was the resort of questionable characters, and such sounds were of frequent occurrence, she gave no further thought to the matter.

The exact spot on which there is no doubt the hapless girl was brutally ill-treated and then butchered was discovered by Mrs. Loss's little children on September 25, exactly two months after the murder. While playing in the woods, they found in a dense thicket a white petticoat, a silk scarf, a parasol, and a linen handkerchief marked with the initials "M.R." The ground all around was torn up and the shrubbery trampled as if the spot had been the scene of a terrific struggle. Leading out of the thicket was a broad track, such as might have been made by dragging a body through the bushes. It led in the direction of the river, but was soon lost in the woods. All the articles were identified as having been worn by Mary on the day of her disappearance.

Every effort was made to trace the "tall, dark-complexioned man," but without success. It was rumored that he was a young naval officer. Mrs. Loss and several witnesses who claimed to have seen him with Mary during the time that she was absent from the cigar store, noticed that he seemed to be a person of a considerably higher social grade than his companion. It was generally believed at the time, that the murdered girl's mother knew more about her daughter's mysterious admirer than she chose to tell.

Daniel Payne never recovered from the shock caused by the awful death of his betrothed. The blow evidently affected his mind, and within a few weeks after the murder he committed suicide.

The crime was ever the subject of more searching and prolonged investigation, but in spite of everything that could be done, the veil of mystery has never been penetrated that shrouded the fate of "the pretty cigar girl."

The Burdell Murder

A severe storm passed over this city on the night of Friday, January 30, 1857, and as the rain was falling and the wind moaning about ten o'clock a piercing shriek of "Murder!" rang through quiet, aristocratic Bond Street. A gentleman living at No. 36 Bond Street heard the cry, but as he was unable to tell from what direction it came, and as it was not repeated, he closed his door and retired. The city was shocked next morning by the discovery of the mysterious murder of Dr. Harvey Burdell, a wealthy but eccentric dentist who resided at No. 31 Bond Street.

Dr. Burdell owned the house, of which he was in the habit of letting the greater part, reserving for his own use only the reception parlors, operating room and bedroom on the second floor.

In person he was a fine portly man of middle age. A man of strong passions and ungovernable temper, he had few friends. In spite of his invested wealth, which was considerable, and his large and remunerative practice, his mode of life was so penurious as almost to entitle him to the name of miser. His house was usually let to persons of questionable character, a class among which he had many intimates.

He kept his own servant, an extraordinary girl, who, although in most respects an ignorant creature, possessed a singular facility for acquiring foreign languages. French, German and Spanish she spoke with fluency, having devoted all her spare time to study. She was devotedly attached to the doctor.

On May 1 preceding the murder Mrs. Cunningham, a buxom widow with two daughters, took possession of the house. Like others of the doctor's tenants, her reputation was none of the best. The other inmates of the house were John J. Eckel, who was generally supposed to be paying court to Mrs. Cunningham; Snodgrass, a youth of eighteen, who was very attentive to the two daughters, Helen and Augusta; Daniel Ulman and Hannah Conlan, the cook.

Mrs. Cunningham appears to have divided her affection between Mr. Eckel and the doctor, each of whom did his utmost to supplant the other, with the result of causing frequent uproars in the house.

On October 28, 1856, Mrs. Cunningham was married by the Rev. Dr. Marvine—to whom it has never been clearly proved. The certificate states that it was to Dr. Burdell, but it is by no means certain that he was not personated on the occasion. As his lawful wife, Mrs. Cunningham would, of course, have been entitled to her legal share of his estate in the event of his sudden death.

Whether they were married or not, however, furious outbreaks between the couple continued to be of frequent occurrence, and matters finally came to such a pass that the doctor determined to look out for another tenant.

While Dr. Burdell was out at dinner on the evening preceding the murder Mrs. Cunningham asked Hannah, the cook, what woman it was that she had shown through the house that day. Hannah replied that it was the lady who was about to take the house.

"When does she take possession?" asked Mrs. Cunningham.

"The first of May," replied the servant.

"He better be careful; he may not live to sign the papers," was the reply.

What time the doctor came home that night is unknown, but the exact moment of the murder is fixed at half-past ten o'clock, the time when the cry of murder was heard.

It was eight o'clock in the morning when the boy came, according to custom, to make the fires in the doctor's rooms. He brought a scuttle of coals from the cellar and setting it down opened the doors of the front room on the second floor. It struck against something which seemed heavy and yet yielding. The boy, who was whistling merrily, pushed it back and stepped into the room. The sight which met his gaze struck him rigid with horror. On its back, with arms outstretched and eyes staring blankly at the ceiling, lay the body of the owner of the house, the head resting in a pool of blood. Blood was everywhere—on the walls, carpets, furniture, splashed five feet high on the door and spurted to the very ceiling. The boy's terror found vent in a shriek that was heard by every soul in the house. Mrs. Cunningham, with her family and boarders, were quietly at breakfast in the basement, apparently all unconscious of the awful scene up-stairs.

On learning what had occurred she gave way to a wild outburst of grief. Eckel exhibited little concern.

The room in which the body was found had evidently been the scene of a terrific life and death struggle. The furniture was tossed about in every direction and hardly an article was found to be free from the stain of blood.

No less than fifteen distinct stab wounds, any one of which was sufficient to have caused death, were counted on the corpse, which was fully clothed. They had the appearance of having been inflicted with a long, narrow dagger.

Around the neck, sinking deeply into the flesh, was the mark of a small cord, showing that strangulation had first been attempted. This failing, resort had been had to the dagger.

The gas was burning full. The bed had not been slept in. A complete examination of the house disclosed the startling fact that there were blood marks on the hall, on the stairs, in the lower bed, on the front door, even in the attic room and on the very steps leading to the scuttle in the roof.

The spirit of murder seemed to have stalked through the house, leaving everywhere the gory traces of its fingers.

At the Coroner's inquest, which was held in the house, medical experts testified that the strokes of the dagger had been delivered by a left-handed person. Mrs. Cunningham was left-handed. The verdict charged Mrs. Cunningham and Eckel with the murder, and they were conveyed to the Tombs.

The case against Eckel was dismissed, but Mrs. Cunningham was placed on trial on the 6th of May. She was ably defended by Henry L. Clinton. District-Attorney A. Oakey Hall conducted the prosecution, but was unable to establish anything against the accused except the existence of a motive. The trial lasted three days, and the jury, after deliberating for an hour and a half, returned a verdict of "not guilty."

Mrs. Cunningham, who had assumed the name of Burdell, immediately returned to her home at No. 31 Bond Street. Not satisfied with having escaped the penalty of the crime, which there is little doubt that she committed, and having become entitled by right of dower to a third of the murdered man's wealth, she determined to gain possession of the whole of it, and in furtherance of this object conceived the remarkable idea of palming off on the authorities an infant heir to the estate.

A Dr. Uhl was taken into her confidence, with the understanding that he was to receive $1,000 for his share in the transaction, but the doctor promptly acquainted the District Attorney with the particulars of the widow's ingenious little plan.

Mr. Hall entered eagerly into the spirit of what appeared to him a huge joke and actually undertook to supply the necessary infant. In due time Mrs. Cunningham announced that all was ready for the interesting denouement.

Disguised as a Sister of Charity she went to a house in Elm Street, where the infant, borrowed by Mr. Hall from Bellevue Hospital, was delivered to her by Dr. Uhl, and carried it to Bond Street in a basket. The next day the arrival of the heir was duly announced, and then Mr. Hall and a policeman stepped in and arrested the "mother."

She was soon afterwards, however, set at liberty. The little girl who was used in carrying out this remarkable fraud was named Matilda Anderson. She and her real mother were placed on exhibition at Barnum's Museum.

Mrs. Cunningham soon afterwards went to California. Eckel was imprisoned in the Albany penitentiary for complicity in some whiskey frauds in Brooklyn and died there.

The house in Bond Street, which is but little altered in appearance, is frequently shown to strangers as the scene of the "mysterious Cunningham–Burdell murder."

The Murder of Benjamin Nathan

The most celebrated, and certainly the most mysterious, murder that has ever been perpetrated in New York City was committed on the night of July 28, 1870, during the fitting accompaniment of the most terrific thunder-storm that ever visited the city. While the thunder rolled, the lightning lit up the heavens with blinding flashes, and the rain fell in torrents, Mr. Benjamin Nathan, a wealthy stock-broker, was foully murdered in his handsome mansion, No. 12 West Twenty-third Street.

Mr. Nathan's family, with the exception of his two sons, Frederick and Washington, whose business kept them in the city, were at the time absent at his country seat in Morristown, N.J. Mr. Nathan was in the habit of coming into town every day to go to his office in Broad Street. On the evening of Thursday, July 28, he left the house of his brother-in-law, in Nineteenth Street, at seven o'clock, saying that he intended to spend the night with his sons in Twenty-third Street, instead of going out to Morristown. His son Washington was then with him, but parted with his father in the street.

The old gentleman went directly home. A bed had been fitted up for his use in the centre of the front parlor on the second floor. Adjoining this room was the library, which was connected with it by a short passage. In the front room was a writing-desk and a small safe, in addition to the ordinary furniture.

A few minutes after six o'clock next morning, a policeman who was patrolling Twenty-third Street heard screams of murder near the corner of Fifth Avenue, and running in that direction, saw two young men standing in their night-dresses on the stoop of the Nathan mansion.

One of them presented a ghastly appearance, blood covering the front of his white night-dress, and even his bare feet were smeared with blood.

"Come in!" they shouted. "Father's been murdered!"

He hurriedly entered the house, and going up-stairs, was shown by the distracted young men the mangled form of their father stretched on the floor of the front room, close to the door leading into the library.

The corpse presented the most horrifying appearance. It lay on its back, clad only in a white night-dress, with arms and legs outstretched. The head lay in a great pool of blood which flowed from numerous gaping wounds in the skull.

Blood was spattered over the door, door-posts, and adjoining furniture. Close to the body lay an overturned chair, also smeared with blood, which had been placed in front of the writing-desk.

The door of the safe stood wide open. The key was missing. On the bed lay a small drawer taken from the safe. It contained nothing but a few copper coins. On the floor, near the desk, lay a small tin box containing papers, also taken from the safe.

The policeman hastened to summon assistance, and a thorough search of the premises was made. On the desk lay a partially-written check to the order of H. Lapsley & Co., on the Union National Bank. The "stub" in the check-book was marked "July 29—$10,000 subscription for 100 shares German-American Bank."

From the position of the corpse and the chair, it seemed evident that the old gentleman had been stricken down from behind while writing this check. The first blow must have been insufficient, for there were evidences of a struggle in the overturned furniture and the blood-stains that were distributed in every direction.

In addition to this, it was found that two of the fingers of the left hand had been fractured, evidently in warding off a blow. No less than fifteen wounds were counted on the head, most of them being on top and on the back of the skull. Brain matter, mingled with small splinters of bone, exuded in half a dozen places.

So much did the injuries vary in character, some having evidently been made with a blunt and others with a sharp instrument, that it was at first believed that they must have been inflicted with two weapons, and this led to the theory that more than one person had been concerned in the murder.

This view of the case, however, was disposed of when one of the policemen picked up, between the inner and outer doors of the front hall, an instrument known as a carpenter's "dog," covered with blood and hair. It consisted of a bar of iron about eighteen inches long, turned down and sharpened at each end, somewhat in the shape of a staple.

It was readily seen how with the sharp end of such a weapon the incised wounds could have been inflicted, while the other injuries were caused by blows from the blunt angle.

Simultaneously with the discovery of the weapon a bloody trail of naked footprints was found leading from the chamber of death, down the main staircase, to the front door and out on the stoop.

The discovery made a tremendous sensation among the searchers until Mr. Frederick Nathan explained that on being roused by the cry of his brother Washington, who discovered the body, he had rushed into the room and knelt beside it, thereby smearing his night-dress and feet with the blood. Finding that life was extinct, he had run down stairs to give the alarm, leaving the trail of blood with his naked feet.

The only persons in the house at the time were the two sons, who slept on the floor above their father; a servant-man, who occupied an adjoining room, and the house-keeper, who slept in the basement. None of these persons heard any noise during the night. Absolutely no trace could be discovered of the manner in which the assassin had gained access to the premises.

The announcement of the murder caused an excitement absolutely unparalleled. For days Twenty-third Street was fairly blocked with dense masses of people, who came to gaze at the windows of the room on the second floor. Stage-drivers either drove slowly past the house or pulled up altogether to give their passengers a chance to stare at the spot. Even private carriages drove slowly through the street all day, forming a long procession, their occupants leaning out of the windows to catch a glimpse of the scene.

Next day the Stock Exchange offered a reward of $10,000 for the arrest of the murderer, and Mayor Hall issued the following circular:

PRIVATE AND CONFIDENTIAL.—$47,000 REWARD.— PROCLAMATION.—THE MURDER OF MR. BENJAMIN NATHAN.

The widow having determined to increase the rewards heretofore offered by me (in my proclamation of July 29th), and no result having yet been obtained, and suggestions having been made that the rewards were not sufficiently distributive or specific, the offers in the previous proclamation are hereby superseded by the following:

A reward of $30,000 will be paid for the arrest and conviction of the murderer of Benjamin Nathan, who was killed in his house, No. 12 West Twenty-third Street, New York, on the morning of Friday, July 29th.

A reward of $1,000 will be paid for the identification and recovery of each and every one of three diamond shirt studs, which were taken from the clothing of the deceased on the night of the murder. Two of the diamonds weighed, together, 1, 1-2, 1-18, and 1-16 carats, and the other, a flat stone, showing nearly a surface of one carat, weighed 3-4 and 1-32. All three were mounted in skeleton settings, with spiral screws, but the color of the gold setting of the flat diamond was not so dark as the other two.

A reward of $1,500 will be paid for the identification and recovery of one of the watches, being the gold anchor hunting-case stem-winding watch, No. 5657, 19 lines, or about two inches in diameter, made by Ed. Perregaux; or for the chain and seals thereto attached. The chain is very massive, with square links and carries a pendant chain, with two seals, one of them having the monogram, "B. N.," cut thereon.

A reward of $300 will be given for information leading to the identification and recovery of an old-fashioned open-faced gold watch, with gold dial, showing rays diverging from the centre, and with raised figures believed to have been made by Tobias, and which was taken at the same time as the above articles.

A reward of $300 will be given for the recovery of a gold medal of about the size of a silver dollar, and which bears an inscription of presentation not precisely known, but believed to be either "To Sampson Simpson, President of the Jews' Hospital," or "To Benjamin Nathan, President of the Jews' Hospital."

A reward of $100 will be given for full and complete detailed information descriptive of this medal, which may be useful in securing its recovery.

A reward of $1,000 will be given for information leading to the identification of the instrument used in committing the murder, which is known as a "dog" or clamp, and is a piece of wrought iron about sixteen inches long, turned up for about an inch at each end, and sharp, such as is used by ship-carpenters, or post-trimmers, ladder-makers, pump-makers, sawyers, or by iron-moulders to clamp their flasks.

A reward of $800 will be given to the man who, on the

morning of the murder, was seen to ascend the steps and pick up a piece of paper lying there, and then walk away with it, if he will come forward and produce it.

Any information bearing upon the case may be sent to the Mayor, John Jourdan, Superintendent of Police City of New York, or to James J. Kelso, Chief Detective Officer.

The foregoing rewards are offered by the request of, and are guaranteed by me.

(Signed) EMILY G. NATHAN, Widow of B. Nathan.

The following reward has also been offered by the New York Stock Exchange:

$10,000.—The New York Stock Exchange offers a reward of Ten Thousand Dollars for the arrest and conviction of the murderer or murderers of Benjamin Nathan, late a member of said Exchange, who was killed on the night of July 28, 1870, at his house in Twenty-third Street, New York City.

J. L. BROWNELL, *Vice-Chairman Gov. Com*

D. C. HAYES, *Treasurer*

B. O. WHITE, *Secretary*

A. OAKEY HALL, MAYOR.

MAYOR'S OFFICE, NEW YORK, August 5, 1870.

Great importance was attached to the blood-stained "dog," and every effort was made to discover where it came from, but without success. It was a tool that is often used in building, and might have been left in the house years before by workmen. It certainly was not the kind of weapon that a deliberate assassin or professional burglar would have carried with him, and this suggested the theory that the murder had been committed by one of the inmates of the house.

Of one thing the police were perfectly sure—that the assassin, whoever he was was thoroughly acquainted with the premises. No one else, they argued, could have so completely covered up his tracks.

Tremendous was the sensation when it began to be whispered that Washington Nathan, then one of the handsomest and most popular young men in the highest New York society, was perhaps not free from the stain of his father's blood. The idea seemed too monstrous for belief, but there were not a few people who clung to it. There was some mystery about the young man's movements during the fatal night that he seemed indisposed to reveal. Then, too, he had been the first to discover the murder and the last one to see his father alive. In addition it was darkly hinted that Washington had much to gain by his father's death. The unhappy young man was closely cross-examined at the Coroner's inquest and fully accounted for every moment of his time from the hour he parted from his father up to a quarter-past twelve o'clock in the morning when he came home. His testimony was corroborated by that of Clara Dale, a young woman in whose company he had passed a portion of the night.

The day after the murder Patrick Devoy, a man employed to take care of the house of Prof. Samuel P. Morse, No. 5 West Twenty-second Street, told the police that at half-past ten o'clock on the night of the murder, a closed carriage had driven up to the entrance of the Nathan stables, which adjoined Professor Morse's house, and had remained there all through the furious storm, until nearly two o'clock in the morning, when it suddenly drove rapidly away.

A gentleman who had come in from Morristown with Mr. Nathan told a story of a rough-looking man who was said to have been seen loitering the evening before about the Nathan country-seat, and who occupied a seat in the same car near Mr. Nathan, and watched him closely until the train reached Hoboken. Nothing ever came of either of these clews.

To enumerate the hundreds of theories propounded would be impossible. While many detectives clung to the belief that the murder had been committed by a member of the household, others insisted that it was the work of a burglar who had secreted himself in the house, and being found by the victim, had slain him to prevent an outcry, while others again held such wild theories as that the deed had been done by some fellow broker who was a rival in business, or that some escaped lunatic had entered the house.

Interest in the murder of the banker was revived by the confession of the notorious burglar, John T. Irving, and the subsequent arrest of Billy Forrester and several other professional cracksmen. Irving in 1873, during a fit of remorse and while in San Francisco, delivered himself up to the authorities for the Nathan murder. He was brought on to this city and made a confession, and promised to produce the necessary corroborative evidence if the District Attorney would consent not to prosecute him for two burglaries—one at Green's pawnshop, No. 181 Bowery, where he had stolen diamonds worth $200,000, and the other at Casperfield's jewelry store. The agreement fell through, and the evidence of the crime was not forthcoming. Irving's confession ran as follows

"On or about the 15th day of May, 1870, I was passing through Madison Park with Daniel Kelly and Caleb Gunnion, otherwise known as George Abrahams, when our attention was called by Kelly to a man standing in the Park. We advanced towards him, and on reaching him the following conversation ensued, Kelly addressing the man:

" 'Well, McNally, what are you doing here? I have not seen you for a long time,'

" 'That's so,' responded McNally, 'and you are the last person I expected to meet. You have not been home long, have you?'

" 'No—a few months. What are you doing now?'

" 'I am at the old business again.'

"McNally took Kelly to one side, about six feet from ourselves. I never knew what transpired at that time; however, a portion of that conversation was overheard by both Gunnion and myself. I give it as follows: Kelly was standing with his back towards Twenty-third Street, McNally facing him. 'Where does your mother live, Mac?' Mac answered, 'Down Twenty-third Street,' pointing with his fingers towards Sixth Avenue. I had almost forgotten to explain how I came to call this man McNally. I and Gunnion were introduced to him by Kelly, at the time when we first came up to where he was sitting. Kelly, turning around toward us, said: 'Come, boys, let us go through Twenty-fourth Street and we will have a drink.' McNally refused, saying at the time that he was going home. We parted and went through Twenty-fourth Street to Eighth Avenue, taking an Eighth Avenue car, and leaving it at the corner of Hudson and Christopher streets. We went into a large hardware store on the same corner that we got out at, which was the northwest corner, and there purchased a bar of steel about four feet long, to be made up into tools. Taking the steel we started through Christopher Street for the Hoboken ferry, and passed over. While on that trip Kelly told me that he had made arrangements with McNally about a job which would turn out well. Nothing further was said until June about the matter, and then, for the first time, I was made aware of this job. I was then told by Kelly that the family was not at home, and that access to the premises could be readily obtained, as we would be let in, and work the safe without any further trouble. Gunnion was also present at this meeting, and it was decided that we work the place. In a very short space of time after this meeting I was arrested at my residence, No. 37 Garden Street, Hoboken, in connection with one Charles Carr, now in Sing Sing, for a robbery in Lispenard Street, where it was alleged that I had broken into and taken laces valued at $5,000; I had no connection with it, so I was discharged, but re-arrested for an attempt at burglary on Wilson & Green's pawn-broking establishment, corner Delancey and Bowery, and held to bail, which was procured, and I was released in the ——part of July, a day or two before the murder of Mr. Nathan. During my stay in the Tombs everything was arranged, so that when I came out all that was to be done was to get our tools and proceed to work. We agreed to meet at eight o'clock, in Madison Park. The evening previous to the morning of the murder we met, according to appointment, and found McNally awaiting us. Kelly took McNally aside, and, after about twenty minutes' conversation with him, he left, going towards Sixth Avenue. Kelly told us that we would have to wait for about ten minutes. He instructed us to follow one after another, a short distance apart, and if everything was right we were to move up close together, by a signal from the man at the gate by wiping his face with a pocket-handkerchief. All was clear, the man was at his post, and we entered the house by the basement door, Gunnion and myself going to the cellar, as we had been previously instructed to do. Kelly went up-stairs, and when all was ready he was to call us. I should judge, from the length of time that elapsed, we must have been in the cellar about four or five hours. It was a very stormy night out, which made the time drag along very slow. At last Kelly made his appearance, telling us to take off our shoes, which we did, and made our way up-stairs (three flights), entering at the side door at the front of the building. I think there was a taper burning. I noticed a person lying on the floor, about three or four feet from the door. In the small room things were scattered about. I stepped on something which at that time appeared to me like a pocket-book, and on picking it up it proved to be a memoranda, or Jewish calendar, with the following names:—Albert Cardozo, Dr. Leo, Samuel Lewis, corner Fourteenth Street; also papers, or rather — stock, which had been —; also Pacific Mail and some — bonds. I think the Pacific Mail has the name of J. Coke or — endorsed on them. Am not positive, but that name appears on some of the stock. In the aggregate the amount is $6,000; $273 in money was also obtained. The safe had been opened before we went up-stairs. There appeared to be a peculiar kind of odor in the house; something like kerosene or turpentine. Altogether I don't think we were in the rooms occupied by Mr. Nathan more than fifteen minutes, and about five of the time was spent by Kelly washing his hands off. I think he said he went to the bathroom. We stood waiting inside the room door for him, and I noticed finger-marks on the jam of the door, as if it were blood.

"Our next step was to descend to the lower part of the house, and there await a favorable opportunity to get out, knowing that we had to contend with more on the outside than on the inside. We waited at the foot of the basement stairs until half past five o'clock in the morning, and then went up to the front door, Kelly looking out of the door to see if all was clear. He passed us once, and we reached the street without being seen, but just as we were about to direct our steps toward Fifth Avenue, a man came along on the opposite side of the street with a dinner-pail in his hand; this man stooped down and picked up something like an envelope. As yet we had not made a start, and on looking at Kelly I observed blood on his shirt bosom, and told him of it. He went inside of the railing to adjust his vest so as to hide it, when Gunnion saw a young woman coming toward us from Fifth Avenue. Just then we made off toward her. I think I saw a person come toward one of the windows in the Fifth Avenue Hotel, on the third story, and look toward Sixth Avenue. We walked pretty fast, so as to get away as soon as possible, keeping on Twenty-third Street until we reached Third Avenue, knowing that would be our best policy, as the streets running east and west in the morning are never so closely watched at that time as the ones running north and south in that neighborhood. Third Avenue was reached in time for a car, and, without hailing it, we jumped aboard on the front platform, leaving the car at Houston Street. It was now after six o'clock, and people were coming and going in all directions. We went into a house on —— Street, and then and there, in the presence of two women, divided what we had got. Kelly seemed to be somewhat excited, and all at once said: 'You know that dog I got from Nick Jones. Well, I left it behind. Do you think it will cost us any trouble?' I said: 'I don't know. I believe Nick is all right. You had better see him, anyhow, in time.' He asked the elder of the two women to give him a shirt, which was done, and he told her to wash the one he had just taken off as soon as possible, and adding at the same time, 'Here is $20, and I will go see Nick Jones.' I left the house and went to my home in Rivington Street. I returned to wait for Kelly. He came back about ten o'clock the same morning. I believe Nick Jones was very much afraid of Kelly or his friends. I never knew of the exact amount of property taken, as Kelly denied all knowledge of the diamonds, which caused a rupture between us. Have had nothing to do with him since. Have heard since I came to New York that he was in Auburn prison; also heard that Gunnion was in prison. In October of the same year I visited Nick Jones at the Brooklyn Navy Yard by permission of the naval commander, he granting me a permit, as during working hours nobody is allowed to hold any communication with those who are employed therein. On this occasion Jones acted rather green, and when I spoke to him about Kelly he upbraided me for having introduced him to Kelly, saying that I had destroyed his peace of mind. I asked him in what respect. All that he said was by placing his mouth to my ear and whispering 'Nathan,' trembling violently at the same time. I did not make any reply, as I saw it might cause him pain. This ended my visit. I intended when I went over to see if he had received anything from Kelly; but then, when I saw how he became affected, I never mentioned it. The conversation I had with Kelly about the killing of Mr. Nathan occurred in the house in Suffolk Street. He said the return of Mr. Nathan was wholly unexpected, and when he found out that he had come home he thought that he would try and get the key of the safe. He got into the room without disturbing any one, got the key, and was ransacking the safe, when the old man awoke and said, 'Who's there?' On the party coming toward him, as if to lay hold of him, he raised the 'dog' as if to strike him. The old man threw up his hands to protect himself, and received the blow on one of them. He then screamed, and was struck several times on the head. He (Kelly) then ran into the entryway, and in going down stairs he found that no one could have heard the noise, as all was quiet. He waited in the hallway some time, and then got us to return to the room with him to see what we could find."

Irving was afterwards placed on trial for the burglaries, and being convicted of the two charges against him, was sentenced to State prison for seven years and a half. He is at present residing in this city.

The Ryan Murders

Nicholas and Mary Ryan, brother and sister, both unmarried, on November 28, 1873, engaged furnished lodgings from Mrs. Patrick Burke, who rented apartments on the fourth floor of the tenement No. 204 Broome Street. Ryan said that he was a shoemaker, and that his sister, who seemed to be a modest, well-behaved young lady, was a "gaiter-fitter," employed at the establishment of Burt & Co., in Thomas

Street. Mrs. Burke sub-let the front room of her apartments to the Ryans. The place was immediately occupied by the young pair, Nicholas and Mary cooking and sleeping in the single chamber. The room, which was about sixteen feet square, was well carpeted and comfortably furnished with a walnut three-quarter bedstead in the southeast corner and a new black horse-hair sofa at the rear and centre of the apartment, against the wall. The walls were decorated with framed prints representing the "Crucifixion," the " Last Supper," the "Immaculate Conception," and other pictures. The door of this room led out on the front part of the landing of the fourth floor, and had a catch lock or bolt which could be pulled back from within, but could not be opened from the outside excepting by a key made especially to fit the lock.

Although the brother and sister lived in the same apartment, they did not sleep in the same bed. Nicholas Ryan slept regularly on the bed—a very comfortable one—while Mary Ryan slept on a large mattress, which was disposed of nightly in this way: the mattress, or one side of it, was placed on the horse-hair sofa, and the outside part of it was supported by two chairs. The brother and sister appeared to live happily together, working in the daytime and rarely going out of an evening. The young woman always seemed to be in a melancholy mood, and her brother was dark and distant. Nothing unusual transpired to attract attention to the Ryans until Monday morning, December 22, 1873. A policeman who was passing the house between half-past two and three o'clock on that morning heard a window raised with a sudden crash, and, looking upward in the direction of the noise, he saw the head of a man protrude from a window on the fourth story of the six-story brick tenement house No. 204 Broome Street, which gave shelter to twenty-four families. The man was shouting "Murder!" and "Police!" violently. The officer ran into the house, giving an alarm rap at the same moment, to which there was a response in a few moments by three other members of the force. They lit matches and held them above their heads. The policemen found streams of blood pouring down the stairs and banisters, but discovered no human body until they came to the landing of the second story, and on that part of it toward the rooms fronting on the street there was discovered by the officers a most woful and terrible sight. A young man, apparently in the full flush of manhood, wearing nothing but his drawers and undershirt, was stretched, life just extinct and his throat across the jugular vein severed by an awful and deep gash. He had bled, even on this floor, three or four quarts of blood, and the worn and soiled oilcloth presented a smoking, red, ghastly spectacle. The head of the slaughtered man rested against the panels of the door of a German named Charles Miller, whose family occupied rooms on the second floor. On examination long rivulets of blood and pools of the same ghastly fluid were discovered all over the stairs and walls of the third and fourth floors, to which the policemen ascended as rapidly as possible. The face of the man, not long dead, lay downward.

Patrick Burke, who occupied three rooms and let the fourth of his suite to the Ryans, was met on the stairway. He was in his shirt-sleeves and was very much excited. Burke directed the officers to the room in which he said there was another dead body. All entered close after one another, with that expectant gait and bated breath that comes of an unknown terror. And there on the mattress, cleanly covered, and in a dark night-robe, lay a young girl, her head thrown back, her throat cut by a deep gash almost from ear to ear, and her tongue almost lolling out of her mouth and slightly black on the surface. The neck—a fair, white one—was marked with the deadly press of fingers, indicating that the assassin had strangled his victim perhaps into an insensible state before cutting her throat. The improvised couch was in itself very clean, tidy, and not at all disturbed. The fingers of the hand were slightly closed, and the face, bearing marks of considerable intelligence and refinement, had an expression of pain and sudden fright. The mattress was fully soaked with the poor girl's blood, and her skirts and underclothes, of remarkably fine texture, were found placed smoothly and in regular order upon an adjoining chair. A little further on was a small lady's gold open-faced watch, with a black composition chain, a lady's gold lead-pencil, and inside the door was a night-key and a small white-handled penknife, the blades shut and the handle spotted with gouts of blood. The blades, on being opened, had not a stain upon their bright surfaces, but were sharpened in that peculiar way noticeable among shoemakers, the heart of the blade being eaten away by grinding on a whetstone.

The bed which had been occupied by young Ryan was tossed about and looked as if something violent had taken place on it while occupied. The sheets and quilts were thrown in a heap, and on an adjoining chair were discovered a pair of pantaloons belonging to the dead man, a white linen shirt, with two small gold imitation studs in the bosom and having short cuffs. This shirt was spread out in an orderly fashion, as was the trousers. There was besides the shirt a pair of linen cuffs and a pair of gold sleeve-buttons. A razor case, made to hold two razors, was found, and but one razor was in the case; the other could not be discovered on the premises.

Out on the landing, and all the way up from the fourth to the sixth story were found pools and clots of blood on the oilclothed stairs, and the walls were discovered to be covered with finger-marks and clots of livid red blood. It was a slaughter house, this tenement, which contained over one hundred souls, hived together in such a small breathing place.

But how to explain this horrible slaughter? Who had done it? Where was the weapon? Had young Ryan been followed home and killed for his money, and had his sister been strangled and her throat cut by the assassin? Was the assassin a resident of the house, full of Poles, Germans, Italians and a curious and mongrel mixture of people whose avocations are uncertain? The latter theory has its possibility. Or had young Ryan, who was said to be a peaceable and temperate man, in a moment of mad insanity, killed his sister and then cutting his own throat rushed out, not knowing where he was going—anywhere into space and eternity?

There was a small rosewood lady's box in the room full of trinkets and which contained a bank book on the Bowery Bank, indorsed by the depositor, Miss Winifred Stapleton, while in Mr. Ryan's trunk was discovered two bank books on the Emigrant Savings Bank, Nos. 64,522 and 97,121, indorsed in the name of the deceased Nicholas Ryan. The Miss Stapleton was said to be a niece of the dead brother and sister. The depositors in the three bank books were accredited with a total of over $700. In the bottom drawer of the rosewood case a small revolver, looking quite new, was observed.

Patrick Burke, who rented the room for nine dollars a month, the first month's rent having been paid in advance by Nicholas Ryan, when questioned stated that he had been awakened by some strange noise about half-past two o'clock on that Monday morning. He jumped out of bed instantly and ran out in the hall, but all was dark. Then he listened for a moment and heard a noise which sounded to him something like the wheezing of a cat. As he was hastily clothing himself he heard the cries of his children, who were sleeping in a hall bedroom adjoining the front room occupied by the Ryans, and his daughter, Jennie Burke, aged eleven years, cried to him, "Come here, father; there is something the matter on the landing." Then his wife said, "Go, Pat, and see what's the matter." He did so, and carried a lamp with him through the hallway, when he saw streams of fresh blood on the oilcloth and walls, and this frightened him and he went back and told his wife that murder must have been committed in the house. Then he went to Ryan's room and saw the door open, and on entering he discovered Miss Mary Ryan with her face downward on the mattress and her throat cut. Then he ran to the front window and gave the alarm to the police, whereupon they entered and discovered the body of young Ryan on the second floor and afterwards saw Miss Ryan lying dead in her room.

Patrick Ryan, a married brother of the murdered pair, was sought out in the hope that he might furnish some clew that would lift the bloody veil. He resided in South Brooklyn, and was employed as foreman in the shoemaking establishment of T. Kalliske & Co., No. 34 Warren Street in this city. He said that his brother Nicholas, who had worked under him, was a sober and peaceable young man, and had supported his sister, who was also employed in Burt's shoe factory.

Mary was an affectionate girl, and the brother and sister had lived together previous to their removal to Broome Street at No. 3 Canal Street, since the death of their mother. They kept house for the mother; Nicholas loved his sister dearly, and if there was any little disagreement it never amounted to anything more than is usual in any family, and would be forgotten. Nicholas and his sister were brought up too religiously to think of suicide or of any other similar crime. Nicholas had attended St. Mary's Church, in Grand Street, and St. Bridget's Church, in Avenue B. He took tea with a married sister and his own two children at the room of Nicholas and Mary on Sunday evening, and all seemed happy, laughing and joking. All six persons then left the house in Broome Street to go out. His sister Mary and brother Nicholas accompanied as far as the corner of Suffolk and Broome streets and there—it was then seven o'clock Sunday evening—Nicholas left them, and he (Patrick Ryan) said to his brother, "Nicholas, you might tell us where you are going and introduce us to the girl that you are going to see." This was in a joke, and Nicholas left and I did not see him again until I was sent for to see him dead. Mary, my sister, left her married sister's in Lewis Street at or before nine o'clock to go home on Sunday evening, and that is all I know, excepting that my brother had a silver watch valued at $15, and a gold chain attached, valued at $35. Would not know the maker's name or what amount of money he had in his pocket. He always carried money and made good wages.

Several hours after the discovery of the double tragedy a girl named Jenny Burke, the daughter of Patrick Burke, discovered Ryan's vest on the roof-top. There were also bloody footprints on the top of the house and on the stairs leading to the roof. There was no trace, however, of the missing watch, or, most important of all, the weapon with which the deed had been committed.

The deputy coroner carefully examined the bodies, and found on that of the sister a cut on the throat nine and a half inches long, beginning at the back of the neck on the left side and terminating at a straight line from the left jaw. The carotid artery and jugular vein were cut, which must have resulted in almost instant death. Blue marks, as if made by fingers, were on the throat, as if tightly pressed against it, causing the tongue to protrude between the teeth. The medical examiner was of the opinion that the young woman was first strangled until she became nearly unconscious, when a knife or some other sharp instrument was used with the right hand, while the throat was clasped by the left hand of the murderer. The autopsy also revealed something wholly unexpected. It was that Mary Ryan was *enciente* at the time of her death, and that three lives instead of two had perished at the hands of an assassin. An old shoe-knife, upon which there was not the slightest trace of blood, was found in the room of the Ryans several days after the murders, and was said to be the weapon with which the crime had been committed. The accepted theory in the case, outrageous and inconsistent as it was, was that Nicholas Ryan was the father of his sister's unborn child, and to conceal his sin he had murdered the young woman and afterwards committed suicide. There were facts, however, which proved the absolute falsity of this conclusion. The murders were not committed by a robber, but the watch and other articles missing were carried off by the assassin to create such a suspicion. Had he left the weapon he had used behind him the scoundrel well knew that it might prove a tell-tale piece of evidence against him, so he carried it off. All the facts go to show that Nicholas Ryan and his sister Mary were cruelly butchered by a young man who had been keeping company with the latter. Having ruined the young woman he refused to marry her, and when threatened with arrest and exposure he resorted to murder to conceal his sin. He was seen in the vicinity of the Broome Street tenement on the night of the tragedy, and after his brutal work he purchased a drink of whiskey to brace up his shattered nerves at a saloon in the vicinity of the house of blood. The bartender noticed that the customer looked wild, and also that his cuffs were stained with the crimson fluid of his victims. There the trail ended, and although nearly thirteen years have elapsed since the slaying of the brother and sister, the whereabouts of their murderer is yet unknown.

• • •

The Murder of Annie Downey, alias "Curly Tom"

As a flower girl Annie Downey started out in life, and the acquaintances which she formed while peddling bouquets along the Bowery doubtless led to her ruin. Small in stature and possessed of a shapely form and a handsome face, she soon made hosts of friends. In time she became a degraded creature, and was entered upon the books of the filthy dens in which she lived as "Curly Tom" and "Blonde Annie." She was naturally a brunette, but was in the habit of dyeing her hair to a light blonde. All her relatives were respectable people, and to save them from the shame of her disgrace she passed under the name of Annie Martin. She was found dead in the house kept by a woman named Smidt, at No. 111 Prince Street, on January 17, 1880, under circumstances so mysterious as not to give the faintest clue to her murderer.

During the day preceding the night of her murder she remained in the house and received a number of visitors, none of whom were known to the proprietress. The young woman seemed to be in unusually gay spirits. On retiring to her room, the second floor front, at eleven o'clock, she called out over the banisters to Mrs. Smidt, saying that she expected a visit from an old friend before midnight, and asked to be called as soon as he arrived. She was never seen alive again.

Up to half-past twelve o'clock no one entered the house, and at that hour Mrs. Smidt's husband locked the front door and went to bed, taking the keys with him, according to custom. The back door was always left unlocked.

The Smidt bedroom was on the first floor in the rear. Rosa Schneider, the cook, and a colored chambermaid, whose rooms were in the attic, were the only other persons who slept in the house that night.

Bertha Levy, a hair-dresser, called at ten o'clock next morning to dress Annie Downey's hair. She attempted to open the door to the girl's room, but found it locked. Being unable to get any response to her repeated knocks she called Mrs. Smidt, who, becoming alarmed, called a policeman.

There were three doors leading into the room, one from the hall, one from the adjoining hall bedroom, and the third from the rear room. The two former were locked. The bed was placed against the latter.

Going into the rear room the policeman forced open the door, pushing the bed back with it, and entered the room. Lying on the bed, face upward and drenched in blood that had flowed from several ghastly wounds in the head, he found the body of Annie Downey. It was cold and stiff.

Tied so tightly around the neck as to blacken the face and force the eyeballs from their sockets, was a thin pillow-slip taken from the bed. The fingers of the left hand clutched one end of the slip with a death grip. The limbs were extended straight along the bed, and the attitude of the body did not suggest that a struggle for life had taken place. The only other marks were two small cuts over the left eye that looked as if they had been inflicted with a blow of a fist.

Everything about the apartment was in perfect order. The girl's clothing was neatly arranged over a chair by the bedside. In the ears of the corpse were a pair of handsome amethyst earrings and a diamond ring flashed on her finger. Evidently the murderer's motive had not been robbery.

The only thing missing was a watch and chain of little value, but it was soon remembered that the girl had disposed of them a few days before.

Search was made for the key of the door, but it could not be found. All the inmates of the house were strictly interrogated, but no information that could throw a ray of light on the mystery could be elicited. No unusual sounds had been heard during the night.

Smidt was positive that no man was in the house when he locked the door for the night. Annie's last visitor had gone away long before eleven o'clock, the hour at which she went to her room. The only theory of the case was that the murderer had entered the house during the evening without attracting attention, and secreted himself in the room until the girl entered, when he surprised and killed her before she could make any outcry.

This view was supported by the condition of the body, which

indicated that the murder took place at least ten hours before it was discovered.

By way of the back door the assassin could easily have made his way to an alley running along the eastern side of the house to the street. The padlock which fastened the door of this alley was found to have been twisted off.

The coroner's examination showed that death had been caused by strangulation, and that the wounds on the head were merely superficial and had been inflicted after the pillow-slip had been knotted round the throat, evidently in an effort to still the girl's struggles for life.

The Assassination of Ching Ong, alias Antonio Soloa

In a little underground shop, with the evidences of his careful thrift about him, within hearing of customers in the store overhead and almost in sight of passers by on the walk without, a man was, on November 2, 1885, in broad daylight, hacked to death.

The horrors of murder were in his case intensified by dreadful mutilations, which happily are rare in the domains of civilization, and the extent of ferocity expended in the deed pointed at once to people of semi-barbaric instincts as the authors. Like most assassinations of this kind it was involved in mystery, and investigation for the truth required to be carried on among people with strange secrets and unfamiliar tongues.

"Antonio Soloa" was printed on the cards of the little eating-house that burrowed under the southeast corner of Wooster and Spring streets, with its single window admitting only such dreary reflections of daylight as straggled down to it through an iron grating. Antonio Soloa had a Spanish flavor about it, and it rather unsatisfactorily indicated a man with unmistakably Mongolian features, who was often seen bustling about there in the dual capacity of cook and waiter. Soloa was a Chinaman, and, according to the words of a countryman, had brought from home the more characteristic name of Ching Ong. But it was not from the West but through the Indies that he had come to New York, and while in Cuba he acquired a Hispano-American name. His occupation, too, had been learned in the South, and he at first went to work in this city as a cigar-maker. As such he had been brought into contact with a lot of West Indian coolies, native Cubans and Spanish speaking negroes of the Caribbean Islands. He went from one quarter of the city to another and finally found engagement in Chio & Soona's factory, in South Fifth Avenue. There he lived, too, in the heart of the district which has of late years become marked above all others as a foreign quarter. There Spanish, French and Italian were commonly spoken and were not unfamiliar to the Chinese who herded among the hybrid population of the place, and through Ching Ong's knowledge of them as Antonio Soloa he became a person well known among them.

He had the aptitude of his race for money making, and several years before his tragic death gave up the drudgery of the workroom for a little shop near the Catherine ferry, whence he removed to No. 81 Thompson Street and No. 51 Wooster Street. At these he catered for the cigar-makers, often bringing their lunches to the factories for them. Later on he removed to the basement where he met his death. Stockelberg, Chio & Soona and other tobacconists have factories on South Fifth Avenue, and some of the workmen used to go to Soloa's place. Nearly all were men of his own race or of Cuban extraction, and the dingy little den, with its cleanly linen and dishes attuned to the palates of its patrons, gained favor among them all. About $10 a day was believed to be the extent of the host's receipts, and out of that he was supposed to comfortably run his establishment and save a snug little penny besides.

Soloa's neighbors knew little of him or his guests. John and Peter Waurchus, the German grocers overhead, only occasionally noticed the stream of swarthy visaged men, who, at meal-time, slipped down the stone steps outside and as noiselessly shuffled away. O'Brien & Ryder, the plumbers next door, gave little heed to the Chinaman or his belongings. And probably the children who played about the place only occasionally caught a glimpse through the iron railing of the lamp-lighted snuggery and the dark, strange-speaking people who sat at the tables in it. Soloa himself was a quiet, affable sort of a man. He dressed rather well for a Chinaman, discarding all the native gear, with the exception perhaps of an alabaster bracelet, and he wore his hair like his neighbors', without a suspicion of its ever having been trussed up in a queue. He appeared to be on the best of terms with his guests, too, and seemed altogether a good-natured and hard-working fellow.

At noon on that fatal Monday he was in his kitchen and bustling about the shop as usual when Julius Dichon, a countryman of his, who had known him for ten years, went down to dine. There were the usual set of men dropping in by twos and threes. The long table by the wall was set for eight. The smaller square table was set for four. There were two tables at one side, to accommodate a couple each. Only one was occupied. The diners at it paid their score and went out. The hand of the clock, ticking over the mite of a counter little more than a yard long was drawing to one as Dichon arose to go. The pair of canary birds, whose gilded cages were strangely bright as they swung in the dimness of the place, were fluttering about as he went up the steps. Soloa was standing alone with a can in his hand and feeding them.

Almost an hour later John Waurchus went out of his grocery to drive over to Centre Street. He saw the Chinaman coming up the steps at the same moment. Soloa had turned the key in the door, and as he returned the grocer's nod he said:

"I am going over to the Bowery to see about my music box."

As he spoke he went off in that direction and John Waurchus turned to his wagon. He never saw his Chinese neighbor again alive.

It was only a little after that—no more than three-quarters of an hour—when Jim Coughlin, a coal-heaver in the Farrar Company's yard, had a surprise. He was lounging on a box watching a peddler named Daly trundle a handcart of vegetables along and voice their quality for the good of the neighborhood, and he had his eyes on the man when he left his vehicle at the curb-stone and descended the steps of Soloa's restaurant. Daly was gone only for an instant. When he stumbled out on the walk his eyes were full of horror and his face pale with excitement.

"My God!" he cried to the coal-heaver; "there's a man dead down there."

Coughlin got up and asked, "Where?"

"Down below on the floor," said the peddler.

"Let's go down and see," said Coughlin, and the other, evidently ill-satisfied with his fortune of first discoverer, lagged at his heels as they descended.

The peddler's words were true. A man was lying there dead, but so horribly butchered, so disfigured with gaping wounds, protruding brains and untraceable lineaments as to betray no facial evidence of identity. Blood welled from his heart and head and lay in a pool about him. There were clots upon his hands. There were marks upon the floor, and a dripping knife lay upon it beside him.

The place at first sight seemed undisturbed. The tables were covered with clean linen, and the glasses and bottles on them were polished and ready for use. On the wall two of those grotesque Chinese pictures representing an Oriental procession and a Mongolian horseman in the act of leave-taking, turned a blotch of glaring color with threads of tinsel upon the incomer. Between them was the photograph of a well-dressed Chinaman, who was pronounced to be Antonio Soloa himself. A lot of unpainted boards, reaching from floor to ceiling, divided the eating-room from a kitchen and dark hutch of a place that was found to have been used as a bedroom. From nails along this partition hung strings of garlic; on a shelf in front of it were cans of starch and preserved vegetables, with lemons, cheeses and spices, and along the wall some cheap prints were swinging. A white table-cover, suspended on one side, shut out the dismal glimpse of a black opening, sinking lower, and suggesting a sub-cellar, and it cut off whatever fugitive rays might intrude on that side from a second iron grating on the walk.

So dark it was within that the prostrate figure lying between the kitchen partition and a couple of tables was not clearly discernible. And it was only when a reluctant lamp was lighted and threw its yellow gleams on the floor that the details of the fearful assassination made themselves visible. It was the host of the little restaurant, Antonio Soloa, who had been with the Chinaman, Chong Ong, that lay there, so far as figure and attire indicated. But the red lineaments that were spread upon the floor had every semblance of life crushed out of them. Only a bloody mask was turned to the light divided by a great gash at the chin, slashed deeply on the cheek-bone and temple, with one eye gouged out of its socket and lying at the apex of a mass of bone and muscle which a cut into the forehead had raised out of the skull itself. The head was crushed nearly flat. A portion of the face held in position by the bones seemed unnaturally swollen by contrast with the dreadful mass of features that were driven in alongside it. The nose had shrunk into a red hollow. The head bulged out in places, and through the tangle of hair could be seen great gapes where the brain was oozing out. The sight was horrifying. But that was not all. The red shirt falling back from the breast revealed a cut. It was turned further back, and directly over the heart, repeated again and again, were nine great holes, where a knife had been thrust up to the hilt. It had cut the heart in two, and some of the blows had severed a series of the ribs. The knife must have been wielded with demoniac strength and ferocity. It had almost cut the man to pieces.

The knife itself was there. It lay on the floor—a big kitchen-knife, with a blade eleven inches long, fitted in a handle of dark wood by brass rivets. Through the blood that covered it the inscription, "Lamson & Goodnew Manufacturing Company," appeared on the blade, and this blade, heavy though it seemed, was bent by the force of the blows that had been struck with it. To all appearance it was a kitchen-knife, and there was a suggestion in a cut loaf of bread lying on the table beside the corpse that the knife might have been caught up from the table for the bloody work. It was the only weapon found. How the head had been crushed in, the bones of the face mashed to a jelly, the skull beaten into over threescore fragments, as was later on discovered to be the case, there was nothing about to indicate. A dent was noticed on a stone and a fleck of blood was on the floor beneath it, but the light sheet iron could never have withstood the force of a falling man nor beaten in his skull. The pockets of the dead man were turned out. Beside him, smeared with blood, was a fire insurance policy for $500 in the Phoenix company. An empty pocket-book was on the table.

In his disordered garments, in the blood mark at the stove and in a shivered pane of glass in the door were evidences of a struggle. But where the body lay with all its wounds nothing seemed out of place, as though the man had been beaten down suddenly and without resistance. Beyond the body an opening in the partition led into the kitchen and bedroom. In the former nothing was amiss, but the sleeping apartment had been fairly ransacked. The contents of a trunk were scattered about. An accordeon lay on the bed, a watch ticked beside it, an opium pipe had fallen on the floor. Heaps of clothing were wildly tossed around. Outside in the dining-room the drawer from the counter lay underneath it, the papers and dinner tickets it contained mingled with some small coins. Plunder was certainly hinted by all this as the motive of the crime. The watch was the only valuable left behind, and in the scurry of such a moment and the horror of such a scene the murderer's neglect was natural. That precautions were taken to examine everything was shown in the red smears upon the clothes in the bedroom and the marks of bloody fingers on the counter cards. Nor had need of security been overlooked. The wash-basin on a stand in the dining-room told its tale. It was full of bloody water.

The coroner on his arrival made an autopsy, which revealed that the heart and other organs had been reached by the knife; that the skull had been shattered to pieces, and the brain again and again penetrated. The excessive mutilation could be due only to the body having quivered after the knife thrusts had been delivered, when, to make death a certainty, the skull had been beaten in. It did seem strange that so fearful a death struggle had passed without attracting attention, and the neighbors were closely questioned. No one had heard a cry. Ryder, the plumber next door, had heard a crash of glass, and had sent a boy out to see what was broken. The little fellow did not look into the Chinaman's basement, and so the pane that had been smashed during the fearful work of that half hour escaped attention. In the place nothing was left that could serve as a clew to the murderer. Not a sign that might serve to indicate his identity or even his nationality or station in life had the slayer of Soloa left behind, except the suggestion that lay in the fearful completeness of his work. A weapon left behind might have betrayed something, but the knife with which the stabs were inflicted seemingly belonged to the dead man himself. The wounds were inflicted with a bread-knife, and such a knife was picked up in the kitchen. The heavy instrument with which the head had been crushed in was not discovered. A deep gash on the brow and some wounds on the head, as well as the traces of sprinkled blood upon the walls and ceiling, suggested a hatchet. A search of the basement and cellar failed to reveal any such weapon, and the assassin was wary enough to carry off his murderous implement lest it should afford a clue. The blood spattered on the ceiling seemed to show that he was upright when the blows were struck. The knife was used to complete the work, and was driven again and again into his heart fairly up to the hilt, a few blows falling upon the face and chin. A slash upon the left arm was doubtless received while that member was raised in defense, but it was as probably inflicted by the murderer in the wild fury of his strokes after it was prone and powerless. The crushing of the bones of the head was, like the excessive stabbing, an atrocity to remove all doubt of dissolution.

There had been a witness to the butchery, but that fact did not become known until long after the discovery of the murder. Then William Schimper, a nickel-plater, came forward with his office boy, who was named George Mainz. Mr. Schimper said that the lad could throw some light on the tragedy. Young Mainz was questioned. He said that he had been sent on a message by his employer, and as he was returning through Spring Street, he saw two men quarreling at the top of the basement stairs on the southeast corner of Wooster Street. "One," declared the boy, "was a short, thin man, who looked like a Chinaman. The other was a tall, strong mulatto. The men were very angry with each other, and their loud voices made me stop. I thought there was going to be a fight, so I watched. I saw the tall man draw a knife and plunge it into the little man's breast. He had hard work to draw it out. When he did pull the knife out, the big man ran down stairs out of sight. The little man followed him, but he seemed to fall down, for I heard a crash as he disappeared. I was so frightened that I ran to the office, and did not tell Mr. Schimper till hours after."

"Do you think you would be able to recognize the tall man if you saw him again?"

"Yes, sir, perfectly well."

"How?"

"Because he had a terrible scar on his left cheek."

The description of the assassin furnished by the lad cleared the suspicion that the brutal crime had been committed by a Chinaman believed to be a "highbinder." The murderer had been seen at his bloody work, and the witness said he was a tall negro. That was definite enough, and it was subsequently learned that a man answering the description given by young Mainz had been seen on several occasions in Ching Ong, alias Soloa's restaurant. He was a Cuban negro, and was said to be a member of a Cuban insurrectionary organization known as "Niazzas." There was a section of that revolutionary society in this city. Its meetings and doings were kept secret, but in a moment of vanity the conspirators, some years before, had had a large photograph of all the leading members taken in a group. A copy of the original picture fell into the hands of the detectives. It was shown to young Mainz.

"There! there!" exclaimed the boy, pointing to a large, dark-complexioned man who stood in the middle of the group, but in the background; "there he is. That is the man I saw stab Soloa."

The photograph was exhibited to many, and at last a man was found who said, "Yes, I know him, (meaning the tall conspirator). His name is Augustus Rebella, but I don't know where he lives or works. He is a cigar-maker." Then for the first time the name of the slayer of the Chinaman was learned. Rebella was sought after, and on November 20, 1885, just eighteen days after the assassination, the tall Cuban negro was traced to the cigar manufactory at No. 161 Pearl Street, and there arrested. Although Rebella had no scar on his cheek, when he was photographed there was the mark of a healed wound on the left side of his face, just as the boy had said, when the suspected man was made prisoner. The scar was very prominent and had been made some eighteen months before by his mistress, whom Rebella had quarreled with at No. 309 Mulberry Street. Rebella said that on the day of the murder of the Chinaman he had been at work in Los Dos Amigos' cigar factory in Washington Street, Brooklyn. There it was learned that on November 2 the prisoner had only made one hundred cigars, while the usual number he was in the habit of making in a day was two hundred. He admitted that he had known Ching Ong, alias Soloa, and gave his address as at No. 118 West Twenty-seventh Street. Young Mainz positively identified Rebella as the murderer of the Chinese restaurant keeper, and the prisoner was held upon the lad's affidavit of identification. Subsequently it was ascertained that Rebella had made two attempts prior to the murder to kill Ching Ong.

That he was the slayer of Ching Ong, was well known to the Cuban insurrectionists, and also the fact that he was assisted by two others in the completion of the butchery. The weapon with which Ching Ong's skull had been battered in was a slung-shot. Still, Rebella's fellow-conspirators were determined to save him from punishment. Although it was a fact that Rebella had only worked the first half of the day on November 2, and returned to the factory just before closing time, nearly two dozen of the cigar makers made affadavit to the effect that he had not left the shop. The few other workmen in the place, who could not be induced to perjure themselves, were threatened by Rebella's murderous associates with death, if they ventured to testify against the prisoner. The men, aware that their lives were in danger, were therefore afraid to come forward, and vanished before their testimony could be secured. Thus were the hands of justice tied, and as the preponderance of evidence, such as it was, was in favor of Rebella, it was impossible to legally convict him on the testimony of young Mainz, and the prisoner was consequently released. It is more than probable that the horrible butchery, owing to the machinations of a secret society, will forever remain unavenged.

One Cop, Eight Square Blocks
by Michael Norman

Former marine Michael Norman (born 1947)
has covered the police beat for the New York
Times and other publications. He spent 60
days on patrol in the Bronx's 54th Precinct with
officer Kevin Jett, a tough cop Norman
describes as "incredibly patient; never cynical."
President Clinton later praised Jett during a
State of the Union address.

I t will always come down to this—one mutt, one cop, eye to eye, struggling for control of the street. The cop is Kevin Jett, Badge No. 19980, Beat 12, Sector George, the 52d Precinct in the northwest Bronx. The mutt is Killer, a Jamaican drug dealer with arctic eyes and a taste for letting blood.

The cop patrols on foot from East 194th Street to East 198th Street, from Decatur Avenue to Valentine Avenue—one man, eight square blocks, perhaps 12,000 people. Most of these, in the officer's words, are "upstanding citizens." They work hard, worry about their children, struggle to survive. Among them, however, boldly encamped on corners or lying in alleyways, is a species of citizen that Kevin Jett has come to despise: the urban predator—Cuco and Sweet Pea, Gravy and Chisel Head, Scarface and Killer.

In the gathering warmth of a summer day, the officer has turned down Valentine in search of a murder suspect, a Jamaican dealer named Leopold. As it happens, Killer is on the street, his first day back after a while away.

Killer shot a man a few months back, a rival in the drug trade, then left the man for dead. The victim, however, recovered. When Killer discovered his blunder, he fled, eventually to Philadelphia, where his nemesis caught up with him. There, Killer was shot. Naturally, neither man sought comfort in the law, so the police had no case. But "we knew the deal," says Kevin Jett.

"Killer's feared around here, so every once in a while I got to bring him down a peg." And today, spotting him around the bend on Valentine, the officer has decided to do just that.

"Hey! Killer!"

The dealer wheels, his face sour, his eyes full of rage.

"What you call me Killer for!" he snaps. "You know my name."

Kevin Jett had only wanted to tweak the mutt, not force a duel. But one word has led to another and a line has been drawn, and now, too, from out of nowhere, come Killer's supernumeraries, five in all, among them a giant in a track shirt.

"Where's Leopold?" Jett asks. He stands squarely in front of Killer, but he can sense that the others are close. "Why don't you tell him to turn himself in?"

Killer lets the question dangle. His hands are deep in the pouch of his hooded sweatshirt—hooded sweatshirt? On a day as hot as this? Maybe Killer has poor circulation. "Don't know where Leopold is." He's sullen and still full of fire. "I'm not into that—that life anymore, man."

Jett closes the distance, closer . . . closer . . . so close, now, Killer can see the flakes of breakfast oatmeal still in the officer's teeth.

"There's no reason for you to get angry," says the cop. "What are you trying to do? Show off in front of your friends here?"

Killer spits and curses.

"You just tell Leopold if you see him," Jett goes on.

"I'll tell him," says Killer, pulling back from the edge, but still sullen, still snarling.

"You know what I like about you Killer? I'll ask you a question and you'll stand there and lie to me."

And all at once, Kevin Jett turns his back and walks silently away.

Around the corner on East 194th Street, the officer looks over his shoulder.

"Guys like Killer will eat you alive, even with the uniform on. They can sense fear, smell it like a dog smells it. Some of the mopes will come right out and tell you you're nothing, and you don't want that, oh, no. If you're going to do this job, wear this uniform, you definitely don't want that. If it gets around that you're soft, that without your nightstick and gun you can't fight, that's bad. If you allow someone to smoke a joint in front of you or curse you out, word will spread throughout the neighborhood like a disease. You're a beat cop, out here every day, alone, so you set standards right away, and for those that don't like it. . . ."

There has always been a sharp eye in the streets: the colonial watch, the gaslight bluebottles, the Roaring 20's copper. Even after the advent of the radio car, most cities still relied on foot patrol, the cop on the beat. By the 1970's however, the role of the police had changed. Department after department, rocked by scandals and racked by recessions, saw their ranks shrink. Many decided to narrow their job to emergency response—911, a cop in a car racing from call to call, crime scene to crime scene. Soon, the police became isolated, strangers in the neighborhoods they were sworn to serve and, worse, little more than a passing annoyance to criminals. Disturbed by this state of affairs, a new generation of police executives began to experiment. In the late 70's, in Flint, Mich., and Newark, they took a lesson from history and put bluebottles back on the beat.

Watching all this was Herman Goldstein, a law professor at the University of Wisconsin in Madison. From his work in criminology, he knew the experiments would fail if the police simply followed form: answered calls, filled out reports, made arrests. They needed to focus on substance, which meant attacking the circumstances that make crime possible.

Goldstein proposed what he called a basic "problem-solving method." Step 1: Analyze the problem. If there is a rash of burglaries in an apartment building, find out when the thefts occur, what floors they occur on and what's being taken. Step 2: Use this information to fashion solutions. Train a tenant watch, persuade the landlord to improve building security, install alarms and show the tenants how to cage their windows and secure their doors. Step 3: Follow up. Watch the building, stay current with the tenants.

In time Goldstein's method and the experiments in foot patrol coalesced in the practice known as "community policing." While some of the early trials in regular foot patrol had little real effect on crime, people in the test neighborhoods embraced the idea. The beat cop was back, and no matter what the statistics said, the neighborhood seemed somehow more secure.

Encouraged by this reception, a number of places, Portland, Ore., and Madison, Wis., among them, adopted the practice. By 1990, Lee P. Brown, then Commissioner in New York, declared community policing "the dominant philosophy" in his department. But in New York, a city of quarreling multitudes, the most densely populated major municipality in the country, community policing has been slow to take hold.

Part of the problem is the size and nature of the force. The N.Y.P.D., with more than 31,000 uniformed officers, is the largest such force in the United States. Its bureaucracy, which includes 8,000 civilian workers, is inflexible. Its rank-and-file officers, wedded to traditions that date from the middle of the last century, resist new ideas. What is more, the new policing demands a special breed of officer, tough but skilled, and smart—an organizer, a planner, an ombudsman. Finally, there are the streets, which seem meaner and more savage than anywhere else—perhaps, say beat cops, too tough for tenant patrols and problem-solving protocols and nuisance-abatement programs.

In New York, then, community policing is a mass experiment in urban order, maybe the largest and most important policing experiment any government has tried to conduct.

The question is, can a city this large, hobbled by chronic budget deficits and a hidebound bureaucracy, make it work in a violent world?

The sky is clear this morning, the sun white-hot. On Briggs Avenue,

Kevin Jett stops in front of No. 2773, an apartment building with an elegant arch. Last summer a clique of teen-agers used the entryway as their hangout; by early fall, three boys in that clique—boys absorbed by drugs—were killed.

"That sobered the others up," says Kevin Jett. "They got jobs. They realized what was going to come of hanging out and doing nothing."

Two teen-age girls are sitting on the steps under the arch. One has a ponytail, the other a gold ring in her nose. Ponytail is talking about getting a job. Gold Ring is talking about her boyfriend, who is "on vacation," a neighborhood term for a stretch in jail.

"I don't need no job," says Gold Ring. "I got a man to support me. He got money."

Jett asks: "Doing what?" She laughs, sheepishly.

"So, what's he do?" Jett again asks, pressing for an answer he already knows.

"He makes lots of loot—that's what he do," says the girl, sticking her tongue out.

"You ought to get yourself a regular man," says Jett.

"A regular man?" The girl shakes her head. "Ain't none of them out here."

In fact, there are legions of men and women leading respectable lives on Beat 12. They pack the aisles of the Roman Catholic Church, they usher their children through the streets to school, they crowd the busy bodegas and Laundromats. Without the regulars—day laborers, office workers, welfare mothers—the neighborhood would surely fall, as have so many others in the Bronx. But more and more of late, the regulars—and their allies, the police—wonder how long they can hold their ground.

So many stores have been robbed so often that many, including the Post Office, conduct business from behind thick Plexiglas partitions. Some streets are so dangerous that the auxiliary police won't drive down them. And when regular patrol officers respond to calls in some zones they are often met with "air mail," bricks and chunks of concrete that rain down from above.

At night Beat 12 echoes with gunfire, much of it random; few here are foolish enough to sleep with their bed by a window. When the gunmen have a target, as they often do, the next morning the neighbors are out with broom and hose sweeping blood from the sidewalk. All this, of course, creates an air of dread, a feeling best expressed by a T-shirt popular among teen-age boys. "Back up," it reads, "and live."

Now and then Kevin Jett does traditional police work—writing tickets, making collars—but usually only in passing. The sector cars answer most emergencies. And special units—narcotics, morals and so on—work the streets.

Jett's main mission is to insinuate himself into the lives of the people on his beat, to walk and talk, analyze their trouble and then find a way to stop it. He's a collector of suggestions, a clearinghouse for complaints. He listens, weighs options, takes action.

Sometimes he attacks the context of crime, the disrepair and disorder that make mayhem possible—drunks on a corner, drug addicts in a lobby, trash on the sidewalk, burned-out cars in the street. And sometimes he moves against the criminals themselves—a burglar preying on a building, a motorcycle gang staking out a block.

All of this seems to take place more at random than by plan. Kevin Jett is not a textbook cop. He has not read the department's new problem-solving manuals and knows almost nothing of Herman Goldstein's methods; his training in community policing was so short and superficial that he barely remembers it. He embraces the objectives of community policing, but seems to work more by instinct than design. In short, he is no poster boy for community policing. He's a street cop, a grunt who relies more on old-fashioned savvy than problem-solving protocols. As an average cop, one who has to moonlight to make ends meet, he stands as a good test of the new police science.

Down East 194th Street, then north on Bainbridge, then west to Valentine. Across the street four young Hispanic Americans are sitting on the hood of a car. "Let's stop," says Jett. "Just stand here."

He hooks his hands in his gun belt and studies the scene. "They've been dealing heroin up here. I've been in the precinct five years and I've watched them grow up from kids. They were about nothing then, so I guess I shouldn't expect much now. You hope things will change, but they don't."

A moment later, the group moves on and the officer seems satisfied. "If they don't know my name at least they know there's a big black cop who's always around. That's my reputation. I like that."

Always around? Not in this neighborhood, or anywhere else. With vacations, furloughs and sick leave, court time, paper work, meetings, training sessions, special assignments and details, the average beat cop can spend as much as half of his regular 43-hour week off the street. To put it another way, if a neighborhood sees its cop 1 hour out of every 10, it's lucky.

Actually, Kevin Jett is hardly ever around. He tries to stagger his shifts to create the illusion of omnipresence—one of the new tactics. But while this gambit fools some people—"Man, you is always working!" says a surprised mutt—it does not mollify the regulars.

Down Valentine toward East 194th Street, half a block from the corner, a middle-aged Hispanic woman with reddish hair corners the officer. A pack of boys, she says, have been smoking marijuana in front of her building.

"I tell them to leave. I tell them I live here 18 years. They say, 'So what?'"

The officer looks down the block. Four teen-agers are standing in front of the Right Spot pizza parlor.

"That them?" he asks.

"That's them," says the woman.

"Yo!" yells Jett. "C'mere!"

They are 14, perhaps 15 years old.

"You keep hanging out all day," he tells them, "and you're going to get in trouble, or catch a bullet. Don't destroy the neighborhood you live in."

"It wasn't us," one of them says. "It was our friend."

"I saw you," says the woman, so angry she begins to shake. "Don't come in our building! You got no business here! I don't want our kids to see the reefer. It's dirty. Dirty!" And suddenly she begins to cry.

Jett leans forward. "You hear her," he tells the boys, in a voice so soft it's almost lost in traffic. "This is somebody's mother."

Saturday afternoon and the station house is quiet. A sergeant mans the front desk. To his right an officer answers the phone.

The sergeant is writing in a log book and complaining out loud. "Another community event and it's pulling officers from the sector cars, but that's community policing. It's great, huh? We're all community policing."

The cop on the phone cups his hand on the mouthpiece. "Yeah, the community policing unit does something and we have to clean up the mess."

"Ten years," the sergeant goes on, "they've had it for 10 years and it's a failure, but the department keeps trying it because it's the new thing."

In one form or another, New York has had a cop on the beat since 1783. Even in the 1970's, when most of the force rode patrol cars, there were still walking posts and trial programs in foot patrol. Today, on average, about 40 officers in each precinct walk a neighborhood: some 2,700 cops on 1,320 beats, or roughly 20 percent of the patrol force. The experiment is broad, and the results, so far, show just how complicated and difficult the job of radically restructuring the police really is.

In the subculture of the station house, the answer to crime is swift punishment, not social work. To many cops, community policing is too "soft" to deal with the mopes and knuckleheads roaming the streets. Even those officers who joined the force because they wanted to "help people," as so many of them put it, do not relish the role of "government liaison," "problem-solving facilitator" and community organizer.

"If you live in Mayberry R.F.D. then it will work, but I don't see it happening in New York," says one cop, speaking anonymously for fear of official censure. Now an undercover man, he walked a beat for more than a year. "I don't think a police officer should be involved in community organizing. The department also wants you to solve long-term problems, but that was impossible—the drug problem, that's never going to go away. Community policing—it sounds great, but I think it's a big waste of time."

The bureaucracy adds to the problems by rewarding cops for "turning numbers," making arrests, not for solving problems. Then there are the dual diseases of brutality and corruption. Beat cops, for the most part, are on their own—historically a risky practice, particularly in New York. In the early 1970's, a commission headed by Judge Whitman Knapp revealed an entrenched system of corruption—thousands of cops on the take, mostly from bookmakers and gamblers. This year, two decades after the Knapp Commission's final report, another commission, this one headed by a former judge, Milton Mollen, found new pockets of corruption: small clusters of brutal cops beating up drug dealers and stealing their merchandise and cash.

Finally, as the most trenchant critics of community policing point out, it makes little sense for the police department to become "client oriented," to take its marching orders from the people it serves, if the rest of the city government continues on its centralized, bureaucratic, self-absorbed ways. To truly reform the police, one must first reform the other agents of government—the sanitation inspector, the Health Department officer and so on—making them problem solvers too, directed by the community and working in concert with the police. It makes little sense, for example, for the Police Department to target a building for action if it's going to take the Department of Housing Preservation and Development a year or more to evict dealers from their apartments. It's not a foothill that has to be moved, it's a mountain.

The day he learned the department planned to hire him, Kevin Jett drove to his parents' house in Mount Vernon to break the good news.

His father was elated. "Go on, boy," he said. "Go on!" His mother, however, seemed heavy-hearted. "A policeman?" she said. "Kevin, are you sure you really want to do this?"

By his own lights, Kevin Maurice Jett, 31 years old, a former amateur boxer and black belt in karate, six feet, 200 pounds, strong and swift, is a mama's boy.

He calls his mother several times a week. She asks if he's wearing his bulletproof vest; she worries the dealers will target him. Not long ago he bought a beeper so she would always be able to reach him. "The beeper makes her feel better," he says. "But I don't tell her half the things that happen on my beat."

Bennie Ruth Jett, an assistant teacher at an elementary school, and her husband, Morris Jett, a supervisor with the city Housing Authority, were born and raised in Mississippi. Twenty-eight years ago they came north in search of a better life, settling in the Bronx on the ninth floor of a 22-story building in a public-housing project, the Mott Haven Houses.

Bennie Ruth's passion was the Pentecostal Church. She sent her children—Bruce, Cheryl and Kevin—to Bible study and encouraged them to sing in the choir. Kevin, the youngest, spent so much time singing hymns and studying scripture his friends started calling him Church Boy.

Mott Haven then was not as mean and dangerous as it is now, but it was still a place to be wary. So the Jetts set down rules: no smoking, drinking or languishing on the corner. After school, there were chores, then homework.

Church Boy went to Christopher Columbus High School, and it was there, one winter day midway through his freshman year, that he learned just how savage the streets can be.

He was on his way home in the late afternoon, walking along Pelham Parkway toward a subway station, when, nearing a corner, he heard footfalls from behind. By the time he turned, he was surrounded.

There were 13 in all, he says, white teen-agers, poised for an attack. He fought off the first, then the second—even then he was sturdy and quick and well schooled in self-defense. Soon, however, the gang overwhelmed him. They beat his face and kicked and pummeled his body. And then he saw a silver blade catch the light, a sharp blade that sliced through his ear and came through his coat, again and again. He struggled onto the subway, then up the stairs to his family's ninth-floor apartment, where he sank into a chair. His mother came into the room. "What happened?" she asked. He looked up . . . then collapsed at her feet.

Roll call. The afternoon shift. Down Webster to East 194th Street, then up a block to Decatur. On the southeast corner looms a soot-stained brick building with Tudor trim, 384 East 194th Street, six stories, 81 shabby apartments—a haven, the police say, for drug dealers.

The sidewalks are empty, the building quiet. "To look at it now," says Kevin Jett, "you wouldn't think it's notorious. Now is when real-estate brokers bring clients to see apartments. Little do those clients know what lurks in the shadows."

Informers say that business is booming, with at least 3,000 packets of heroin and hundreds of vials of crack sold every day. The dealers use women—mothers, wives and girlfriends—to fetch their stock. They are organized and they are ruthless. "You get personal with these guys," an informant told the police, "and they'll just blow you away."

The building is just outside Kevin Jett's beat, but he regularly slides a block east to check it. Sometimes he stands on the corner, as he is doing now, his thick arms folded across his chest, a bugbear in blue frightening away flocks of buyers.

Occasionally he'll cross the street and wade into the circle of young mutts who do the dealers' work—the lookouts and ushers and cashiers. He'll ask for identification, demand to know what they're doing there—question after question until he forces them to scatter. But a beat cop has to circulate, so he'll move on, up the hill toward Valentine, knowing, without looking back, that the boys have returned and the next sale is already under way.

The police in the 52d have tried everything to rout the dealers from Decatur Avenue, all the tricks from the old book, all the techniques from the new. Narcotics squads have conducted operations and made arrests. Building inspectors have issued 800 housing-code violations to prod the landlord to fix the building and evict the dealers. Police lawyers have invoked the city's padlock law and closed down crooked storefronts. Beat cops have talked to the "good" tenants, mining them for information; they've also used traffic tickets and miscellaneous summonses to harass the dealers and scare off their trade. Nothing has worked.

The tenants are terrified, and all the tickets and citations are like so many "flea bites," as one cop put it, "when you consider the volumes of money," the profit from drug sales, the revenue from rent. (The building is owned by L. P. East 194th Street Realty. Its lawyer, Irwin Cohen of Brooklyn, says his client knows of no tenants who are selling drugs.)

Still, every month when the precinct captain, the community-policing lieutenant, the sergeants and beat officers gather to identify the precinct's five most pressing problems, 384 East 194th Street is near the top of the list. They hope one day to build a case with enough arrests and complaints to convince a Federal court that the building is a "crime instrument" that should be seized, cleaned out and turned over to a nonprofit community group. But such a legal procedure takes time. Meanwhile, Kevin Jett's supervisors urge him to look for a "creative" solution to the problem.

"Here's the creative solution to that problem," says Kevin Jett, shaking his large fist at the building.

Up 196th Street to Valentine. School is out and the street is crowded with children.

"Excuse me, Mr. Policeman."

There are two of them, dark-eyed girls with wan smiles.

"Hey, hi," says Kevin Jett.

The taller of the two is holding a plastic cage. Inside are two hamsters, one very large, one very small. The large one is chasing the small one, round and round and round. And their keeper is worried.

"Do you think," she asks, "do you really think the father will eat the baby?"

Bennie Ruth Jett was afraid of animals, save the goldfish she allowed in the house, so Kevin Jett knows nothing of hamsters. But a beat cop must have an answer for everything, even a head-hunting rodent.

"I don't think the father will eat him," says the officer, watching the chase. "But you got to get the mother to help."

"Oh," said the little girl, her voice fading. "I just wanted the baby. I gave the mother away."

Down East 196th Street to Decatur. Across the street comes a short, stout boy leading a short, stout dog, both scowling. The dog is a pit bull, the boy is J. J.

"Oh, my, my, my," says Kevin Jett, "here comes the terror of the neighborhood. Now J. J. lives at 384 East 194th Street, so you can guess what he's into. He told me he's raising that dog to hate cops. He used to be the balls of a gang that robbed kids. Now he's a steerer, leading customers to the dealers at 384. He was away for a few months in a juvenile detention center. They should have kept him until he was 40."

Off the beat, for the moment, on Kingsbridge Road, headed for the New Capitol diner and lunch.

Kingsbridge Road is like a suq, or bazaar, clothing and shoe stalls as packed as old closets, produce stands with the world's fruit piled high. In the stacks of sugar cane and mangoes, there's a little Santo Domingo; in the cans of rambutan, a breath of Bombay. No neighborhood in New York is more eclectic: Koreans, Puerto Ricans, Albanians and Mexicans, Irish, Jamaicans, Italians and Guyanese.

Up the street comes Joanne Pritchard of Valentine Avenue with her companion and son.

"How you doin', Kevin?"

"Doin' fine, how about you?"

"Well, do you believe they shot a dealer in the chest on our street?"

"I heard a little about it this morning."

"We knew him," she says. "He was a nice guy, real nice to the kids. I'll tell ya, we're getting outta here. I got to get the hell out. It's really changed, the neighborhood. People have tried to bring it back, but. . . ."

"Yeah, ah huh, I hear you."

As it happens, two of the precinct's detectives are sitting across the street in a dark sedan. Jett walks over and leans down to the open window.

"What was the deal on Valentine?"

One dealer shot another, says one of the detectives. The victim was Tony Manning.

"Tan-gray Maxima?" asks Jett.

"Yeah," says the detective, "that's the car."

"Why did he get it?"

"Some kind of dispute. Don't really know yet. You know the saying, 'Dead men tell no tales.'"

For the moment, the murder troubles Kevin Jett. The drug dealer, his line of work aside, gave the police their "props," their respect. He was discreet about his business and well liked by his neighbors. Still, Jett says, "I guess if you live by the sword, you die by the sword."

Turkey burgers, yellow rice and marinara sauce. He eats light, lifts weights, runs to keep trim. After the meal, three more turns of the beat, then down to Webster to catch a bus back to the precinct.

Aboard climbs a young Jamaican, a thin man with a toothy grin. He looks toward the back for a seat, but, spotting the officer, decides to stand in front, by the door.

Jett looks up and smiles. Toothy Grin is new to the neighborhood, an apprentice in the drug trade.

"Let's go up front," says Jett.

Toothy Grin loses his glow. He looks at the driver. The bus isn't stopping. He's trapped.

Jett slides up next to him.

"What is it?" says the officer.

"I just be riding here, man," says the Jamaican, the grin now a faint smile.

"Guess you heard what happened to Tony Manning."

"I don't hear no-ting, man."

"You heard."

"No, man, what you say?"

"Better stay out of trouble or you might end up the same way."

Back at the station house, the shift is changing, with cops coming, cops going and the first arrests of the late afternoon crowding the cells. Jett climbs the stairs to the second floor and finds the detective in charge of the Manning case, a stocky man with a square face.

"What happened?" Jett asks.

The detective digs in a large folder and fishes out a stack of snapshots.

"Enjoy," he says.

Tony Manning, in blue jeans and a denim jacket, is lying face down on a white tile landing in front of an apartment at 2685 Valentine Avenue. The landing is covered in blood. Next to the body is a large red V-shaped smear, as if the victim had tried to raise himself before he died. He was shot twice. The first bullet entered his chest and struck an artery. This was the fatal shot. The second bullet hit him in the groin. This was a message.

"My, my, my," says Kevin Jett, shaking his head. "Look at that."

"How old was he?" someone asks.

The detective looks at the folder. "Thirty-two," he says. "But don't feel sorry for him. He wasn't one of the good guys. Shouldn't even investigate this one. Waste of the city's money."

Kevin Jett wasn't so sure. That night at home, he did his laundry, cooked some fish and wondered to himself how Tony Manning, by all accounts a polite and civil man, came to "waste his life" selling drugs. "I kept thinking, he wasn't a bad, bad guy. He wasn't a real thorn in my side. Maybe I'm getting soft."

He boxed his way into the Golden Gloves. He ran track. He played football. At the end of his senior year, Kevin Jett graduated with honors, but when it came time to sort through the scholarships and choose a college, he stayed home, close to his church and his mother, and enrolled at the City College of New York. He studied education, then began to think about the law. Along the way, he married a woman from his church and soon had a daughter, Charisse. Then he began to drift, away from his studies and out of his marriage.

He ended up in front of a sorting machine at the Post Office, "brain dead" and desperately wishing he were somewhere else. He took the test for the Police Department and passed, but when he was called to report, his wife protested that she was afraid. Before long the marriage had dissolved, and in April 1987, Kevin Jett reported for duty with Training Company 8746 at the New York City Police Academy.

Across the six months that followed, he heard lots of advice. "They told us: 'It's a war out there. You're going to lock people up on a Monday and on a Wednesday, they'll be back on the street looking for you.' That was true. We were also told that someone you know on the job will get killed in the line of duty. That was true, too."

Some of the training was easy. "Being from Mott Haven I already knew how to treat people in the streets—like you want to be treated, even the bad guys, until they show you disrespect." The book work, however, left him struggling, so much so he almost gave it up. "I just kept thinking about graduation, that day when you wear the white gloves and stand and salute with your family watching."

His first day on the job, he left for work from his parents' house. "My mother said, 'Be careful.' I turned around and said, 'What do you mean?' Then I realized, Wow—I'm a cop."

After six months of field training, he was assigned to the Five-Two, a precinct of about 300 officers on Webster Avenue in the northwest Bronx. He walked short foot posts at first—back and forth on the same stretch—then rode in a sector car. In 1991, he volunteered for the precinct's small community policing unit. He liked the flexible shifts— beat cops set their own hours—and, he says, "I like to work alone with no one looking over my shoulder." He was assigned to Beat 12, one of the most dangerous in the precinct.

He surveyed the neighborhood and sized up the "players." Then he did what beat cops have always done to make the terrain theirs—he set out to establish a presence.

"You have to project an image, especially if you work alone. So you have a little talk with the knuckleheads, introduce yourself and tell them where you're coming from. You say: 'I'm Officer Jett. This is my neighborhood. If you mess up and I see you around, I'm going to take care of you.'"

His background, of course, helped him do his job. "The average white rookie out of the academy on a beat like this is terrified. I grew up in Mott Haven, and the mutts understand that that's different from East Cupcake, Long Island. They feel that guys who came from there are soft.

"I also tell the rookies that sometimes you can use bluff, trickery and deceit with the bad guys. Some of the knuckleheads say, 'Without that gun you ain't nothing.' I say, 'If we have to do it, let's do it.' Then I say: 'This is my job. Let me do my job and you get on about your business.'

"If I have to fight, I'm the type who hits first and radios for help second. Most cops don't know how to fight. My technique is to pick you up and body-slam you to the concrete. Bam.

"Of course, you got to remember that no matter who you are, there will be somebody bigger, so you have to have the gift of gab. Once at the corner of Briggs and 194, I saw a guy I hadn't seen in the neighborhood before. He was only about 5 feet 8 inches, but he had muscles coming out of his ears. I said, 'Damn, that guys's got some muscles.'

"I go into a video store for a routine check and pretty soon this woman comes in and says there's a guy outside who had slapped her and had some money that belonged to her. I went outside. She says, 'Officer, officer, there's the guy who slapped me.' It was the guy with the muscles—I mean, muscles in his neck, in his knees, in his toes, muscles everywhere. I said, 'Damn.' She says, 'They call him 'Grape Ape.' I said, 'Damn.' Then she said, 'He just got out of jail.' I said, 'Oh, no.' Then she leans over to me and whispers in my ear: 'The last time it took 10 cops to lock him up. His arms were so big they couldn't get them together to cuff him. They needed two sets.' I said, 'Lady, you ain't helping me none.' I could see myself going through the plate-glass window.

"I said to myself: 'Shoot, you don't want to get into a fight with this guy. You don't know how many of those 10 cops got hurt.' I said, 'I better do some talking.' I wasn't going to walk up and say, 'Look, give her the money or I'm going to lock you up.' So I said: 'Excuse me, fella. Could you come here for a minute.' I said: 'Look, I heard you just got out of jail. Here's the charges you face so far: robbery, assault three, and if you want to fight me, it will be assault on a police officer. Why don't you give her the money and you can walk.' He said, 'O.K., officer.' I was so happy."

Kevin Jett keeps his uniform spotless and neatly pressed. He carries a .38-caliber Ruger revolver with a four-inch barrel, two extra cylinders with six rounds each, handcuffs, a can of Mace and a radio. He also packs two additional pieces of equipment not listed in the regulations.

The first is a pair of black leather driving gloves. In the beginning, he wore the gloves as prophylactics, to search addicts and dealers, anyone with cuts or open sores. Then, perhaps acting on his boxer's instincts, he began wearing them for trouble. Now the gloves are a kind of signature. "When people see me with my gloves on," he says, "they know it's not about talking to anyone." Another part of his kit is a pocketful of quarters, which, every day, he slips into the hands of the small, often thirsty fold that tugs at his trousers or trails him wide-eyed and silent along the street.

It is just after 7 p.m. and Ted Husted is calling to order the monthly meeting of the Bainbridge-Marion Community Association, a neighborhood group bent on beating back the mutts.

Kevin Jett is at the head of the table. Meetings like these are part of his routine. Last month, the precinct commander, Capt. Raymond Redmond, was there. So were 150 angry and emotive citizens.

Tonight, the mood is different. There have been some changes in the neighborhood. "We've seen more police on the beat and more sector cars," Ted Husted is telling his neighbors. "And now that they've put helicopters up, there's not as much gunfire at night. We've even seen Captain Redmond on patrol in the neighborhood, so it's not just show. We don't have any promises, but they're doing something."

Kevin Jett leans back and smiles.

The meeting is in the parish center of Our Lady of Refuge Roman

Catholic Church. The church and the church school are on one side of 196th Street. P.S. 46 is on the other. Together they anchor the neighborhood and are a large part of the reason that Ted Husted, a teacher, and Milton Mendoza, a carpenter, have not fled.

They own homes on Bainbridge Avenue, across the street from the public school. They are neighbors and friends. In the fight for the streets, they are also a flanking force for police. If they and others like them leave, the knuckleheads will overrun the neighborhood.

Ted Husted teaches second grade at P.S. 46. He and his wife, Jo Anne, will not let their three children walk the streets or visit the homes of their friends. "Maybe a drug dealer might be living next door to the apartment they would go to and maybe someone looking for that dealer will get the wrong address, break down the door and start shooting," Ted Husted says. The Husteds lead a Cub Scout pack, a Girl Scout troop and the local Little League—recreation for 600 children. Without them, there would be nothing but makeshift basketball in the street. More and more, however, the Husteds talk about leaving. To them, the neighborhood seems lawless.

"If a guy can drive down the block with his radio blasting so loud it shakes the buildings and no one stops him, then he might as well drive down the street with a megaphone announcing, 'I have drugs.'" It is a neighborhood with a hollow heart, says Husted, a place with no moral center. "Parents in this neighborhood teach their children they're entitled to certain things, like if the local bodega is price-gouging, it's O.K. to take what you want and walk out without paying." And children, of course, tend to absorb the worst of society, not the best. "I talked to kids who've seen movies like 'Sleeping With the Enemy.' One of my students said: 'Yeah; my Dad took me. It was great. The guy slapped the [expletive] out of that [expletive]'—I'm talking about a second grader here."

Their values have become so warped, so twisted that violence, in the end, is the only ethos most people know. "I have one student in class who refused to do anything. One day I said, 'Joey, why don't you do what I tell you to do?' He said, 'Because you don't really want me to do that.' I said, 'What gives you that impression?' He said, 'If you really wanted me to do it, you'd hit me.' "

Milton Mendoza grew up in the Bronx. His father was a laborer, his mother worked in a sweatshop. Five years ago, he and his wife, Aurora, a nurse, and their two children moved into a house a few doors down from the Husteds'. It's a fine house, with a modern kitchen and parquet floors. Milton Mendoza the carpenter knows his trade. He has worked hard getting his place in shape. In a year, he says, he hopes it is owned by someone else.

It was winter when they arrived and the neighborhood was quiet. Then came the spring and the mutts emerged from their dens. They urinated on the sidewalk in front of his house, burglarized cars along the curb and filled the street with gunfire. One morning Milton Mendoza found three bullet holes near his front door.

He is 39, a man who has taken his lumps. "I come from the streets," he says. "I know how to handle myself." And yet:

One evening in November 1990, as he was driving home from work, something crashed against his car. He pulled to the curb to see what had happened and discovered that a teen-ager had tossed a brick at him. "I asked the kid, 'What are you doing?' He looked at me and said, 'Get the hell out of here or I'll put you in a body bag.' I thought of my family and said to myself, 'This guy is a moron.' So I started to walk away. Suddenly, seven or eight guys were surrounding me. The kid slapped me. So I grabbed him and slammed him against the building. I got in the car and took off.

"I was only a couple blocks from home. I stopped at the house to pick up the wife. When I came out, I saw them on the corner just down from my door. I figured I'd better try to talk to them. All of a sudden someone hit me from behind with a baseball bat. I went down. They sat me up and gave me 25 or 30 shots. Just about then the mailman came by and yelled at them. I was trying to block some of the blows with my arms. They broke my forearm, my wrist, my fingers. They dislocated an ankle and a knee. I had pins in my hand, a carpenter with pins in his hand. When I grew up we had fistfights, but today you look at the wrong person the wrong way and they want to shoot you, stab you, beat your brains out—they want to kill you. These kids are like time bombs."

Street cops call him Popeye. He is short and muscular, with a balding pate and a canny smile. He worked his way from cadet to Commissioner—the cops' cop. This year, an election year, is Ray Kelly's last as the top cop. New York's Mayor-elect, Rudolph W. Giuliani, has appointed William J. Bratton, the Police Commissioner in Boston, New York's next Police Commissioner. All three men support community policing.

But Giuliani's campaign promise to push the police to make more street arrests contradicts the whole idea of the new police science. The professionals know that wholesale arrests are a pointless exercise when courts are overbooked and prisons are beyond capacity. "Turning numbers," as the police call it, does little to lower fear or restore order.

Ray Kelly believes that the upstanding citizens he has served all his professional life are more perceptive than most politicians grant. He's walked a beat, he ought to know. "The public," he says, "wants a more personal relationship with the police."

So the Commissioner committed himself to community policing. It's a "work in progress," says Ray Kelly. And progress is slow.

It has not been easy to sell the rank and file on the value of problem-solving protocols. Young cops have the lights-and-siren syndrome; they're all action. And the veterans, those who have been on the job five years or more, suspect that community policing is a smoke screen for "social work." They're angry at the courts, the revolving door of justice, and they're careworn by the suffering they see in the streets. Many are so cynical, so demoralized, they echo the ethos of the streets: justice is swift and sure, some say, only at the end of a nightstick. Kelly knows too that many of his beat cops are ill trained and poorly supervised. Field officers get just two days of training in community policing, and the sergeants who direct them on the job frequently do little more than "scratch," or sign, their log books.

Even Kelly's executive corps has often failed him. Who knows how many tradition-bound captains, inspectors, commanders and chiefs have issued daily orders that sabotaged the new philosophy. Recently two such commanders—apparently convinced that a cop out of sight is a corrupt cop—stopped their beat officers from patrolling in apartment buildings, an essential tactic in community policing. "They're paranoid about integrity," says one precinct commander. "The whole idea is to watch your back, to make sure nothing happens, so you can move up to the next slot."

But it is the Commissioner who directs the department, not a small corps of cautious traditionalists. And it is unlikely the new Commissioner will change policies. "We're moving," says Kelly, "there's no going back."

Out in the precincts, the rank and file watches and waits. Some cops long for the old days. Others believe Kelly is right: community policing is here to stay.

On most mornings the troops under his command find Capt. Raymond Redmond, the precinct commander at the Five-Two, an amiable boss, one worthy of respect. He jogs through the precinct and every week spends hours walking a different beat. "The old precinct commander," says Jett, "could barely walk to his car."

Redmond runs the Five-Two with an even hand, an approachable autocrat. This morning, however, the word has spread that the boss is grumpy.

"Well, yeah, I am grumpy and I don't care if my cops don't like it."

He's piqued, in part, from a trip he made the day before to 1 Police Plaza. He had traveled to headquarters for a ceremony to honor the good work of several community police officers, among them one of his own.

"They take them down there and give them a certificate. A certificate? I would have given them a detective shield. That's a reward."

• • •

Early afternoon and Kevin Jett is back on the job, in the cool, wood-paneled rectory of Our Lady of Refuge, conferring with the pastor, the Rev. John Jenik.

Father Jenik is a multifarious man, 49 years old, a fire-brand from the 1960's who abandoned his bourgeois background, joined the church and, some 20 years ago, began a career with the poor in the Bronx. The archetype of the urban priest, he can quote from St. Augustine, plot urban policy, curse like a drunken marine.

He arrived at Our Lady in 1978 and formed the Fordham Bedford Housing Corporation, a nonprofit group that restores and runs buildings seized by the city or the courts. Then he went after the dealers. He organized boycotts of the stores that were drug fronts, then held marches and Masses and vigils at the neighborhood's "hot spots."

The dealers were angry; the priest was hurting business. And before long, John Jenik—blond-haired, blue-eyed John Jenik, who daily walks his parish unescorted—had a price on his head. "There's big money out here," he says. "You get in the dealers' way and you get killed."

Which is why Kevin Jett has come to the rectory today. Father Jenik has planned another all-night vigil and Mass—this time at the hottest spot in the neighborhood, 384 East 194th Street, the six-story heroin house on Decatur.

"Well, Father, we're going to bring in big lights and flood the building and we're going to put people on the roof to make sure you don't get any airmail," says Kevin Jett.

"Good," says the priest. "We'll gather in the church and walk down from there. Thanks, Kevin."

Out on the street, the cop looks back at the rectory. "Father Jenik is a thorn in everyone's side," he says. "But he's a good thorn."

Across the street at P.S. 46, the afternoon session has just started. "Let's pay them a visit," says the cop, and he heads up the steps and though the gray Gothic arch.

Kevin Jett "owns" P.S. 46, and everyone in the neighborhood, including the school's principal, Aramina Ferrer, knows it. "He's told the bad element in the street, 'You don't come into my school and mess with my teachers and my kids,'" says Ferrer. "I feel like he's part of the staff."

The patron of P.S. 46 is always on hand. He speaks to classes about safety and drugs; he roams the peach-colored halls under the big clocks to keep the building secure; and when the final bell rings, he's on the corner, chasing away dealers and ne'er-do-wells.

Last year, when an angry parent confronted the assistant principal, Ferrer turned to Kevin Jett.

"I got five cops and went to the house. I asked him what happened, 'Why did you assault a teacher?' He said: 'I didn't assault him, I moshed him.' I said: 'Oh, you moshed him. Well this is my school, you hear me? Mine. And I don't like nobody coming into my school and moshing the teachers.' I said, 'You do it again, and you'll be getting locked up.' I said, 'If you really have an urge to fight, we can accommodate you.'"

When Kevin Jett surveys his career, three days come back to him: the morning he helped close the smoke shop on Briggs, the evening he saved the life of an asthmatic struggling to breathe and the afternoon he addressed the final assembly of fourth graders at P.S. 46.

"Come on into the auditorium," he is saying now. "Let me show you where I stood." He climbs some stairs, turns a corner and steps onto the stage. "Here, right here by the piano. See, this is where you stand. Then you have to shake everybody's hand. I wore my best dress shoes that day. Patent leather. Really shines."

He steps forward for a moment and stands silently on the apron, looking out into the quiet hall and the long rows of empty seats.

"I love what I do," he says. "But I'm not going to make detective here. No, that's not going to happen."

Any day now, Jett is scheduled to be transferred, most likely to a job as a narcotics officer in the Organized Crime Control Bureau. In New York there's no reward for walking a beat; no detective's gold shield, no sergeant's stripes, no cash bonus. The path to promotion and a raise is still through the special units—narcotics, vice, organized crime. And Kevin Jett must move up: to support his three children he supplements his base pay of $3,100 a month with his earnings in a supermarket as a part-time fishmonger.

By all standards, his own and those of his superiors, Kevin Jett has succeeded. Crime statistics in his monthly community policing log show that when he was off the beat for any substantial period, there were more burglaries, robberies, car thefts. His sources on the street have told him that when he's sick, injured or on leave, drugs sales go up, too.

He attributes his success to his size, strength and background: a black belt in karate, a Bronxite wise in the ways of the streets. "Not every cop can work single patrol," he says. "I grew up in the city. I faced everything the knuckleheads faced."

The advocates of community policing, however, would argue that even a less streetwise cop, one from East Cupcake, could have assumed ownership of Beat 12. It might have taken more time, but a smart, determined cop armed with the penal code can, they say, "establish a presence" anywhere.

To be sure, the baneful reality—the swarms of drug dealers, gun merchants, loan sharks, pimps, robbers, burglars and extortionists— powerfully suggests otherwise. But no one knows for sure. After rising inexorably for more than a generation, reported crimes have declined in New York for two straight years, to the lowest level since 1985. Yet officials are reluctant to ascribe the trend to any one factor, or even to recognize the existence of a trend based on such notoriously unreliable statistics. There is no data on community policing either, and the case studies are too narrow and anecdotal to serve as proof.

The basic idea of community policing—marrying a cop to a piece of ground—seems sound. If a cop can move onto a beat, roust the bad guys and teach the upstanding citizens how to resist their return, then that's one piece of ground where crime is unlikely to breed. But the job of organizing and educating places like Beat 12 is more daunting than the job of patrolling them. As one insider put it, "half the community is cheering the cops on, but the other half is still throwing things at them." And without the community, there is no community policing.

To imagine an N.Y.P.D. devoted entirely to community policing is to understand how far the department still has to go. It might have to be twice as large, perhaps 60,000 or 70,000 officers assisted by 15,000 to 20,000 civilian workers, with an annual budget of about twice the current $1.7 billion. A third or more of the force would be on foot patrol, covering the most dangerous and crime-plagued beats 24 hours a day. Cops would be community leaders, practiced in the political art of pushing city bureaucrats—in sanitation, health and human services—to do their jobs.

The officer on the beat would patrol where and when he wanted. His supervisors would be true colleagues, teaming up on tasks. The department would be decentralized; most decisions would be made by precinct commanders and supervisors in concert with neighborhood groups. All the support services—from the sector cars to the vice squad—would be organized around the beats and would work closely with the cop on the street.

In reality, of course, the municipal budget is tight and growing tighter, and the municipal mind is ill disposed to bureaucratic reorganization. Cops want to be crime fighters not problem solvers, Alexanders whacking the Gordian knot rather than unraveling it. The average cop sees himself as a lone agent, isolated and besieged, the mutts in front of him, his department nipping at his heels.

And there is more—the overwhelming issues of crime and punishment, rehabilitation, new prisons, disintegrating families, murderous teens, turbulent schools, immigration, the economic isolation of the inner cities, racial warfare, gutter politics, urban alienation and fear so rampant it threatens to make the idea of compassion a concept from another age.

Can community policing work? Yes.

Does it work in the tough precincts of New York? Again, yes, though, at the moment, only by degrees and, at times, as much by accident as design.

Will the entire force—detective squads, patrol cars, narcotics division and so on—adopt the new science? Will the "dominant philosophy" ever become dominant practice? Herman Goldstein says that David Couper, the recently retired Police Chief of Madison, Wis., spent 20 years trying to reform that city's tiny 311-member force. By that measure, New York won't have a comprehensive community police force until the year 4000.

Perhaps the problem-solving and organizing can wait a bit. In the Bronx, at least, it seems enough for now just to have some bluebottles back on the beat.

from Brooklyn Bounce
by Joe Poss and
Henry R. Schlesinger

Most cops never fire their guns in the line of duty—but many do. Here Brooklyn cop Joe Poss, with the help of writer Henry R. Schlesinger (born 1957), describes his reaction to shooting an armed suspect.

I never saw the muzzle flash. I can't remember if I even heard the shot. But I knew I was the one that fired because I felt the jolt at my wrists. The familiar recoil sent the gun jerking back, then I saw the guy spasm and fall into the darkness.

The scene froze. Everyone within my field of vision suddenly turned into a statue. And everything had this weird maroon tint to it, like looking through a piece of stained glass. I remember turning towards Tommy, the other cop, up on the row house's stairs. And for a long time he didn't move. His face pale, registering a look of horror and disbelief.

As the haze began to fade, Tommy was the first to move, his face unfreezing and expression shifting just slightly as he turned and began coming down the stairs towards me. But even then, it was in slow motion. Each frame passed agonizingly slow. Every detail sharply focused. The way his hand held the flashlight as it swung. The gun in his other hand at hip level. The equipment on his belt bouncing. It was like a movie without sound.

All around—everyone—cops, people hanging out their windows, myself, we were all moving incredibly slow.

The strange maroon tint narrowed down to a dot. Then everything snapped back. Instantly everyone was moving at normal speed, and slowly I began to hear the sounds.

People were yelling. I was yelling, my voice tight in my throat. I was screaming, "I can't see the gun! I can't see the fucking gun!"

From over my left shoulder I could hear running, other cops coming towards us. They were shouting too, wanting to know what happened. Who'd fired? Who was shot? Trying to sort it out as they run up on us.

"Put your gun down! Put it down!" Tommy shouted.

I was still "covering" the guy with my gun, holding it out with two hands, ready to shoot again if the shadow at the bottom of the stairs flinched. I screamed back, "I don't see the gun! I can't see the fucking gun!"

"It's all right, man," Tommy said. "It's okay, you shot him."

A sickening panic washed over me. The gun that the guy was pointing at Tommy's face just a couple of seconds ago had vanished. I'd shot an unarmed man.

"I can't see the fucking gun! Get it! I can't see it! Get it!" As the panic rose, I could barely talk. I couldn't catch my breath. The words were coming out strangled as I began to hyperventilate.

Another cop turned my way, pushing my gun down as more cops rushed past. He was trying to take it from me, but both my hands were tight around the grip, one finger glued to the trigger.

Then someone from below said, "I got it! I got the gun!"

I saw a hand pop up, holding the gun the way cops always hold a recovered weapon. He was holding it up so everyone could see it, like a trophy. Thumb through the trigger guard, two fingers up on the slide, another behind the strap—displaying it like the guy on TV holds the American Express card.

I released the grip on my gun and my partner took it. A moment later they were hustling me into an RMP.

I felt the isolation as soon as the door slammed. I was sitting in the back seat, getting the same view the perps get, only my hands weren't cuffed.

I watched the two cops climb in the front. And it was like a wall went up between us. I could feel them distance themselves from me, not much, but enough. I could almost hear the questions going through their minds. Was it a clean shoot? Did Poss panic? Who the fuck was that guy he shot? If there's a problem—if the shooting was fucked up, nobody wants to know you. But if it's clean, they'd want a little piece of the story to tell.

A second later we were moving, heading towards Jamaica Hospital. Standard procedure; any cop involved in a shooting has to get treated for trauma.

All the way to the hospital I kept saying, "I had to do it. He had a gun. Piece of shit pointed it at Tommy's face. You know, I had to do it."

The cop behind the wheel said, "Relax. Just don't think about it, okay?"

Don't think about it? Relax? Fuck you, I thought. I just fucking shot a guy. Get a grip. But even as I'm thinking this, his partner was on the radio saying, "Five base, you on the air?"

Someone at the precinct responded with, "four," abbreviating the 10-4 to the suffix, just as the cop had foreshortened the 7-5 to 5.

"Make the call," the cop said. "Get a delegate."

As we moved along the empty streets, I remember thinking, "So it's come to this? Why me? Why the fuck me?"

At the hospital they rushed me to the head of the triage line. Blood pressure, medical history, pulse, and temperature. When I unbuttoned my shirt and took my vest off, it was like I was drawing my first breath since firing the shot.

Out in the hallway, the other cops swarmed around me. Protectors, bodyguards. They weren't letting anyone get to me, not before the PBA delegate showed up. And all the time they're reminding me, "Don't say anything. Not a fucking thing."

When the sergeant arrived, I was relieved to see it was Sergeant Glass, a veteran who knew what the deal was and knew to keep procedure simple. I volunteered my revolver without saying anything, and he checked the "state-of-load," acknowledged only one "spent" round, then handed it back. This in itself was a good sign. It signalled to me, and everyone who might have been watching, that it was a good shoot.

If he had kept the gun, it would have meant lost trust, suspicion, and the worst kind of doubt.

Then the intern arrived. Luckily it was a doctor who's known in the precincts. He's an 8-3 cop who's studying medicine, working two jobs. "Do you know your name?" "Do you know what day it is?" "Do you know where you are?" "Do you know what just happened?" "How are you feeling?"

I can tell you this, right from the jump. Maybe they won't admit it, but *all cops* fantasize about shoot-outs. Some of them can't wait to get into a shooting. They have a hard-on for it. Maybe because deep down, that's what they thought the job was all about, cops and robbers. Heroes and villains.

The ultimate scenario is one where you come out the hero; maybe with a nick that draws a little blood, just to show that you're lucky, but still the hero. Unscathed, but salted, cherry-busted.

I had those daydreams. I'll own up to them. Maybe it's all the movies we saw as kids. Maybe a lot of people have those fantasies about coming out the hero. But I never thought it would happen to me, just in my head.

Where the fuck does a kid from Shaker Heights get off shooting anyone?

Shootings are for those other cops. The ones who put in their twenty years and open a bar in Queens. Heroics are for those kids from Long Island, third-generation cops, who'll have a story to tell their friends and families. Maybe it would even be something that brought them a little respect and acceptance.

I didn't know what my friends back home and family would offer me when I told them, but I was pretty sure it wouldn't be a pat on the back and a knowing nod. As it turned out later, a lot of them didn't know how to respond. They didn't even know how to mouth the right words or fake the right attitude. Even for my parents, it was beyond their realm of etiquette.

This is the way it started.

It was one of those sticky August nights where the humidity is pushing up toward 80 percent and everything has a haze over it. Nights like that are markers. You know there's going to be action in the street. People hang out in front of their homes. People start drinking. Everyone's nerves wear a little thin from the heat. Cops, EMS crews, and emergency room staff prepare for these nights on the way to work.

I remember breaking the unwritten, unspoken rule, when I turned to my partner in the rear lot of the precinct and said, "You know, I think something heavy's gonna happen tonight."

It kind of startled him when I said it. Premonitions could turn into omens if you talk about them. It's like asking for something to happen. He kind of gave me a quick look, poked me in the chest, and asked, "You got your vest on?"

On hot nights I've been known to go out on tour without a vest. Maybe it's tempting fate, or maybe I just don't like sweating into it. But on those sticky nights, I'd usually think twice about slipping it on. That night, I didn't. I wasn't thinking about premonitions, but put it on without thinking about it.

We'd just begun the tour when a call came over the radio. A 10-13 (officer needs assistance) citywide, Essex and Atlantic. We tried to get more information, but there wasn't any available. We didn't have a clue what we were dealing with or getting into. It could have been real, bogus, or anything. But then we pulled up to the corner and there was a lone RMP, lights flashing, engine running, doors ajar, and nobody in sight. The scene was eerie, and it gave me a hollow ache right in the pit of my stomach. That's when I knew we'd come into something real.

Then the sergeant and his operator, Tommy, pulled up.

The street was lined with row houses, two and three stories. There was a power station for the elevated subway down at the far corner. It was surrounded by a fifteen-foot-high chain-link fence topped with

razorwire. And there, sitting atop the fence, was a cop. He was strad-
dling the thing, barbed wire right up in his crotch, yelling and
directing us by waving his arms—not in pain, but pumped up on
adrenaline. He'd tried to follow a perp over the fence and got hung up.

"There's one down there, and two other guys, one went that way and
the other over there! They got guns!"

The sergeant and my partner went one way, and me and the
sergeant's OP (operator), Tommy, started walking the other way. I'm
being cautious, partnered with Tommy, checking porches, between
cars, and under cars.

Tommy was walking just a little ahead of me. We both had our guns
drawn, and we're working our flashlights into all the dark places. Then
I passed this particular house and something hit me. It might have
been a noise, something. I turned back and looked into darkness,
down a stairway to a basement apartment, and unknowingly, right at
the perp.

"Wait a minute," I called to Tommy and he walked back, as I turned
my light on the basement apartment's stairway. The light hit right on
the top of the guy's head. He was crouched down, concealed by
shadows.

I pointed my gun and yelled, "Don't move!"

Tommy jumped the gate, rushed up the front steps, and shined a
light on him from above. We saw the gun. It wasn't hard to spot, it was
a black automatic, but the thing that stuck out in my mind was that it
had this strip of white tape on it around the barrel.

I took a few steps toward the guy, so that now I'm maybe three feet
or so away, and yelled, "Drop it! Drop the fucking gun!"

Then Tommy yelled, "Let me see your hands!"

Soon we were both shouting at the guy to drop the gun, drop the
gun, and to see his hands, over and over again. Tommy is above him
and I'm two or three feet away, face-to-face and without cover.

It seemed like it went on forever, both of us yelling at the top of our
lungs. But the guy didn't move. And the more we yelled, the more he
didn't move and the more pissed off I got. Until finally, I'm not even

pissed off anymore. I'm still yelling at him, but I feel this kind of despair come down on me. This asshole is just not going to listen. He's not playing by the rules.

We caught him, fair and square. He's supposed to drop the gun, come out with his hands up so we can cuff him, take him back to the precinct, and toss him into the system. That's the way it's supposed to work. But by just crouching there, not moving, he cancelled all the rules.

One thing I know is, I'm not going to jump this motherfucker. There just wasn't enough room. In six years, I've jumped guys with guns, tackled them on the run, and night-sticked them. But with this guy, not a chance. He was down a stairway with a gun out. Even in the shadows I could see his hands wrapped around the stock and his finger on the trigger.

Then the guy did a quick look over his right shoulder, positioning me in his mind, and unbelievably, as we're still yelling at him, with our flashlights on him, he pivoted around and brought the gun up over his left shoulder, so it's pointing right at Tommy's face.

That's when I shot him.

Up to that night I'd handled every call there was: rape, robbery, assault, attempted murder, murder, sodomy, child abuse, child molestation, family disputes, and auto theft. I'd handled maybe three quarters of every felony in the New York Penal Law. With all of those, you just show up and follow Patrol Guide procedures.

Broken window. Door is ajar. Somebody's inside: *burglary.*

Popped door lock. Broken steering column. Broken ignition: *grand theft auto.*

Woman's face is beaten bloody, and his knuckles are bruised: *assault family.*

But when a guy's got a gun and he's pointing it at somebody, you don't think of the charges. You think of what you have to do to stop him. It's on a different level. You're not thinking of paperwork or over-time, or court-tour changes. What you're thinking about is getting the fucking gun away from him. Eliminating the threat.

• • •

When a cop shoots someone, procedure puts into motion the department's official machinery. It's like turning on a switch. It begins with phone calls. The DA's office gets a call. The duty captain is notified. FIAU (Field Internal Affairs Unit) is summoned. And the PBA delegate arrives with a lawyer.

By the time we'd arrived back at the precinct from the hospital, an "unusual incident" investigation was in gear. A few minutes later, the PBA delegate showed up, and both he and the nightwatch detectives brought me into the back office to get my story of what happened. They checked the state-of-load of my gun, emptied the cartridges, and made a visual check of each chamber, looking for powder residue that signifies rounds fired.

The full investigation would come later. But little by little the facts started filtering back to me from other cops.

The guy I'd shot and three others had robbed a White Castle at gunpoint. The cops that saw it go down weren't even from our precinct. They were from the 4-7 in The Bronx, "flying" to the Crown Heights riot detail in the 7-1. As they drove by, they spotted guys with guns running out of the White Castle. They didn't know the neighborhood and didn't know for sure what they had, so they put the call out over citywide.

Later, the guy I shot climbed onto the gurney himself. One of the victims from the holdup, after making a positive ID, kicked him. Another spit on him.

A Spanish guy from across the street, hanging out his window, witnessed the whole thing and told the detectives, "I don't know why those two cops kept shouting at the guy? I'd'uve shot the motherfucker right off."

Later, the perp took a turn for the worse. The shot had blown out his shoulder and bounced around inside. It was only a matter of time before he died. A background check showed he was 26 and a recidivist (repeat) felon who'd just finished seven years upstate for armed robbery. He'd been out almost a week.

After a shooting, it's standard procedure for a cop to get a few days off.

The department figures it gives you enough time to pull yourself together and to see the department psychiatrist for what's called "early intervention." A couple of days after the shooting, I went and saw the shrink. He asked if little things bothered me more? Was I getting violent around the house? Had I broken anything around the house? Had I taken my gun out at all? Had I dry-fired the gun? Had my eating habits, sleeping habits, *any habits* changed? Did I start drinking or get drunk more than usual?

I gave him all the answers the department needed to assure itself I was sane and stable, which I was. The whole thing, what it meant, didn't really hit me until later. I stopped hanging out with my friends, other cops, assistant DAs, and defense lawyers. I could feel myself withdrawing. None of it seemed connected to the shooting, yet I knew it was.

You just don't shoot someone and walk away. For me it built up slowly, all the anger and all the questions. Strangely, I was even pissed off at the guy I shot. He could have put the gun down, come out quietly, and gone back to prison. It could have gone either way, right up to the time he pointed the gun at another cop's face.

Yeah, right, I'd answer myself back. There you go again, thinking like a white boy from the burbs.

Then there are the personal questions. And for me, there were a lot of them. Another person had ended up dying at my hands. I was born, baptized, and raised a Catholic. What right did I have to take away another man's life? Even as a cop? Even if that person was posing a threat to another person?

The guy was a criminal—a piece of shit. He'd just gotten out of jail for doing the exact same thing. And he was posing a clear threat against another blue uniform, something that stands for law and order. I could be cleared by the department and dead right in the eyes of the law, but there's still that part of me that contends it was wrong.

Four months after the shooting, the letter from the police commissioner's office clearing me arrived. But now, a couple of years later, there's still that conflict. Nothing painful, no sobbing remorse, but irritating and probably there forever.

The dreams about it haven't been nightmares, but more like instant replays. It's not something I think about everyday, but when I do think about it, it's always uncomfortable. And it's always vivid.

What it comes down to are questions left unanswered. It's a test you take and never know if you've passed or failed. It's a feeling of unfinished business. And all the schools you attend, the academies you pass through, the friends you collect, the church sermons you hear, none of them can prepare you for this. And nobody, not your partners, teachers, friends, priests, or your parents can give you the answers after the fact.

Not even my father, who, for everything he's offered, by suggestion or advice, never taught me to pull the trigger.

from Will the Circle Be Unbroken?
by Studs Terkel

Oral historian Studs Terkel (born 1912) inter-

viewed 61 year-old Bob Gates, a retired NYPD

officer, for Terkel's 2001 book Will the Circle

Be Unbroken. *Gates' career included stints with*

Emergency Service and the homicide squad.

E mergency Service is like a rescue squad. You respond to any call, any incident: a man under a train, trapped in an auto, bridge jumpers, floaters, psychos, guys that murdered people and then barricaded themselves in. We go and get these people out. It was sometimes a little too exciting. On a couple of incidents I felt I wasn't going to come home.

Ever hear of the Statue of Liberty job? We had a guy climb to the top of the statue, break through the center port window of the head, and stand on the top of the crown. For over an hour. He's there for a cause, and he's jeopardizing our lives by doing so. He was threatening to jump from the crown to the head.

After speaking to him for a while, my partner and I saw an opportunity and pinned him down, handcuffed him, and held on. We were tied in through a rope, but the tie was below us. If he had thrown either of us off, just the stress from the rope would have killed us.

Did I mention the World Trade Center job? That's a hundred and ten stories high. We had a guy, he defeated the tower security system. There was a rabbi there, with a priest on the way. The guy had climbed over the top of the World Trade Center and dropped approximately a foot onto a window washer's ledge, which was about four inches wide. My partner and I were looking down from above, trying to talk him into coming in. His problem is he was born a Jew and is now a Christian. He was mad at the Jews because, he claimed, they were responsible for the crucifixion of Christ. I said to him, "Well, suppose they'd only sentenced him to seven and a half to fifteen years? We wouldn't be Catholics today." He said to the rabbi, "I'd like that officer to come down and talk with me." They rappelled me over. I kept on talking to him. As I handed him a cigarette, I grabbed him in a bear hug and we both swung over, up on top of the World Trade Center. Besides being dangerous, it was *such* a beautiful sight . . . At a hundred and ten stories up, the East River is a half-inch wide. Talking to him, I just wanted to concentrate on him not grabbing me. I wasn't sure if he had a knife. At that point, it was life-threatening. I thought briefly about dying, but I had partners there to back me up—and it happened so fast.

You don't have time to have fear because you have to prepare psychologically, get focused on what you're gonna do—you got a job to do. With the sirens and the lights around, you're thinking about equipment, about who's gonna get the rope, who's gonna wear the Morrissey Belt, that looks like a safety pin . . . You're so hyped up, keyed up, you can feel and hear your own heart beating.

If it's a barricaded psycho, and he's got a gun and he's threatening to go out and kill somebody, you're focused on that person, on not killing him. They don't like the word "kill" anymore—you're gonna *stop* 'em. But you're there to try and save his life. If not, you have to take other measures.

You always look at them as another human being. You try to get into a conversation and tell him what he's giving up, find out if he has a family. Sometimes it's not so good if he has a family, 'cause they're the ones he could be mad at. When they show up, that's when he may jump, or shoot himself.

Then there's the floater that drowns and eventually comes up. We pulled this kid out of the pond. You look at him with the hook in his eye. A woman asked me, "What color was he?" I said, "Lady, he's ten years old—what *difference* does it make?" She said, "You pulled him out, you should know." I just walked away from her. It never entered my mind whether he was white or black. He was a life that had to be saved, but it was too late. And people that hang themselves . . . if the body's there for a certain period of time, it decomposes. Sometimes we call that "the smell of death." You come into an apartment, the body's been there for a couple of weeks, and the acids are floating through the air. The body swells up and the gases inside penetrate the air and stick in your nostrils while you're cutting the person down. Maybe people should ride with emergency service, get into the shoes of a cop and see what it's like, see what they go through. The average life span of a cop today is fifty-nine years old—twelve years short of an average person.

Death . . . The most vivid case in my mind is a space case I had. A guy was caught by the train and rolled between the platform and the train. When we got there, the transit police were in conversation with him. He had a family, several children. He was caught in a four-inch space. The reason he was still alive is because everything was still intact above, keeping his heart pumping blood into his system. So you could converse with him while he was sitting there. There wasn't much else you could do. The medical people said the minute that we start to jack this train away from the platform, he would pass away. You could almost predict his death, but meanwhile you're talking to him.

I thought about the family as we jacked the car away from the platform with what we call a journal jack. You fit it between the supports of the train, the subway car, and the platform. As you start jacking, it pushes the train away from the platform, giving you another six inches to take the body out. The body is rolled like a bowling pin. He just went off to sleep, he passed away right there. Was he wondering, "What are they gonna do to get me out? What's the story here?" I was talking to him: "We're doing the best we can." "I don't feel my legs. . . ." "We're handling that now—we got people under the train . . . Where do you work?"—just questions to take his mind off what was happening.

We get to go in where your heart is pumping, your adrenaline is running and you've got your hand just off the hair trigger. You're in there because this is your job, and if you have to kill you will—but you don't want to. You have fear of accidentally pulling the trigger. You think about these fears afterwards. If you can save a life, you'll save that life. Thinking about the death end of it and your safety end of it usually comes after.

Since the time I first met you, I found spiritual solace and guidance. I stop off in church once in a while now. I believe in the hereafter. Yeah. But I have questions, too. Why do young people have to die? Why do people have to threaten to kill themselves?

One of the jobs I had was a private house where a man placed a twelve-gauge shotgun under his chin and blew his head off. Half of it went onto the ceiling and half onto the walls. We had to take the photographs and notes. I noticed the serenity of a death scene, how quiet. I was writing notes on this body, sitting at the kitchen table, when part of the skull and face drops onto the table and onto my shoulders. All I said to myself was that it was raining death, *raining* death in that kitchen. Sometimes you're a little annoyed because if somebody is going to kill themselves, why do they want to make such a mess? If they're gonna do it, if they made up their minds . . . *[Suddenly]* Police officers are one of the highest rates of suicides in the country—because of the strain, the stress, the problems. I knew a guy that committed suicide, a cop. I went to the scene. He was on the top of the stairwell. He had a picture of his wife and kids leaning against the wall, and he shot himself in the head.

I never had that thought, thank God. But if I ever get to that point where they put the tubes in me, and the IVs, and I'm gonna vegetate, I want to have mind enough to tell them, "Pull the plug." If I'm put in an old-age home and I still got my faculties, I want my kids to bring me up some chocolate chip cookies, wipe my mouth, and wheel me out of the sun.

acknowledgments

Many people made this anthology.

At Thunder's Mouth Press and Avalon Publishing Group:
Thanks to Ghadah Alrawi, Will Balliett, Sue Canavan, Maria Fernandez, Linda Kosarin, Dan O'Connor, Neil Ortenberg, Paul Paddock, Susan Reich, David Riedy, Simon Sullivan and Mike Walters for their support, dedication and hard work.

At The Writing Company:
Nate Hardcastle did most of the research, with help from Sean Donahue. Nat May oversaw rights research and negotiations. Taylor Smith, Mark Klimek, March Truedsson, Brad Kelly and Kate Fletcher took up slack on other projects.

At the Portland Public Library in Portland, Maine:
Thanks to the librarians for their assistance in finding and borrowing books and other publications from around the country.

Finally, I am grateful to the writers whose work appears in this book.

p e r m i s s i o n s

b i b l i o g r a p h y

The selections used in this anthology were taken from the editions and publications listed below. In some cases, other editions may be easier to find. Hard-to-find or out-of-print titles often are available through inter-library loan services or through Internet booksellers.

Asbury, Herbert. *The Gangs of New York*. New York: Thunder's Mouth Press, 2001.

Byrnes, Thomas. *Rogues' Gallery: 247 Professional Criminals of 19th-Century America*. Secaucus, New Jersey: Castle, 1988.

Davidson, William J. and Steven Allie Collura. *Collura: Actor With a Gun*. New York: Simon & Schuster, 1977.

Laffey, Marcus. "Cop Diary". First appeared in *The New Yorker*, November 11, 1997.

McAlary, Mike. "The Last Cop Story". First appeared in *Esquire*, December, 1997.

McAlary, Mike. *Buddy Boys: When Good Cops Turn Bad*. New York: G.P. Putnam's Sons, 1987.

Norman, Michael. "One Cop, Eight Square Blocks". First appeared in the *New York Times Magazine*, December 12, 1993.

Poss, M. Joseph and Henry R Schlesinger. *Brooklyn Bounce*. New York: Avon, 1994.

Sayre, Joel. "With the Meat in Their Mouth—I". First appeared in *The New Yorker*, September 5, 1953.

Sayre, Joel. "With the Meat in Their Mouth—II". First appeared in *The New Yorker*, September 12, 1953.

Terkel, Studs. *Will the Circle Be Unbroken?: Reflections on Death, Rebirth, and Hunger for a Faith*. New York: The New Press, 2001.

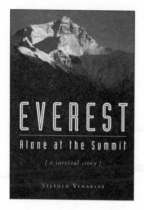
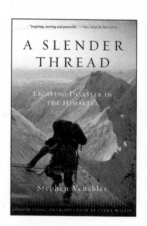

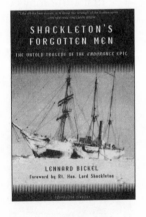

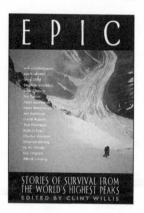

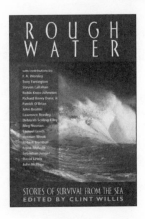

Exciting titles from Adrenaline Books

ROUGH WATER: Stories of Survival from the Sea

Edited by Clint Willis
A unique collection of 16 pieces of great writing about storms, shipwrecks and human resourcefulness. Includes work by Patrick O'Brian, John McPhee and Herman Wouk, as well as a Sebastian Junger story previously unpublished in book form.
$17.95 ($29.95 Canada), 368 pages

WILD: Stories of Survival from the World's Most Dangerous Places

Edited by Clint Willis
The wilderness—forest, desert, glacier, jungle—has inspired some of the past century's best writers, from Edward Abbey and Jack London to Norman Maclean and Barry Lopez. *Wild* contains 13 selections for people who love the wilderness and readers who love great writing.
$17.95 ($29.95 Canada), 336 pages

RESCUE: Stories of Survival from Land and Sea

Edited by Dorcas S. Miller; Series Editor, Clint Willis
Some of the world's best adventure writing tells stories of people in trouble and the people who come to their aid. *Rescue* gathers those stories from mountain ledges, sea-going vessels, desert wastes, ice flows and the real Wild West. It includes work by some of the world's best writers, from Antoine de St. Exupéry to Spike Walker and Pete Sinclair.
$16.95 ($27.95 Canada), 384 pages

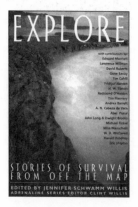

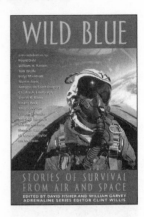